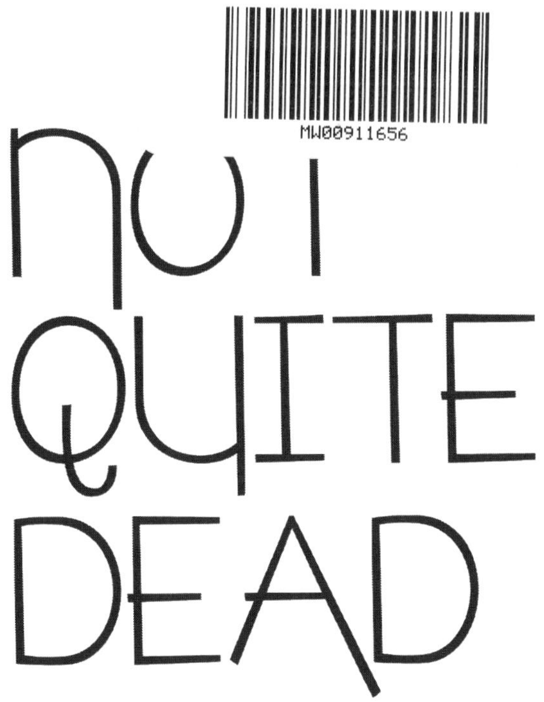

A Lowcountry Ghost Story

by:

USAToday Bestselling Author

LYLA PAYNE

Cover Photography by Iona Nicole Photography
Cover by Eisley Jacobs at Complete Pixels
Copyediting: Lauren Hougen

not quite dead

A Lowcountry Ghost Story

To Anne Bonny, for letting me imagine the end of her story. Here's hoping she doesn't haunt me for it.

Chapter One

In retrospect, perhaps drinking myself to sleep in my grandparents' driveway hadn't been the best idea.

The epiphany arrives with a blast of sunlight and a knock on the driver's-side window that explodes my brain into pain soup. I manage to make out a shadowy form through the tightest eye squint in history, its elderly, feminine hand shading a gaze that's directed more or less toward the two empty wine bottles on the passenger-side floorboard.

Annoyance mingles with nostalgia, because the hand can belong to no one but Mrs. Walters. She's made a career out of being the neighborhood busybody, and spent half my childhood chasing me back toward this very house with a garden hose turned on to full blast.

After driving for almost a full day with no sleep, last night's alcohol spectacular only amounts to one of this morning's problems, and my face and breath would be more at home on a hooker who just came off a double shift. Not the fancy kind of hooker, either.

There's nothing to do but crank down the window, which ushers a refreshing wash of cool morning air into my oven of a car. Late May in South Carolina isn't exactly temperate. Regardless of the thin, disapproving line of her mouth, no amount of childhood memories can summon a smile.

"Good morning, Graciela."

"What time is it?" I ask without acknowledging her greeting.

The grooves beside her lips deepen. "A little after seven."

"Christ. It had to be sunny." I shove the door harder than necessary but she steps back, avoiding a good smash to the knees. I press my toes to the concrete, taking a few gulps of fresh coastal air before grabbing the doorframe and wobbling to my feet.

"Are you ill?"

"What? No, not exactly."

"Is Martin well?" She crosses her arms over her chest, her faded brown gaze flicking toward the house.

"I just got here. You're the one who called me, remember?" Maybe Mrs. Walters had gone batshit crazy since I'd last spent any real time in Heron Creek. Maybe I should have considered that option before packing my entire crappy life into my crappy car and hauling it from Iowa to South Carolina.

"He's no worse off than when I called. I just wondered why you arrived in this . . . harried state."

"Oh." I put my back to the rising sun, refusing to follow her eyes as they take in the giant pile of clothes and shoes and hangers and toiletries crammed in my backseat. The distaste curling her lips toward her chin says she might be wondering how many Iowa City rats hitchhiked with the rest of the mess. "I was in a hurry."

I straighten my shoulders and run fingers through my limp hair, wishing I'd taken the time to put it in a braid or a ponytail, anything that would have lessened the tangled brown waves that fall past my shoulders. Maybe Glinda still cuts hair in town. If I ever get around to making a to-do list, that's going on the top.

The path that leads to the front door is uneven, the red bricks dipping and jutting, fighting with green grass and mud for the right to send me falling on my face. They all manage to fail, my passage to the front stoop ending in safety. Up close, the old two-story house sags, more tired and run-down than it appears in my mind. White paint flakes off the shutters and columns, and even the porch swing, making the house seem as bone-weary at the prospect of standing upright another day as I feel.

My keys are somewhere in the mess of my purse but the door swings open, hinges creaking, before I gather the energy to go dig for them. The sight of Gramps, half bent over his walker, brings tears to my eyes. He must have been watching, because he can hardly hear a thing anymore, and the thought shames me in the light of my behavior.

I throw open the screen door, ignoring the fact that nosy Mrs. Walters hovers behind me, and sling my arms around his neck. Right here, enfolded in his embrace, is the closest thing to home. He smells like Gramps, a combination of sunshine and earth and sea that's as elusive as it is comforting, and my limbs droop with relief.

Home.

"Hey, Gramps." My words are muffled against his shirt, and he leans his head close to mine until his hearing aids squeal in protest and we both laugh.

Even though my throat throbs, for Gramps I wrestle loose a smile and he gives me a lopsided one in return. His pale blue eyes twinkle like always but, like the house, they seem dimmer than they do in my vision of the past. Far away.

Grams passed almost six months ago. I've stayed away too long.

"Gracie-baby, don't you go frowning. I might look like a fish dryin' out in the bottom of a hot tin boat, but get a load of your own mug and you won't find me so offensive." He wrinkles his nose. "Not to mention the stink about you."

The laugh his comments knock loose hurts. Rusty flakes shudder off my lungs and throat as the hurt cackles its way past my lips, and it finishes with a grimace. "I drove straight through and slept in the driveway. Didn't want to wake you."

He raises an eyebrow to acknowledge my lie, but doesn't turn his disapproval into words. We both know he wouldn't have heard me if I drove a dump truck through the front of the house with a full marching band as a lead-in, then finished off with a fireworks display.

He peeks around me as I wander into the foyer. "Mornin', Stella."

"Good day, Martin."

The kitchen is far enough away to relieve me of listening to Mrs. Walters rant about my inappropriate return to Heron Creek. There's grape soda, water, milk, and a pitcher of sweet tea in the fridge, along with an assortment of fruits, vegetables, lunchmeats, and condiments that there's no way he prepares for himself. Gramps has a housekeeper in twice a week, and my Aunt Karen hired her to do the grocery shopping now, too.

The grape soda tastes like being ten years old, like Grams and Gramps and summers spent splashing in the intracoastal, and barely squeezes past the lump in my throat. Tears, which have never been quick to come for me before, have become my constant companion since the public, humiliating demise of my engagement.

They're under control by the time the bump of metal on ceramic tile announces Gramps' return from his banal chat with Mrs. Walters. "You hungry, Gramps?"

"Eh?"

"Did you eat breakfast?" I ask, a little louder.

He shakes his head, which means he hasn't eaten, or he doesn't want to eat, or that he didn't hear me. I'm worn too thin to ferret out the correct interpretation, even though the primary motivation for my return to Heron Creek is taking care of Gramps. Mrs. Walters had called my Aunt Karen, threatening to contact the authorities about putting him in a home if we didn't do it ourselves.

My aunt has no intention of leaving Charleston, ever. When I got wind of Mrs. Walters' threat during a weekly phone call with Gramps, it happened to be the exact same day I caught my fiancé fucking his teaching assistant. On the desk in his office. During school hours.

The decision to move back here to take care of Gramps and get the hell away from anyone and everyone who knows both David and me—people who knew about his affairs, plural, for years and never said a word—made itself.

Maybe I'm technically running away, but since Gramps needs me, or someone, I'm running toward something, too. A new life, my old pre-David one, it doesn't matter. I can hide here.

We wander into the living room, and Gramps eases down into his worn, comfy recliner, one that's tan and shiny in the bald spots, before pinning me with his perceptive blue gaze. "You come to put me in a home, Gracie-baby?"

"Don't be silly, Gramps. You'll probably have to put me in one first."

He nods, his expression serious except for the sparkle in his eyes. "I can see that by the looks of you. Gonna be a crazy home, or one for booze hounds, though, not a place for old folks."

I'm ready to collapse, spent from the night of driving and the bottles of wine, not to mention the sunrise wake-up call. Or the contents of the past two weeks of my life. Either way, I can't find the energy to argue with him, especially because he's not wrong, the way things are going.

"No need to answer. You should never defend yourself, girl. Those people who would believe you already know better and those who won't aren't listening anyway. Best to keep your mouth shut." He huffs. "At least something your Grams and I taught you lodged between your ears."

"Oh, come on. I learned more than that around here. How to make applesauce, how to make every person in a twenty-mile radius love you unconditionally, that it's okay to shoot things that annoy you."

"That last one is all your grandmother." The wistful sigh in his voice tears at my heart. He's lonely, and no wonder. We are all terrible people for having left him alone.

I need a few minutes, an hour, a week, to try to find the chunks and strips of myself that have ripped off, floated away. Hopefully they're still tied to me, like balloons, and can be tugged back. "I'm going to take a shower and get some things from the car. I'll make lunch in a few hours, okay?"

He waves a hand my direction and nods, his eyes glued to the *Creek Sun* he picks up from the end table. I take my cue and head for the foyer, but a rustle of newspaper and the sound of my name turns me back around.

"Yeah?"

"Karen called yesterday. Amelia's pregnant again. Three months along this time, so they're hoping it's going to stick."

The mention of my cousin's name seizes every muscle in my body. We grew up here together, more sisters than cousins, but it's been five years since we've spoken. Since the night of her bridal shower.

Through my pain, layered thick with the loss of Amelia close to the bottom, comes a geyser of joy. Amelia never wanted anything more than to be a mother, and there have been four miscarriages. That I know about. It had killed me to not be there for her when they happened, but our rift had been Millie's choice, not mine.

There have been an inordinate number of miscarriages and stillbirths, going back to at least our great-grandmother.

Odd, but it had never occurred to me to worry. Amelia was the one who always wanted kids.

"That's great news," I manage, the words a little strangled but sincere.

Gramps huffs, his gaze wandering back to what passes for news in a town of less than two thousand. "I'm disappointed you two still haven't put aside whatever came between you, Gracie-baby."

My heart sinks, his words carrying the same impact as they have for all of my twenty-five years. "It's hard to talk with only one person in the room, Gramps."

He doesn't answer, and this time I'm pretty sure he's pretending not to hear me. He has a point. "She won't talk to me" isn't much of an excuse, but like everything else in the shambles of my life, thinking about actually taking steps to fix it makes me so tired I almost curl up on the carpeted steps climbing upward from the foyer.

Fat pants, clean underwear, maybe a toothbrush, then no more requirements until lunch.

My old Ford waits in the driveway, as patient and loyal as ever. Better than any dog, I used to tell David when he wanted to bring home a puppy. Not that I have a problem with dogs, but he would've gotten bored within a week and all of the cleaning and walking and playing would have fallen to me. One day, I'd promised myself, he'd be more reliable, I'd be done with grad school, and things would be different.

Well, I'd finished grad school. Maybe one out of three isn't bad.

I rummage through the backseat in search of my necessities, coming up with my toiletry case and yoga pants before finally discovering clean underwear stuffed inside a ratty pair of running shoes. My skull cracks on the car's frame on my way out, making me rethink the loyalty of my hunk of junk. I pause to rub at the pain and catch myself staring into the woods toward the creek.

Heron Creek is situated around an intracoastal waterway about twenty miles from Charleston. There's a dock at the back of my grandparent's five-plus acres, and the town itself has three public access piers.

Even now, I can see Amelia and I streaking into the morning, our bellies full of Grams' banana-and-honey pancakes. A warm, muggy mist curling around our tiny bodies, lifting us to Mel's porch down the street, and then sweeping up Will from the big house along the water. We laughed away entire days, lazing in the sun, splashing in the salty river, making up a variety of adventurers that most often ended up in the old graveyard.

I would never have believed when I left my childhood behind that not a single one of their friendships would follow me into the future. My heart split in two at the memory of Will, even though I had been the one to let go.

Mel and Amelia . . . the miles that separate us are more complicated.

Closing my eyes does nothing to erase the years of memories twirling through the early morning fog. Turning my back helps a bit more, and once the front door clicks shut behind me, I almost believe I'll be able to shut out the painful days of my past as easily as the piercing sunlight. That I'll be able to live in Heron Creek and cherry-pick the pieces of the past that comfort, not the ones that remind me that the person I'd dreamed I'd be is not the person the mirror says I've become.

ଓ

I don't remember falling asleep, but the smell of my hair on the pillow insists I didn't make it into the shower, or out to unload my car, before stretching out in my old room. The scent of fresh linen—the same laundry detergent and fabric softener Grams used—permeates the crisp, light blue sheets and handmade quilt. The sight of the blues and creams, the gauzy curtains blowing in the salty late-spring breeze, had stolen the last bit of my will to act like a grownup.

My stench, a faint trace of salt and fish, forces me to shift, at least enough to remove my nose from my armpit. Something black shudders in the corner of the room and I shriek, sitting up and scrambling backward, pulling a fluffy sham to my chest. My heart pounds and the stink in the room increases, morphs into an unfamiliar odor that's impossible to place.

No matter how hard I stare into the shadowed recesses of my familiar room, they remain empty.

I shake my head, snorting at my panic. It's like I'm ten years old again, clutching at sheets and straining to make out invisible faces after a night of Amelia's impressive retellings of local legends. Like every small Southern town, Heron Creek's chock full of ghosts. Supposedly. As hard as we'd tried, as many hours as we'd spent in cemeteries, none of us had ever seen one.

The sound of Gramps shuffling around downstairs propels me out of bed and into the bathroom, my legs hot and tingly from the unexpected nap. I'd slept the better part of the past twelve hours, which, while not uncommon for me in the past week, was pretty much unheard of during the six years before that. Not that sleeping drunk in the front seat of a car is particularly restful. Or good on my twenty-five-year-old lower back.

The mirror reveals an atrocious rat's nest of dark waves and an impressive array of pink crease marks on the right side of my face. My eyes look as though they belong in the face of a girl who drove nineteen hours, guzzled two bottles of gas-station wine, and passed out in the car, so at least the mirror doesn't lie.

I'm not tempted by the shower, instead choosing to wrestle my hair into a lopsided bun, then brush my teeth and throw on some deodorant. It won't fool Gramps, but he's not going to get on me about it. Today. He's an advice giver, but has a knack for knowing when a kind word will help or push me over the edge. I'm already dangling.

Soft snores fill the living room, even though it only took me about fifteen minutes to get downstairs. Gramps' mouth hangs open, head drooping onto his shoulder while an Atlanta Braves game blares from the television. I turn it down and head into the kitchen, deciding to whip up something fancy, such as grilled cheese sandwiches. He's awake when I return; I plop a plate of gooey goodness on his lap and a grape soda on the end table next to him, then settle on the couch.

"Have a nice nap?" I ask.

He nods. "How was yours?"

I don't know why I'm embarrassed about napping mid-morning. Maybe because I'm a girl in my mid-twenties with a doctorate, not an infant. "Yes. I didn't mean to fall asleep, but there's something about that room. It still smells like Grams."

"The woman buys the same laundry detergent."

"I'm pretty sure her name is Laura," I venture around a steaming bite.

He grunts, swallowing half of his sandwich in a couple of bites, then taking a swig of his soda. "There's a new couple down the street, invited us to dinner tonight. Not new to me, new to you. Been here about five years."

"I don't really want to—"

"Already said we'd be there. I can roll my old ass down the street with my walker alone, if you'd rather."

I roll my eyes. "Fine. What time?"

"Five."

Old people and their eating habits. I'm going to have to start eating lunch at ten-thirty in the morning if my meals are going to be taken with Gramps and his friends. Which, since I have none of my own and little desire to leave the house, seems likely.

"Braves are winning," I observe, setting my empty plate on the coffee table and snuggling back into the sagging cushions. They smell like my Grams, too, among other vestiges of the past.

"They're ahead, sure."

We watch in silence, the easy togetherness warming me in exactly the way I'd dreamed since deciding to come back here. He doesn't ask me what happened with David, why there's a pale ring of skin on my finger instead of the flashy diamond I'd worn to Grams' funeral. I don't bug him about his diet, or needle him about being nicer to his cleaning-slash-laundry-slash-grocery-shopping woman.

There are a million questions surrounding me, waiting not-so-patiently on the sofa at my hips and thighs, that need to be answered. What I'm going to do with myself, with my graduate degree in Archival Studies here in Heron Creek. When I'm going to take a good hard look at my part in what happened in Iowa City, because there's always two sides. Whether I'll be able to live here without falling so deep into the past there's no way to generate a future. But for this afternoon there is acceptance from Gramps, and the scents of my childhood, and these things allow me to pretend those little piles of insistent words and letters don't peer up at me.

And the Braves. There's always them, too.

Chapter Two

By the time five o'clock rolls around, I'd rather be anywhere than on the Freedmans' front porch. Preferably my bed, though.

According to the brief two sentences Gramps shared regarding his new friends on our walk, they're recently retired, have two sons that live down around Atlanta, and he enjoys their company. When a perky, makeup-slathered face and perfectly coiffed hair appear on the other side of the screen door, it makes me wonder whether Gramps has started to go senile.

Of course, since I prefer no company, it's not like anyone would have excited me.

Mrs. Freedman's lips are painted a bright, berry fuchsia and spread wide at the sight of us. The scent of her perfume tries its best to push me backward off the porch. "Martin! It's so lovely to see you, we're so glad you were able to come." Her wide, dark eyes shift to me. "You must be his granddaughter. We've heard so much about you!"

"Ain't she as pretty as I said, Meredith?"

"Gramps, sheesh. Stop."

"No, you are, dear. Simply beautiful, and he talks about you all the time." She extends a hand my direction, pumping and pulling me forward into the house at the same time.

It hurts, this interaction. The stimulation. The quiet of my own thoughts has filed down my nerves, exhausted my tolerance for faking normal, but if I'm going to get along in Heron Creek without getting tossed into the loony bin, learning to at least fake it will serve me well.

My teeth grind together but muscle memory finds me a smile. "It's nice to meet you, too."

"Roger! The rest of our guests are here already. They're a nice young couple that you're just going to love. Come and say hello!"

The *rest* of her guests? Crap on a cracker, *more* people.

Gramps meets my gaze, his blue eyes sharp and full of concern. Maybe I'm fooling Meredith Freedman with my faux relaxed friendliness, but he knows better. His presence soothes me with an ease born from years of practice and I do my best to calm down. It's just people. I used to love them all, the way Gramps does.

A balding man rounds the corner, wearing the retirement uniform of khaki shorts, a colored polo, and Sperrys. His smile is as big and genuine as his wife's, his handshake a little weaker but no less enthusiastic. "Hello, Martin! How're you feeling?"

"Still vertical!" Gramps quips, appearing stronger this evening than he had this morning. His voice booms the way it does in the cobwebbed corners of my mind, his presence curling out to fill the corners of the rooms.

"And you must be Graciela. We're so happy to welcome you to Heron Creek."

"*Back* to Heron Creek," I reply absently, my mind still stuck on who might be in the kitchen. Whether I know them, or they know me. If Mrs. Walters has already gotten to them with rumors of my drunkenness.

Mr. Freedman's brow wrinkles, but his smile doesn't falter. "I'm sorry. I was under the impression you were from Iowa."

"I went to college in Iowa. I was raised there, but spent every summer here between the ages of six and eighteen. This is pretty much home, to me." I soften my slew of words, which sound kind of lecturey even to me, with a shrug. "But thank you."

"Of course. You might know our other dinner guests then—they're about your age."

"Roger, I think you may want to check on the meat—" The man—it's a man, I realize, not a boy—stops short when he sees the Freedmans are no longer alone.

When he sees me.

My heart stops beating, and the shock wraps a thick down pillow around my head. It blocks reality, slows my thoughts until my ears register sounds as far away, a million packed-together feathers between me and the rest of the scene. The Freedman's other guests, the *nice young couple,* is one-half William Gayle.

Which means the other half is Melanie.

Our eyes stick together, his dusky blue gaze swirling with the same confusion somersaulting through me, tearing me apart in the process. I haven't seen Will since the summer after high school graduation. Since he asked me to stay and I said no, since I took it one step further—a final step, off a cliff—and said college would be better for both of us without any attachment holding us hostage.

"Gracie." His lips taste my name, roll it around in a way that's familiar but also strange. As if it's a drink he doesn't like, but takes another sip because a friend promises it's an acquired flavor.

I want to reply, to diffuse the tension crackling in the room with so much force we're probably about to give the old folks a triplet of heart attacks, but the feathers drift down, coat my tongue.

"William, boy, it's good to see you." Gramps swoops in, rescuing me, at least for the moment.

Will tears his attention from me with what looks like effort. He shakes his head once, then twice, and finally digs out a genuine smile for Gramps, along with an embrace. "Gramps. I didn't know you were coming tonight! You should have told me and we could have picked you up."

"Got Gracie to babysit now, so you and the boy are off the hook."

The boy?

As though on cue, two more blond heads round the corner. One, a shiny dirty blonde bob, belongs to the former Melanie Massie. We'd become fast friends at six, during my first summer in Heron Creek, and her, Amelia, and I had shared everything. Of course, we'd never dreamed that would include Will.

The second head only comes up to my knees. It belongs to a little boy who can't be older than two. He sports a head of cornstarch curls that came from Will, but his chocolate brown eyes are a gift from his mother.

If forming words in the face of Will is impossible, this is something else. I know they have a kid, but meeting him hasn't been on my list of things to do. Ever. The ring on Mel's finger catches the light from the declining sun as it streams through the screen behind me, winking at me as though to say, *see what you threw away, Gracie? And what do you have now?*

Nothing. You have nothing.

The kid stares up at me, the stranger, and pops a finger in his mouth. I don't know anything about kids, not things like when they talk or can carry on conversations or whatever, but since this one walks he can probably say a few things. He's fucking adorable, like some kind of toddling angel.

Melanie finds her voice, her face white at the sight of me. "Gracie. We had no idea you were coming to visit." She's the same ol' sweet, friendly Mel, and nothing feels off about her reaction. Not until she shoots Will a suspicious glance. "We didn't know she was coming to visit, right?"

"He didn't know," I clarify, finding my voice. It sounds as far away as everything else, but other than that, fine. "And I'm not visiting. I'm here to take care of Gramps."

"You're staying?" Will's strangled question earns him the focus of everyone standing awkwardly in the foyer, and his cheeks turn red.

It almost makes me smile, the reminder of how easy it is to embarrass him. We had fun with that on more than a few occasions, but today I take pity on him. Because the responsibility for this mess rests mostly on my shoulders, maybe, but it's best not to examine my feelings too closely right now.

"And who's this?" I ask, forcing a perkiness to my voice that hasn't been there naturally since I discovered sarcasm around the age of eight. It's not easy to look at his kid, at this tiny replica of the boy I was supposed to marry, but squatting down to his level relieves me of facing either of his parents.

Mel's hand, that damn ring sparkling, toys with his curls. "This is Grant. Grant, honey, can you say hello to Aunt Gracie?"

My stomach tangles like two ropes twisting together in a ship's rigging—one love, one hate. Love, because it's so Mel to act as though no time as passed. As though she didn't marry my first love. Hate, because it had, and she did, and I don't want to be a part of this kid's life.

"Hi," he says, soft but clear.

"How old are you, kid?"

He holds up two fingers with a solemn, serious expression that's so much like his dad's that it breaks me in half.

"Two? Wow." It's all I can do, and I straighten up before he notices the tears in my eyes. My throat burns, as though someone poured gasoline down it, then struck a match.

"So, you all know each other?" Meredith Freedman asks the dumbest question in the history of dumb questions, but it breaks the tension, which has pulled so tight my cheeks hurt.

"We grew up together, Meredith." It's Melanie again, the only one of us that has regular access to her tongue.

"How lovely."

It's all I can do not to snort.

"Roger, how about we go check on those steaks? I'm afraid to leave them alone with you for too long."

Roger laughs at Gramps' comment and gestures him through the living room. The sound of the clumping walker disappears beneath a child's voice, and I look down to find Grant tugging on the hem of Mel's dress.

"Mommy, I have to potty."

"Okay, baby." She sweeps him up onto her hip and smiles at me. For some reason, it makes my throat burn even hotter. "Welcome back, Graciela."

Mrs. Freedman walks Mel and the kid out of the foyer, leaving me alone with Will. It seems I was wrong earlier today about never having seen a ghost in Heron Creek, no matter the stories.

Now I have, and he's mine alone.

"When did you get back?"

"Just this morning."

Silence. Then, "It's good you're here. Gramps . . . he's not doing too well."

"What do you mean?" We're having a conversation as though it hasn't been a lifetime since the last one. As though we're robots programmed to default to the last known setting. At least, I feel that way.

"I take Grant by and see him on Tuesday nights, when Mel's in school. We bring dinner, watch a game or play cards. He tries to hide how bad off he is, and he fools most people, but he shouldn't be alone."

Guilt gushes through me until it lands in my stomach. The idea of eating dinner is less desirable than ever. I shouldn't have stayed away as long as I have, knowing that Aunt Karen is a dubious caretaker at best. Alongside the shame spurts a geyser of irritation at Amelia. She's better than her mother.

At least, she used to be.

"I'm here, and I'm not going anywhere until . . . you know." Tears sting my eyes, refusing to obey my demand to stay away now that my audience is smaller. Or maybe because it's just Will. "I can't imagine not having him."

"Me either, Gracie. The whole town's going to grieve, you know that."

I nod, swallowing hard and stepping around him toward the living room.

"Listen, Grace . . ."

It's too much, the tone in his voice. The one that promises he's about to say something I don't want to hear, can't handle. Some stupid platitude about how things worked out the way they were supposed to, or no hard feelings, or he hopes all three of us can find a way to be friends again.

Instead of stopping, listening and accepting and dealing with the things neither one of us ever wanted to say or hear, I leave the foyer for the crowd, now a solace. Even though there's no escape. I've been back in Heron Creek less than twenty-four hours, but I'm starting to believe that that line about not being able to go home again is an absolute truth.

Dinner goes about as well as expected, which is to say that the Freedmans do most of the talking. Gramps hears about 25 percent of the conversation at best, and spends more time nodding with a goofy smile than adding anything. Melanie tries, regaling our hosts with a few tales of our more daring childhood exploits, but it's clear that Will has as little interest in reminiscing as I do, and she gives up before dessert. Grant helps, adding a word here and there, and making zooming noises with his green beans, but there's a palpable sense of relief when the dishes are cleared.

"Well, I hate to be the party pooper, but I'm still pretty tired after driving yesterday. I think Gramps and I had better call it a night."

Gramps looks peaked, and says his good-byes and thank-yous without further prodding. Dinner was good, and it's obvious the Freedmans retired after a lucrative working life, because Meredith is a pro at hosting. Everything, down to the last freshly pressed linen napkin, had been perfect. Like having dinner inside an issue of *Southern Living*.

They've been good to Gramps, though, befriending him and checking in, having him around to dinner. It's obvious that even though busybody Stella Walters was ready to ship him off to a home, he hasn't been alone. Will and Grant stop by, the Freedmans look in on him, and Melanie mentioned something about the town's new mayor being a big Braves fan and watching games with Gramps, too.

"Everything was wonderful, Meredith. Thank you." My robot voice is starting to freak me out.

"Of course, dear. Oh! And I almost forgot, but Roger's brother is the chairman on the library's board of trustees and he was able to get you an interview, like your grandfather asked."

I shoot Gramps a look but he's shuffling toward the front door, pretending not to hear.

It's strange, but I don't have it in me to ask what on God's earth she's talking about, even though I do not want a job. Not yet. I'll get it out of Gramps later, and let him know that I plan to spend at least a couple months' worth of savings hanging around the house before facing the big, ugly world again.

Gramps is halfway down the street by the time I escape the well-meaning clutches of the Freedmans. When Melanie calls out for me to wait, I wish for a second I could pretend not to hear things I'd rather not address, too.

Instead, I stop at the end of the driveway. My fingers curl into fists, my fingernails pressing little half-moons into my palms while she strides toward me. I never used to be this way—doing anything to avoid spending time with people, scared of standing tall. It sucks. David did this to me, made me feel like an idiot at even the prospect of explaining how exactly I could drop everything and move halfway across the country with no job. Confronting the reason there's a winking diamond on Mel's finger but a shadow of a tan line on mine.

He changed me, but if I'm being honest, I'm mostly angry that I let him.

"Hey, sorry. I know you're ready to go." Behind her, Will carries Grant out to the car, leaning in to put him in a car seat. It's weird, because in my mind, they both still live less than a five-minute walk away.

Which is dumb. Of course they live somewhere else. In their house. Together.

"What's up?" I force out, mostly to stop from folding in on myself and imploding.

"I just . . . I know it's none of my business, but have you talked to Amelia lately?" She bites her lip, glancing over her shoulder as though Mrs. Walters can hear us from here. Maybe it's habit, but her paranoia infects me.

"No. Not since before she married Jake." I pause, not wanting to ask. Having to ask. "Why?"

"I don't know."

"You know. Come on, Mel. I'm tired."

"The last time I went down to Charleston, I called to ask if we could have lunch or just visit. Catch up, you know?" Another glance, over my shoulder this time. "She said yes, but then later Jake called back and said Millie couldn't make it. And one of my sorority sisters from state knows his family and said there were accusations against him in college. Violent stuff, swept under the rug. With all the miscarriages, I kind of . . . I'm worried about her."

All of this is news to me, and yet it's not a surprise. I've never seen any indication of Jake being violent, but know for a fact that he's lower than the cow shit we used to scrape off our bare feet after cutting through the Jefferson's' farmland to get to the creek.

Worry for my cousin squeezes me tight, digs sharp claws into my heart and lungs and everything else I need in order to live, no matter how hard my brain protests that she's made it clear she doesn't need me. Millie didn't even show up for Grams' funeral last winter, for God's sake.

"I don't have any illusions that Millie's married to a great guy or anything, but you know her as well as I do. I can't believe she'd sit back and take something like that without saying a word." The words seem right when they form in my mind, but by the time they fall off my tongue they sound less than convinced.

Maybe it's just that the past few hours have forced me to face the fact that nothing is what I thought, or expected, or assumed during the twelve summers I spent in this town. There's nothing about life now that I saw coming. What makes me think I ever knew my cousin at all?

"Well, she never seemed like the kind of girl who would have her husband call and break a date with a friend, but I didn't imagine it." Her lip is red where her teeth worry at it. Without warning, Mel's hand snakes out and wraps around my forearm. Her dark eyes fall to my naked left ring finger but she makes no comment.

The gossip is going to be all over town before the end of the week. That I'm back, with no ring, no fiancée, and a drinking problem. "No, I'm not engaged anymore. I don't want to talk about it."

She pauses, avoiding my face. Maybe it hurts her, too, to realize that there was a time when I wouldn't have wanted to talk to anyone else. "It's good you're here, Gracie. Gramps needs you."

That's all she says, and we both walk away. The parting words are innocuous enough, but there's more left unspoken. I heard it all the same. It's okay that I'm here because Gramps needs me. But falling back into old relationships, particularly with her husband, isn't going to be part of that equation.

Fine. I didn't come back here for Will, no matter what Mel thinks. I came back here to spend time with Gramps, and to hide. Having no friends, and no expectations, suits me just fine.

Chapter Three

It's been two weeks, and even if I had gotten around to making a to-do list, very few things would be checked off. The car is emptied, but the majority of my things remain in giant yellow trash bags in the corner of my room. They look like lumpy, fat cartoon chickens roosting. Luckily for me, Gramps can't make it up the stairs and Laura the housekeeper hasn't ratted me out.

Yet.

If she finds my growing collection of empty liquor bottles squirreled away inside nests of sweaters that no longer seem practical, that could change. There's not a doubt in my mind that she reports to Aunt Karen, and between that and whatever Mrs. Walters has already told her, I'm sure my aunt and uncle have had some colorful discussions regarding my choices.

I'm not an alcoholic or anything; I've only been toying with the idea of developing a drinking problem. I don't want to come out to the family and the town until I'm sure that's the direction I want to go. It's nice to fall asleep without hours of tossing and turning, and the vodka erases the endless loop of obsessing over all of the ways I surely drove David away. That's all.

"Gramps! You want a zucchini muffin?" I shout from the doorway to the kitchen, hating that this is how we have to communicate but loving spending my days with someone who makes me feel as though I'm not a loser.

Not that he never has anything to say about my sloth, but Gramps has a way.

"Did you make them?"

"No, Laura."

"Then yes."

"Nice, Gramps. Real nice. Maybe I'll learn how to cook, since I have all this free time on my hands."

I toss two of the muffins in the microwave; when they're warm I slice them in half and butter them before joining him in the living room. We ate dinner several hours ago and now *The Lawrence Welk Show* is on, which I swear is only beamed into the houses of people over the age of eighty, because I never saw it on the *Guide* in my apartment, ever.

"That interview is tomorrow, Gracie-baby. Make sure you get there on time."

"So, ten minutes early?"

He nods, chewing on his muffin in a thoughtful manner. "On time is late, that's right."

Protests burble up, insist on having a voice, even though getting out of the house can't be the worst thing in the world. I can't wallow in my shame and misery forever. But, mature or not, having the interview and interaction forced on me digs in my heels. "I'm overqualified for that job, you know. I'm an archivist, not a librarian."

"Not a job for a librarian," he grunts in response, not looking toward me. "Assistant-type thing. Cleaning, reshelving, maybe reading to the kiddies a couple times a week."

That makes me smile. It reminds me of when he and I used to press our noses against each other until our eyes watered, waiting for the other person to pull away first. He's used to winning, but I'm not a little kid anymore.

But for some reason, this news makes me feel better as well as worse. Maybe because it won't be like pretending things are hunky-dory. It's pretty much announcing my surrender to the world, like when men wear sweatpants in public.

It feels right.

"What time?"

"Nine-thirty. You remember where it is?"

"Yeah, Gramps. There's one stoplight in this town and I've been over every inch of Heron Creek in my bare feet. I think I'll be fine."

"Can never tell with you these days, Gracie-baby. You sleep more than a drugged bear in the dead of winter, and don't think I can't smell you feeling sorry for yourself all the way down here." Now he does catch my gaze, his pale blue gaze sympathetic but stern. "Time to saddle up and ride again."

"I'm not going to take that metaphor and run with it, but I get your point. I'll go to the interview."

"Don't go acting like this new you and make everyone there run in the opposite direction."

ಽ

It's weird waking up to the sound of an alarm. Gramps and I have a schedule, one where he's responsible for his own coffee and breakfast, since there's no way 6:00 a.m. and I are ever going to be acquainted. I stumble downstairs and make a fresh pot around eleven, just in time to make lunch.

Today, though, the hot spray from the shower hits me before eight. It leaves me as grumpy as a bathed cat, and I don't look much different than one, either. I glimpse another moving shadow as I shiver my way out of the tub and grab a towel, but I ignore it. It's happening more often than I care to acknowledge, probably due to the increase in mornings shrouded in hangover fuzz.

I dig through my bags of clothes, emerging with a knee-length knit dress in a subdued shade of purple that won't look too terrible once a cardigan covers my bare shoulders. It's wrinkled, but so is everything I own, and the thought of taking the time to iron it actually cracks me up. It takes me less than twenty minutes to swipe on some foundation, blush, and mascara, then eyeliner as an afterthought—it does its part to make my eyes appear more open than closed. I get bored with drying my hair halfway through and twist it into a French braid that lands between my shoulder blades, then grab a cardigan and call it good.

You can hardly see my depression without looking closely. It's there in the smudges under my eyes that press through the light foundation, and in the red lines spinning webs through the whites of my eyes. Even so, as long as I mind my tongue, it shouldn't matter. No one knows me well enough to tell the difference. Not anymore.

There's hot coffee in the kitchen, which I dump into a travel mug along with a healthy load of creamer before wandering into the living room to say hi and good-bye to Gramps.

"You look nice, darling girl." His mouth is full of raisin bran that must have been soaking in milk for at least half an hour. It might as well be raisin oatmeal at this point.

"I do not."

"Well, that's maybe true, but you look a hell of a lot better than you have since you dragged your ass in here two weeks ago, that's for sure."

"It's nice to see your charm hasn't abandoned you." I give him a smile, feeling better than I have since I got here, too. Maybe there is something to that fake-it-until-you-make-it nonsense. "I'm going."

"Good girl. You're going to kill 'em with that gorgeous brain."

I lean down to kiss his cheek, a spot that had once been ruddy and warm but now crinkles under my lips like a worn sheet of paper. The manifestation of his aging makes me want to scream and cling, shout to God that I'm not ready to lose him, too, to be alone, not yet. It's coming though. Since our dinner with the Freedmans', the truth behind Will's concern has glared, bright and loud. Things aren't good, and even though he mostly still acts like himself, there's not much time left. Not enough, anyway.

Maybe there's never enough time.

"Okay, well, I'll see you in few. I might even bring you back some lunch."

He waves a hand. "Don't go wastin' your money feeding me. I'm gonna be dead soon and you'll never get it back. Bad investment."

I refuse to dignify that with a response. Either I use my money to buy us food or spend the next few months or a year slowly drinking it away, but at the moment there's enough for both.

The morning is warm, but not overly hot or muggy, which is something for South Carolina in early June. It's almost enough to tempt me to walk into town, except for the fact that I don't have an excess of time before my interview. The warm air feels good in my lungs, against my skin. Like it wants to promise that even out here, things are going to be, well . . . if not good, maybe not bad.

I swing open the door to my car and slide in, holding my breath to ward off the smell of stale nachos, a scent of unknown origin but one that refuses to be expelled from the old Ford. When I give up and breathe, the horrible smell I'm expecting isn't there.

But there is *an* odor, the same one that lingers around the edges of my room on occasion but hasn't been strong enough to place. Until now.

Briny. That's the word that pops into my mind. It's like the scent of rotting wood and wet, salty ropes aboard a ship, tangling in the wind. Like a face full of a barnacled hull, or last week's catch sunning on the deck.

"What in the actual . . ."

My eyes catch another pair in the rearview mirror. She's pale, her skin hosting a greenish tinge. My mind registers that and a mane of matted red hair as my flight instinct propels me out of the car. My throat aches, suggesting I may have screamed even though it's not coming back to me, and the path to safety reaches up and snarls my feet. The bricks bite into my knees and hands, leaving stinging patches and bits of clay and dirt behind as I find my footing and race for the front door.

I push it open so hard I trip again, over the threshold this time, and land on my butt on the foyer rug, kicking the door closed with my shoe. There aren't any rushing footsteps over the sound of my jagged breathing, and no pale fist slams into the polished wood. My heart hammers against my ribs so hard they feel as though they're about to splinter. The more focus I place on trying to breathe the more impossible it becomes, my lungs and heart and everything else I need tripping over one another trying to save my stupid life.

"Gracie? I thought you left." Gramps looms over me, his knuckles white on his walker.

"I can't . . . I saw . . ." It's too hard, the talking. My lungs won't fill up, they're holding onto the gulp of brine and terror from the car—apparently the last time I breathed fully.

"Spit it out, doll. You're scaring me, and you know this ol' ticker's half plastic the way it is."

His heart, a knee. The man's practically bionic. He sat Amelia and me down with popcorn when were ten, promising a great movie, and instead popped in his knee replacement operation. Even though we didn't choke down much of the popcorn, neither of us gave him the satisfaction of wimping out.

Oxygen wriggles back into my lungs a few drops at a time. With it comes the question of what exactly I had seen. The smell in the car was more powerful than the one wafting through my bedroom on the night breeze, but it was the same. Could the figure in the backseat be my moving shadows?

"There was a lady in my car. In the backseat."

"A lady? What lady?"

The wall feels cool against my back, and I soak up its strength as I inspect the scrapes on my palms. My heart settles into some semblance of a steady beat and my hands stop shaking. "I don't know, but she scared the shit out of me. It was like some kind of horror movie."

He doesn't answer, just studies me with an inscrutable expression. I can't tell if he believes me or if he thinks I hit the sauce before my interview, but now that it's been a few minutes, the scenario seems less than likely. It's time to consider my own lack of sanity as an option, as opposed to a simple depression or bad dreams. Tricks of the eye. I think I'm seeing a real ghost.

"Never mind. I'm probably just nervous or something, saw a shadow."

I didn't imagine that smell. Couldn't have. No one could conjure something so rank from their mind.

"Well, you want me to walk you out this time?"

The thought of saying yes heats my face and makes me angry—I'm a grown woman, at least as far as years on this earth—but the indignant refusal won't come. "Maybe just watch from the porch?"

He reaches down a hand but I don't take it, getting to my feet without hauling my ninety-year-old grandfather onto the hallway floor alongside me.

There's no one on the porch, or the path, or in the backseat of my shitty car, which smells like moldy nachos again. Gramps waves from the doorway, waiting for my thumbs-up before retreating into his sanctuary. The weather's so nice that I make a mental note to make sure the chairs on the screened-in porch are clean enough for him to sit on, and maybe pack a picnic for us to take down to the dock on one of my day's off.

Strange, but my mind assumes this job will be offered. Not only that, but that I'll take it.

The drive to the library takes fewer than five minutes, the same distance as pretty much every trip in Heron Creek. There's a single stoplight, as I reminded Gramps, and it's red for me this morning. Of course. Even so, there are still eight minutes before nine-thirty when I walk into the library, an unassuming one-story tan stucco building nestled between the post office and a gas station. Like everything in Heron Creek, it's a couple years overdue for a facelift but not falling down.

An unfamiliar woman sits behind the front information desk, draped in a crankiness that makes her seem even older than she is—which must be over sixty. Her ebony skin flakes in the creases on her face, dark age spots like chips of obsidian mar her cheeks and throat, and tufts of gray crowd out the jet-black in the plaits gathered in a bun atop her head. Despite the facts that she can barely see over her desk and that there's no way her feet touch the ground from that giant chair, she's a frightening, grouchy greeter.

"Yes?" she snaps, looking up from her computer as though I've interrupted a project that will cure cancer. A hint of an accent tickles my ears. It's impossible to place with just the one word.

"My name's Graciela Harper. I'm here for an interview . . ."

She leaves without another word before I'm done talking, as though maybe she knows what I'm going to say. Or, more likely, she's uninterested and going to find someone else to listen to my yammering. The reference desk holds little of interest except for her personal touches of family photographs and a couple of weird stick figurines that look vaguely humanoid situated around some kind of burning incense. When she shuffles back around the corner five minutes later she's still alone, and remains silent. Seconds later, the sound of her fingers resuming their banging on sticky keys jams in my ears and stirs the beginnings of a headache. Too much excitement, not enough food.

A man hustles into the lobby before I can ask about my interview. He's harried, wearing a fixed, impatient smile. He's the spitting image of Roger Freedman, who failed to mention the man that would be interviewing me is his twin. "I'm Ralph Freedman, the library director."

I smother a giggle. *Ralph and Roger.* "Graciela Harper. Your brother Roger said he set up an interview for me? An assistant's job?"

"Oh, right. Grace."

"Graciela." I spell it for him as we make our way through some stacks, as though he gives a shit. He pretends to listen. The dance continues.

His manicured fingers press open a heavy, paneled door at the end of the hallway. Door holding remains one of the few Southern traditions that don't annoy the crap out of me. In fact, I've run into quite a few doors back in Iowa expecting the same, as though they've magically opened for me my whole life.

Once I'm settled in a cushy, high-backed chair he rounds an oversized oak desk and flops into his own ornate seat.

"I brought a resume."

He waves away the single, half-assed sheet of paper, the purse to his lips suggesting it might contain a smear of cholera. "That won't be necessary. You come highly recommended, and you and I both know you're far overqualified to be shelving books. Although, if you find yourself with spare time on your hands once the dusting is done, the library does have an impressive collection of local historical documents that could use a professional touch."

My ears perk up at that before I can remember that I don't give a shit about anything anymore. It also occurs to me that Mrs. Walters must not have spread the news that I'm a total crackpot around too far, since the Freedmans are still sticking their necks out. *Highly recommended.* It takes all of my effort not to snort.

"Well, thank you. I'm here in town on short notice, of course, but plan to stay for the foreseeable future. I appreciate the chance to get out of the house and get reacquainted with the townspeople."

"We do story time every Tuesday and Thursday afternoon at two, and I'd appreciate you taking that over," he continues, as though he didn't hear me. "Mrs. LaBadie doesn't get on too well with the children."

If Mrs. LaBadie is the woman doing the Oscar the Grouch imitation at the information desk, I can imagine why. Instead of voicing that particular opinion—or any of my opinions, actually—I nod. He blathers on about responsibilities for another fifteen minutes before dropping the bomb that Mrs. LaBadie will be in charge of my training and oversee the assigning of my duties on a day-to-day basis.

"We don't need you full time, I'm afraid. Thirty hours a week, and you can pick your day off. We're closed Sundays, and the woman you're replacing had Mondays, but . . ."

"Mondays are fine." What on earth do I care?

"That's fine, then. You'll start tomorrow."

That was easy. It almost pisses me off that he made me drive over here at this unsaintly hour when he had no intention of refusing to hire me. A job is a job, and as I pass the front desk, ignoring the pointed, curious glance of my new boss, the realization that I don't want to go right back to the house surprises me.

The fresh air, the cracked sidewalks shaded by live oaks, the breeze running fingers through the Spanish moss—it all tempts me for a walk. I'd promised Gramps lunch, anyway, and one of our favorite restaurants is only a couple of blocks away on the riverfront. The combination of margaritas and fish tacos proves too heady to ignore, and no one has better offerings in either department than the Wreck.

I glance down at my watch to find that it's not long past ten thirty, which means a half an hour until lunch—and alcohol—will be served. It's only a ten-minute walk, but I can wait. There's not one single thing in my life at the moment that requires hurry, and as much as the circumstances suck, the reminder that a world exists that's not racing at breakneck speed is nice.

The streets are quiet, the sun high, and my mind takes leave of the task at hand, tracing maps through my past on the stroll through town. My thin dress sticks to my chest and back before two blocks are behind me, and even tossing the cardigan into my purse offers little in the way of relief. The morning's reprieve from humidity and heat disappeared with the morning, and I wonder for the thousandth time in my life where my genetic proclivity to sweat like a Sasquatch came from.

Dripping perspiration aside, it feels as though my world is starting to slowly tip back upright on its axis. There's the job, with the exception of Mrs. LaBadie, but maybe she can be won over. Or bought. Gramps and I are settling in. I haven't seen Will or Melanie since the night at the Freedmans', and I'm fine—grateful, even—with the unspoken agreement to steer clear.

Of course, either a homeless person or a ghost has taken up residence in my car, but that's neither here nor there. There's still a good chance that's my inebriated imagination.

I turn onto Oak Lane, pushing my face into the cooler breeze coming off the water. My eyes are closed, which is why the brick wall is invisible until I smack right into it. It bounces me backward and onto the ground for the third time that day, where I sit for a moment while my head spins, wondering when and why the good people of Heron Creek decided to erect a wall in the middle of Oak Lane.

Then a hand reaches through the dizziness, palm outstretched, offering assistance.

Chapter Four

I ignore the hand, getting to my feet and brushing dirt off my dress before confronting its owner.

A man with an overly strong jaw and wavy, sun-kissed brown hair watches me with humor sparkling in his hazel eyes. Too bad he picked the wrong girl in the wrong year, because nothing about getting knocked on my ass strikes me as humorous.

Undaunted by the cocked eyebrow I shoot his direction, he keeps a hand out, now poised for a shake. "Beauregard Drayton."

"That's a mouthful," I mumble, searching the ground for my purse. It's lying in a puddle, which stirs up more irritation, as does the fact that he hasn't moved. He's tall, at least six foot three, and even under the blue pin-striped suit and red tie, there's no secret why he felt like bricks. His face is hard, too—all rough angles and sharp cheekbones.

His eyes are soft, though, and the enticing mixture of green, blue, and gold still reflects amusement. "Well, what do you think?"

"About you?" I shrug, even though I didn't mean to study him quite so openly. "Typical."

"Interesting."

"Actually, typical is the opposite of interesting." I shoulder past him and continue toward my destination, annoyance tightening my chest when the sound of expensive shoes clicks on the sidewalk behind me.

Beauregard Drayton catches up, then slows his pace to match mine. It would have behooved me to drive to the Wreck, apparently. Or skip it all together, no matter how the thought of their fish tacos makes me drool.

"You can call me Beau, everyone does," he comments, as though we've been carrying on a conversation.

"Thanks."

"What should I call you?"

It's clear my rudeness isn't going to make him go away, and the part of me that was raised below the Mason-Dixon Line blushes in shame at my behavior. Grams would tan my hide if she could see me now. The thought of her stern, loving expression makes me relent, along with the fact that my eventful morning has worn me out. I don't have the energy to outmaneuver him.

"Graciela Harper."

"Lovely to meet you. Where are you going?"

The fact that he doesn't comment on my different name moves him up in my estimation. Still, his nosiness makes me sigh. Loudly. "To get some lunch."

"Are you meeting someone?"

"Yes. His name is Vlad and he lives to drink the blood of persistent, well-dressed men, so I suggest you run along."

"Really? Dracula's making a midday appearance in Heron Creek? Did you call the paper? Danny's going to be mad if he misses out on the interview opportunity."

His quick knowledge of history surprises me, and if liking men was something that interested me, he might be intriguing. As it is, I'm forced to concede he's *not* typical, which for some reason makes my fingers curl into my palms. I breathe deep a couple of times, through my nose, and they relax.

"I'm not meeting anyone. I'm grabbing some fish tacos from the Wreck and taking them home. To eat them in peace."

"Best fish tacos in the world, but kind of a local secret. Did someone point you in the right direction?"

"Did anyone ever tell you you're nosy?"

"Not really. Mostly because we all know everything about each other already." He shrugs, leading me around the final turn. "Which means you're not from here. One, no drawl. Two, I'd know you."

My irritation gets the better of me at last, spurred by an irrational anger about the fact that it seems as though no one in Heron Creek remembers me. As though I were never here. As though with everything else in my life, the town means more to me than I ever did, ever could, to it.

The thought makes me want to cry, which stops my feet and I whip around, planting my hands on my hips as Beauregard Drayton stumbles to a standstill as well. "Look, what do you want?"

"Maybe I'm headed for lunch at the Wreck myself."

"Except you aren't. You were walking the opposite direction when you ran me over."

"Maybe *you* ran *me* over. Can I take you to lunch?"

"What in the hell for?"

His eyes dance, as though this tit-for-tat exchange with me is the best thing that happened to him since his first girlfriend got up the nerve to give him a hummer. I can't remember the last time a single part of me felt as happy as his eyes are, and in that instant, my anger begs to dissolve into tears.

"I'd like to apologize for ramming into you. Walking and texting isn't cool, and if you're living here now, I should get to know you."

"What in the hell for?" I repeat, the words scraping my raw throat. It's not an empty question. I want to know.

"I'm the mayor of Heron Creek. It's my job."

All of the fight bleeds out of me, leaving me wondering whether or not he can see the gooey, stale alcohol–scented remnants of the girl I used to be littering the sidewalk. I smile, because the other option is running, and the ability to stand back up isn't a foregone conclusion. "Well, if it's your *job*. I mean, how can a girl resist an invite like that?"

We fall into an easy pace for the duration of the walk, which lasts less than two minutes. The Wreck of Jack and Anne, named after a couple of famous local pirates who fell in love, or so the story goes, sits out on the boardwalk that faces the Charles River. It looks like a hole in the wall, which isn't false advertising, and the inside decor reflects the waterside culture of Heron Creek. It's as cheesy as it sounds, which in no way is a comment on their outstanding fare.

Beau greets the hostess, a pretty blonde probably a few years younger than me, and asks her for a table for two. She bends over to get the menus, displaying way too much of her chest. It's not for my benefit, obviously, but a sneaked glance at Beau reveals he's not looking, either. More points.

The girl straightens up and catches him not looking, and the direction of my gaze. She frowns at me, as though it's supposed to hurt my feelings. "Right this way, Mr. Mayor."

I fight the urge to mimic her snotty tone, Mayor-chaser or not. A grown woman mimicking people falls under the category of inappropriate, I'm guessing. Even though inappropriate is kind of my thing, these days, for some reason I'd like to keep that a secret from Beau as long as possible. It won't be long before he figures it out on his own, and then will remember fondly the time he had lunch with that funny girl who didn't seem too touched in the head at first glance.

The waitress greets us before either of us can open a menu. Handsome Mayor Beau orders water and asks for soup and salad, I ask for two baskets of fish tacos, one to go, and order a margarita. Maybe if he thinks I'm a lush he'll back off the gentlemanly interest.

"Soup and salad, Mr. Mayor? How manly of you."

His mouth curls down as he watches me, the first sign of distaste. "You don't have to call me Mr. Mayor, Graciela. Call me Beau like I asked. Please."

"Sure thing. Now that you've got me sitting in this booth, how about you entertain me. What's your story? You didn't grow up in Heron Creek, but based on the accent and the manners, maybe . . . Charleston?" Something occurs to me that gives me a moment's pause. "Wait, are you a Drayton or are you a *Drayton*?"

"I'm sure I don't know what you mean. How do you know I didn't grow up in Heron Creek? Are you psychic?"

No, but I see ghosts. "I spent my summers here growing up and I'm guessing we're about the same age. I would know you." I pause. "Are you avoiding my question about your name?"

"No. Who'd you spend your summers with in town?"

"My grandparents. The Harpers." I offer the information without prodding, then take a sip of water. Twenty Questions is tiresome. Or maybe it's the having to use my brain for more than ten minutes at a time.

"I'm sorry about your grandmother's passing—she was a fantastic lady, even though I'm afraid we disagreed about her liberal use of a shotgun. And Martin's a good man. Braves fan."

I roll my eyes even though I'm a fan, too, even though preferring them over the Cubs or Cardinals is a sin for an Iowan, and fight a smile over the shotgun reference. My grams tended to find shooting annoying critters like chipmunks or snakes or woodpeckers simpler than ignoring them.

We chat for a little while about nothing—baseball, Heron Creek, the weather, boring shit that somehow seems more interesting falling off his too-full lips. By the time the food arrives we've lapsed into silence, the poor mayor likely regretting his decision to ask me and my inane blather to lunch. If he thinks I'm asking about his family a third time, he's wrong. Draytons are a dime a dozen, and chasing after guys with money doesn't interest me, anyway.

David's family had money. Asshole.

"How long are you planning to stay in town?"

The question startles me out of my downward spiral, and I ask the waitress for a second drink when she checks on us. "As long as Gramps needs me."

The flicker of knowledge in Beau's eyes says he's not unaware of my grandfather's failing health. He nods but doesn't inquire further, as though maybe he senses the fountain of tears a breath away from ruining my surface calm.

"I even have a job now, I guess." I keep talking to move away from the subject of Gramps. I can't stay too close to it for long, not without it slicing the last tiny pieces of my heart into ribbons.

His face brightens, as though he's happy for me. As though he hasn't met me an hour ago, or been about to fall asleep in his soup trying to have this conversation. "Really? Where?"

"The library."

"Oh, right. June just moved down to Savannah to be closer to her grandkids."

His knowledge of the citizens of Heron Creek charms me, no doubt. The smile he flashes a moment later catches me by surprise, and the deep dimples in both cheeks lend him a boyish air, despite his expensive suit, that tries to prod awake parts of me better off dormant.

Gramps' food arrives in a plastic sack and Beau grabs the bill, handing over his credit card before I can intercept.

He waves away my protest. "Please, consider it an apology for both running into you and then forcing you to have lunch with me."

"Well, it was pretty rough." My lips turn up in an honest-to-goodness smile. "I hope that wasn't your business card. I'd hate to have to report the mayor for purchasing alcohol on the clock."

It's gut instinct, my desire to remind him that I am the kind of girl who takes low-paying library jobs and drinks in the middle of the day. It's okay that he's going to walk away. Nice or not, I *want* him to walk away.

I pick up the food and we both stand, making our way to the front of the restaurant. His hand rests gently on the small of my back, warming my blood, and the hostess shoots daggers my direction. It takes all my willpower not to stick my tongue out at her, but I can't resist giving her a thousand-watt smile as we pass.

The sticky breeze makes breathing a chore, but relieves the chill from the air-conditioning inside the Wreck. I've never been a fan, and after living in Iowa during the winter, I prefer the heat over the cold any day of the week. "Thanks for lunch, Mr. Mayor."

"Of course. I'm sure I'll see you around." He pauses, making no comment on my continued refusal to call him by his first name. Point for me.

"And Graciela?" His dimples crease his cheeks and kick at my knees until they turn to jelly. Saucy, presumptuous dimples.

"Yes?"

"It's very nice to meet you."

He climbs into a town car idling at the curb. I stand there, my sour expression reflected in the tinted window, trying to decide whether I'm annoyed or relieved he didn't offer me a ride. My pissy mug disappears little by little as he rolls down the window, and I swipe sweaty strands of hair out of my face.

The bright natural light shades his eyes mostly green, and they're alight with devilish glee. "I'd offer you a ride, but you've made it clear that spending even this much time with me has been a hardship. You've endured my torturous company and incessant questions with such grace that I'm sure the hike back to the library is something of a gift."

With that, he motions to his driver. They pull away from the curb, leaving me speechless, every sassy response stuck between my brain and my lips. Out of practice, is what I am. Of course he waits until we're alone on the street, out of the sight of chesty hostesses and other doting constituents before showing his ass. Typical. He's definitely a *Drayton.*

The walk back to my car is less than a mile, but it's hotter than blue blazes. Heat shimmers in waves off the sidewalks and street. The breeze dries up the farther my stroll takes me from the waterfront, and by the time the library comes into view there's a fair amount of sweat dripping between my boobs. It'll be interesting to see whether or not the fact that I could wring a day's worth of sweat out of my clothes will be the incentive that pushes me over the laundry hump.

My stomach twists at the sight of my car, and the memory of this morning's scare, but no one's in the backseat. My windshield wipers trap a little yellow piece of paper, though, which I tug free with a sigh. A damn ticket. Maybe I should have been nicer to Handsome Mayor.

Getting out of tickets and possibly some future drunk-and-disorderly arrests might be a reason to let him flirt with me.

C'est la vie. That ship sailed.

The note crinkles as though it's written on old parchment instead of paper. I turn the car on and roll down the windows before taking a look, bracing myself for a fine I don't want to pay.

Instead, there are just three words, written in thick, dark lines with a calligraphy pen.

Be Ye Warned.

The threat—warning, whatever—freezes my muscles in the blink of an eye. It stops my blood, my heart, my lungs. It's so juvenile, so vague, that it has to be a joke, and yet it freaks me out. The people wandering on the streets, some heading home from the market, others going back to work after a lunch break, combine with the bright sunlight to ease my fear. Heron Creek isn't scary. My mother, my grandparents, all of my friends' parents let us roam unsupervised for hours—often overnight—without worrying for our safety.

It's the woman from this morning, still festering in the back of my mind, who is sawing away at my nerves. And now this.

I stare down at the note, putting on my archivist eye. The parchment looks authentic, but it could be fake. Between the parchment and the handwriting, it looks like it could be from a couple of kids playing pirate games. That it's a joke on the new girl in town seems as likely as an honest threat.

Why would anyone threaten me? I haven't left the house in the two weeks I've been back, and the only people who remember me are Will and Mel. And Mrs. Walters, but no way she'd waste time writing notes. She tells everyone what she thinks of them right to their face.

I toss the scrap of parchment into my purse, then put the car into first gear and merge onto the street. As hard as I try, it's impossible to stop myself from checking the backseat a second time, just to be sure it's empty. There's no one back there, of course, but as the library slides past, the woman, Mrs. LaBadie, watches me through the plate glass windows on the front, her lips pulled down into a frown.

Chapter Five

The sound of the doorbell wakes me from some kind of dream, and based on the fact that my chest is heaving like a varmint racing from a coonhound, it included either sex or running. It's hard to say which would be less likely given my current state of affairs. A draw, maybe.

My mouth tastes like acid and feet, and there's no way my hair isn't a mess, but Gramps isn't going to get the door. He can't hear it, for one thing, and for another, he won't go through the trouble of getting up out of his chair now that I'm here to do the walking things.

It's probably Mrs. Walters or Mrs. Freedman, neither of whom seem convinced of my ability to care for Gramps without their eyes over my shoulder. They both drop by on a daily basis, sometimes with food, other times with pitchers of tea or, in Mrs. Freedman's case, the latest romance novel. It's good that they've been watching out for him, but it rankles my pride that they continue to check in so often. This is my time with my grandfather, and Mrs. Walters only comes by so she can spy.

I'm ready to tell her off, protests and indignant rhetoric forming a disorderly line, when I swing open the door. They dissolve, frightened away by the sight of Mayor Beau on the porch holding a six-pack of beer. My prepared expression of annoyance shifts, and by the lines that crinkle around his eyes, it's closer to dumbfounded. Emphasis on the dumb.

"What are *you* doing here?"

"Charming. Is that how they answer the door in Iowa?"

My sputtering attempt to shift from shock to smart-ass fails miserably, and when I realize that I'm wearing the exact same clothes as the last time he saw me—with additional wrinkles—the hot flood of embarrassment doesn't help. The thought of what my bed hair and smeared makeup must look like makes me want to run, but instead I jut out my chin. I don't care what Mayor Beau or anyone else thinks. I came back to Heron Creek to wallow, and nosy neighbors and handsome mayors aren't going to stop me.

"How do you know I'm from Iowa? I never told you that."

"I'm the mayor."

"Is mayor interchangeable for stalker here, because— - Hey!"

Mayor Beau steps over the threshold and past me without an invitation, disappearing into the living room. He shouts a greeting at Gramps, who hollers back at him with a familiarity that suggests he spends more than a little time here. I don't have much choice but to shut the front door before every mosquito in the county shows up for a feast, then head back upstairs. The realization that the mayor spent his afternoon either thinking or asking about me tingles under my skin, and I change clothes and run a brush through my hair, forgetting already that I'm not supposed to care what he thinks. I do draw the line at fresh makeup, but concede to wiping the smudges of mascara from under my eyes before heading back downstairs.

The cutoffs and University of Iowa T-shirt I change into are comfortable, so it's not as though I'm trying to look nice. Especially since, like the rest of my clothes, they've been crumpled in trash bags. There's probably no coming back from being the girl who didn't bother to change clothes before sleeping away the afternoon, but the last thing I need is someone else who doesn't think I'm fit to be the one caring for Gramps.

The Braves game gets underway on the television, the announcers pontificating on the day's matchup with the Nationals loud enough that the closest neighbor, three lots away, can probably hear. Mayor Beau sinks into the couch, one arm slung up on the back of the cushions and an ankle crossed over a knee. Companionable silence hangs between them, a reminder that they've done this before, and that Beau showing up tonight may not be about running into me.

Neither of them has noticed my presence in the threshold, behind them and off to the side, and the moment of invisibility affords me the time to study the mayor. He traded his impeccable suit for a pair of worn jeans and a crisp pink polo, and wears each with equal comfort. The perfectly combed hair from this morning is softer, with a slight curl around the collar of his shirt that makes me think he showered before stopping by—he probably did something insane, such as exercising after work.

I enter the room with as much dignity as possible and offer them both a drink. Beau asks for a beer, ignoring my raised eyebrows. I fetch two, popping the tops in the kitchen, and grab a grape soda for Gramps. The only place to sit is on the other end of the couch, which sets the tips of my nerves to a slight hum. Which is stupid. I'm twenty-five years old, and I lost my virginity nearly ten years ago. Why am I freaking out about sitting next to him on the couch?

Sitting next to him does not, in fact, lead to him ripping my clothes off and doing me right then and there. Or vice versa.

Beau gives me a sideways grin that makes me wonder if he's some kind of mind reader, then shifts so he can talk to Gramps. "Martin, I bet it's nice to have your granddaughter here."

Gramps nods, breaking into a familiar, goofy grin that goes straight to my heart. "Yup. She's gorgeous, ain't she, Mayor?"

"Gramps, please." Heat burns up my neck and nests in my cheeks.

"She most definitely is, Martin. Ran into your Graciela in town today and the whole experience knocked me right on my rear end." He tosses me a wink, which I catch without meaning to, like an unwilling single gal forced onto the dance floor for the bouquet toss at a wedding.

I give him a look that leaves no doubt that his attempt at humor is not appreciated, then roll my eyes at Gramps. "He's exaggerating."

"He's a slippery one, Gracie-baby. You know how politicians are." Gramps takes a sip of his soda and coughs for a solid minute. Concern tenses the muscles between my shoulders and Beau sits up straighter next to me, but the fit passes, leaving watery eyes in its wake. They warn us to keep our mouths shut. "Did you tell the mayor here about your scare this morning?"

It's a way to shift the focus, but it doesn't stop me from wanting to throttle him. If Mayor Beau didn't question my sanity after lunch today, admitting that I see people that aren't there will seal the deal. His eyes, though, reflect nothing but interest and mild concern—the second of which might be residual after Gramps's little coughing fit. The golden brown that rings his irises reaches farther into the blue tonight, and my heart flips like a pancake on the griddle.

My laugh sounds forced, even to me. "It was nothing. Just my mind playing tricks."

"Don't listen to her. Found her sitting on the floor in the entryway, gasping for breath like a ninety-year-old woman running a marathon."

"Gramps, cripes. Can't anything stay between us?"

"Not when it makes for an amusing story, nope."

I sigh. Amelia and I, along with our friends, learned the art of grace under embarrassment at Gramps's hands. It made me into a woman almost impossible to offend or shame, which typically makes me thankful. Right now, a break would be welcome.

Suck it up, Gracie. "I thought I saw someone in the backseat of my car this morning, so I ran back into the house. End of story."

"Dropped her purse on the lawn and left the keys in the car, mind you."

Gramps winks at my sour expression, his humor as endearing as ever. Beau looks charmed, for some reason, either by Gramps—like everyone—or by the story. Likely the former.

"Sorry I'm not up on the proper procedure for handling a smelly homeless person in the backseat of my car. Cripenanny, Gramps. I'll do better next time." I brush my bangs out of my eyes, thinking again that I needed to make an appointment with Glinda. "Anyway, she was gone when I went back outside. Or, more likely, was never there to begin with."

It's on the tip of my tongue to bring up the nighttime visits, and the note from earlier today. If nothing else, maybe it'll give the police somewhere to start when they find my body tied to a broken grave in the local cemetery. I don't say anything, though, because one admission of hallucinations is more than enough for today.

"What did the woman look like?" Beau seems to think there's nothing odd about this conversation.

"I didn't stick around to get a good look. She definitely smelled like unwashed body and kind of . . . briny." The same word that stuck in my brain this morning rolls off my tongue. There just isn't a better one.

"Briny?"

"You know, like an old, wet boat, or nets and rigging. Lobster traps. Salty and halfway rotten."

"I know what it means." He looks thoughtful, except for the mischievous twinkle in his eye, which makes me twitch. "You don't remember anything about her appearance?"

I close my eyes and conjure the brief glimpse before my feet hit the bricks. Along with the rest of me. "Red hair, but she wore some kind of leather hat. I really don't recall anything about her face, other than she seemed pale."

Gramps and Beau stare at me with twin expressions of mirth.

"What?"

The mayor swallows his amusement first, settling back into the couch and extending his arm again until his fingers almost brush my shoulder. I lean away and cross my arms, sure whatever coming is going to test my ability to withstand humiliation for the tenth time today. Also sure that nothing good will come from his touching me.

"I can't believe you didn't recognize her, since you *claim* to have grown up here in Heron Creek."

"You know her? Is she dangerous?"

"Yes, very. Killed, like, a hundred people or something."

Gramps coughs again, but this time it sounds suspiciously like a covered chuckle. The words coming out of Beau's mouth turn my blood cold, but the tickle of a smile on the corners of his lips doesn't match.

"Seriously?" I squeak in a voice that's unfamiliar, but appropriate in the face of almost dying twelve hours ago. Gramps puts a hand to his face, but as big as it is, it can't hide his smile. I stand up, facing them both with my hands on my hips. "Okay, funny men. What am I missing?"

"Now, don't panic, Graciela." Mayor Beau scoots to the edge of the sofa, rearranging his face into a serious expression that doesn't sit well on him at all. "The woman's name is Anne. Anne Bonny. Do you know her?"

My shoulders relax, but my irritation spikes. "Very funny, Mr. Mayor. It might be a little hard for her to have been in my car this morning, given that she's been dead two hundred years."

"Closer to two-fifty, depending on which version of history you like best."

It's self-preservation, my instinct to pretend as though I don't understand the implication that I've been visited by her ghost. In Heron Creek, seeing Anne Bonny has always been something crazy folks claim. For the rest of us, she's a fun urban legend, something that makes our little town unique. As kids we looked for her at night, in the graveyard and in the corners of our closets and under the bed, but never saw a thing.

"Okay, I'll bite. I've heard the stories, but when did she start asking people for rides? What does she want?" It's a question that's never entered my mind before--to ask *why* Anne Bonny haunts Heron Creek.

As a kid, the possibility of seeing a ghost was all that mattered. Now that we're discussing it as if it's normal to accept the premise that dead pirates wander the town streets, the foundations of the story hold intrigue.

"What Anne wants and why she's still with us have always been mysteries. No one knows what became of her, of course, since she officially disappeared from prison after Mary Read's death." He shrugs, wiggling his eyebrows my direction. "Maybe she likes you. I could see that."

"You don't know me very well."

"Never heard of her climbing in cars, though," he continues, determined to like me, apparently. "Most people claim to see her wandering around the library or the docks, a sad look on her face. Sometimes they see her closer to

Charleston, on her father's land. She's harmless, Graciela. I wouldn't worry."

Except she's not haunting *him,* and there's more to worry about than whether or not the dead can pose a threat to the living. Seeing her at all makes me sick to my stomach, makes me wonder if I left more than my future plans and my dignity behind in Iowa City. The thought sparks the slightest flicker of something inside me and I know that I don't want to be like this—listless, lost, without hope—forever.

"Gracie-baby, I forgot to tell you your Aunt Karen called. Amelia went to the doctor today and everything's going fine. She's about thirteen weeks along now, and feeling fine."

"You answered the phone?"

"Nope. She left a message."

"Hmm." The legend of Anne Bonny has taken root, driving out the concerns of real life, and the archivist struggling to surface from underneath the depressed, budding alcoholic can't stop asking questions. I turn back to Beau, hungry for details. "I knew Anne and Calico Jack pirated around here, but I didn't realize she grew up in the area. For some reason I thought she was European."

"You're not wrong. Her father, William Cormac, left Ireland in disgrace with the servant who was Anne's mother. His wife never forgave him, but he did fine here in the States."

Gramps starts coughing again, and this time he doesn't stop. Bright red veins pop out in his cheeks and neck, and when they darken to purple, I move to his side. Fear grips my heart, lifts it into my throat. There's nothing I can do for him, and watching his skin turn gray and water drip from his eyes makes me feel so helpless I could scream. The hacking rattles in his dry chest, banging around with such force that it must hurt like hell.

He's a giant in my memory—towering over Amelia and me in the garden, grabbing all four of our arms in one hand—but now he's weak, folded in on himself, and the reality shakes the house under my feet. Gramps is the last person I have in this world who makes me feel safe, wanted. Good enough the way I am.

And I'm going to lose him.

Beau's at my elbow, his warm hand on the small of my back. "Give him a minute, Graciela. He'll work through it."

The murmur begs to offer comfort, but with the rug out from under me and the world spinning around, it doesn't have much of a chance. His hand anchors me, though, and reminds me that I'm the healthy one. I can't fall apart because Gramps needs *me,* now.

"How do you know?" My voice is small, as lost as I feel. My fingers grip my grandfather's big toe, propped up on the recliner's footrest, my eyes searching his face for signs that it's not getting better.

"I spend a several evenings a month with Martin. He's got some time left. Don't give up on him."

He reaches out and squeezes my wrist, letting go before the sensory overload turns me into a vegetable. Gramps recovers in the next several moments, taking sips from his soda and wiping his eyes on the Braves blanket covering his stiff legs. I kiss his head, trying not to make a fuss. There's nothing he hates more, at least when it comes to his health. He loves a fuss if it's over his birthday, or some other Gramps-focused celebration.

He peeks at me, and in that quick glance I see something beyond pain. It's resignation, and the implication fills my body with a sorrow so complete everything else disappears. Gramps shakes his head at the tears welling in my eyes, but loneliness claws at my insides, makes me wish for someone to help me through this. Right now the loss of Amelia hurts more than ever, like a million shallow, stinging slashes across my skin. The combination of grief and anger burns, but mostly I wish she could help me shoulder this responsibility. We loved each other best, loved Gramps with equal ferocity, but she's not here.

It's like by leaving me to deal with this on my own she's choosing Jake over me. Again and again and again.

"I think I'll take off, Martin. I can see you're in good hands here."

Beau's eyes meet mine and relief cools the storm of pain and rage thundering inside me. He trusts me with Gramps, even after hearing my hitchhiking ghost story. At least that worry can be shelved since he doesn't seem inclined to call…whoever you call to report an elderly person in need.

"I'll be right back, Gramps, okay?"

He squeezes my hand and reaches for the headphones that allow him to hear the television without broadcasting the game for the tourists all the way down in Charleston. I lead Mayor Beau to the front door and thank him for stopping by, and for taking care of Gramps. The pause between us lengthens, the air between us thick with some kind of indecision, but he finally nods and steps backward over the threshold.

"Graciela?"

"Hmm?" My mind is in the living room, on Gramps. On my family, or what's left of it.

"If I had tried to give you a hug right then, would you have slugged me?"

"Yes."

I slam the door in his face, but not before those dimples do their part to salve my frayed nerves. In the living room, Gramps seems better, chewing on his bottom lip as he watches the Braves' pitcher try to get out of a two-on, no-one-out situation.

His pale eyes are sharp again instead of hazy with pain and flick my direction. "What are you smiling for, girl?"

"What? I'm not smiling."

But damned if I'm not.

Gramps falls asleep in his chair before the game ends. I leave him there while I clean up the kitchen from our dinner of cereal and toast, inventorying the fridge and pantry in the process. The homemade jelly is running out—only four jars of strawberry left in the freezer. That might be a reason to call Aunt Karen, and pick her brain about Amelia in the process. She used to help them make it, so I know she'd be able to teach me, if I can pry her out of Charleston.

I help Gramps to the bedroom a little later, and make sure he gets out of the bathroom and under the covers before heading to my den of blue-and-cream comfort. Moonbeams tumble past the gauzy curtains and lay on the bed like an extra set of blankets, but for the first night since returning to Heron Creek, sleep isn't the first thing on my mind. Anne Bonny is, followed closely by the fact that my resentment of my cousin slips toward concern. Melanie's words from the other night fester in the back of my mind, because even though I've done my best to act as though nothing she said made a difference to me, she's not wrong about Amelia. Ignoring Mel, having Jake return her calls . . . none of it seems right.

She hadn't come to my mother's funeral, or Grams', and at the time it had sent me into an indignant rage. Now, thinking harder, it could reflect something more than just a lack of caring. A different problem. Knowing what I know about Jake, it doesn't take much to imagine what exactly might be changing my cousin's personality.

There's no good course of action. When we fought five years ago, it ended with her informing me that, as far as she was concerned, we are no longer family. I can't just waltz into her house and demand answers for her bizarre behavior, especially not now that she's in the second trimester of a healthy pregnancy. It's all she ever wanted, and upsetting her now would be a worse transgression than the first.

I take off my shorts and crawl into bed in my T-shirt, deciding that my teeth can wait until morning. I tell myself it's because we barely had anything for dinner, but in reality, I'm a little bit spooked that there's going to be a ghost reflected behind me in the mirror, or lurking behind the glass shower doors. Once the cool sheets rustle over my legs, my thoughts wrestle with the possibility that the smelly woman in my room and my car is a long-dead lady pirate, and that maybe she's not going away.

I wish I'd paid more attention to the stories about her as a girl, but perhaps it doesn't matter because, as Beau says, the details regarding her lurking around Heron Creek are scant. Amelia, Melanie, Will, and I performed as many séances and spent as many nights scaring the pants off one another with ghost stories as the next group of kids—maybe more—but we mostly made up histories for the patches of gravestones in the ancient local graveyard. It was more interesting to have the full tale, and as someone who now has a graduate degree in the subject, I know that history rarely affords that kind of full accounting. Real people are harder to pin down, in life and in death.

The memory of my interview, and Mr. Freedman the Redux telling me about the extensive local archives, makes me look forward to going to work. Miracles will never cease.

Sleep should come easier knowing tomorrow could hold at least a few answers, but every time I close my eyes, the image of Beauregard Drayton shimmers behind them. He's such a strange mixture of kind and cocky that he intrigues me far more than he should—far more than expected, given that I haven't even thought about a man other than David for over five years.

I shove the thought of the mayor away and refuse to think about how long it's been since anyone other than me got my blood pumping below the waist. He may not know me well enough to realize it, but I'm the exact opposite of the kind of girl a politician would want on his arm, and the idea of turning into one of those fembots, a younger version of Mrs. Freedman, makes me itch all over.

The minutes tick away on the clock beside the bed, turn into hours. I stare at the moon and the stars, not thinking about much of anything, really. The whiskey hidden in one of my trash bags tempts me, but with work coming up fast, it doesn't seem like the smartest idea.

Jesus, I even fail at being a depressed alcoholic. Any girl serious about giving up on life in general wouldn't give a squirrel's shit about the consequences.

Somehow, despite my best efforts—or nonefforts—tomorrow still matters.

Chapter Six

"That Mayor Drayton's really something, huh, Gracie-baby?"

I roll my eyes, even though it's exactly what he's expecting. It seems like the right thing to give Gramps what he wants every chance I have. "He's okay. A little overconfident."

"You know, I think he thought you were prettier last night, without your makeup and fancy purple dress. He's no dummy, and you can bet most of the single gals in town have made a pass. Not interested, though. Nope." He slurps a bite of oatmeal doctored with a healthy dose of brown sugar and syrup.

He could be gay. The thought stays where it belongs, in my head, both because Gramps would argue and I don't believe it for a second. The way he looked at me, the not-quite-hidden suggestion of interest in his gold-flecked eyes, betray him. I might not have been able to tell that my fiancé was sleeping with half of his graduate students, but surely I haven't lost the ability to sense when a man is genuinely interested.

"Well, I'm sure it'll be the same with me."

Gramps shakes his head. "You're just like your Grams. Don't see the truth of how pretty you are—look just like her, too."

The comment lifts the corners of my lips and swells my heart in my chest, even though it's far from the first time he's uttered some form of it. The fact that Grams and I bear such a strong resemblance to each other might be part of the reason Gramps has always had a special affection for me, and my Grams was a beautiful woman, even in her eighties. Regal. We do share features, along with a kind of prickly countenance, but she had grace—a quality that, despite my name, continues to elude me.

I get up and rinse out our bowls, helping Gramps take a quick stroll around the front yard, then into his chair. He's situated with remote controls, blankets, his pills, and a drink all within easy reach, not to mention Mrs. Walters saw us outside, so she can't say he's not getting enough air. It's an hour before the library opens when I step out the front door, taking a moment to breathe in the fresh morning air before it turns stagnant and sweaty.

Maybe it's lingering fear of Anne's ghost, or a sudden urge to burn some fat, but my feet find the sidewalk instead of my butt finding the driver's seat of my car. I have an hour, and the walk will take fifteen minutes. I'll regret it later, when the trek home in a hundred muggy degrees drenches me from head to toe, but that's then.

I'm out to prove that I don't give a shit about consequences after all. Fuck adulthood.

Avoiding my car turns out to be a moot point when, less than two blocks from Gramps' house, the scraggly redhead from my backseat joins me on the sidewalk. Her gait matches mine, but her feet don't make any sound on the concrete despite her clunky, knee-high leather boots. Lord if she doesn't smell bad enough to gag a maggot, even outside.

Yesterday, I ran. Today, for some reason, it's as though none of this is happening in real life and I don't go faster, or slower, just keep going, eyes forward, clinging to the hope of waking up. It's like swimming through the air with my blood pumping through me ten times too fast, depositing a chilly sweat on my brow and palms.

She doesn't talk, but based on my sideways glances, the premise that she's Anne Bonny seems legitimate. The smell and her stiff men's shirt, trousers, and boots, combined with the sword and dagger belted at her waist, convince me that she's Anne Bonny or that I'm going nuts. Or both.

The expression on her face wavers between frustration and sorrow, but nothing about it or her posture suggests causing harm is on her agenda. We walk side by side a few more steps, me and my reeking ghost, before my nerve returns out of nowhere.

Dead or not, she's kind of starting to bug me.

"What do you want?" The question would sound more at home in the mouth of the first victim in a horror flick, but it has to be asked.

Even so, Anne—if it *is* Anne—doesn't reply. Maybe she thinks it's a dumb thing to ask, too.

"Okay, obviously you left your tongue in your grave. Let me guess, you want to grab a coffee and a bagel? I'm thinking about stopping at Westies, but I'm not sure . . . Oh," I gasp as my body turns to ice.

My blood freezes in place, sluggish in its attempt to continue flowing; the soles of my sandals frozen to the pavement. When the chill lands in my chest it's impossible to breathe.

The cause of the cold seems to be Anne's fingers wrapped around my wrist. Below it, my hand may as well have disappeared, because there's no feeling at all. Terror races as fast as the cold, enveloping me with equal strength. I'm going to die in the street, frozen into an ice sculpture in the middle of summer, and end up on one of those shows about unexplained alien murders on the Science Channel.

The ghost's eyes reflect confusion at the look on my face, which must be horrible. Her gaze falls to my arm, and her fingers reflexively set me free. It takes several minutes for my skin to thaw out enough to allow movement. My teeth continue to chatter. For her part, the ghost doesn't look the slightest bit apologetic. That, more than anything else, makes me sure she's Anne Bonny. If even half the stories are true, she's not the type to care much if she made the poor living girl uncomfortable.

Curiosity begins to trump my fear. For whatever reason, having a ghost stalker scares me less than if an alive person started following me, and aside from the unbearable cold of her grip, she seems harmless. A tad annoying, perhaps, but since she hasn't tried to kill me yet, I'll assume she doesn't plan to.

Her expression changes again, morphing into a twist of desperation that's so intense it makes me sick. She snakes a hand toward me again, but she snatches it back when I recoil.

Note to self: Ghostly types and touching do not go together.

"I don't know what you want. I'm guessing you can't tell me."

Like her boots, her matted red hair makes no noise when she shakes her head. Grime smears her from head to toe, as though she climbed straight out of a grave for today's visit. She points a cracked, blackened fingernail the direction I was headed before she turned me into a proper ice sculpture.

"You want me to keep walking the same way? That's super helpful. Thank you so much."

Her lips twist in a display of distaste that might make me laugh if our lack of ability to communicate didn't frustrate me as well. It's looking as though she's not going away until I figure out what she wants, but the answer to how to make that happen sits outside my grasp. Less drinking and wallowing, more thinking.

Anne's head snaps up, her eyes fixed down the empty street. I follow her gaze, but see nothing. When I turn back, she's disappeared, and a heartbeat later a young mother appears around the corner, jogging behind a stroller. Fantastic. She seems to like *me,* as Beau suggested in jest.

Why, I haven't the slightest.

☙

By the time I order my sugar-free iced vanilla latte at Westies—named by an owner obsessed with the dogs she breeds—my thoughts are completely consumed by the mystery of why Anne Bonny has taken an interest in me. There's nothing special about me, nothing that relates to her as far as I know, but there must be a reason.

Unless I'm batshit crazy and don't even realize it. That seems more likely than her picking me for some mysterious, specific reason.

My mind drifts so far from the comfortable coffee shop that I don't see Melanie until she perches in the chair opposite mine and sets down a hot drink on the round table between us. The marker on the side of the cup declares it a decaf mocha, which sparks my interest. Mel's been a caffeine addict since we could buy our own from the Kwik Stop.

She appeared so fast and so silently that if we hadn't been friends since first grade I might assume she's a ghost, too. "Hey, Gracie."

"Hey, Mel. You're up early."

She gives me a wry smile. "Things change. Can't exactly sleep past noon once there's a baby in the picture."

I nod toward her decaf mocha. "Or two?"

"Plus I have class this morning. Had to drop Grant off first," she continues, ignoring my suggestion.

"Will mentioned you were going to school. What are you studying?"

"Accounting."

"Hmm." Silence invades the space between us, but we were friends for so long I can read her like a book.

She's uncomfortable, and she sat down here to talk about something specific, not shoot the shit or catch up. We shared every secret for most of our lives, and even the fact that she married Will can't erase twelve years of friendship. Over six years have passed without a single word, but despite the fact that it's been as much my choice as hers, I hate that we're uncertain around each other—like strangers, but not.

"Whatever you want to say, just say it, Mel."

"I want you to stay away from Will."

"Stay away from Will?" Incredulous disbelief begs me to laugh. "Are you serious? He's your husband. You have a little boy together. Why should you feel threatened by me?"

Especially by me. The loser whose fiancé cheated, who ran away so she didn't have to face the fallout. The one too stupid to realize that sometimes first love *is* the real thing. Was, I guess.

"I don't need any uncertainty in my marriage right now, Gracie, and you and I both know why I should feel threatened by you." Her dark gaze falls to my left hand. "Where's your ring?"

She asks the question like it's been burning a hole in her pocket since we ran into each other at the Freedmans'. It kills me that she and Will have likely been discussing what might have happened to send me scurrying back here to bury my head in the marsh. Heron Creek is a small town, and I don't want to talk about it.

"I didn't come back to Heron Creek because of any lingering regrets over what happened between Will and I, if that's what you're thinking. He seems happy. Have some fucking self-confidence for once in your life."

She cringes, maybe because of my language but probably because of the remark. It's unfair to throw that in her face. Melanie lost her mom before I met her, and her father's one of the most critical men I've ever met.

But I don't want to think about why she feels threatened by me. About the force Will and I had been, or all the times he called after I left—crying, begging, demanding to know why we couldn't be together. There wasn't a good answer, then. The week before I left for college it had hit me that if Will and I stayed together nothing new, nothing exciting or adventurous, would ever happen to me again.

He and Melanie were engaged less than a year later. The regret hit me like a ton of bricks, and the fact that he and I never talked about it made moving on harder than I could have imagined.

All of the explanations, the *I still love you*s, the *I'm sorry*s and *Let's try again*s hung in the empty years between us, forever stuck in our mouths and hearts and souls. We would never say them. It used to bother me, but now I think it doesn't matter. We had been close enough, once, that we know.

We know what we had was real, and rare. And we know it's over.

"Will and I had a thing, and it was important to both of us. But that was a long time ago, Mel, and we were stupid kids. If you want my reassurance, you have it. I promise I'm not interested."

It's the truth. It took me years to let go, to really move beyond the hope that he'd find his way back into my arms, but when it happened, it was permanent.

Relief oozes out of her pores, which is nice for Mel but does nothing to relax the knot between my shoulder blades that's been throbbing since Anne touched me a half an hour ago. As she sips her coffee, a different regret threads through me. I might be past wishing things could go back to the way they were with Will, but I would kill to have the old Mel. It would be so nice to be able to talk through what happened with David, or to get the scoop about Mayor Sexypants from my oldest friend.

As sweet as Mel's always been, she's not quite ready to trust me. She's not sure what my reappearance means in her life, and the mama bear in her can't decide whether to believe me about Will. I sense all of this, and accept it, because the thought of spending time with her and Will together fades my desire to rekindle our friendship. My fragile emotional state can't handle happy couples, especially not them.

"I thought about what you said about Amelia," I say, feeling my way along the frayed, damaged thread that used to connect us. Surprised to find it's survived at all.

"Yeah?"

"I don't know what we can do about it, if anything, but I'm worried, too."

She pauses, closing her eyes as though maybe she's searching for how we used to be, too. "What happened between you two?"

It's easy to forget that no one knows except Amelia and me. And Jake. Being able to release that burden from my shoulders, to let Melanie carry a piece of it, tempts me more than Beau's dimples. The fact that telling Mel means telling

Will almost stops me, but in the end, it doesn't. "Jake made a pass at me when I was in town for her shower. It's the only time in my life I felt in honest-to-God danger of being raped."

"Sweet Jesus."

"Yeah. Anyway, I told Amelia, but Jake had gotten to her first and said it was the other way around, that I came on to him. She believed him. Instead of me." A lump throbs in my throat, begging to be let loose.

Melanie's mouth falls open, and she tucks pieces of blond hair behind her ears, taking several breaths before finding a response. "I can't believe it. I mean, I believe *you*. But you and Amelia were like sisters."

I swallow hard. "I know."

"She believed Jake because she couldn't face the shame of calling off her wedding. You know that deep down she doesn't think you could sleep with her boyfriend."

"Either way, I lost her." Breathing gets easier. The tears recede. To my surprise, letting Melanie in on the deep, dark secret lightens the weight dragging down my heart. "Things might have gotten worse with Jake. The guy definitely has a dark side."

The memory of his assault on me, from which I escaped only because the heel of my hand accidentally found his nose, sends shivers down my spine. I'd thrown up all over myself once I'd gotten away.

"But obviously you can't check on her." Mel chews on her lip. "I'll try calling again. Tell her my news."

That makes me smile. Secret for secret, just like old times.

Melanie gets up to leave, tossing her cup in the trash can. I follow suit, since my shift at the library starts in a few minutes and I'm pretty sure the mean front-desk lady won't be forgiving any tardies. We're outside, where the morning's cool is starting to give way to the humidity, when she gives me a real Melanie smile.

"It's good to see you, Gracie. It really is. And I'm sorry things ended badly with David."

"Life isn't turning out the way we all thought it would as kids, I guess." I shrug, and summon an honest smile for her in return. "See you around."

"Yeah. I hope so. And Gracie?"

"Hmm?"

"You didn't lose Amelia. Or me, or Will. It's impossible. We stick together. Until the end, remember?"

I do. The reminder of our old friendship pact brings a faint smile to my lips, rolls the required echo right off them. "Until the end."

Chapter Seven

I manage to make it to the library without being accosted by any more confrontational women. My heart feels buoyant, almost as though it's in one piece, after my unexpected coffee with Mel. Things are different, for sure—she's a mom, for heaven's sake—but maybe different doesn't have to mean dead and gone.

The woman at the desk, whose name I've forgotten, glowers as though I stomped a kitten to death and splattered the entrails all over the glass windows on my way inside. She obviously has a problem with me, though what it is, I haven't the slightest idea.

But being intimidated by grouchy grandmothers—or anyone, really—isn't my thing. "Hi, my name's Graciela Harper, we met yesterday. Mr. Freedman hired me to be the new assistant librarian."

"Mr. Freedman ain't here, but he said I'll be in charge of training you up." She sneers at me, her trace of an accent still eluding me. "Says you're some kind of big-shot smarty-pants, so you'd better not take up too much of my time."

"I don't know if I'm a big s—"

"Follow me, please."

She tours me around the library, reminding me twice that I may call her Mrs. LaBadie and nothing else. There's a scent in her wake, not offensive like the ghost's, but strange. Spicy and earthy. Smoky. It trails behind her, finding its way up my nose during the brief walk-through. The building isn't big, and the sections are organized in a familiar enough way. I bite my tongue while she drones on about reshelving, barely managing to fight off the desire to inform her that understanding the fucking Dewey decimal system isn't rocket science, and also that there are inventions called computers that are well on their way to replacing it in the rest of the known world. After her thrilling explanations of the coffeepot, break room, and cleaning supplies, she leaves me with a cart full of books to shelve.

Based on the number of people that live in the town versus the number of books on the cart, she either hasn't done any reshelving since June What's-Her-Name left for Savannah, or she pulled these just for me.

"Where are the archives? Mr. Freedman said there are local history documents here."

"No need to worry about that. We keep 'em locked up unless there's a special request, and that room's my responsibility. Won't be needin' your help."

With that, she stomps back to the front desk, leaving me to wonder how big a bug flew up her ass and how long it's been there. Before long, the books nestle back in their rightful places, my sense of accomplishment at the completion of the small task giving me a strange, simple kind of pleasure. Mrs. LaBadie catches me wandering a few minutes later, trailing my fingers over random embossed titles, and hands me a feather duster.

"Is the kid's reading time thing today?"

"Baby Book Club?"

"Okay."

"Yes. It's at two, and you're in charge. Try not to negatively influence any youth."

I can't help rolling my eyes. Luckily, she's already turned her back. Again.

Lunchtime rolls around before all of the dust falls prey to my ministrations. My stomach keeps growling and since not a single patron entered during the morning hours, the sound echoes off the empty walls. There's a deli down the block, and I even make another attempt at friendship with an offer to bring something back for Mrs. LaBadie. She ignores me altogether this time.

Even though the temperature outside has risen to approximately ten degrees hotter than hell, the air smells fresh compared to the musty dust bunnies lodged in my nose.

"On your way to lunch?"

The voice startles me out of my head, and my trademark grace tangles my feet. The only reason my ass doesn't find the pavement again is the strong pair of hands that catch me around the waist. I look up, ready to stammer thanks through my embarrassment, to find Beau's laughing hazel eyes.

I reach for some smart-ass bitchiness, but find that it's all used up after a morning with the Witch of the Heron Creek Library. Yes. That's the reason I smile. "That makes twice that you've knocked me off my feet."

"You know, you're not the first woman to say that to me, but I never tire of hearing it."

So goes my reward for harnessing my smart-ass instincts. I turn my eyes heavenward, asking silently of God if he listens to complaints about pain-in-the-ass men.

He probably doesn't. It would take up too much of his time.

"Asking God what you've done to deserve my charming company again today?"

"I most certainly am. Also asking why he allows his public servants to engage in stalkerish behavior. Isn't that illegal?"

"I hear." We fall into step toward the deli, as though we had plans ahead of time. "I'll admit I came looking for you. I wanted to see how your first day is going."

"Do you roll out the welcome wagon like this for everyone who returns to town after a seven-year absence?"

"No." His hand brushes mine, sending sparks and sizzles across my skin. "Where are you headed?"

"The deli, I think. Let me guess, you just happen to be grabbing lunch there, too!"

"Funny, isn't it?"

The deli is less than a block away, a bonus and a curse because it means my lunch break won't go over the prescribed time limit. As we draw closer, the haunting strains of a guitar twist through the air. Something about the melody tickles my soul, and when the guy starts singing, his voice brings my feet to a halt. Beau stops at my side, saying nothing as the guy finishes the song and I fish a dollar out of my back pocket, hoping there's enough left for lunch.

"Graciela Harper."

My name emerges from somewhere under the musician's long black hair and above the scratchy-looking beard. It doesn't sound particularly pleased, that voice, but it does sound familiar in the way that a dream seems real during the first moments awake.

Beau stiffens beside me, and for the first time since we met, he seems uncomfortable. It's not as interesting a mystery as who the guy is, and I squint and tilt my head like a curious puppy. It comes together after a bit of concentration—it's the combination of guitar playing and sardonic attitude that spells it out.

"Well, good night nurse. Leo Boone."

He smiles then, putting the guitar down and standing up. His gaze slides to Beau and he gives a stiff nod. "Mr. Mayor."

"How do you two know each other?" Beau asks, apparently in way of response.

I smack Leo's bicep, wondering when it got so hard, then grin at Beau. He doesn't smile back. "Leo here and I are sworn enemies."

"*Mortal* enemies."

"That's right. Mortal enemies."

Leo and I are both smiling like morons, even though the explanation is true enough. If Mel, Will, Amelia, and I were thick as thieves, Leo headed up a rival group of sorts, which contained only more Boone children. Their poor mother pushed out eight or nine of them, all boys except one, and the oldest four were constantly at war with the four of us. Leo and I, the unofficial leaders, hated each other. At least during hostilities.

Actually, we became grudging friends during one of our "peace talks" when he'd saved me from a fallen wasps' nest. It had been our little secret, probably more embarrassing for him than me.

The look on Beau's face can only be described as pained amusement. "Care to explain?"

"It's nothing, honestly." I squint at him. "What's the matter with you?"

"Not a thing."

"Hmm. Anyway, my little group of friends used to have regular battles with Leo and his three closest brothers. We spent the better part of three or four summers thinking up pranks to play on each other."

"Each more disgusting than the last," Leo adds, packing up his guitar.

"Wait, you still live here?"

"Of course."

"And you play the guitar on the street?" We abandoned the wars as we got older, but even through high school our two little groups kept space between us. Tradition or habit, I didn't know, but we did attend more than one party that featured Leo and his band. They were good.

"I do many things, Graciela Harper. What are you doing here?"

"I just moved back."

"Oh?"

"Graciela, you're more than welcome to continue your reunion, but I'm afraid I need to grab a sandwich and get going. Duty calls and all that," Beau comments, his tone too stiff for the offhand comment.

"Oh." I nudge Leo with my hip. "It's my first day at my new library job, and I'm about to run out of lunch break, too. We'll catch up, though, yeah?"

He shoots Mayor Beau a look that I can't come close to deciphering. Beau may think he fooled me with his lame excuse of having to get back to work, and Leo hasn't said a word, but there's definitely some kind of wonky blood between the two of them. Heron Creek gets more interesting every day.

Shit, every hour.

"Yeah, Graciela. I'd like that." He gives me a mock salute, which makes me giggle, and hauls his guitar down the street.

I follow Beau into the restaurant and we get in a line seven people deep. My brain tries to formulate the best way to bring up the awkward unfriendliness outside, but comes up with nothing before he changes the subject. I really need to start using the lump on my shoulders for something other than dreaming. It's out of practice.

"So, how are you and Zaierra getting along?"

"Zaierra?"

"Yeah. The other librarian?"

"You mean Mrs. LaBadie?" I snort at his nod. "Oh, she's a peach."

Beau's relaxed during the two minutes we've been inside—his shoulders have sunk back into place. They were glued to his ears outside. My sarcasm raises his eyebrows.

"What, you're going to tell me she's a sweet little grandmother who spends her weekends baking peach pies and canning tomatoes from the garden?"

"I don't know about the peach pies and tomatoes, but she does have grandchildren. And great-grandchildren, for that matter."

Huh. She must be older than she looks, not younger.

"Is she mean to all of them, too?"

"She's not mean at all. What'd you do to her?"

"I didn't do anything to her. She doesn't like me."

"Now, how is that possible? You're so consistently friendly and charming!"

I give him a look as we take a couple of steps toward the counter. "You're a real ass."

Beau grins, his teeth straight and white except for one crooked one on the bottom. *So, he's not perfect after all.*

The thought relaxes me a little, even though I'm only vaguely aware that he makes me nervous. It's just that with so many faults of my own, it's intimidating to be around someone who seems to have it all together. It's nice to know he has flaws, even if it's just a tooth.

We order our sandwiches and wait at the end of the counter, in unspoken agreement that we won't be able to sit and eat. Especially now that I know Mrs. LaBadie has it in for me in particular. The mayor insists on paying again, and the girl behind the counter gives me a half-curious, half-envious stare.

"How's Gramps today?" Beau asks as we step back out onto the surface of the sun.

"Better. We had breakfast and took a turn around the yard. I think I'll drag him down to the dock on my day off. The fresh air is good for him, and he must miss the water."

He must, because he loves it as much as I do, and it calls to me in my dreams when I'm in Iowa.

"And Anne Bonny, have you seen her?"

A glance around reveals that no one's close enough to overhear, but he's being a little too cavalier, going around talking about ghosts. I mean, there's no reason to worry about *my* reputation, but he must have some sort of respect for his own. It won't be long before he realizes that being seen with me in public is going to wallop his poll results. And not in a good way. Mrs. Walters' tale of my public drunkenness, among other things, is sure to have wandered to church and beyond by now.

"No, and I wouldn't tell you if I had. Next thing I know you'll be tossing me in the nuthouse and swallowing the key."

"First of all, I would never swallow a key. That's disgusting." His expression turns serious, a rare thing in the two days we've known each other. "I don't think you're crazy, Graciela."

"You don't know me all that well yet. Give it time."

He guides our path until we turn onto the street where the library lives. "How has your day been, aside from angering the sweetest old woman in town?"

I snort, which is totally unladylike but impossible to hold in. "Besides not getting any sleep because of wondering whether or not a freaking *ghost* is following me around, I spent the morning in an awkward conversation with my ex-boyfriend's wife over coffee. Apparently, I smell like a husband-stealer."

The silence seems to indicate he's contemplating this information, which isn't what I expected, and stirs a bit of anger.

"Did you plan on stealing her husband?"

"That's insulting," I snap, quickening my steps back toward work, something I hadn't imagined wanting to do twenty minutes ago.

Beau shrugs, as though insulting me ranks pretty low on his list of things to avoid. "First loves are hard to let go."

"I never said first love, I said ex-boyfriend. And not that it's any of your business, but my coming back to Heron Creek has nothing to do with William Gayle."

Not entirely correct. My coming back here has nothing to do with wanting to rekindle the flame with Will, but the memories we share weave thick through the tapestry of my childhood and this town, the tapestry that made it seem, through hindsight, at least, safe and warm.

"You used to date Will Gayle?"

It's the first time the mayor has shown surprise since we met, and that rousts my suspicions. "When we were kids. So what?"

His hand circles my wrist, pulling me to a stop at the library steps. It has the opposite effect of Anne's chilly grasp, though they touch me in the same place; this time heat pours into me, swirling and pumping its way to my heart.

Those eyes, green this afternoon, project desire, with the tiniest bit of guilt swimming in the middle. "I'm sorry for pushing. We just met. You don't have to talk about your past with me if you don't want to."

"You asked about my morning and I told you. There are a lot scarier things in my past than my relationship with Will, but I'm not hiding anything. Ask away."

It occurs to me that perhaps he's giving me space because *he's* hiding something. Or plans to. The tension between him and Leo springs to mind, more interesting now that the situation is relegated to memory and not playing out in real time. Along with the fact that I don't know much about him.

"I plan to. How else shall I solve the vexing mysteries behind those pretty green eyes?"

I snort again, unable to stop myself. Beau looks startled, and I pull my arm out of his grasp. Now it's easier to think. "Sorry, Mr. Mayor, but I can solve one of those mysteries for you right now—I'm only a fan of romance in books and movies. In real life, it's almost always trumped-up bullshit."

"You realize that a true Southern gentleman can only see that as a challenge."

"Please don't. I beg you."

"Graciela . . . would you like to go to dinner with me tonight?"

It's weird to be flabbergasted at his request. I haven't been out of the game long enough to miss the cues he's been giving me, but it's hard to believe he can't see how wrong we are for each other.

"I mean, I've coerced you into spending time with me on three occasions now, so I think it's high time I act like a man and ask you outright. Of course, if you say no, there's always the chance I'll keep popping up here and there. This is my town, after all."

This is as much my town as Beau's, no matter his job or how long I've been away. "You realize if I had that recorded it would be grounds for an approved restraining order."

The smile that breaks out over his hard features, dimples and all, tries hard to crush my resistance. It makes me think that, wrong for each other or not, we'd have a pretty good time figuring out all the reasons why it will never work.

"Judge Mike would never dare. He enjoys his weekends off for fishing far too much."

His persistence, which likely charms most women, drags an exhausted sigh from my chest. "Mr. Mayor. Beau. It's not that I don't like you, and for sure as hell you're attractive—a fact that can't escape your notice, with the way every female in this town starts drooling whenever you're around—but I'm a mess. A big disaster of a woman at twenty-five, and I don't think, as much as I'd like to spend more time with you, that it's a good idea."

"Hmm. I have to admit, like most fool men, I can lose track of things while a beautiful woman's in front of me. Something about your mouth—your lips, likely—but either way, I'm afraid I heard nothing except that you'd like to spend more time with me. So, I'll pick you up at eight. Wear a dress."

"Wait, Beau—"

But he's gone, hands over his ears like a small child, deaf to the remainder of my protests. It's equal parts adorable and frustrating, and it's possible he's lost as much of his damn mind as I have, given that he's the mayor and he's walking down the street with his hands over his ears. People have stopped to watch, and whether or not they've overheard our conversation, the scene sets my cheeks on fire.

I can't wait for Mrs. Walters to get wind of this.

The library offers respite from the onlookers, but it also harbors Mrs. LaBadie's pointed look toward the clock, which shows that I'm three minutes late. It's on the tip of my tongue to blame the mayor, since she likes him, but I let it go instead. At least there's story time to prepare for, and after I wrangle a list of the most recent reads from the head librarian, I spend the next hour scouring children's books for the right one.

And considering Mayor Beau and his proposed date.

It would be smart to blow him off. Stand him up, spend the night curled up in my blue-and-cream bed with a bottle of vodka and maybe a book on local history. Even taking a chance on another visit from Anne.

Spending time with him tempts me far too much, but I'm nowhere close to ready for a new relationship. There's no way half the date wouldn't be dedicated to me embarrassing myself in one way or another. Then again, he'd been warned.

No. Even just on principle, I had to refuse him. Handsome or not, charming or not, he can't force me to do anything I don't want to do. I'd spent way too much of the past four years playing the dutiful subservient to David and his demands, and look where that had gotten me.

A broken engagement, buckets of shame, and the complete loss of myself.

I'm sitting on a folding chair in the children's reading area, a pile of slender illustrated books balanced on my knees, when Anne appears by the window.

"Holy shitballs!"

The books slump to the floor in a quiet but noticeable flutter of pages. We stare at each other, the ghost and I, my heart struggling to stay in my chest. If it were possible, it'd be halfway to the door.

"*Why* do you insist on sneaking up on me like that?" I hiss at the apparition.

"What in tarnation is going on back there, girl? You makin' a mess?" Despite the fact that Mrs. LaBadie hollers to check on me, it's clear from her tone of voice that she couldn't care less if I'm hurt. She's probably more worried about her books—not that I can blame her.

"Fine," I manage, not taking my eyes off my new ghostly BFF.

I take a step toward Anne, trying to keep my sandwich down in the presence of her stench. Her reek grows with each encounter, but the expression in her eyes—smoldering anger laced with sad desperation—doesn't change.

It hits me that I've started calling her Anne, and given up "the ghost." *Ha.* It's easier than referring to her as the woman, or the ghost, and at least this way when I inevitably start referring to her in public it will take longer for people to realize I've lost my ever-loving mind.

She doesn't move, just stares at me as something like pleading strains her expression, and my frustration at our inability to communicate grows. "What? What do you want?"

That thing again, with her finger. Pointing, beckoning, all of it too vague to be helpful. Except this time she moves, shuffling until her mournful gaze focuses on the locked door to the local archives.

"The archives? You want to go in?"

Anne disappears without answering, leaving the lingering smell of fish slime in the air. When Mrs. LaBadie's weathered, lined face glares at me from around a stack, it's clear why she scooted. Apparently Anne's a little shy around strangers, a fact that again leaves me wondering, *Why me*?

"Who you talking to back here?"

A nervous giggle escapes my lips, and it occurs to me that she makes me even jumpier than Anne Bonny's ghost. "No one. Myself. I do it all the time."

"I've heard you're crazier than a shithouse rat, and a drunk, too." She huffs, her gaze falling toward the mess on the floor. "Makes no difference to me, as long as you keep the beasts quiet during story hour. Clean that up."

"Yes, ma'am."

"I'm going into the archives while the children are here. I expect you'll be able to handle it."

She stalks off into the other room, leaving me to wonder why she came to tell me about her afternoon plans. She's in charge here, not me, and it's almost as though she knew what Anne wanted me to do. Knew I planned to find a way to sneak through that door the moment her back was turned.

The sounds of laughter and chatter tumble through the stacks, stick to the books like gooey little smiley faces, and a moment later the reading nook under the big, west-facing windows fills with children under the age of five. Their grins and shouts turn to curious looks peeped from behind their parent's legs, and the joy of the moment steals away my suspicions and curiosities.

"Well, fancy running into you twice in one day."

The voice comes from behind me, but its familiar, teasing tone brings a grin to my face. Leo grins back when I turn around, his hand engulfing a much tinier one attached to a little girl with black pigtails. Her huge, dark eyes make her the spitting image of Leo, but there are so many Boone offspring that all look alike. This one may or may not belong to him.

"Hey, Leo. I'm glad you're here for story time—all these years I wasn't sure you could read."

"I can see that time hasn't improved your manners."

I turn my attention to the girl at his side, who gives me a tiny, shy smile. "Who's this?"

"This is Marcella." He squeezes her palm. "Ella to most of us."

"Hi, Marcella." I squat down, then hold out the two books clutched in my hand. "I wonder if you can help me decide what we're going to read today? I can't decide between *Ballet Shoes* and *Do Pirates Take Baths.*"

The second reminds me of Anne, and makes me grimace. Pirates most definitely do not take baths. The little girl considers the titles with a serious expression, one finger between her lips. I didn't know Leo when he was quite this young, but I've never known him to sport such focus. Finally, she pokes the pirate book.

"Pirates it is! I would have chosen the same one, little lady."

I straighten up, my gaze meeting Leo's. He's watching me with something new in his eyes, as though he's never seen me before, even though we were so sick of each other's faces in middle school I would have bought him a new one if I could have afforded it.

"Is she yours?" I ask in an attempt to nudge things back to normal.

"She's my niece, but she's my responsibility, yes."

The answer births a million new questions, each one more insistent than the last, but none of them are appropriate in Marcella's presence. I wonder which sibling she belongs to, what happened to them, and how she fell into Leo's custody. Maybe he'll tell me one day, but for now, the crowd at my back is getting unruly.

Heaven forbid the "beasts" and I disturb Mrs. LaBadie and her communion with her precious archives. That room is a big reason this job appeals to me, and if she continues to block me from it we're going to have words.

The rest of the afternoon goes off without a hitch, if I ignore the looks several of the mothers launch in my direction. The slant of their eyes, the way they glance at me from underneath their lashes, as though meeting my gaze might mean having to talk to me, suggests Mrs. Walter's rumors have spread past our little riverfront neighborhood. Damn church. The soil in that fellowship hall grows excellent cookies, true, but also gives gossip and hearsay a place to put down strong roots. From there, it spreads like ivy over stone.

Mrs. LaBadie spends the rest of the day hidden behind that locked door, but based on the fact that no noise comes from the archives, it seems likely she's using the time for a nap. I could use one, too, and given that exactly one patron comes in before five o'clock, quitting time, I have to walk a few laps to make sure I don't nod off at the front desk. I spend the rest of the time plotting the best way to get into those archives. Because if that batty old woman thinks she's going to keep me out while I've got a ghost that won't quit who wants in, she's got another thing coming.

Chapter Eight

In the end, I decide to go along with the date with Mayor Beau not for him, or me, but for Gramps. The memory of the looks from the mothers in the library tweaks my stomach for the rest of the afternoon. My being back in town is stirring up gossip and rumors, and sooner or later they'll find their way to our house. Make Gramps worry, which is the last thing I want.

Beau showing up and me refusing to go out to dinner would only cause another scene. Gramps wouldn't understand, and with Mrs. Walters' ability to rival the U.S. Department of Homeland Security on spying, word would get out. It could mature into any number of monsters by the time it reached the end of the line—not only am I crazy, but if I'm not interested in the most eligible mayor ever to grace Heron Creek with pin-striped suits, maybe I *am* back in town to steal William Gayle back from sweet Melanie Massie.

And that would be the nicest result. I came here to help Gramps, to spend whatever time he has left together, not to make his life harder. Throwing a fit, clinging to the banister and screaming like a little girl determined to avoid Sunday school, won't do. I'll go, I'll smile and pretend it's my idea to be there. For Gramps.

At the end of the night, when we're alone, I have every intention of letting Mayor Beauregard Charles Drayton—of the Charleston Draytons; I couldn't help Googling him at the library—know, in no uncertain terms, that this isn't what I want. I'm not ready. I want to be alone, with my memories and my failures and my booze.

And my ghost, if she insists.

Regardless of why I'm going or what I mean to say at the end of the night, my nerves refuse to back the hell off. My palms sweat so much the tube of eyeliner slips from my fingers twice, and I get ready in a bra and underwear to keep my armpits aired out. No need to start the rumor that I smell like a rotting pirate corpse.

The dress is new, bought on the way home since my laundry still waits in trash bags. That stupid to-do list haunts me more than two weeks after pulling into town, and everything is still wrinkled to hell and back. Mrs. LaBadie's going to give me shit, probably, if I don't show up in clean, pressed things at some point.

Tomorrow. I'll do the laundry tomorrow, swear.

My purchase satisfies me, and the mirror reflects a girl who looks something like me. She's skinnier than the Gracie I used to be, and the weight loss has flattened my boobs more than I care to admit. The black dress is cut well, though, and shows off the legs that have long been my one vanity.

Those and my hair, which after a wash and dry and curl with the flat iron, looks better than it has in a month. Maybe longer. My appearance leaves a bit to be desired, with the bones too prominent under my skin and the smudges that won't vacate my under eyes, but I won't embarrass the mayor. If we can keep it short enough, maybe my mouth won't, either. My stomach flip-flops, then cartwheels as though it's trying out for the next summer Olympics. A shot of vodka stops my hands from shaking, or maybe it's my tight grip on the bathroom counter.

I stare my reflection down, checking briefly for Anne in the space behind me. "It's a date, Graciela. I know it's been, like, five years, but I'm sure it's like riding a bike."

Not that I've ridden a bike in better than five years.

The doorbell rings and startles me out of my skin. Gramps answers it, having been prepped as far as my night out, and his booming voice tangles with Beau's smoother one. I pat my hair, swipe on some lip gloss and an extra coat of deodorant, then say a quick prayer that Gramps' attempts to embarrass me will be minimal. He lives to tease his grandkids, and the fact that we're both girls never slowed him down.

My mind wanders to Amelia on my way down the stairs. I wonder whether, based on our family's history with childbearing, she expected the issues she's having conceiving and carrying to term.

I was happy with dreams of adventures. I think I can be, again.

Beau's face lights up, though whether it's because of the sight of me or the fact that I manage to get all the way down the stairs without falling is hard to say.

"Graciela Harper, you look more gorgeous than ever. Thanks for not giving me any trouble about the dress."

I bat my eyes at him, doing my best impression of innocence. "Me? I would never dream of giving you any trouble, Mr. Mayor."

Beau rolls his eyes, and Gramps snorts. I turn to him and squeeze his hand, more than a little concerned about leaving him alone at night, even if it's only for a couple of hours.

"You going to be okay? There's a snack on the counter if you get hungry, and I'll be home in time to help you to bed so just stay in the living room until then."

"You'd think I can't wipe my ass without help. We're not there yet, Gracie-baby. Stay out as late as you want, and I promise I'll be snoring away when you get home." He leans down and kisses my cheek, then cups it for a second. The calluses on his hand scrape against my skin, sending me spiraling backward in time to a place where things were simple, smeared with marsh mud and love.

My eyes fill with tears as he turns away to give Mayor Beau's hand a shake. "You kids have a good time. I'd get all fatherly and give you a lecture about treating my girl with respect, but you'll learn Grace can take care of herself. If you haven't already."

He clumps into the living room and I dab the wetness from my eyelashes and cheeks, determined to try to enjoy the evening. It's been a long time, and even if it can't continue, there's no reason not to enjoy tonight.

"You okay?"

"I'm fine."

"Things change, Graciela. You can't stop it."

His presumption that he knows what thoughts are clanging around in my head annoys me at least as much as the fact that he's guessed correctly. "So, where are you taking me that requires a dress?"

If Beau notices the change in subject, he doesn't call it out. And he notices. I'm not sure he misses much of anything, though he's well-bred enough not to comment on most of it.

"Just dinner. I wanted to see if you'd actually dress up."

"Are you kidding me? You're a cad, Mr. Mayor, and I'm not sure I should go anywhere with you."

His eyes twinkle, golden in the late-evening light. They make it impossible for me to stay angry, a smile twitching the corners of my mouth, but I manage to hang on to my composure. Barely.

"Well, the joke's on you, because I like wearing dresses."

Mayor Beau suggests we walk, which suits me fine since I decided on flat sandals. Dresses are fine, but I draw the line at heels, especially for a date I didn't technically agree to. But the evening is warm, the setting sun determined to put on a sexy show as it slides down toward the horizon on silky sheaths of indigo and blush, and the man at my side smells amazing, like soap and sea and maybe a hint of some kind of pine cologne. He's gone to some trouble with his appearance as well, choosing a dark pair of jeans, shiny brown shoes, and a lilac button-down rolled to his elbows. The muscles in his forearms shift with every movement, and are pleasant enough to look at. All in all, the night could be worse.

Our stroll leads us to one of the two nice restaurants in town. Gallants sits on the water, but unlike the Wreck, the decor includes table linens, silver place settings, and nice china, and boasts a wine list that would make half the restaurants in Napa Valley green with envy. There's a host, not a hostess, who throws me a merely curious look as opposed to one full of venom. It's kind of nice, but also a tad disappointing. I do better reacting to outright adversarial attitudes than to feeling like an animal in a zoo.

He nods to Beau, then grabs two menus from the stand in front of him. "Right this way, Mayor Drayton."

"Thank you, Jerry. How's that new litter of pups?"

"Doing good, thanks. When are you going to let me hand one over? Best hunting dogs in the state!"

"I know, believe me. When I have time to squeeze in some hunting trips again, or to take care of a dog, I'm coming to you." He claps the man on the shoulder as we stop at a quiet table that boasts a spectacular view of the sunset over the Charles.

The sun itself has retired, leaving fingernails painted lavender and fuchsia clinging to the waves in the distance. Beau's voice, relaying how much he wants to have a dog again, drifts to the corners of my mind as the scenery floods my senses. So many memories. Good ones, bad ones, scary ones. Painful ones. I'd spent my formative years getting older in Iowa, but this is where I'd grown up. Where every experience that formed me, pushed me forward, or gave me understanding happened on these streets, on this water.

That's what makes a place home, I suppose. The fact that all of the memories add up to the person you've become, or the one you wanted to be and might find the strength to be again. Despite everything, my summers in Heron Creek left me with far more good than bad. Unlike life with my mother, or the father who died before any memories of us together could take root.

How on earth had I ever thought returning to Heron Creek would be easy?

"How about a bottle of wine? Graciela?"

The question snaps my attention back to the man across the table. His eyebrows are raised, an amused crinkle forming between them.

"What?"

"Wine. What kind do you prefer?"

"It doesn't matter."

"Now, that can't be true. White or red?"

"Red," I concede. "A gamay or a red zinfandel, please."

The server, who had appeared sometime during my reverie, nods. "We have an excellent and rare gamay in stock, one of my favorites."

"We'll try that," Mayor Beau says.

The server scurries off, leaving the two of us alone with our menus. I bury my face in mine, hating to be one of those people who aren't ready to order, and also starving. Eight o'clock is late, especially when I've been eating on a ninety-year-old's schedule. Early-bird specials all around.

It's also a good excuse to avoid talking, which means avoiding saying something embarrassing or getting all teary-eyed over one thing or another, which has become something of an unwanted specialty of mine of late. As soon as I put my menu aside, Mayor Beau pounces.

"Where were you before? When we first sat down?"

My cheeks feel hot. He reads me too easily. "Old Heron Creek. Which is the same as new Heron Creek, with the exception of aging friends. Aging me."

"And a new mayor."

"Of course, how could I forget." I give him a smile, but it feels strained. I'm kind of tired of putting on my teasing, sarcastic face for Mayor Beau. It's exhausting, and maybe the way to make him go away is to act more the way I feel—lost and depressed.

"Tell me about your summers."

"It's not that exciting. Nothing different from anyone's childhood summers, I'd wager."

"I'm not a fan of gambling." A glint in his eyes tells me the comment isn't offhand, but the energy to prod him about it is nowhere to be found. "You were friends with Will and Melanie, an enemy of Leo Boone. It seems you're better connected here than my family ever has been in Charleston."

That makes me roll my eyes. "Doubtful. My friends' families don't have Drayton clout, though my cousin, Amelia, did marry a Middleton."

"Which one?" Shadows claim parts of Beau's face, and it squeezes my lungs with fear.

I don't want to say Jake's name, but I do. "Do you know him?"

Beau nods, slowly, taking a sip of the wine he approved while we studied the menus. "Our families are old acquaintances. Sometimes friendly, sometimes not, depending on the generation. They've got quite a bit more stature. And money."

My mouth twists, sourness coating my tongue in spite of the sweet, fizzy gamay. "I'm aware."

We'd all been treated to extensive Middleton family histories when Jake had first come into Amelia's life. Their roots trace all the way back to the foundation of the country, with Arthur Middleton, the grandson of the original patriarch, signing the Declaration of Independence. His grandson Williams Middleton signed South Carolina's order of secession, an act that might be considered less honorable by some, but not necessarily by South Carolinians.

"Anyway, the four of us were pretty inseparable as kids. All the way through high school, really."

"Then what happened?"

I shrug, draining the rest of my first glass of wine. "What happens to anyone when they grow up? People move away, others move on . . . same old story, it just happens to be mine."

The idea of talking about what happened with Will and me makes the wine turn to vinegar in my stomach. It may be true that I long ago accepted the finality—the inevitability—of our ending, but it's still a part of my past that seems best left undisturbed under a glass case. A piece of history relegated only to those who lived it.

A change of subject can't come fast enough. "What about you? Where did you grow up?"

"Charleston, but I didn't have the carefree summers or close friends you seem to have had. I didn't find my place until I went to boarding school in England at fifteen, and still keep in touch with most of my mates."

"What brought you to Heron Creek?"

"I spent time in several coastal towns when I finished graduate school, but couldn't get this area out of my mind. I love the people, mostly, and when they offered me a job in the local police department I jumped at the chance."

"Wait a second, how old are you?"

"Twenty-eight." He sips his wine, content to let me put the numbers together.

Even with finishing graduate school in a couple of years, he can't have lived here more than four. It's impressive, rising from entry-level cop to mayor in that amount of time, but knowing him even a little, it's not surprising. Everyone likes him, and he makes it his business to remember details about everyone's lives.

It's not my favorite thing about him, because now he's intent on uncovering mine.

"Impressive," I offer.

"I don't think any more impressive than finishing a doctorate in archival studies, complete with a fluency in Latin and Greek, in less than four years."

My academic achievements are impressive, without the reason for my motivation being revealed. I'd wanted to be on David's level, his peer, too badly to slow down.

"You've been reading up on me." There are other things easily located with Google—my engagement, for instance—but as usual, he doesn't bring up anything unsavory. It's as though he's determined to see me in the best possible light, which works against my plan to make him understand that this will never work out.

The topic turns to lighter fare as the food arrives, and as our bottle of wine disappears. It's on the tip of my tongue to suggest we order another, but the thought that I'm going to need every last ounce of my wits to deflect his charm on the walk home makes it a bad idea. Plus, it's time to either commit to or give up my drinking problem, and I find that solving the mystery of Anne Bonny encourages sobriety.

She doesn't come up in conversation, and neither does Will. We chat a bit about Gramps, all stories that bring a smile to my lips and an ache to my heart, as well as the Braves' chances to make it to the play-offs this year. I learn that Beau laughs loudest when it's surprised out of him, that he's close to his mother and sister but doesn't get along with his dad, and that he has political aspirations beyond Heron Creek.

"You know, that makes three meals you've bought me," I comment as he signs his credit card slip.

"Don't worry. I'm sure you'll find a way to repay me."

He offers his arm, which I take because my brain is doing a backstroke in the wine, and threads his fingers between mine. The air outside has cooled to a mostly comfortable degree. Moonbeams bounce off the gently moving water of the Charles River, lighting the uneven sidewalk as well as the pale streetlamps.

I take a deep breath, sucking down courage and blowing out the lust that had infected my nether regions when his fingers locked with mine. "Mr. Mayor, I had a lovely time tonight."

"As did I. But if you don't start calling me Beau it's going to ruin everything."

"There's nothing to ruin." I chance a look at his profile, and get caught in the expression he's using to kill my resistance. "I'm sure that you uncovered a few things besides my doctoral work at the University of Iowa. I came back here for Gramps, that's true, but I'm also here to kind of . . . hide away. Heal. Figure out where I go next, and if I go there alone."

He says nothing, and the comfort of his strong silence almost flings me into his arms. Which is the opposite of what I've been saying, and what I thought I feel. Want.

Maybe need.

"What I'm saying is that I'm not ready for romance, or a relationship, or probably even a roll in the hay. I don't know if you have any or all of those on the agenda, but I want you to know where I stand. When I say I'm a mess, I'm not trying to be cute or coy. It's the truth. You shouldn't get caught up in it."

Beau stops, turning to face me. The moonlight sweeps across his face, pale shadows dancing with dappled light that catches every strong angle. They should be too sharp, too hard, but for some reason it works with the softness of his hazel eyes, the gentle squeeze of his fingers around mine.

"I know we don't know each other all that well, and I've been pretty silly, popping around and looking you up so I felt more ready for our date tonight. But the truth is, it's been a long time since anyone has walked into this town and snagged my interest. Since anyone has been brave enough to look me in the eye and tell me what they think, not what they assume I want to hear." A crooked smile appears, along with a single dimple and an endearing expression of chagrin. "But most anyone in town—including your friends the Gayles—could tell you that I'm not the type of guy to go out of my way for a roll in the hay. I'd go into this wanting more, but if you're not ready, I'll settle for a new friend."

Friend. Without Amelia or Melanie close at hand, just the word makes me aware of the empty caverns inside me. They used to be filled with laughter and secrets, love and generosity. It hits me hard, the craving to have that again, but the way he affects me, it's unlikely I'll find it in Beauregard Drayton. Or *only* that, at any rate.

Maybe that's not fair. Will and I had been friends, once. It's not a bad place to start, and for all my bravado and pushing away, I don't like the idea of passing the mayor on the street with nothing more than the same tip of the head he offers everyone else in town.

We start walking again before I decide on an answer, but my heart knows I need a friend. I've said as much as I can manage; there won't be any more protests from my lips. It's sweet of Beau to care.

All thoughts of romance and friendship and loneliness flee my brain when we get within shouting distance of Gramps' house and see my car. Starlight glints off a bed of glass that used to make up the windows. My mouth falls open and my feet stumble to a stop, but Beau keeps going, his stride quick and purposeful as he checks the area and then surveys my car. It's too dark to make out his expression, but his tight movements communicate both efficiency and concern.

His reaction mirrors the one flashing through my mind, which is that this is Heron Creek. Cars don't get vandalized in people's driveways. Even as kids, the worst thing we did was toss a few eggs or rolls of toilet paper. Nothing that cost people money, or frightened them.

Beau leans over my missing windshield, plucking a square of yellow paper that looks familiar from the wiper blade. My stomach sinks, landing somewhere around my knees. It wasn't a joke, the note at the library. Now they—whoever they are—came to my house. To Gramps' house.

I wish Mayor Beau hadn't seen the note. It's going to make an explanation necessary, but explaining things I don't understand doesn't rank very high on my favorite things. If at all. Not to mention I feel like an idiot—likely the first person in the history of Heron Creek to be left vaguely threatening love notes.

"Someone left you a note, Gracie."

It's odd, but my first thought is how nice my nickname sounds covered by his honeyed drawl. No proper response comes to mind as his fingers toy with the crispy parchment, folding it open. My feet move, though, carrying me to his side in a few steps, wishing for a way to steal the note away before he can read it.

Not possible, of course.

"Stay away from the archives. This be not only your second warning, but your last," he reads aloud while I follow along. Clouds of anger thicken on his features when he's finished. "What the hell is this? What does it mean, second warning?"

His demanding tone leaves no doubt that he's not often ignored. It's beyond my capability to do so now, and if we're going to be friends, this seems like a good place to start.

"I don't know, okay? After we ate at the Wreck yesterday, there was something similar on my car. Except it didn't say anything about the archives or staying away from them. Just some vague crap about me being warned." I take the note from him, mentally comparing the paper and handwriting. "Looks like it's from the same person."

"I certainly hope so. One note-writing vandal in town seems to be quite enough." Irritation swirls in his hazel eyes, dark in the deepening evening. "Why didn't you tell me about this earlier?"

I feel defensive, which makes me hate everything about this situation, including the man standing in front of me. David had me on the defensive all the time, even when he'd imagined whatever upset him in the first place. I never want to feel that way again, never want to have to explain myself, yet here I am.

"Oh, I don't know, Mr. Mayor, maybe because you're about the only person in town who doesn't have me pegged for a girl with only one oar in the water the way it is? I wanted to keep it that way a little longer, and confessing that I'd received a weird note the day after deciding I'm seeing the ghost of a goddamn eighteenth-century pirate seemed like the fastest way for you to grab your own pitchfork and light me on fire." A chill sinks into my bones, leaving me shivering in the eighty-degree evening.

"This note is real, Graciela. It's not some figment of your imagination, and as far as Anne Bonny's ghost, I'm sorry Martin and I had a laugh at your expense last night. You certainly wouldn't be the first person to see her, and you won't be the last." He reaches out, snagging my hands and squeezing tight. The slight pain in my knuckles focuses my attention. "We can figure this out. We'll talk to Gramps, I'll notify the police, and I won't let them relax until they find who did this."

"No, please. If we report it, it'll just get around even faster. And as far as Gramps, I came here to ease his burdens, not make them bigger and more embarrassing." My tone turns pleading, and it makes me feel disgusting and weak. But this is my life, and my call, and some stupid vandal that leaves stupid notes isn't going to ruin what little I've got. "I'm not scared, Beau. Whoever's doing this is a coward, leaving notes and making messes."

His lips pull down into a deep frown, eyes burrowing into mine as though they're looking to dig up a different response. "I don't like it. This person could be dangerous. But it's your decision."

Relief floods me, so fast and potent my knees want to buckle. I refuse them, because I just made a show of being strong and unafraid, and most of all, that's how Beau sees me.

If nothing else, it's nice to have someone else believe in me again.

Chapter Nine

It's been a week since someone smashed my car, and even though I managed to get it fixed without Gramps noticing the damage, I haven't driven it since. Anne's ghost continues to freak me out at least once a day, the note incidents leave me checking over my shoulder far too often, and besides that, the evidence of my sneaked alcohol and too many meals with Gramps is starting to show on my waistline. Not that I can't stand to gain a few pounds, but being in shape has always been a borderline obsession, and I've spent too much of the last couple of months curled up under the covers.

The fact that I even have that thought makes me wonder if maybe, just maybe, I'm headed in the right direction as far as my heart. My life, of course, remains a shambles.

The notes and Anne Bonny do give me purpose, as crazy as that sounds, and the second warning does nothing to dissuade my desire to get my hands on those archived documents. The fact that Anne's creepy ass pops up at work about every day and spends as much time as possible casting mournful looks at the locked door encourages me further, because even though I'm no expert, all of the movies suggest that ghosts go away when their business is finished.

I'm starting to miss her when she's not around, but she makes me sad, too. As though her moods have started to affect me.

Beau's dropped by for a few lunches, but he's backtracked to friendship territory. He's not the kind of guy who could ever be friend-zoned against his will, though, and his approving glances and slight touches have set my blood to a simmer that would leap to a boil with the slightest nudge.

Mrs. LaBadie is worse than ever today, and truly has some kind of sixth sense when it comes to that damned locked door. She calls me away, assigns some additional menial task, anytime I even pause outside it. Quitting time isn't far off now, and she'll be waiting for me by the front desk. I stop in the bathroom first to wash the dust from my hands and wrists, partly because they feel gross but mostly as a passive-aggressive attempt to gain the slightest foothold of control in our relationship by making her wait.

The powder room is small, with one toilet, a single sink, and a window that's about shoulder high and covered with frosted glass. An idea pops into my mind, maybe something I read in a Nancy Drew novel as a girl, and without thinking too hard about it, I unlock the window. I'd left behind the law-breaking period of my life with the start of college, but Mrs. LaBadie's hawk eye makes it impossible to follow Anne's finger. She has no good reason—the archives are accessible to the public with an appointment, but even when I came in on my day off she refused to let me in, saying there was a cleaning crew present.

She lied, but calling her out on it won't get me inside. Sneaking is my only option.

The witch herself waits impatiently by the front door, her lips twisted in distaste. "Where have you been?"

"Bathroom. Listen, do you think I could make a copy of the key to the archives? Mr. Freedman did promise that I would have full access, since archival history is my area of study."

"You saying I don't know how to manage that room? That you can do it better?" She squints at me, her black eyes glittering in a way that makes me want to jump backward. It's not just a bad mood—it's like she hates me for a real reason, something I've done, but it's as mysterious as Anne's for choosing to haunt me.

I stand my ground. "No, but it's my area of expertise, and it's open to the public. I'd like to take a look."

"Only Mr. Freedman can authorize a second key, and he's going to be gone another ten days. You're welcome to ask him when he returns."

Old Ralph took a week of vacation and combined it with some librarian conference down in the Caribbean. Sounds like *two* weeks of vacation to me, but it's hard to blame the guy. I met his wife.

Mrs. LaBadie pushes into the early evening, then waits for me to walk down the steps before locking the door and pocketing the key. It's probably not smart to hoist myself through a window in broad daylight, which means I have a few hours to decide whether or not to chicken out.

I've been arrested in Heron Creek before, and breaking into the library is small potatoes. It's not as though it's going to damage my sterling reputation, though it may put the final nail in the coffin of my potential relationship with Beauregard Drayton. Imagine a Drayton, the mayor, dating a common criminal.

I push him from my mind, sure that he's already given up on the inkling that he'd like to get to know me better. Gramps is waiting for dinner, and I'm anxious to sit and chat with him. The thought—the hope—skitters through my mind that perhaps Aunt Karen called with an update on Amelia and the baby, leaving a throbbing behind in those empty caverns of friendship inside me.

Amelia doesn't have to be my friend anymore—that's her choice. We'll always be family, though, and she can't stop me from caring about *her*.

☙

Gramps falls asleep in his chair before the supper dishes are clean, and I watch the last four innings of the Braves game to the sound of his raspy breathing, a laptop in front of me. He looks comfortable, snuggled underneath his fleece blanket, mouth hanging open as his snores drown out the postgame analysis on the television. He'll be fine there until I get home, then we can get up to bed together.

The night makes me jumpy, an undeniable fact that colors the edges of my vision with red. Heron Creek shouldn't scare me. It shouldn't scare anyone, yet I glance behind me, sure there's going to be a ghost or a crazy person dogging my steps at every turn. No one's there, though, and aside from the few restaurants that stay open after nine and the one bar I pass on my way to the library, the Creek is as sleepy and deserted as ever.

No one notices me leave the sidewalk and traipse around to the rear of my place of employment. It's darker back here, away from any street lamps and lit signs. The unlocked window slides up under the pressure of my palm with no resistance and, most importantly, no noise. I have to jump a few times before my hands hook the sill, and it's clear that I need to do more than walk to work if I'm going to get back into shape.

My grunts don't carry far, and after a few more minutes of trial and error, I manage to hoist my hips over the painted wooden lip. It digs in, scraping hard enough that it'll leave a bruise, but there's no time to worry about that while my body is dangling half in, half out. The chance that anyone will wander back here seems slim, but there's no excuse in the world that will work if I get caught like this.

I kick my feet and use my forearms to tug my body forward, which doesn't work, until it does. I fly through the rest of the way, toppling face-first into the edge of the toilet.

"Holy shitballs, that's gonna leave a mark." Quoting *Tommy Boy,* even to myself, is usually good for a chuckle, but at the moment my face feels as though it's made of broken glass and pulsing pain.

My nose throbs, my vision blurs, and it takes more than five minutes of sitting still with my head between my knees before the dizziness subsides enough to allow me to stagger to my feet. The mirror reveals a weeping red line across the bridge of my nose, which promises to turn into at least one black eye. So much for Gramps not noticing I went out.

Oh, well. Onward and upward.

There's no alarm system in the library, and no one else is in the building. Neither fact makes me slow down or feel less watched, and my steps move quickly toward the front desk. Mrs. LaBadie keeps her key in the locked top drawer, but she doesn't know about my long and storied career picking locks with nothing but unbent hairpins. Another Nancy Drew–inspired talent. The multiple Carolyn Keenes had no idea what kind of delinquents she would spawn with those books.

I palm the key after making quick work of the weak lock, then move toward the archives. It's like forbidden fruit, this room—literally, if I take the note seriously, figuratively if I consider all the times Mrs. LaBadie has gone out of her way to keep me away. She's crazy protective of these stinking files.

The flashlight app on my phone offers plenty of light to work by, which saves me from the risk of turning on the light. My favorite scent in the world, the combination of weathered paper and cracking glue, washes over me as the door swings open and I take a moment to breathe it in. To remember that this is where I imagined I belonged—wandering among history—before David sold me a different version filled with academic glory and babies on the side, only to steal it from under me.

It's funny that Anne Bonny should choose me. She's kind of a manifestation of my first love—history. Although I'm not sure I prefer my history quite so alive. Words on pages, primary sources are good enough.

There's another smell in the room, and it takes a moment before I place it as the same incense Mrs. LaBadie burns at the front desk. It, combined with her little stick figurines, has me half convinced she is some kind of voodoo witch, except no one around here would be so accepting if she is.

The question of where to begin vexes me for a moment, and curses stream through my mind. With any luck, they'll float through the air, out the front door, and straight into Mrs. LaBadie's dreams. This would be so much simpler if I'd had the opportunity to familiarize myself with the cataloguing system ahead of time. In daylight.

The better part of an hour skitters away before I locate the boxes containing documents related to Anne Bonny and her father's family in the local history section. Anticipation makes my breath too quick and my palms more damp than they should be while handling these kinds of things, but it's exciting—she's hanging around over two hundred years after her death, pointing toward this room, and the mystery of why is about to be solved.

Nancy would be proud.

The box contains fewer things than I expect. The moment the lid slides off, the feeling of being watched grows so intense that I glance around, sure Anne or maybe even Mrs. LaBadie lurks over my shoulder. There's nothing, not even a sound save the wheezing air conditioner working its ass off to keep the room at an appropriate storage temperature.

I don't want to take anything out of the room that's not imperative to my search, that I need to help the ghost cross over or whatever, but at first glance, there's nothing that seems important. There's a family tree, some information on her father's holdings in the Charleston area, including a land survey of his property, which was sold more than fifty years after his death.

It takes me longer to read the couple of oral histories attached to Anne, but they amuse me so I take the time. It seems the girl was destined to be a criminal from a young age, perhaps because her father treated her as the bastard she was, or perhaps because it was simply her nature. Either way, she certainly didn't fit the mold constructed for young ladies of her circumstances and time. There's one story about her stabbing a maid who displeased her, and another account of a stabbing, this time a man attempting to take certain liberties with young Anne. Hard to blame her for the second. And since I've never had a maid, maybe I shouldn't be so quick to judge on the first count, either.

Another recounting, this time how her father disowned her after she began her affair with James Bonny, and how she responded by burning down his entire plantation. Her father turned out to be right about ol' James, though, and I'm sure admitting her mistake really burned Anne's lady breeches when the time came.

There are multiple newspaper articles that chronicle the falling-out between father and daughter; they were a high profile family, William Cormac a respected lawyer. Not the kind of man who expects to have a child turn pirate, never mind his only daughter.

A noise from outside the archives catches my attention, pulls me from two-hundred-plus years ago and deposits me back in the present. It's not a figment of my imagination, not this time. My gaze strays longingly to the bundle of information, which isn't nearly plumbed, and I make the snap decision to take it with me. Once it's back in the protective plastic, air dismissed and seal reinstated, I poke my head back out into the main library.

No one's around, that I can see. If there *is* someone in the library, it's imperative I get out of here as soon as possible, especially since there's a good chance it's my equal parts scary and annoying boss.

It's not a big place, and I feel well-hidden among the maze of the stacks, but not well enough, as it turns out.

"Gracie?"

The voice, combined with the sudden glare of a flashlight in my face, almost makes me pee myself. That it knows my name—speaks it—at least suggests this is no kind of spirit.

That it doesn't sound pissed off all but proves it doesn't belong to Mrs. LaBadie.

I put a hand up to shield my eyes, but can make out nothing but a shadow. "Turn that damn thing off before I go blind."

The absence of the light doesn't do any good, at least not right away, and whoever busted me stays silent until my eyes adjust. Once they do, they almost fall out of my head. "Leo?"

My old friend sports a navy blue security guard uniform, pepper spray at the hip and everything.

"It's weird that you sound more surprised to see me than I am to see you. What are you doing here?"

"You sing on the street by day, security guard at night . . . anything else?"

"Yes. I pump gas on the commercial docks three days a week and bartend at the Royal Oak on the weekends, plus a few shifts here and there during the week."

"Oh." His answers lead to more questions, like why he doesn't have just one job, or whether he's struggling with money since taking on his niece, but they all seem a little prying, seeing how we've barely spoken for years.

"You're avoiding my question, which is obviously: What are you doing in the library after hours?" His gaze slides to the plastic bundle still clutched in my hands, then back to my face, patiently awaiting a response.

It sucks that Leo and I spent years parlaying with each other on behalf of our respective clans. He knows my tricks, and lying to him has never been easy—at least, not getting away with it.

"I left this here." I wave the packet in front of me, hoping that keeping it moving means he can't get a good look. "I'm having trouble sleeping lately. Thought I might as well work on this project, but realized I left it here."

"And you thought crawling in through the bathroom window and busting your face seemed like a good plan?" He shakes his head, but even in the shadows his struggle not to smile bleeds into my vision. "You look like hell, by the way."

"Thanks, I know. Gramps is going to freak out."

"How is the old coot, anyway?"

"He's good. Just old. Probably could still catch you and paddle your ass, though."

"Now there's a pretty picture."

We fall silent as the familiar patter dries up, flakes off, and drifts away. I can see him clearly now, even without the light. The moon shines through the windows and illuminate the spines of thousands of books, little motes of dust, and empty tables and chairs. It's creepy, actually, but less so with Leo here, too.

"Are you going to tell on me? Mrs. LaBadie already hates me and I'd really prefer not to be fired."

"Because you're a loony, depressed drunk and no one else will hire you?" Leo arches an eyebrow, humor evident in his still twitching lips.

"You've heard about my tumble into town, I see."

"Yes. And the empty liquor bottles in Gramps' trash."

"Mrs. Walters has stooped to going through the trash? Yikes. How the mighty have fallen."

"It's unclear whether she goes through the garbage herself or pays poor old Luther to tell her if anything interesting falls out when he dumps it."

"Pays him in blackberry pies, you mean."

"I sure hope so. Can you imagine if it was anything more . . . deviant?"

"If you make me throw up, we both lose. You'll have to clean up vomit and I'll get busted after Mrs. LaBadie finds the wet spot in the morning."

He snickers, and the uncontrollable sound makes me giggle. Somehow—perhaps from the too many hours I spent at frat parties my first couple years of college—I know Leo's holding back a joke containing the phrase *wet spot.* It takes us both a moment to get our juvenile senses of humor under control, but when we do, a warm familiarity replaces my mirth.

It may be true that you can't go home again, but laughing with Leo Boone feels pretty close.

"I'm not going to turn you in, Graciela. It goes against our Rules of Engagement, after all." I breathe a sigh of relief, even though it's dubious that our childhood war games extend into adulthood.

And if they do, I now owe him big-time.

"Thanks, Leo."

"And I'll even let you out through the front door."

My lips snake into another smile, and with it comes relief—that spontaneous happiness still has the ability to trump what I've started to worry is a permanent cynicism. "I don't remember you being quite so gracious when you've got the upper hand, Leo Boone."

"We all grow up, Graciela. Some more reluctantly than others, and some only when we have to." A sadness threads through his words, winding and tugging them into a sweater that can't quite keep a person warm.

"Marcella is beautiful, Leo. And she seems happy."

It's a guess, that his niece is his reason for growing up, but a safe one. Even though my words were almost a whisper, he winces.

"She's as happy as she can be, with no father and a mother in jail."

"Whose daughter is she?" My curiosity gets the better of me, even though he would be well in his rights to tell me it's none of my goddamn business.

" Lindsay's."

I struggle, but barely recall her face. The only Boone girl is years younger than me. It's not as though remembering what she looks like would give me any additional insight. I knew no details about any of them, save Leo, and even that was a long time ago.

"If you have what you need, let's get out of here. I still have to make the rounds through the government buildings and the bank before I can call it a night."

"Sure, Leo." I pause. "But could we go out the side door?"

The look he shoots over his shoulder overflows with suspicion, but he changes his path through the stacks without pause. To his credit, no follow-up questions slip out. It's unthinkable to me to talk about the threats I've received with a second person within a couple of hours, but they're the reason for avoiding the front door.

Maybe if one person had to know, it should have been Leo and not Beau. The thought surprises me, but once it settles in, it makes sense. Leo knows me. We'd solved a few mysteries in Heron Creek, even if it was just who made out in the seven minutes in heaven closet and who just made whispered pacts to never tell that they didn't. He's different than Beau.

Leo's more like me—not willing to let adulthood body snatch us yet. Not in total. Together, we'd be more likely to turn over stones that don't include official reports and policemen.

He pauses after unlocking the glass door that leads into the alley between the library and the post office. When he turns toward me, there something shimmering on his face that's never been there before, not in my presence. Nerves. "Gracie, I'd really like to get together sometime. Have dinner, catch up."

My heart stutters, and his nerves dance off him and tango around me, little army men intent on causing me discomfort with their tiny pellets and miniature bayonets. It's my nature to be gentle in these situations—when they can't be avoided entirely—but too many people are trying to infringe on my self-imposed solitude since arriving in Heron Creek. Too many people determined to make me feel things, and only a small percentage of those feelings are good.

"I'd like to catch up, Leo, but I have to be honest—I'm not looking to date anyone."

One eyebrow shoots up. "Who in tarnation says I want to date you, Graciela Harper? I just thought . . . well, you're short on friends these days, and so am I, if you don't count the siblings. It'd be nice to chat with someone who knows all my secrets, that's all."

"Oh." Embarrassment singes, so hot I can almost smell my burned hair. "That'd be nice."

He lets me out into the evening with a snort, leaving me looking forward to seeing him again. But if Leo Boone thinks he ever knew all of my secrets, or that he's going to get access to them now, he's got another think coming. It'd be stupid to think he doesn't feel the exact same way.

I get about three steps onto the sidewalk before my name bleeds from the semidarkness for the second time in less than half an hour. This time, it makes me jump sideways, turning my ankle in the process.

"Jesus, Gracie, what happened to your face?"

Will. Will Gayle, the once love of my life, stealer of my virginity in every possible connotation of the word. He's as handsome as ever, hair tousled and blowing in the slight breeze, arms stretching the limits of his worn Clemson University T-shirt.

I hate that my heart still reacts to him with a leap and twirl, as though he's the greatest thing in the world, or as though it's been waiting a lifetime for him to come home. It makes me frown, and I wave him away. "It's nothing. I tripped and hit my face on a cart at work today."

"You look like ten miles of bad road."

"I'm sure. Well, it was nice to see you."

I quicken my pace but he does the same, and given that he and Mel no longer live in the old neighborhood, it seems suspect that we're walking the same direction.

"So, you're working at the library, huh?" He waits, but when silence greets his question, soldiers on. "What are you doing out so late?"

"It's, like, nine o'clock. How old *are* you?"

"How is Gramps getting on? Grant misses hanging out with him."

A twinge somewhere in my chest tries to force me to be nice, to stop and chat with him, tell him they can come by anytime. It's the right thing to do, because I'm sure that Gramps loves spending time with the little boy, too—he's always loved children—and if I'm being honest, he's always loved Will, too. My presence is squashing his happiness, and maybe in another couple of days the maturity to call and invite the Gayles to dinner will find its way into my heart. "He's about the same. Putting on a good face, like you said."

"Mel's pregnant again. She told me at dinner."

I wonder if that's the reason for his solitary late-night walk, but can't see why. What I told Mel the other morning is true, that he seems happy. No one can doubt his love for that little boy, and responsibility has long been the biggest difference between Will and me.

"Yeah, I know." I keep walking, because even though the predominant feeling among my jumble is peace with this whole thing, it's not a situation on the top of my "dissect every nuance of" list.

"How do *you* know?"

"We had coffee the other morning. It was delightful, even if her threats and my subsequent promises not to seduce you away didn't pair all that well with my sugar-free latte." I pause, sliding a glance his direction. The shock on his face appears genuine, and discomfort tugs at my gut. That was a breach of girl code, and if he mentions it at home, will set back whatever Mel and I patched over the other day. "In fact, I'm pretty sure we shouldn't be seen alone together, and you know the Creek's streets have ears and eyes."

"What? Mel said that?"

I stop walking, and he does the same. Staring at his face, feeling the familiar intensity of those gorgeous blue eyes, isn't doing anything to make me feel better. I hug the historical documents relating to Anne Bonny and William Cormac to my chest, a sensation of loss running like a fissure through my soul. It will never heal, never fill. It's the hole left behind by the tearing apart of Will and me, two people who were like one, and the scar has only faded, not disappeared.

"It's no big deal, Will. She's a mama bear now, and we both know Mel's never backed down from a challenge, real or perceived." He startles at my smile, which appears from some part of me still able to love him—and her—and not fall apart in the process. "I'm not mad. I kind of hoped that we could find a way to be friends again, even if it can't be like it was, but it's going to take time, Will."

"I miss you, Gracie. I know Melanie does, too."

The confession spears my heart, leaves it wriggling and wounded. "I miss you guys, too."

Even though we're as alone as we'll ever be, even though those unspoken words from seven years ago surround us like a swarm of bees, we say nothing. They make no noise, as though our past, and the people we were inside it, live on the other side of a glass curtain.

In another dimension, relegated to an alternate reality, perhaps.

"I appreciate everything you've done for Gramps, Will. I do."

He lets me go this time when I walk away, my eyes on the clouds assembling on the horizon. Maybe he's choking on the same sweet sadness that's drowning me. It's nice to imagine that he is, for some reason. It makes what we had seem solid. Not a dream.

As much as it hurts, having the past disappear altogether would be so much worse.

Chapter Ten

It's later than I meant it to be by the time I get home, having been waylaid by not one, but two ghosts of Creek past. When Gramps' snores greet me in the foyer, relief drops my shoulders from their tense position around my ears. The sound breaks off before I make it into the living room, though, and his sleep-hazed eyes poke me with reproach. It changes to concern in a blink, reminding me of the state of my face.

"It's okay, Gramps. I tripped and caught the edge of a cart, that's all."

"Always were clumsy. Get that from your mother. That girl couldn't go half a day without breaking something in the house or on her body. Cost me a bloody fortune." He pulls his thoughts from the past, and points at his watch. "Been worried, Gracie-baby."

I lean over and kiss his papery cheek, then put my arms around his neck and lay my head on his shoulder. "I'm sorry. I felt like a walk after that meatloaf, that's all. I didn't want to wake you."

"Leave me a note next time, please." His smile is wry. "I know you're not a little girl anymore, but humor an old man."

"Okay, Gramps." I kiss him again, press my ear to his hearing aid, then pull away with a grin. "You want some ice cream?"

It's a silly question. Ice cream is never a bad call, and I dish up two bowls of Neapolitan. There's extra strawberry in Gramps', not enough that he'll call me out for cheating but enough to make him happy. The baseball games are wrapped up for the night, so we eat our bedtime snack to the quiet cadence of the local news. I've heard that in big cities the news is depressing, all about murders and violence and missing kids, but in towns like Iowa City and Heron Creek, it's about people taking food to the flood victims up the coast or the guy determined to open a farm and fill it with abused rescue animals, with the occasional scary story ripped from national headlines.

On really good days, we'll get an awesome story about a local hillbilly getting drunk on his own moonshine and giving the cops hell during an arrest.

"Haven't seen William for a while. You two aren't going to let an old romance ruin a fifteen-year friendship, are you?"

Fifteen years is an exaggeration, but it's a different way of looking at things. Will and I were friends longer than were a couple, and if I'm being honest with myself, it's his level head and commonsense advice that I'm missing the most. Have missed the most, since we said good-bye.

David was never particularly interested in my problems, or in reigning in my wild side with any kind of patience or love. Will adored my tendency to play the daredevil, even as he tried to point out the obvious downsides to my misadventures. David tended to favor disdain and the liberal use of the word *stupid*.

"We're going to be okay, Gramps. If you want to see him and Grant, I'll invite them over for a game. Or maybe a picnic? I was thinking it might be fun to traipse down to the docks for lunch on Sunday."

"Fun, maybe, but you're not getting these old legs through the swamp."

"It's a marsh, and you leave that to me." I take his bowl and mine into the kitchen, rinsing them out and wondering if Will's parents still have a smart car. They'd let me borrow it to get Gramps around, for sure.

He holds up a hand when I get back to the living room, letting me haul him to his feet. His weight, or lack thereof, saddens me as I support him easily into the hallway and up the stairs, then run back to bring his walker while he's in the bathroom.

My face aches and throbs, the three Advil I popped in the kitchen doing little to take the edge off. I'm going to try Aleve next time, and maybe wash it down with some vodka. I think I deserve it, but despite the pain, my eyes are heavy. It's been a long day, and as much as reading over the files from the archives in good light appeals to me, sleep sounds better.

Then a smell drifts into the hallway, leaving no doubt that there's a visitor in my room who might have other ideas. It doesn't startle me like it has in the past, given the warning, but it does wake me all the way up.

Inside my room, the sight of Anne's ghost perched on the edge of my clean, soft, blue-and-cream down heaven pisses me off.

I close the door and cross my arms over my chest, letting my anger build unchecked. I've already smashed my face and gotten busted trespassing in the service of her wild-goose chase tonight, and now she's funkifying my favorite place in the world.

"What do you want, woman? You can't just pop in and stink up my life whenever you feel like it. I mean, maybe you think I don't have much of a life to begin with, and you might be right, but at least I'm not dead." Guilt twists my stomach, even though she's a stupid ghost and whether or not she even had feelings while she was alive is up for debate. And she *is* dead. "I mean, I'm just saying I could use a little help here. If you're showing up just to cuddle and point fingers, I'll pass."

It's nice to talk to her in a normal tone of voice instead of a whisper—or in this case, a louder than normal tone of voice—without fear of being overheard. When she climbs off the bed and lumbers silently toward me, a bolt of uncertainty makes me wish I hadn't yelled. Or insulted her. Or basically acted as though she's everything that's wrong with my nonlife, when in truth she's only a small percentage.

My body shrinks back, not bothering to ask if I'd like to go out of the world cowering like a little bitch, until the doorknob jabs into my spine. The ghost doesn't take her watery gaze off my face, and bares her cracked, yellowed teeth at my obvious fear. She's part woman, part animal, all instinct, and leaves no doubt in my mind that in life, Anne Bonny must have been a fearsome creature.

She stops a foot away, the smell of unwashed skin and salty rope gathering in my nose and on my tongue. My stomach begs to rid itself of dinner and ice cream, but gets distracted when she unclasps her hands from behind her back and swings them around to the front. It's on the tip of my tongue to tell her that if she plans on more pointing, I'd rather she go ahead and torture me, but the last scraps of my sass dry up at the sight of my car keys dangling from her fingers.

What the hey?

Despite my moment of dumbfounded shock at the revelation that my ghost can pick up inanimate objects, it's clear what she wants. And I am *so* not on board.

"Oh, no. I'm not going anywhere with you." I eye her, managing to ease off the doorknob and relieve the knot in my back. "I have a feeling you've not exactly a reliable GPS."

She ignores me, and I don't reach out to take the keys. My lack of movement relates partially to the idea of accidentally touching her, the memory of the last time chilling my bones all over again. We're at a stalemate, but she moves her chess piece first. The ghost gives me a shrug, as though telling me she doesn't care what I say or do, then walks through the door, each body part disappearing as it touches the flimsy wood. With my keys.

I open it and peer out in time to see her white-gray figure stomp noiselessly down the hall, then float over the top step and out of sight. I have no idea what she'll do if I don't follow, but seeing as she lived in the eighteen hundreds, I doubt she's going anywhere with my car.

Even so, the inaction of the past couple of weeks and the lack of obvious answers at the library tonight taunts me. There's too much inaction in my life, too little of the old, impulsive Graciela. I wonder what Will would say if I told him I'm considering hopping in the car for a ghostly road trip. I feel sure David would throw me in a straightjacket and lock me away forever, which is the thought that sends me hustling after her.

It's not as though I have anything better to do, unless I count sleeping or drinking. Sad, but true.

By the time I reach the foyer, Anne's out the front door. *Through* the front door, whatever. Trepidation and common sense try to urge me back to my room, but the reality is that Anne's not going to leave me alone until we figure out what exactly she wants my help with—and if I can figure out why she's so keen on it being *my* help in the process, so much the better.

The wind has picked up since I got home from my little breaking and entering excursion. It blows strands of hair from my haphazard bun into my smashed-up face as the fronds of the palmetto trees rustle a loud greeting to the approaching storm. The electric scent in the air obscures Anne's briny odor until I climb into the car.

She's in the backseat. I meet her impatient, sorrowful gaze in the rearview mirror, wondering if she'd let me stay home if I asked. So far she's been insistent, but not forceful. There's no way to know what she's capable of, or if the inclinations of our living bodies follow us into death. If so, a visit from a quiet Southern belle would be preferable to a deadly pirate.

"You know, you can sit up front if you want. I don't even have a chauffeur license." She doesn't reply, and I know she won't, but the nerves bouncing around inside me have control of my tongue. "Are you afraid someone would see you? *Can* other people see you? Am I crazy?"

Her eyes gleam bright like a cat's, but hold nothing in the way of a reply. Part of me is glad she's unable to answer that last one, and I know the answer to the second. Other people *have* seen her, or at least claim they have. Never heard of her stalking anyone else, though. Graciela Anne Harper, the Heron Creek stalker magnet.

I sigh. "So, where are we going?"

She leans forward and points to the passenger seat. The plastic bag of documents I took from the archives lies on the stained cloth, which is weird because it *was* on the dresser in my bedroom.

"You're getting a tad bold, ghost lady." I put the packet gingerly on my lap, worried all over again about taking them out of the temperature-regulated environment. She watches as I pull the documents out one at a time, holding them up for her perusal before getting a tight shake of the head. "This sure would be simpler if you could talk, you know. Or knew sign language. Then again, *I* don't know sign language."

Her big green eyes pop open at a particular piece of paper, the deed and land survey detailing her father's original property.

"This? You want to go home? That's pretty cheesy." I poke some coordinates into Google Earth, then glance at Anne while a map of Charleston pulls up on my cell phone. "Especially for someone who burned her home down and ran away."

The look she gives me could curdle milk, but then again, not one of these documents, or any of the online histories, suggests she had even the barest sense of humor. The map finishes loading while I rethink this whole thing, all the way back to the possibility that I'm having a complete psychotic break by seeing her in the first place.

The land where her father once lived is still intact and now exists as a plantation home and museum. Rebuilt, obviously. I snicker at my second joke at the expense of Anne's teenage psychotic episode but keep my mouth shut as she glares at me harder. I steer the car out of Heron Creek and onto the road toward Charleston, concentrating on the map and not the fact that I'm basically not only off my rocker, but impaled on the splintered remains. Following a damn ghost into a stormy night.

In the past week, between my job and spending time with Beau, not to mention quite a bit less drinking, I've been feeling better. Maybe I've passed the midway point of my tunnel, with the tiniest pinprick of light winking at me from the far faraway distance. The thought of sexy Mayor Beau makes me wish my lifeboat moved a little bit faster, but it goes as it goes, my Grams would say.

Anne and I pass the rest of the thirty-minute drive in silence, which is expected, but her jaw is hard and she refuses to even try to respond to my conversation attempts.

Fantastic. Even though I'm her chauffeur, the woman doing her bidding at midnight on a Wednesday, she's apparently big on holding grudges. I'm also too wimpy to say any of that to her pasty face, since she does have a sword.

A ghost sword. I wonder if it's still sharp.

I pull off the road just past the entrance to William Cormac's former property. It's gated and locked, at least to cars, and my feet crunch too loudly on the gravel. Anne's out of the car and standing inside the gate, waiting for me with an impatient set to her strong shoulders.

The wind blows harder here, snatching dirt and particles from their perches and flinging them into my eyes. The storm marches forward, gathering force on the horizon before making its full-on assault, but there's no doubt it's coming. It would be best to take an umbrella, but there isn't one in my car even though I'm sure there had been when I'd left Iowa. Maybe she stole that, too, and her goal is to get me soaked and laugh it up.

No. Whatever Anne is, whatever she wants, it's not about pranks or haunts. She has a purpose.

The ghost moves on, hiking down the lane that would eventually lead to the house and museum. Giant live oaks with trunks so wide it would take ten of me to ring them tower over the path, playing unwilling host to heavy curtains of Spanish moss that twist in the wind. Anne turns off the path before the house comes into view and I follow, despite the fact that the wind rustling the trees grows stronger. The world blurs no matter how hard I blink, making me wish I'd gotten Lasik the twenty-seventh time David mentioned how dorky I look in glasses, instead of contacts. Perhaps stubborn defiance has not always served me well.

Anne Bonny realizes I've stopped to try to wipe the dirt from my eyes and pauses, turning back to watch me. My vision clears for a moment, and when our eyes meet, there's nothing of her previous smoldering anger, or even the frustration of our previous meetings.

Tears roll down my face before my brain registers that I'm crying. Her anguished desperation is palpable; it pounds me with more ferocity than the wind, with more poignancy than even my own depression. It pushes me to my knees, the heartache that crashes into me, ripping at my heart with a kind of torment that seems too pervasive, too merciless to be real.

It starts to ease when our gazes pull apart, but even the memory of it makes me gasp. Several moments pass before I climb back to my feet, ignoring the globs of dirt and pine needles sticking to my bare knees. Jeans would have been a better choice, but she didn't inform me the evening plans included hiking.

I follow Anne with renewed dedication, suddenly finding a purpose of my own. If I can help fix whatever tortures her after two-hundred-plus years, I'm going to do it. I haven't the slightest idea what plagues her, but I couldn't be happier it didn't happen to me.

We trek through the trees, sticking close together. She'd better know where she's going, because after five minutes of twists and turns, there's no way I'm finding my way back to my car on my own. It's hard to know how far our hike has taken us before she stops at the edge of a clearing, staring across a pond of waist-high grasses crawling with who knows what kind of bugs and other creepies waiting to infect me with tropical diseases.

The only tree is on the far edge, a magnolia so huge it doesn't look real. Moss creeps up its trunk, and its thick branches twist and turn in a gorgeous, somehow threatening display of nature.

The ghost steps toward it, her pace faster, almost running now. She slips around to the opposite side, the girth of the trunk more than enough to hide her wispy form, and I follow, scared to lose sight of her in this strange place. My feet tangle in the roots, sending me crashing to my hands and knees, twisting my ankle in the process. It's the same one that betrayed me with Will earlier, but this time the pain that shoots right up the bone is no joke.

I sit on the ground, breathing through the pain and poking at the new scrapes up my legs, not realizing right away that Anne's disappeared. Panic sets in, because it's about to storm and I'm trespassing for the second time in the same day, with no way to get out, but I squash it down. She'll be back.

Instead of curling up in the fetal position and crying, which might make me feel better for a second but won't do a smidgen of good in the long run, I turn on the flashlight app on my phone and go searching for what tripped me, mostly so I can chuck it against the tree.

Or at least spit on it.

My free hand finds a cool, smooth rock three-quarters buried in the damp ground. Then another, and another, and I put down my phone, exploring with both hands until I've uncovered a dozen grapefruit-sized stones embedded the soft ground, glowing pale in the strikes of lightning.

They're too perfect to be naturally occurring accidents, not to mention that nothing but human hands could have placed them so carefully between the magnolia's twisted, exposed roots. They almost look like marble against the backdrop of the velvety black night.

The first drop of rain maneuvers its way through the thick canopy of leaves, plopping on my cheek with a good measure of defiance. Great. Anne Bonny's ghost brought me out here, watched me trip over some weird rocks, and then left me trapped in a coming rainstorm. The tree will provide some cover, because the number of splashes hitting the leaves outnumbers those dropping onto my skin, but it's a small comfort.

Uncomfortable or not, without Anne or good light, there's no way I'm finding the car.

My attention turns back to the rocks, if only to use the mystery to calm my panic, which still teeters on the edge of a screaming freak-out. I'm enough of a country girl to know that the first rule of being lost in the woods is to not lose my shit.

I brush away leaves and dirt from the sleek white rocks, until I've uncovered all of them—sixteen in total, that shape a crudely formed X. It almost makes me laugh, because for all Anne's bluster and evil looks, I'm following around a pirate cliché.

Then again, are you a cliché if you're one of the people who set the standard?

It's a question for another, drier, possibly saner time. If I have any of those left.

"Anne! What am I supposed to do now, you sadistic bitch? Sit here and get soaked? What'd you drag me out here for?"

No answer, but of course the answer lies in front of me. X marks the spot, after all, so as more fat, chilly raindrops decorate my goose-pimpled skin, I search for a stick for a minute before finding one thick enough to help me dig. Time passes and mud builds up on my arms and legs like a second skin as I work the four rocks in the middle loose with my stick and my hands, sacrificing four fingernails to the effort.

The stick scrapes against something that doesn't sound like dirt or roots, and I toss it aside in favor of the gentler ministrations of my fingertips. It's a trick I recall from a couple of archaeology classes, to abandon sharp tools when unearthing artifacts.

My hands find the smooth wooden surface that turns out to be the top of a small box. The bottom is half rotted away, but an oily piece of cloth covers the item inside, protecting it from the elements with a fair amount of success. It goes against all of my training to open such a thing in the rain, so I leave everything inside the smelly, half-damp box and tuck it under my shirt.

Anne's traitorous ass is nowhere to be seen, and fear or not, I'm going to give her a piece of my mind the next time she shows up. Of course, if this little present is all she wanted me to find, maybe she won't come back.

The thought saddens me, which makes me shake my head at my idiocy. I need to take Leo up on that dinner offer, because if I'm looking for a sign that I need friends, missing a pushy, abandoning ghost is a big one.

The clouds blot out the moon and stars, draping the night in complete blackness save the occasional flash of lightning. Each clap of thunder shudders the earth beneath me, transferring the booming shivers up my spine. Thunderstorms are one of my favorite things, but not so much when I'm trapped inside one.

I could use the GPS on my phone, maybe, and send the location to . . . who? There's no one I can call in the middle of the night to bail me out, and as with the horrible expression on Anne's face on our trek out here, the realization that even a ghost has more passion for life than I do gives me a reason to change. It's no way to live, clinging to the past and my hatred of David.

Of myself.

My phone's dead, anyway, I realize when I try to turn the flashlight back on for a little bit of light. That's not good, because in the morning Gramps is going to panic when I'm not there, and more when he can't get ahold of me. Aunt Karen will give me the business if he ends up having a heart attack because of me, the very girl who claims she moved back to the Creek to help him.

Not to mention I'd never forgive myself.

My ankle aches where I turned it, and whatever help the Advil lent to my face earlier has worn off. Chills creep over me as the errant drops of rain join together to make rivers on my skin, then little cold lakes under my skin. I draw my knees up to my chest, my back against the tree, which helps keep my body heat circulating and the box as dry as possible, then put my head down on my arms. It's not much, but it's enough to thwart my shivers. I think there's no way I'm going to sleep a wink, but close my eyes anyway, just in case.

Chapter Eleven

My eyes open to a brilliant, cloudless morning and the first streaks of golden light across the sky. Even with the clear weather, my bum ankle and the fact that I have no idea where my car is ensure it's almost noon by the time I make it back to Heron Creek. My phone lies useless on the passenger seat, and every time it gleams in the corner of my eye my stomach clenches harder, knowing there's no way to tell Gramps I'm fine.

He's got to be worried sick. There's no telling who he called, either. Maybe Mrs. Walters. It kills me to think people are going to say I'm not good for him, even more so because they're right. They're so right.

Gramps's house appears at the end of the block like a mirage. I want nothing more than to reassure him I'm fine, then take some painkillers and a shower, and go to bed. In that order.

There's someone sitting on our front porch, and the figure jumps to its feet at the sight of my car. It's Melanie, I realize as I park and open the door, watching Grant leap after what might be a frog in the side yard. She strides toward me, worry pinching her pretty features. Red circles rim her eyes and bloom on her cheeks, and she calls Grant to her before she gets close enough to startle at my appearance. If it was horrific yesterday, there probably aren't words now.

She makes no comment. "Get to the hospital, Gracie. They took Gramps a few hours ago."

"Who took him?"

"He called Mayor Drayton when you didn't come down this morning, and when he got here he found Gramps unconscious in the living room."

"What are *you* doing here?" It might be a rude question, but I can't tell. My brain stopped functioning at the news that my disappearance and subsequent failure to have a charged cell phone like a goddamn adult hurt the one person who never stopped caring about me.

"The mayor called Will. I guess you must have mentioned we're all friends. Were all friends, whatever, and he thought someone should be here to tell you. Will went with Gramps to the hospital."

The smallest bit of relief filters through my mountain of grief, trickling down like a cool river. "Thank you."

"Go. I'm going to feed Grant lunch and then stop by and check on you."

☙

It takes ten minutes to get to the Creek's rinky-dink hospital. It smells like the worst things in the world—antiseptic, false hope, and death. I'd add doctors to the list, but at the moment they're sort of a necessity and I don't want to offend the universe. It hates me enough as it is.

My ankle throbs as I limp-hop to the information desk and get Gramps' room number. He's lying on a bed by the window when I burst through the door, fast asleep and hooked up to a few monitors. At first glance I can see there's nothing invasive, no tubes in his nose or down his throat. The other bed, the one closest to the door, is made and empty.

Mayor Beau sits on one side of Gramps, reading papers probably culled from the briefcase on the floor next to his uncomfortable-looking plastic chair. Will's on the opposite side, his eyes focused on the Cubs game playing on television. They both look up, then jump up at the sight of me in the doorway, which makes me realize I should have at least wiped my face in the car. The weirdness of seeing them here, together, sticks my feet to the spot while they rush over, helping me into the chair closest to Gramps. Will grabs the seat Beau had been using, sliding it over to support my ankle, which looks even worse than it feels.

"Jesus, Gracie, where have you been? And what happened to your foot? And your hands and legs?" Will's gush of concerns washes over me, snapping me out of my trance.

"Her legs? What happened to her *face*?" Beau's voice sounds strangled, and holds a trace of restrained anger.

He *should* be mad at me. Everyone should hate me for this.

"Who cares what happened to me, what happened to Gramps?" His face is pale, too pale, and the shallowness of his noisy breathing seizes my three-sizes-too-small heart. It's going to disappear altogether when Gramps leaves me, I know it.

"He had a coughing fit that wouldn't stop, I think. His face was all red after I came down from checking upstairs for you."

"What do the doctors say?" My land, I hate doctors.

"Pneumonia. They did a bunch of tests and haven't gotten the results yet, but they've got him on strong antibiotics and some steroids for his lungs. What happened to your face?"

"I'm going to let you explain that to Beau while I find a doctor to take a look at that ankle." Will excuses himself, likely because he knows two things the mayor doesn't: how I busted my face, and that if I've been outside, me tripping, falling, and generally getting scratched up isn't an interesting or new tale.

It makes me feel so much better to know that Will's here. Things might be awkward between us, but it's nice to know that when it counts, there's still love and friendship in the bedrock of our relationship. With Mel, too. A flare of hope, small but bright, catches in my chest. If Will, Mel, and I can find our way back, maybe Amelia can, too.

Exhaustion obscures the flame, blots out everything but what's right in front of me. I'm left with Mayor Beau, whose tight, guarded expression smolders like hot coals around the edge of a fire, so I cough up a story for him. "I fell at work yesterday and hit my face on the corner of a cart."

Lying to him hurts a little in unexpected places, like a corner of my heart that's somehow made room for him. This is no way to start even a friendship, but I've told that story so many times now there's no way to change it without starting a domino effect.

Plus, he doesn't need to know I broke into the library. It's called plausible deniability.

"Well, it looks awful. Your eyes are both black, your nose is swollen, and it doesn't look like you've cleaned it up. Not to mention your legs are scraped all to hell—did you go rolling in a rosebush?"

My shoulders slump as the last bit of energy, the surge that got me to the hospital, bleeds out onto the floor. It makes sense, what he says, because I feel as though I've been chewed up and spit out.

Beau sighs and disappears into the bathroom, where I hear the water turn on a second later. With the sun warming me through the window, it's hard not to fall asleep to the sound of Gramps' steady breathing. The mayor reemerges with a wet washrag, a dry towel, and a couple packets of alcohol pads. He pulls the chair Will vacated around next to me, then sits, his knees straddling my curled body.

"Look at me."

I do what he says, because it's nice to have someone take care of me for a change. I do such a shitty job of it on my own. The washcloth is warm against my face, and feels good as he swipes at dirt with a gentle hand. He lays the other one at the base of my throat, his long fingers reaching up to rest on my pulse as he steadies me for his ministrations.

"I went for a walk," I say softly as he towels me dry and then goes to work with the alcohol pads, which sting enough to make me grit my teeth. "I got lost when it started to rain, so I had to wait out the storm."

Will's voice slips in from the hallway, wriggling between us and holding the rest of my story hostage. There isn't much more to tell, if I don't count Anne's insistence on a road trip, her subsequent disappearance, and the buried treasure on her father's land.

Beau watches me as Will explains to someone that I need a doctor to examine my ankle, his typically good-humored eyes serious now. "We're going to discuss this further. You know this town like the back of your hand. Where exactly were these attack woods that trapped you all night and half the day?"

A gaggle of shivers force themselves upon me, my skin chilly in the filthy, damp clothes from last night. It could be the ragged, worried tone of his voice, or the certainty that he's going to wrangle the truth out of me one way or another. I've told him too much already; he knows my getting lost in Heron Creek is impossible. I couldn't get lost in Charleston, either, but the surrounding acres of plantations, marshes, and river lands are a different story.

Will comes back in with a middle-aged, bald man in a lab coat. His beady eyes gleam with annoyance, as though Will grabbed him from a more important patient, and they sweep over my injuries.

"I'm Doctor Michaels." He pushes a pair of spectacles up his beak of a nose. "If you can get into the other bed, it will be easier for me to examine that ankle."

Before I can move, Will bends over and scoops me into his arms. It's warm there, and familiar. The smell of him hasn't changed a single bit since the last time I was close enough to breathe him in—he smells like salt air and sweetgrass. Like the Creek.

His heartbeat quickens under the press of my palm, and when he speaks, the words are breathless enough for me to guess he's under assault by memories, too. "Jesus, Gracie. Gain some weight already. I bet you barely have a shadow."

He sets me on the other bed, wisps of peppermint breath following me down onto the pillows, then grabs an extra one and lifts my foot onto it. I close my eyes and, just for a second, enjoy the heavenly nature of being horizontal on a soft surface. There will be plenty of time to continue berating myself over leaving Gramps alone later. Like the rest of my life.

Over Will's shoulder, Beau's face tinges red. If he were a cartoon character, steam would be blowing out of his ears in streaming white clouds. I have no idea what his deal is, or why he's so angry, and staring at him isn't doing much good as far as figuring it out goes.

Now that the lingering adrenaline from getting lost and then coming home to the news Gramps is in the hospital has worn off, my ankle throbs. Dr. Michaels lays a hand on my foot, shooting pain up my shin.

"I don't think it's broken," he relays after a quick examination. "We'll take some X-rays just to be sure, but most likely a sprain. We'll get you wrapped up and back on your feet."

Not broken is good. No way would crutches and I get along.

"I'm not going anywhere until we find out Gramps' test results. I can wait."

Dr. Michaels shrugs, as though he couldn't care less whether or not my foot rots and falls off. His honesty refreshes me, as far as my opinion of doctors, and there's no way he doesn't have more pressing issues than a wrenched ankle on his plate today.

"Fine. I'll send the nurse in with some ice, and we'll do the X-rays when you're ready. We can't admit you, though."

He leaves, and Will does, too, to call Melanie back in response to a text message. My ex-boyfriend shoots a look toward Mayor Beau that's impossible to translate—it shifts too quickly through envy, protection, sorrow, and finally something primal, as though his eyes are bared teeth.

For my part, I summon my sweetest, most innocent expression and turn it on the mayor. I'm not surprised when it doesn't work. That expression is more than a little rusty.

"Don't go giving me any cute looks, Graciela. I want to know what happened last night." He runs a hand through his dark hair, leaving a few pieces sticking up.

The thought crosses my mind that he might look similar after an evening of rolling around in the sheets, and my mouth goes dry. I shouldn't be thinking things like that. Not now.

"Run out to my car, will you, and grab the little wooden box and plastic bundle in the trunk?"

"What? Why?" Beau crosses his arms, muscles showing under his short-sleeved polo. He peers at me like a little boy who suspects he's being tricked by a clever parent.

"I'm not avoiding your question, but I need those things in order to explain properly. I get the feeling you don't appreciate half-assed answers." I don't owe him anything, except since he took care of Gramps this morning, I sort of feel as though I do. And I'm tired of doing this alone. He already knows about Anne.

He growls on his way out the door, the sound low and frustrated, and it shoots heat straight between my legs. It's been too long, obviously, and the mayor is dreamy. Finer than frog's hair, my Grams would have said. The right balance of protective and supportive, at least from where I'm sitting. Laying, whatever.

Will returns, without his wife and son, with a bag of ice and bottle of water. He holds the latter out to me, then uses the towel from the bathroom to arrange the other on my foot. "You really do look like shit, Gracie. Mayor Drayton's been more freaked out about you being missing than about Gramps. I told him you're kind of . . . headstrong sometimes. Do your own thing, but he's been worried."

My lips twist at the descriptor *headstrong,* and he has the good sense to look ashamed. "Does this little speech have a point?"

"Not really. Guess it's none of my business anymore." He puts a hand on my head and comes away with a couple of small sticks and a wry smile. "It's nap time for Grant, so Mel's not going to come up until later. I'm going to head to work for a couple hours, then we'll all come back and check in on Gramps after dinner, okay?"

I nod, unable to speak around the lump in my throat. Will leans down and kisses my cheek, then squeezes my hand. "We'll get him through this, Gracie."

Then he's gone, and it's just Gramps and me. His steady breaths pull my eyes closed, even though Beau should be back with my artifacts any minute. My worry over getting home took precedence this morning and I didn't open the box, so whatever's wrapped inside the oiled cloth remains a mystery to me, as well. Right now, it's the last and least of my problems.

☙

The sun that wakes me is vivid and glowing, low in the sky. It's not the bright shine of midday that lulled me to sleep, and the nap had been an accident in the first place. Gramps snores away, his skin pinched with a tad more color and his breathing less noisy. The fact that no one woke me shoots a bolt of anger through me and it lands on my tongue, begging for someone to blame.

My gaze falls on Mayor Beau, who slumps in the chair between the beds, his eyes closed and fluttering. The sunlight hits him at an angle that makes the honey tones in his hair glint, and his long eyelashes cast shadows on his strong cheekbones. Between that and staring at his slightly parted lips, I waver between letting him sleep and waking him up to holler at him. For about five seconds.

"Hey, Mr. Mayor! Wake your ass up."

He starts at my raised voice, cracks one eye to peer at me, then closes them both to stretch. When he's done he rubs strong fingers through his hair, then digs them into his eyes before sitting up. "I can't say that's how I've been imagining you waking me up."

"What?" The word slides off my tongue in a breathless gasp that would make a porn star jealous, but I manage to recover with some dignity. "Nice, Mr. Mayor."

"Graciela, for God's sake, stop calling me Mr. Mayor. It's annoying."

"We're even then, because I'm annoyed you didn't wake me up when the doctor came in."

"Who said anyone came in? I've only been asleep for about . . ." He glances down at his watch. "An hour. No one came in before that."

The clock says it's almost six, and the late hour refuels my ire. "Did they forget about us? Aren't you, like, the mayor or something?"

My ankle throbs, ending my tirade, and I look down to see it's graduated to deep purple streaks that run on the underside of the bone, up the outside of my leg, and along the outside of my foot. Gorgeous. The ice pack Will left has turned to water and I wouldn't say no to a couple of ibuprofen, if they were offered.

"I am the mayor or something, and when I checked earlier they informed me the lab is backed up with some kind of issue but they expect to have results by dinnertime, which is in thirty minutes. How's your foot?"

"Hurts. Has Gramps been awake at all?"

"For a few minutes. He was relieved to see you."

The tears that have been swirling into a tight lump in my throat all day break loose, streaming down my cheeks in the kind of hiccupping, snotty gush that's embarrassing even when no one's around to bear witness. They're not the pity party tears that have plagued me for weeks. These are big, and rip loose from a place inside me that's been sealed up since I caught David with that girl, and with them comes a torrent of guilt, loss, and failure that stems from every aspect of my life.

I don't realize Beau is moving until he's on the bed, pulling me into his chest. The heat and strength from his arms hold me up, make me feel more than ever that I'm not capable of holding myself together right now—and grateful he's here to make sure all the pieces stay in one place. It probably means he's never going to see me romantically ever again, but at the moment, his friendship is more than enough and I sob into his shirt until it's soaked through, wrinkled inside my clutching fingers.

Hot breath tickles the top of my head, which must smell less than wonderful. "Gracie, I'm sorry. I didn't mean anything, bringing up Martin. He wasn't that worried, honest, he thought you'd overslept but wasn't feeling up to climbing the stairs to check."

My sobs slow to hiccups while his voice trickles down the back of my neck, warm and smooth and wrapping massaging fingers around my tense muscles.

"He looked at me with his eyes sparkling—you know how they do, right?" I nod against his soft shirt, a smile darting to my still-trembling lips. "Anyway, and he said, 'You gotta keep your eye on my Gracie-baby, Mayor.'"

My attempt at a giggle turns into a cough and a sniffle, and he rubs my back and chuckles in return. I pull away enough to wipe my eyes and pat down my hair, embarrassed now that my meltdown is over.

Mayor Beau's eyes meet mine, and they're amber, filled with fire and concern, desire and gentle care. They flick to my lips, and I lick them instinctively, thinking that he's going to kiss me despite the crying.

And I'm not going to stop him.

He puts a hand on my collarbone again, the way he did earlier while he cleaned my face, and the tips of his fingers brush the throb of my heartbeat in my throat. The forefinger of his other hand traces my injuries with a touch lighter than a feather, trailing down my bruised cheek until it lands at the corner of my mouth.

"I think you're terribly interesting, Graciela Harper. I'd be honored to keep my eye on you."

Before I can smile, or roll my eyes, or figure out how or if to deflect his cheesy, sweet, husky statement, Mayor Beau lowers his lips to mine.

Chapter Twelve

They're soft, as gentle as his fingers had been a moment before, and taste like sleep and a faint trace of maple syrup. The heat between our mouths makes me sigh into him, and warmth spills down my throat and into my belly, where it starts to simmer. It sizzles as he scoots closer, moving his mouth against mine and testing half a dozen ways we fit together before sliding his tongue along the seam of my lips, begging access I'm too willing to give.

It's brief, as kisses go, and our tongues meet for a brief caress before he eases back just in time for a nurse to breeze through the door. It's possible he heard her coming, but I didn't hear a damn thing but the sound of water roaring between my ears and the world.

My lungs struggle to get us a good amount of oxygen and the world's a little black around the edges, and from the way Beau's molten gaze clings to mine, the effect of our chemistry isn't all in my head.

The nurse, a perky, short girl with red curls that remind me of little orphan Annie, notices that she's interrupted something but, other than a curious glance or two, acts as though nothing's amiss. "Martin, dear, it's time to wake up and have your dinner!"

I like the way she talks loud enough for him to hear but doesn't resort to the kind of cadence some people take up, as though they're speaking to an infant or someone mentally deficient. He might be old and half deaf, but Gramps is sharper than a lot of people twenty years younger. That she understands that makes me take to the girl despite her overperky attitude.

Beau helps me off the bed and to Gramps's side, and when he wakes up and sees me, the way he lights up stabs me with so many holes my soul could strain pasta. I'm not trying hard enough, not doing enough, not being a good enough granddaughter. There might only be weeks or months left with Gramps, so why has it been so important to me to minister to the silent, bossy requests of a woman who is already dead? Anne Bonny has waited two hundred and fifty years for whatever closure she seeks; it's not going to kill her again to wait longer.

But the notes surround the archives, and Anne wanted me in that room. They could be connected, which is all the more reason to let it lie for now.

I shake off the thoughts of my ghostly bestie and take the tray from the nurse while Beau gets Gramps' bed into a good position for eating. The food doesn't look as bad as it could, and my stomach growls at the scent—I haven't eaten since the meatloaf last night, and Gramps probably hasn't, either. He only picks at his food, though, and the worry twisting my heart reflects in Beau's concerned gaze.

"What's wrong, Martin? Not a fan of cubed steak?" He grabs the remote and flicks on the television, turning to the

Braves game that's just started as though his question is nothing more than general conversation.

I look toward him and lower my voice. Not that Gramps can hear either of us without his hearing aids. "You can go, Beau. It's been a long day and you don't need to stay. I'll be fine, and Will and Mel are going to stop by later."

"First of all, I'm not leaving until we hear from the doctor and then get you down for X-rays on that ankle. And second, even though the events that began the day were unexpected and unhappy, I've enjoyed spending time with you. Even asleep."

The compliment, frank and unexpected, makes my whole body hot. A glance toward Gramps reveals him watching the two of us with far too much interest, and Mel and Will's arrival flushes me with relief.

My ex-boyfriend steps around the bed and grins at Gramps, ignoring the tension in the room. "Cripes, Gramps, you gave us a little scare. It's good to see you awake!"

When Gramps bobs his head up and down with a wide grin, we all know he didn't hear a darn thing. Melanie picks up Grant and rounds the bed to stand next to her husband, she and the boy wearing matching expressions of concern, though Grant's is tinged with a tad more curiosity.

"Hey there, little boy. Whatcha frowning for? You know what happens to kiddos with scowly faces?"

Grant's eyes get huge and one finger finds his mouth.

"Uh-oh, Grant. You'd better give him a big ol' smile or he's gonna paddle padooks!" I assume that, after spending several evenings with my Gramps, Grant's well aware of the phrase, one that means Gramps is going grab you, throw you over his knee, and give you a couple real or fake whacks, depending on his mood.

I've guessed right, as evidenced when the kid squeals and smiles at the same time, using two fingers to keep his lips tipped up in a grin. It makes us all laugh, including Gramps, but there's a rattle in his chest that turns into a cough. We all sober as a doctor walks in, flipping through a chart.

"Good evening, everyone. I'm Dr. Fields."

This doctor looks as though he's been cast as a surgeon on *Grey's Anatomy* or something, as opposed to being an actual physician. He's attractive, probably in his forties, with blond hair that's just starting to gray around the temples and some of the straightest, whitest teeth I've ever seen in my life.

I step forward and introduce myself when he asks for Gramps' family, returning his strong grip as best as I can. He gives me a once-over, from my bruised face down to my swollen ankle, and purses his lips as though he finds the entire package distasteful.

"We'll get you down for an X-ray, then get that ankle wrapped so you can avoid any ligament damage."

"I'm fine. What do the test results say about Gramps?"

He glances around at the menagerie of people, now aware that I'm the only family present. "Should we talk in private?"

"It's fine. Gramps can't hear you, and everyone else is fine to hear." Beau's fingers wriggle into my palm and I clutch them like I'm drowning in the middle of a hurricane.

"I'm afraid it's not good news. He's suffering from pneumonia, which we diagnosed when he was admitted earlier today. Unfortunately, that's not the primary issue. He's been aspirating food into his lungs because his muscle function is failing."

"What does that mean?" It's a disgusting picture, and there's no doubt food in the lungs is a bad thing, but it doesn't sound like something that can't be fixed.

"He's not chewing or swallowing properly. In order to fix the muscle memory issue, he'll need physical therapy, and during that period, he would need to be on a feeding tube."

"Okay, great, we'll do that."

His eyes, which I realize are black, like lumps of glittering goal, soften with real empathy. "Your grandfather has a directive on file that specifies no extreme measures or artificial machines are to be used in order to extend his life. A feeding tube falls under those categories."

"Yeah, but that's like if he's unconscious and never going to get better, right?"

"You'll need to speak with him to determine his wishes, Ms. Harper. It may be that he wishes, in this situation, to use the mechanisms we have in place to deal with his problem. If not, his directive must be honored." He pauses, watching me in order to make sure his words sink in before continuing. "In the meantime, I cannot recommend he eat, since eating is effectively killing him."

"If he doesn't eat, he'll starve." My tears start again, but they're silent this time. Defiant. A glance at Gramps reveals him watching the television, but the tense bunch of his shoulders tells me he knows that this is about him, and that it's upsetting.

"You see the dilemma. Speak with Martin and decide how he'd like to proceed. The staff here will be able to assist with either course of action."

Sadness bleeds from his gaze into the air, where it creeps toward me. Before long it's aspirated into *my* lungs, thick and cloying and wet. I can't breathe around it, like Gramps can't breathe around his food, and Beau eases me down into the chair as Dr. Fields leaves us alone.

Then Melanie crouches in front of me, her hands covering mine where they're clasped in my lap. She gives me a squeeze, forcing me to focus on her dear face, which is better than the horror going on inside my head. Heart. Everywhere.

"I'm so sorry, Gracie. We'll clear out and let you talk to Gramps, but whatever you need, or he needs, all you have to do is ask. You know that." The ferocity in her dark eyes reminds me of a million little moments that have always added up to the fact that though Mel looks like a sweet little pixie, she'll protect the people she loves until her very last breath.

It catches my breath to see it for me, after all this time, and my arms go instinctively around her neck. She hugs me back and we stay that way for a while, saying all the silent *I'm sorrys* and *you're forgivens* that we'll ever need to trade.

"I love you, Gracie."

"Love you, Mel."

"Call us, please. Let us know what's going on." Will squeezes my shoulder with one hand, supporting Grant with the other arm, his eyes wet with a mirror image of the coming loss ripping me open.

"I will."

They say good-bye to Gramps with long faces and kisses, but when I find the courage to swivel and look him in the face, I find that he's nodded off. My friends leave and I gather up the food tray, trying and failing to contain the fat tears dripping down my face. I elbow Beau out of the way when he tries to help, setting the tray on the floor outside the door and wanting to scream at the pain in my foot with every single step.

A different nurse almost runs me down in the doorway, a guy this time. He startles and manages to right himself with a hand on the wall, the glances down at his chart. "Graciela Harper?"

"That's what they tell me." If only I was someone else tonight. Anyone. This could be their life.

"Supposed to take you for X-rays." He grabs a wheelchair that's pushed up against the wall outside the door.

I glance back at Gramps, who's started to snore again, my heart breaking.

"Go ahead, I'll sit with him," Beau urges, settling into a chair.

The Braves are on, and they'll both be okay. But leaving hurts, even though it's silly. Nothing's going to happen while I'm getting an X-ray, except that I'll miss one more hour with Gramps. It's dumb. I can't spend every waking and sleeping moment with him, but it's my gut reaction to try.

"Go, Gracie. You're no good to Gramps if you can't walk."

Despite my stubborn inclination to argue, it's obvious he's right. I need to get my ankle tended to so that I can help Gramps when we get home. The internal admission doesn't improve my mood, and I flop into the wheelchair with a loud enough huff to telegraph my impatience to both Beau and the nurse, who takes off down the hall with me.

My attitude isn't fair to Beau, who's done nothing but be helpful and understanding and an incredibly skilled kisser, but it's my truth at the moment. The most important thing in my life, the relationship that picked me up after I lost David, that tugged me back to the place that's trying its best to heal me, is disintegrating before my eyes and there might not be a damn thing I can do to stop it.

Tears reappear by the time we get to the X-ray room, but the nurse doesn't mention them. He doesn't say much of anything, actually, while he completes his torture regime of prodding and turning my ankle for what feels like a hundred different photos. By the time he's done I'm biting back tears for a different reason, but at least he hands over a few mild painkillers before depositing me back in the room.

Beau drops Gramps's dinner roll at the sight of me, but the crumbs on his face give him away. He's sheepish, like a little boy caught with his hands in the cookie jar, and the expression endears me to him. Odd, that he can shift between sexy and sweet with so little effort, with a pit stop at bossy and annoying, but never lose a step as far as making me comfortable in his company.

"Sorry. I'm starving."

"Beau, you heard the doctor same as I did. It's better you eat that food than Gramps."

"We're slow, so you should be fine to stay here with your grandfather tonight if you'd like. The radiologist should be up with your X-ray results in an hour or so." The previously quiet nurse helps me from the chair and onto the second bed.

It feels as good as it did earlier today. That four-hour nap had been nice, but it didn't make up for sleeping against a tree last night.

"Thank you," I say to his retreating back.

Beau finishes the roll and picks up Gramps's pack of Jell-O, stuffing half of it in his face with a single spoonful, then looking guilty again. "Did you want some?"

"Ugh. Definitely not. I don't eat anything that moves voluntarily on a plate."

He shrugs and keeps scarfing, and it's on the tip of my tongue to tell him again that he doesn't have to stay, but he's made it clear he wants to. And also, maybe I want him to, a little.

"What are you planning to do, Gracie?"

"Talk to Gramps when he wakes up. It'll be useless if he's already made up his mind, but I'll try. Probably need to call my Aunt Karen, too, and have her give it a shot."

The mayor falls silent while he finishes his disgusting lime green dessert. I watch the game, wondering how he knows when his opinion might be important and when he has nothing to add. The sound of his plastic spoon scraping the bottom of the carton makes me hold back a smile.

"I brought your things up from the car," he comments, changing the subject.

As tired as I am, having something to think about other than Gramps's medical issue—or calling my Aunt Karen—makes me grateful. I hold on tight with both hands.

Beau nods toward the stand beside my bed, where the little box and bundle of archive documents wait for my attention with far more patience than the woman who led me to them has ever shown. My fingers itch to grab it, to dig through the treasure for clues as to how to rid myself of the spirit. I can't explain why, but I want to do it alone. Anne trusts me, I feel that with every instinct, and it surprises me how much betraying that bond, unwanted or not, bothers me.

Not to mention that, as much as I enjoy avoiding adulthood, I'm in charge of Gramps, and Aunt Karen needs to know what happened today. What we're facing. Making that call with Beau in the room isn't going to happen. I do a fine job of embarrassing myself in front of him, and Aunt Karen's always a little too willing to help in that department.

I don't realize how long I've been silent, staring at the box, until Beau throws up his hands.

"Are you going to tell me where you were and what that's all about or not?"

"I'll make you a deal. You go home, get some dinner and a good night's sleep. I'll do the same, after I call my Aunt Karen. If you want to come back tomorrow, I'll tell you what's in the box and what's going on."

"Throw me a bone here, Gracie. I'm worried about you. How do I know you're not going to disappear again and hurt yourself worse this time?"

"I'm exhausted, for one thing. For another, I'm going to have to talk to Gramps when he wakes up, and even though he loves all of you people as much as you love him, he has his pride. He's not going to want you here for that conversation—hell, he's not even going to want *me* here. Let me deal with that first?"

He runs a hand through his hair again, his eyes burning into mine. It's clear he doesn't want to leave, but my argument is valid and he can't really rail against me for wanting time alone with Gramps to discuss whether he wants to lay back and welcome death with open arms.

I do plan on confiding in him what happened last night, since he already knows I see ghosts and doesn't seem inclined to run away screaming, but not tonight. I push that truth into my gaze, let it tumble out of me and through the air between us, until he can't miss the honesty. The promise.

"I can't thank you enough for being there for Gramps today, and for calling Will."

Mayor Beau stands, giving me a rueful smile. "Calling your ex-boyfriend wasn't high on my list of things to do, no matter how much I enjoy beating him at golf."

"Trust me, Beau, Will and I are a long way in the past."

"Doesn't look that way from here."

Jealousy might be too strong a word for the emotion swirling off him, but it's definitely something like that. Closer to envy, perhaps, but either way it strikes me as touching. He's really interested in me. Me, the hottest mess to ever splat on the streets of Heron Creek.

"We're always going to be friends, I think. Even if we aren't."

He nods, slowly, then takes the couple steps between the chair and the bed. His lips brush my cheek, lingering, then sweep down to taste the corner of my mouth. "That's profound, Graciela. And enviable. Get some rest, please."

It takes me several minutes to gather my scattered wits from the blankets and sheets, as well as a few chunks that I worry might have left with Beau. Once I'm back together, at least for the most part, I pick up the phone and dial Aunt Karen's number. Dread drops roots in my belly, reaching deeper and causing me more discomfort with each passing ring.

"Hello?"

I pause, wondering how this day could get any worse. It's not Aunt Karen. "Millie?"

My estranged cousin sucks in a quick breath, and when she replies, there's a tremor in her voice that's entirely new. "Grace?"

My heart grows arms that try hard to reach through the phone, to fold her in a hug and ask why she's afraid to even speak my name, but of course it's impossible. "Is your mom there?"

"No, they're out of town. Is it urgent?" She knows it must be, for me to call at all.

"It's Gramps, Millie. He's in the hospital, and we've got some big decisions to make very soon. I can handle it, but I thought your mom would blow a gasket if I didn't at least give her the chance to be here."

"Oh, God. Is it bad?"

The emotion in her voice clogs my throat for the millionth time today, but I swallow hard in a valiant attempt to keep it together. "It's bad."

She clears her own throat, and then the take-charge, no-nonsense cousin that ran the first ten years of my life like a drill sergeant emerges. "I'll call them right now. They're just down in Savannah for some R & R, so I'm sure they'll leave first thing in the morning."

Savannah's only three or so hours away; if I know Aunt Karen and Uncle Wally, they'll be in Heron Creek before breakfast. "Thanks."

Silence hangs on the line, bigger than the physical and emotional space between us. It's vast, and full of accusations and lies and heartbreak that can't even begin to rival what I've lost with David, or even Will. It doesn't dissolve, isn't broken even though we both have the opportunity, and a moment later she hangs up.

Millie will always be the one to hang up first. Practical, real-world Amelia.

I sigh, then patch up the weeping holes in my heart as I fluff up the pillows behind me and reach for Anne's wooden container. Gramps's snores knit a comfortable blanket over the room, and combine with the soft murmur of the Braves announcers to relax my stiff back into the bed. Pieces of dirt and softened wood rub off under my fingertips even though I apply as much of my training as possible in the situation. It's not old enough or weathered enough to fall completely apart, but it's not going to last long without some preservation efforts, and soon. There are no markings on the outside, nothing that makes it unique.

The lip flips up with little resistance, no lock or even a clasp to keep it closed. The oily cloth feels slippery between my fingers, and whatever it's covering is hard but also pliable.

It's a book, I realize as the cloth falls away and the little leather-bound volume sits on my lap. Smooth, worn by hundreds of touches by human fingers, and tied closed with a matching leather string. Excitement, the kind that drew me to complete a master's degree, then a doctorate, in archival studies, shakes me fully awake.

It's old, clearly, and the fact that Anne led me to it makes me believe it's part of her history. I should wait until I procure the correct equipment, but my curiosity gets the better of me. I grab a tissue from the box beside the bed to protect the old pages from the oils in my fingertips, then open the cover.

My breath catches in my lungs when I see that a diary or journal entry begins on the first page, no title or introduction or explanation. I'll begin with the assumption that the words are Anne's and go from there. With another gulp of air, and then a quick check on Gramps, I dive into Charleston's past.

Chapter Thirteen

December, 1732

I have no way of knowing whether the person who finds these words will know any part of my story, and so I'll start at the beginning. It may already be too late for me, but I have to try. For Jack, and for our son. The child has no ownership in the misdeeds and sins of his parents, and no matter what, deserves to live the life he chooses.

Whether or not this tale makes a difference, I'll tell it. Because it cannot die with me.

I know that the true beginning of my story rests in Cork, Ireland, and with the scullery maid my father forced to lie with him, an atrocity that resulted in my birth, but surely after all I've done, and the prominence of my father in Charleston society, those details will survive. It matters not that I was a miserable child after my mother died, or that my father hated the fact that his daughter, the one child he had left to him, preferred to run around barefoot in tattered clothes as opposed to the fine dresses he brought home from his frequent trips abroad.

It matters not that I never loved him, that no one bothered to love me, not until much later.

I am guilty of many of the transgressions that stirred my father's hatred, even stabbed a few people under his employ, but none of them were innocent. I've never harmed a single man, in all my life, who can claim to be that.

Who among us can?

When James Bonny arrived in my life, he appeared as a lifeline. A preserver, a way out of the hell on William Cormac's plantation, or of the marriage he would eventually force on me. If I give my father credit for anything, it is that he was able to see through James's facade immediately, while my first husband's cowardly nature did not show itself to me until after we had wed and moved to New Providence Island around my sixteenth birthday.

It was then I learned, in a personal way, of the pirate life. James Bonny was small-time, in brains and heart and courage, and lacked the grit to become a great corsair. He was nothing more than a cutthroat and a common thief, and later a betrayer of the men who had once crewed ships through the Caribbean alongside him. He got me with child against all of my efforts, but the girl was dead when she slid from my body. Weak, like her father, and probably for the best—I would never have harmed my child, but loving anything half James Bonny would have challenged my heart.

It was shortly afterward that I met Jack Rackham—Calico Jack, to most. I sat on the docks, drowning the sorrows of my life in a bottle of rum and contemplating how I could have been so stupid, trading the prison my father constructed to one gaoled by James Bonny, when a man sat beside me. Despite the fact that I hadn't showered in days, that I wore breeches instead of a dress, my feet were bare, my hair a mess, Jack's first words to me were "You're a beauty."

I think I fell in love with him then, before I ever chanced a look at his face. The mud caked on his hands and under his nails told the tale of a working man, the kind of man who didn't expect others to do for him. I had never known a man like Jack, and I am never like to again.

When I did look up, into eyes so midnight blue I spent days of my life searching them for the stars, I was lost—and also found. Jack Rackham was everything I'd searched for in another human being—alive, filled with vigor and lust, starving for the next adventure. His filthy, matted hair, bronzed skin, missing teeth, and stench would have sent polite society ladies shrieking in the other direction, and the fact that the sight of him filled me with such desire I struggled to keep my hands to myself proved to me, once again and beyond all shadow of a doubt, that I was not like other women. Could never be, and was never born to be.

When Jack asked me to come with him when he put the Revenge *to sea, I said yes without a moment's hesitation. I would have the life I'd always wanted, with a man by my side who wished to put my proud, fighting nature on display instead of squashing it until it shriveled and died.*

There was, of course, the small matter of my marriage to James Bonny. When I informed him of my plans to leave he dragged me in front of the governor, who suggested Jack purchase me in a divorce. But I'm no cow, and the night we put the sloop to sea, James Bonny threatened me, promised that one day I'd be back to the real world, begging for help.

He was right, though not for any of the reasons simmering in his half-wit head.

The night Jack and I left port and set sail for the smaller islands, where he gathered a crew, was the best of my life. We decided it would be best for me to dress and act as a man, with one exception—he would not have me cut my hair, because he loved to tangle his hands in its waves while we made love.

The crew didn't question my authority as first mate, and if they suspected my womanhood, none made any advances. I knew how to use a sword and a blade, and it didn't take long to learn a pistol as well. The next few times we returned to Nassau I begged James for a divorce under the cover of night. Not because propriety concerned me, per se, but because I'd recently learned I was pregnant again and wanted to give the baby Jack's name. No one knew better than I the stigma that came from an illegitimate birth, and even though my concerns probably seem silly, for the baby's parents were both wanted outlaws, the desire to give him or her a good start plagued me.

In the beginning of 1719 our little crew experienced the kind of abundance and good luck that led to a need for expansion, and so we took on more crew and another ship in Port Royal. Jack was ill with the scurvy, so while the training of new hands generally fell under his purview, this time I took the new ones to task.

That's how I discovered right away that one of our new men was not a man at all, and I'll tell you that the discovery of another woman who desired the same life as I seemed to me an impossible gift from the heavens. A treasure bigger than any we'd ever stolen from a passing merchant or from one crown or another. Mary Read and I became fast friends, and the months we marauded together were the happiest of my life.

It all came to an end, strangely, the night Jack learned I carried his child. The pregnancy had grown thick around my middle, and unable to hide it any longer, the news had to be shared. He'd been elated, full of happiness that burst from him in unexpected smiles and affection. He'd ordered a celebration, and the entire crew had gotten slobbering, deck-hugging drunk. It was the reason the lookout never saw the ship until it was upon us—not that our ragtag crew could have succeeded against the British Navy were we sober as the day we were born.

The trials were short, the lot of us sentenced to hang. I advised the judge of my pregnancy, and was the only person in the courtroom not shocked when Mary advised the judge of her like condition. English common law demanded we be spared long enough to whelp our babes. All I could do was hope he would have my strength and Jack's strength, and make a life for himself even without our hands to guide him.

Some might say he would have been better off, even, away from the influence of the likes of us.

The let me say good-bye to Jack Rackham, and my lack of grace in that moment will haunt me until the last breath of my life. I was angry—at him, at how things had turned out, that none of the days and years we'd planned together would come to fruition. We both knew not leaving a sober lookout was a mistake. I shouldn't have pointed it out again.

Instead of letting my anger have its head that day, I should have hugged him and told him I loved him, made sure his final memory of me was good and right. But I guess that's just not the kind of woman I am. My last words to my love were that if he'd fought like a man perhaps he would not have hanged like a dog.

Terrible thing to say, but Jack only smiled and squeezed my hands through the bars before they dragged him away.

I never saw him again, but I know one thing—no one knew me better than that man. He knew how much I loved him. It's a small comfort, but one I have clung to with desperation more nights than not.

Mary and I rotted in adjoining cells. Her pregnancy was further along than mine, and even during all of those endless days with no other company, she never named the father. Perhaps she herself didn't know.

One day she told me she had a fever. The next, no answer came to any of my questions. I screamed for days, until my voice went away and came back and went away again, before anyone came to check on us. By that time Mary had gone into early labor, and that night delivered a small but healthy baby girl. The stress of the delivery and the illness killed my friend, though, and the day left me totally and utterly alone. They even took the baby, even though I begged to keep her with me.

I lost track of days and months, and the shock when my father's clerk showed up to bail me out almost sent me into early labor as well. I didn't want my father's help and would have turned it down, accepted my fate, but for the child almost grown inside of me. If I could give him a chance, protect him a little longer, it was worth sacrificing my pride yet again. In the end, I only asked for one thing in return for leaving the prison under the cover of night—that Mary's baby came back to Charleston with me.

It took some negotiating, I was told, but the British government had no use for a suckling babe that would just as like grow into the same sort of heathen as her mother. In order to secure this favor, and my release, my father paid a handsome sum to the governor of Jamaica, and I signed a document swearing that upon my return to the mainland I would change my name and never speak of my previous life. My father's additional demand was that Mary's babe be sent away. He located a cousin willing to take and raise the child. I would rather have kept her, of course, but knew that my father's charity was likely near breaking.

I still have no idea why he saved my life at all.

He arranged my marriage to a wealthy local man with a strong family history. Joseph Burleigh, from a less affluent and less respected line of that great family, is nothing but an abusive piece of scat who has no regard for the beings in this world weaker than him. I am not weaker than he, but have allowed him to take his rages out on me rather than my son.

Jack, so named after his father, of course, is Joseph's son, as far as anyone suspects. My husband—though I shudder to use the word—had spent time abroad and the community believes we met and married during his time in London. My boy looks so much like his true father, though, and nothing like the British ass who shares my home. If only Jack favored my Irish roots a little, if he could pass as a boy from the British Isles, or if I'd been able to bear Joseph a strong son of his own, it might not have come to this:

Joseph Burleigh has always despised my son, both for his parentage and his fiery temperament. The latter has been a trial for me, as well, but a secret joy as well, as the fruit of my love with Calico Jack Rackham could not have created anything less. He's almost thirteen now, and loves me so well it hurts my heart to look into his eyes at times. In public, the boy has never claimed to be anything but the son of Joseph and Anne Burleigh, but in private he and I share tales of his true father, of all of our exploits and love, and how living life on our own terms was all we ever wanted. A boy deserves to know where he came from, especially when that place is much nobler than the one he's been living inside the whole of his life, despite what the rest of the "respectable" world has to say about it.

Last night, Joseph came to me and said he's arranged for Jack to leave our house. He blames it on a false concern for our other children, our little girls, asserting that Jack can be no less a murdering psychopath than his father and namesake. The real reason is that he's ill, and the thought of turning over his holdings and estate to a bastard eats him alive. He's arranged it with the local officials, even showed me a signed death certificate for James (Jack) Burleigh, but he's leaving it up to me where to send my son, with the stipulation that it must not be nearby.

I have thought of taking him away myself, of course, but Joseph has threatened to hunt down and kill us both if I try it. There is the matter of my girls, to consider as well, though I must say I've never loved them as well as Jack's son. I've been thinking how to do right by my love this one last time, by this child who has made all the trials of my life worth suffering.

I've decided to write to Mary's cousin, the one who took in the baby girl when I returned to the mainland. I know she lives in Virginia, and am sending Jack to her with new identification naming him Cormac McElroy, along with what money I've been able to siphon here and there from Joseph's accounts.

He's a strong boy, and will be a man grown before long. I have to believe that he will be okay, that this woman who took in one pirate child will find room in her heart and home for another.

I have written all of this to convince you that I am the real Anne Bonny, and that I did not die on Port Royal Island as some continue to claim. The rumor exists, too, that I disappeared from my cell, but as time passes and people forget what amounts to little more than idle local gossip, I suspect neither will be remembered as true, or false, or of enough consequence to be remembered at all.

This has all been the tale that has taken me here, to a life that is not better than any before Jack, and one that, save my son, is no better than the death I earned aboard the Revenge.

This next part is important. It's the reason I wrote down my story. My confession.

Whoever you are, if you've been nodding off or losing interest, this is where I beg for your attention.

There is a woman who works in our kitchen—Zolarra. She's of Caribbean descent, most likely Jamaican, though she pretends to not understand me when I question her directly. Her skin is as black as night and matches her eyes, as well as the braids that dangle halfway down her back. Inked paintings, markings, decorate most of her skin that's exposed on a daily basis; none of the language or marks are familiar to me. She is a fearsome creature, not due to her African heritage, or the fact that she's been sleeping with my husband for years, but because her heart is blacker than the rest of her put together.

The facts I know about her have been dragged from the rest of the staff in tiny crumbs and morsels, dropped in my waiting palms and brushed against my eager ears in whispers, eyes always darting around and white with terror. They believe she's a priestess of one of the island religions that's forbidden and feared. There are others, more transplants in the low country, and all live in secret, practicing under the cover of the darkness that serves them.

I encountered the strange, frightening religions during my time in the Caribbean. I witnessed things that cannot be explained by any natural law or spiritual truth. Their beliefs are ancient, brought from the heart of their home continent, and they protect their secrets with a ferocity that shrouds their practices in mystery, which only amplifies the fear of the uninitiated. In the islands they call it voodoo, a conglomeration of hexes and curses, dark and light, and even speak of returning the spirits of the dead to life. I have no way of knowing if this religion is still active, or if it has disappeared from the pages of history, but I can tell you this true—I never feared anything in my life the way I feared this woman and her ways.

And she's put a curse on my Jack.

I heard bits and pieces of a conversation shared between the woman and Joseph as they were abed together, and one thing I heard clear enough—she said, "The descendants of Calico Jack Rackham will never flourish, never outnumber those from your own loins. I have asked, and the spirits have agreed."

I'm burying this diary as soon as the ink dries on the page, but in the weeks between now and when Jack is forced from my arms, I vow to discover the contents of this curse and detail it in a second journal, which I'll send with my son to his new home. If you're reading this, and you're able, please deliver these words to my descendants. I have a feeling that whatever this woman has arranged for the years to come, it will affect every Cormac and Rackham that lives.

I hope I'm wrong, I truly do. I hope my son finds health and happiness in the hills of Virginia, that he marries a nice girl and she bears him sons and daughters, so many they fill up his home and bring him joy, then turn around and do the same, in time. If that's what he desires.

I can't explain it, but my gut says this is not to be. That this woman, because of the hatred Joseph bears my son and me, has ruined any chance my children have to be bountiful and happy. It kills me that there isn't any more I can do, but I swear I will not rest until I unearth the truth of this thing, and find a way to set it right.

Chapter Fourteen

"Ms. Harper?"

The voice sounds far away by two hundred or so years, but eventually my brain remembers that's where I belong, too. I blink a few times, then look up to find Dr. Fields—the good-looking one—eyeing me with the same kind of worry Mrs. Walters displays. The kind that suggests they'd be only too happy to make me an appointment with the best shrink they can find on short notice.

"Yes?"

"You're certainly into whatever you're reading there. What is it?"

I cover the diary with the tissue, feeling protective of Anne's hopes and devastations and fears. "Nothing, just a journal."

"I have the results of your X-rays, and as we suspected, your ankle isn't broken. You've stretched and bruised a few ligaments, but it should be back to normal in a week or so. You should stay off it as much as possible, and I'll have a nurse wrap it for you." He rips a piece of paper off the top of his pad, scribbled with a prescription for painkillers. "Have you had a chance to talk to your grandfather about how he'd like to proceed?"

I shake my head, sneaking a guilt-laced glance toward the other bed. Gramps still sleeps, but has he been out this entire time? I've been reading for the better part of an hour.

"No, he's been asleep. My aunt will be here in the morning, I think. We'll discuss it with him then."

"Martin's daughter?" His look of relief bubbles irritation in my blood.

"Yes, why?"

"No reason," he covers smoothly. "It's just good to involve as much family as possible during these times. The support is invaluable."

I barely stop myself from snorting. If he knew my Aunt Karen, he wouldn't utter her name and the word *support* within six paragraphs of each other.

"I'll check in around lunchtime tomorrow to see what you've decided," he finishes lamely when I don't respond to his comment about the comforts of family.

The nice aspects of small towns such as Heron Creek are always the same things that grate on my nerves during times like these. Everyone thinks they know you, considers themselves friends, and therefore feel not only free, but obligated, to proffer unwanted advice. Apparently that extends to doctors I've never met, but I'm willing to admit my prejudice against physicians in general might be coloring my opinion.

In the last twenty-four hours I've gotten lost, found out my grandfather is dying, and read a two-hundred-year-old journal that left me feeling heavy inside, as though pregnant with sorrow that has no intention of leaving in nine months, or at all.

It's more than possible I'm not being fair to the handsome Dr. Fields.

"Thank you," I manage, mostly just to get him the hell out of the room.

He leaves, and I give myself a badly needed mental pep talk. I've been slacking on those of late, since there hasn't been much about my life or my future to paint in a positive light, but today definitely calls for some pump. And my own personal problems don't seem like much to write home about after learning of Anne's. And hers are two centuries old.

Her story intrigues me, for sure, but I'm not sure where it's going or why she needed so badly for me to find it. I'm convinced the woman who penned this journal is who she claims, and the true story of her life and what happened to her when she disappeared from the jail in Port Royal is invaluable, historically. It needs to be authenticated, cleaned, preserved, and filed with the rest of the things I stole from the archives.

Thinking of Mrs. LaBadie's hands on it makes me want to fling what's left of Gramps' dinner. I'm not sure why, or if it's residual from Anne's healthy paranoia, but I'm not at all convinced the mean old bag would take very good care of it. Whoever I turn it over to isn't going to buy the story that I found it because her ghost led me to the spot. I'm going to have to make up some tale about stumbling upon it in the dark, which isn't *technically* a lie. Either way, it can be authenticated.

What I really want to know is why Anne led *me* to it. Why does she think I'll be any more willing to believe her, to track down the other half of the diary, to care about her and Calico Jack's descendants than anyone else?

It could be my background in history, but there are plenty of people in town obsessed with local lore—and more that would be faster to believe in her ghost, too. Mrs. LaBadie, even, seems like a more logical choice, with her access to the archives and all the time she spends in the library.

The image of the kitchen woman she described pops to mind, and makes me think perhaps Anne's a little skittish around African-American women who, for all intents and purposes, do kind of resemble voodoo priestesses. In fact, I'm not going to be able to face her now without thinking the same thing.

My sympathy—and empathy—for a confessed murderer and pirate surprises me. It could be that I identify a little too much with a girl who never desired a life of convention, a girl who felt stuffed into too-tight dresses and pinching shoes, nothing ever fitting right. Anne wanted adventure, a different kind of life, and in the early seventeen hundreds there wouldn't have been many options available to her. It's kind of amazing, actually, that she had to guts and the knowledge to turn pirate at all.

I wonder when I stopped dreaming of a bigger life. It had been my reason for leaving Will behind, the idea that I wouldn't be free to search for something special, to trip and fall without bringing someone else down with me. In the end, I'd stumbled straight into shackles forged by my sophomore year ancient history professor. It had seemed exciting to me, at first, but from the moment he proposed and I said yes, the relationship started to chafe.

Now, with perspective, I wonder if I would have walked meekly down that aisle, knowing in my heart it wasn't right. Or if I, like Anne, would have had the courage to hunt until I discovered the life, the person, that would let me be the most myself.

I must have dozed off with those scintillating, self-absorbed thoughts running through my head, because when I wake up my ankle is wrapped and the room is dark, save the very first pale sheen of morning peering through the gaps in the cheap hospital curtains.

And I smell her.

She doesn't startle me, even though she's sitting in the chair between my bed and Gramps like just another concerned family member who couldn't stand the idea of going home for the night. I breathe through my mouth, wondering if Gramps' nose is as deaf as his ears, because that's the only explanation for not waking up to the stench.

Anne's ghostly green eyes travel in a deliberate arc between my face and the journal where it rests on the stand next to my bed. I'm still sore at her for abandoning me in the woods, though, and for some reason reading the diary makes me less scared of her.

She needs me. Or someone, but she seems to think it's me in particular.

"Nice of you to show up."

I know she can't respond, but she doesn't even react. The sweep of her eyes between me and the details of her life doesn't change. It's exhausting, but the gal has a one-track mind. It makes me scowl, but that doesn't earn a reaction, either. "I read it. I still don't understand what you want me to do with it, and I'm guessing you don't know what happened to the other half or where I can find Mary Read's mythical descendants."

I can only assume the girl-child that came home got a name not given to her by Mary or Anne, as well, and if her cousin never told her about her mother, there won't be any way to discover that line. It might be possible, with online genealogical records these days, to find trace Mary Read's living relatives at the time of her death.

If that was even her real name.

Anne's gaze settles on me, eyes almost iridescent with what's becoming a familiar but no less potent mixture of sadness, fire, and anger. She shakes her head, maybe in response to my statement.

"You don't know what became of the girl? What about Jack? If he lived with them after he left you, it's possible his family—if he has any—might know where hers is. They had a unique bond, after all—" I stop talking and stare in shock at the tears leaking from her eyes.

They roll down her cheeks but disappear before they can drip off her chin and land in this world that no longer belongs to her. The horrible grief that attacked me in the woods slams into my chest again, twisting my heart like a rag. I close my eyes, trying to breathe through the pain, when the sounds of footsteps and voices flutter in from the hallway.

The torturous desperation dissolves, and before I open my eyes I know Anne must have left, too. I can't for the life of me figure out why she's so flighty, and the mystery of why she trusts me is starting to intrigue me far more than what happened to her son.

I close my eyes again, in case I want to pretend I'm asleep when the people in the hallway enter the room. Whispers, too soft at first to be discernible, tickle my ears like feathers, but as the figures sneak through my door they bleed into familiar frames and faces, unforgettable no matter how long it's been.

My first instinct is to keep acting like I'm asleep, but Aunt Karen has no volume knob so the ruse will be up sooner than later.

"Wally, I told you we had time to stop for a doughnut and some decent coffee. We could have stopped at the craft store, too; Dad's still sleeping."

"Karen, the craft store isn't open. You made me get up at the ass-crack of dawn. Waffle House isn't even open. And keep your voice down. Your dad can't hear a damn thing, but Graciela's not deaf." Uncle Wally's voice warms over my name like a hug. He's always been sweet to me, even after my falling-out with Amelia.

I watch Aunt Karen glance at me through the slit in my eyes, her lips pursed as though she's sucked on a lemon. To be fair, that's pretty much her default expression, and least she has a reason this time, because as everyone and their mother has pointed out, I look like hell.

A sigh snakes its way free of my lungs and runs into Aunt Karen, letting her know I'm awake. Her fake smile almost makes me gag, but Uncle Wally gives me a real hug, which feels even better than the verbal one. My aunt pats my knee when I swing my battered legs over the side of the bed that faces Gramps. The chair where Anne sat smells normal, sits empty, and for the briefest moment, I miss her.

"Good morning, family."

"Humph. What's he done this time? Refused to use his walker and fell? Forgot to take his meds? Isn't this why you came to take care of him, so he could stay at home and things like this wouldn't happen?" Her words are a branding iron in the shape of my failures, glowing red and searing my skin.

It hurts to breathe them in, to hold them in my lungs while they eat me away from the inside out. She's not wrong. This *is* why I'm here, but I wasn't there yesterday, when he needed me. It takes all of my effort to keep the shame from my face. Aunt Karen is a predator—she can smell fear.

"It wasn't any of those things, Aunt Karen. And I'm sorry we interrupted your vacation."

My return jab hits home and she flinches at the suggestion that her trip to Savannah is more important than caring for her ailing, elderly father. She's made it clear that most things are more important. It's a small victory, because everyone knows Aunt Karen doesn't have feelings.

"Never mind that. We're retired now and travel quite a bit."

"Fantastic. Would you like to know why I called?"

The gesture she flicks my direction feels dismissive and commanding at the same time, but it makes no difference. They're here to help me convince Gramps to get the feeding tube, not so we can all hug and sing "Kumbaya" while looking at old photo albums.

I tell them about the pneumonia, and the food aspiration, then Gramps' directive before taking a pause to study their expressions. Neither of them looks surprised, but even Aunt Karen can't hide her dismay. *Huh. She does have feelings, after all.* "We have to convince him to do it."

The room is quiet except for the soft beeping of Gramps' monitor. We all watch him, as though he's going to disappear before our eyes. Maybe he's already started to.

"He won't agree to it. You know that, Graciela."

I might know it, but hearing her say it, not hearing Uncle Wally argue, makes me angry. They should at least want to fight to keep him.

"We have to try, Aunt Karen. We can't just lose him." Her gaze shifts to me, edged with the anguish spilling into my blood. "He's going to die. Is that what you want?"

Her green eyes, so similar to mine and Amelia's, go cold at my accusation. When she speaks, ice crusts around her reply. It freezes the air between us, making me shudder even though the room is warmer than is comfortable, in truth. "Of course that's not what I *want,* Graciela Anne. Do you think I'm a monster? I want him to live forever, but that's not going to happen." She bares her teeth like the badger she is. "I can see you still haven't mastered the maturity to know when it's time to let something go."

Her harpoon hits home but I grit my teeth, more determined than ever not to show her how it hurts. I swallow, glad they're here for Gramps but wishing I had some support of my own. "Where's Amelia? She didn't think this warranted an appearance?"

"For one thing, you didn't provide any details on the phone, so she had no way of knowing if you were exaggerating your concern or not. Second of all, Jake returned early from his conference and wanted her to himself for a few days."

There's something about the way her voice trembles at the root of her disdain, especially at the end of her explanation, that makes me thing she's lying. Maybe not about Jake coming home early, but something. It settles a hard cramp in my stomach that refuses to leave, and eradicates the rest of my doubt that something is seriously wrong. I whisper a quick, fervent wish into the void that it's nothing to do with the baby.

"If Gramps won't agree to the tube I know she'll want to say good-bye. Make sure you tell her everything."

"Do not presume to lecture me on how to handle my daughter. I'll tell her what I see fit and she'll do as she pleases."

"She usually does," I mutter, more nostalgic for my cousin's bossiness than disgusted.

Gramps stirs and Aunt Karen rushes to his side. Uncle Wally stared out the window during our snapped exchange, but he focuses on the bed now, too, and I limp over to the foot as my grandfather's blue eyes open and find focus. He smiles at his daughter, because he has always been and will always be a better person than I.

I can't forgive Aunt Karen for leaving him alone so soon after Grams died, or for missing her own sister's funeral two years ago. Then again, Amelia had missed that, too.

"Hiya, Martin." Uncle Wally breaks the silence with his typical booming greeting. "You're looking fine."

"Wally, you've never been one to piss on my leg and tell me it's raining. No time to start now."

"Daddy, we came as soon as Graciela thought to call us. I wish she had done it sooner."

Gramps shoots me an apologetic look but I smile and squeeze his big toe. The last thing he needs is to be worried about me, and I've had a few years experience dealing with Aunt Karen's snottiness. It didn't start in earnest until after Amelia and I fell out, but she'd never been overly fond of me. She's nothing if not a social climber, and thought for years that Amelia's attachment to me prevented her from making more appropriate—read, Charlestonian—friends.

"Gracie's been taking good care of me, Karen, don't you worry. Just got a little cough that won't shake loose, that's all."

She shoots me a look, her thin eyebrows raised in question. I take the hint and a deep breath, steeling myself for however this conversation is going to end. Praying for the strength to be the kind of person who does what's best for Gramps, regardless of my heart.

"The doctor came in with your test results while you were sleeping yesterday, Gramps. You have pneumonia."

He looks at me with squinted eyes, then shakes his head and points to his ears, looking old and helpless.

"PNEUMONIA." I repeat in a tone closer to Aunt Karen's normal decibel level. Grief pulses in my throat, choking the word.

"Oh. Well, even if it means they pump me full of crap, I can't say I'll be sorry to get rid of this cough." He's never been a complainer—it's a trait he passed on to me. The pain dimming his eyes and paling his cheeks betrays him, though, and it's clear he's hurting.

I take a deep breath and plunge in the rest of the way, telling him about the aspirating, and that he can't eat on his own until they adjust his muscle memory with physical therapy. He frowns halfway through my explanation, and by the time I'm done, he's shaking his head. Determination finds his jaw, setting it hard as he clenches his teeth and shifts to cross his arms over his chest.

"Gramps, it's just for a while, until you're better. No different than medicine."

Before he can tell me no aloud, not only with his posture and expression, handsome Dr. Fields strides in looking as though he got eight hours of great sleep and maybe a little good sex in the on-call room, even though it hasn't been that long since the last time I saw him. He pauses, taking in the growth in our party, then Uncle Wally extends a beefy hand from his spot in front of the windows.

"Wally Cooper. This is my wife, Karen."

"Dr. Fields. I'm sure Martin is happy to have you both here." He nods, and flicks a glance toward me that seems to say he wasn't sure of my capability on this decision on my own. Aunt Karen sucks harder on her imaginary lemon in silent reply.

"Hey, Doc. You know what we've talked about. No machines." The comment, as well as the nonverbal exchange that takes place between them, gives me a start. I hadn't realized Fields was Gramps's regular doctor.

"I understand, Martin, but this is a bit of gray area. The tube wouldn't be because you *can't* feed yourself, only because you shouldn't for a while."

"How long?"

"A week, maybe two. Your lungs will shut down if you continue to eat. The rest of you will throw in the towel if you don't. Excuse me." He steps past Aunt Karen and checks a chart that lists Gramps's vitals through the night. His frown deepens, and Gramps' eyes never leave the doctor's face. "Running a bit of a fever, Martin. How are you feeling?"

"I'm a little chilly. Chest hurts, too, like that ayatollah nurse is squatting on it."

That makes the doctor chuckle, even though he tries to hide it behind a yawn. "I'll send her in with some stronger antibiotics and some painkillers, just for you, my friend. Talk things over with your family, and don't be too hasty. This place would be far too pleasant without your company."

Dr. Fields scribbles a few notes and walks out of the room. Aunt Karen lays into Gramps, giving him the hard sell for the feeding tube, but it all sounds far away. An argument all but lost.

My brain scrambles for purchase in a world that refuses to stay the same. I said my reasons for coming back to Heron Creek revolved around caring for Gramps, and while that's true, it's also true that I wanted to come back so he could take care of me. I need a hand to grasp while I find my footing, work out a way to step forward without falling into the deep well of regrets in my past, maybe even rediscover the brave girl I'd always thought I'd become. To make sure I can find my way back.

Now he's going to leave me alone. I know it, have known it, and I love him too much to make him feel guilty for being ready to go. He's been sick more often than not over the past ten years, and has hardly been comfortable. Part of me knew, after Grams left us that he wouldn't be far behind.

It's selfish of me to stand here and cry. To want him to decide to fight this one last thing because I need him.

"Come here, Gracie-baby."

I limp forward, shouldering past Aunt Karen, and flop into the chair closest to my grandfather. The sheets underneath him are cool on my face, his hand is warm in mine, and for the moment, my feet stop slipping. It's hard not to let him see how badly I'm hurting when he knows me so well, and trying only makes him smile.

He pats the top of my head. "How's your foot? Because your face ain't too pretty."

My laugh sounds a little like what it is—a sob. Exhaustion threads his voice even though he's been awake for less than a half hour, after almost an entire day of sleep, a fact that tells me if he doesn't elect for the feeding tube, we're probably down to days together, not weeks.

"And the mayor, how's he?" He's trying to distract me, maybe even irritate me a little, but it doesn't work.

At least not on me.

"You know Mayor Drayton, Graciela?" The incredulous, aghast way Aunt Karen asks the question wriggles under my skin. It only took half a dozen insults to get to me this morning.

"I thought I felt my ears burning."

Chapter Fifteen

I twist around, wondering how on earth I'll ever seduce him after he's seen me banged up, crying, and full of snot more often than he's seen me clean. The warmth in his eyes as they seek mine suggests maybe it doesn't matter, and somehow his presence pours energy into my limbs.

He looks like he stepped off the pages of *GQ* with his shower-damp curls, crisp purple tie, and pressed pin-striped suit that's tailored to skim every hard line of his body. His slight smile shows off a hint of his dimples and squeezes me in places I can't talk about in front of my family. He still irritates me with his insistence on coming around even when no one asked him to, but I can't pretend it's not nice to see a face that's 100 percent on my side this morning.

"Mayor Drayton, this is my Aunt Karen and Uncle Wally, from Charleston. This is Beauregard Charles Drayton, the mayor of our fine little town."

The mayor rolls his eyes toward the heavens at my overdone introduction, which is, of course, my whole purpose in doing it. Aunt Karen shoots me a sour look and reaches out a hand, and Uncle Wally does the same.

"It's nice to meet you, Mr. Mayor," my aunt gushes. "I don't know if you remember, but your mother and I worked together in the Junior League for years."

Now it's my turn to cheek the ceiling for pockmarks. She's more transparent than dead Anne.

"I'm afraid I don't, but I know those things kept Mother busy for many years." The way he says it, as though Junior League isn't worth many words, tickles me pink. "Martin, you're looking much better. You'll be back to watching those Braves games and talking me into bringing you buffalo wings in no time."

Gramps does the smile and head bob thing, but I think he did hear what Beau said, because he makes a face at being ratted out over the buffalo wings. Those are definitely not on his heart diet, but I've been known to get a mad craving myself, once in a while. Every week.

Beau pats Gramps' hand, the one still covered by mine, and I worry the jolt of electricity is going to set off my grandfather's pacemaker. It doesn't.

"Graciela, since your family is here to keep Gramps company, I was rather hoping to take you to breakfast." He glances down at my wrapped ankle and his eyes darken. "Wait here a moment, if you would."

My emotions jerk back toward annoyed, since he doesn't even wait for me to *agree* to go to breakfast. The time away from Gramps' beloved face argues against it, while the fact that I've done nothing but stare at these four walls for almost twenty-four hours argues in favor, but either way, actually being asked would be nice.

"What's going on here, Graciela Anne?"

The question snaps me out of my internal argument about whether to get out of the room for a while or stand on my principles and be hungry. Aunt Karen's query doesn't make a lot of sense, but that's never been a prerequisite for speaking, as far as my aunt is concerned. "What do you mean?"

"Are you dating the mayor? You've only been back in town a couple of weeks!"

"Yes, Aunt Karen, I work fast. We're already married, actually. Your invitation must have gotten lost in the mail. You should really figure out how to use your phone." The sarcasm comes out of nowhere but it feels good. Maybe all of the worry and depression and vodka have been keeping it down.

"Don't be ugly, Graciela, it was just a question. I think it's a bit soon to be dating after everything that happened back in Iowa don't you?" She trails off, mostly, I figure, because she has no idea what happened in Iowa. Gramps knows, but he's the only one—or he was, before nostalgia opened my mouth with Mel. Neither of them told Aunt Karen anything, so she's fishing. Which really boils my blood. "Anyway, I was only asking because you blushed the moment he walked through the door. That shade is quite unbecoming on you, did you know?"

I ignore her, but file away the slant of jealousy in her words for later consideration. Even if I *did* marry Mayor Drayton, he wouldn't be a bigger prize in her eyes than Jacob Edward Middleton III. Amelia had landed the son of a U.S. senator, and her husband would probably be one himself sooner or later.

He'd fit right into Washington, the little skeezeball.

Beau returns, rescuing me doing five to ten years for attempted murder—only attempted, because there's no way

I'd take Aunt Karen in a hand fight. Beau's dragging the little redheaded nurse from last night, and she doesn't appear to mind his hand on the small of her back one bit. The set of his jaw makes it clear he's not enjoying anything at the moment.

"Mayor Drayton says we forgot to bring you fresh ice for your ankle, Ms. Harper, and a wheelchair. I've left one outside. Here you go." She holds out a bag of ice.

I take it while she peers up at Beau, waiting for approval with all the subtlety of a puppy who just took its first dump in the backyard. She scurries out after he gives her a tight smile and a thank-you. He's standing up for me, throwing his weight around like I asked him to do for Gramps yesterday, and that uncomfortable feeling, one unsure whether or not I like anyone taking up my cause without asking first, dances into my belly.

"You didn't have to do that, Beau. I could have—"

"What, hobbled down to the cafeteria? Hitched a ride on my back?" His smile softens the words, and my resolve. "I was nice about it."

"It's a good thing you've taken on the task of caring for our Graciela, Mayor Drayton. She's smart enough about certain things, but sometimes I think she hasn't got the good sense God gave a goose."

I flinch at the words, which are obviously true, but the silence that transforms into nervous energy makes it clear that her attempt at a joke has fallen flat.

A glance at Beau's face reveals a bemused expression, as though he's being badgered by a small child selling cookies on his front porch. "I think she does a fine job, Mrs.

Cooper, but of course we're all entitled to our opinions. Gracie? Breakfast?"

I nod, wondering when I lost the ability to give Aunt Karen what for on my own. It's not a mystery, though. Everything changed the night of Amelia's bridal shower. Me. Her. All of it.

"Sure. But can we eat outside? I have a few things I'd like to talk to you about. In private." I can't help but throw in that last bit, along with a slight eyebrow raise and a suggestive bite of my lower lip. It'll be quite the explanation later, but at the moment, annoying my aunt is too tempting.

He seems to catch on, evidenced by a twinkle in his hazel eyes. "Of course. I have a few things I'd like to say to you as well, though most of them will have to wait until you're feeling better."

Uncle Wally chokes on the oxygen in the room, and Aunt Karen's eyes grow as big as grapefruits. The mayor tucks my hand under his arm and supports my weight until we're outside the door, where he settles me in the waiting wheelchair. It's not ideal, but he's right about me not being able to walk without limping.

We're in the elevator before I break the silence, feeling more than a little ashamed of myself. "Thanks for helping me out back there. She's impossible."

"I'm sure I have no idea what you're talking about, but good Lord above, is she always like that?"

The image makes me giggle, but the gravity of our morning sobers me quick enough. It might have given me temporary satisfaction, to stick my friendship with Beau in her craw, but the truth about Gramps and where this whole thing is headed hangs heavy on my heart.

"It's silly. Her sun rises and sets with her daughter, Amelia, and for some reason she's always kind of viewed me as competition instead of family. But I shouldn't let her chap my ass the way she does."

"Does Amelia feel that way, too, or just your aunt?"

Tears start to gather again, but there has been too much of that. It's time to be the strong one, to stop crying. I've been crying for weeks, it seems like. "Amelia and I were best friends. Sisters. Until we weren't."

"What happened?"

"It's kind of a long story."

"I've got time."

The elevator dings and the doors swish open, emptying us into the large cafeteria. Beau pushes me toward the buffet line, waiting on my response with the patience of a man who has nowhere to go and nothing to do. Which is silly, since he has a town to run. Presumably. I mean, people call him the mayor but I've never seen him do anything particularly mayorly, unless we count charming his female constituents to within an inch of their lives.

It occurs to me that we've spent the majority of our time together talking about me—that my knowledge of his childhood, his professional goals, his thoughts on national healthcare and immigration, et cetera, lacks serious depth. That although I'm attracted to him, and the way he cares makes me feel warm, there's not enough evidence to decide whether or not we might be compatible on a different level.

Turning the tables deserves a little more of my focus, but sadly, that's already spread a tad thin.

We both fill Styrofoam boxes with hash browns and scrambled eggs, and I add a couple pieces of toast with jelly while Beau opts for an English muffin. The silence feels nice, especially after the loudness that surrounds my aunt, and the fact that, if I count Anne, quiet and solitude has been pretty elusive the past several hours.

It's cloudy when Beau wheels me up to a circular concrete table in a little courtyard and helps me onto the semicircle bench. He settles next to me, but not too close, and pops the top open on his container.

"You don't have to tell me about what happened with your cousin if you don't want to."

The comment, meant to sound offhand but failing, curls my lips up the tiniest bit. "You know, you say that I don't have to tell you things but you keep asking questions."

"I know. I'm sorry. I'm afraid you've got my curiosity at an all-time high, and you act like you're putting me out by talking, so I have to ask." He has the good manners to look sheepish, which combines with the salty breeze tousling his hair to paint a rather adorable picture.

"It's not you. I've never told anyone what happened, except Melanie. And Amelia, of course. Which went over like a lead balloon."

"I promise to stay friends with you."

I would give up a million years of kisses from men even handsomer than Beau to have my cousin back in my life. But he's here, she isn't, and maybe Aunt Karen's right about one thing—it's time to lay the past to rest, so it can stop wrinkling under my toes and sending me crashing down.

"Amelia and I were pretty typical girls, growing up. We thought we'd do everything together—go to college, join the same sorority, marry brothers and be each other's maids of honor." The memory of our silly conversations hurts my heart. "Our plans started to fall apart right away, when my mother got sick and I decided to go home to Iowa for school, and Amelia stayed in Charleston. Will and I had broken up anyway, my consideration of an early marriage and house full of babies postponed. It didn't matter. Amelia and I visited every chance we got, and talked on the phone or Skype or text message about every day."

I take a deep breath, then chew a mouthful of cold hash browns, somehow finding the strength to swallow them as though they don't taste like wet cement. Once the eggs are down the hatch, it's time to continue. I'm feeling lighter, in a strange way, letting go of my secret. Like with Mel.

"Anyway, she met Jake, her husband, not long after we started school. I met him over New Year's our sophomore year, in Charleston. We'd all gone to a party and he drove us home; Amelia was passed out in the backseat and he hit on me the whole drive."

"You didn't say anything to her?"

"No. Not then. I mean, they were just dating, no big deal. Amelia's smart, and I figured she'd see him for what he was eventually. But then she called and said they were engaged, and asked me to be the maid of honor. I agreed, with a fair amount of reluctance, but she's my cousin and I love her. What could I do?"

The rest of my hash browns disappear, and a triangle of toast slathered in blackberry jam. Beau says nothing, just eats his own breakfast as though it's as fake delicious as mine, and alternates between watching the birds yapping and fluttering in the bushes and checking on me.

"It was after her bridal shower when Jake came into my room and tried to . . . he tried . . ." I swallow, trying to find the word for the second time. Failing. "He tried to force himself on me. Despite what my Aunt Karen thinks, I can take care of myself; I left him squirming and holding his crotch."

"Oh my God, Graciela." His face goes white, and it looks as though his cement breakfast might make a reappearance. "I'm so sorry that happened to you."

I avoid his gaze, staring down at the remnants of my food instead, and nod. "Thanks. That's not even the worst part of the story. I went to Amelia right then, with blood under my fingernails, my nightgown ripped, but Jake had gotten there first. She didn't believe me. Told me I was jealous because she was getting married first. Said she hated me for ruining everything, threw me out of her house and her wedding, and we haven't spoken since. She didn't even come to my mother's funeral."

His hand covers mine, warm and reassuring even though nothing can fix this. Not as long as she's married to Jake. "You know she believes you, Gracie. She just doesn't want to admit it."

"Melanie said the same thing." I shrug. "*I* would believe *her*. I want to think I would trust twenty-plus years of friendship over a brand-new relationship with a guy who's more than a little sleazy, but . . ."

"You would, Gracie. You're not the type of woman who lies to herself. Or anyone."

That makes me stop and think. Perhaps that had been true of me five years ago, before I turned the reigns of my life and brain and everything else over to David. Perhaps it could be true of me again.

If I'm not lying to myself, then it's time to admit I'm worried about Millie, whether she hates me or not. Everyone's acting a little weird when they mention her, and it can't only be her pregnancy that's making them skittish. The memory of Jake's dark gaze, of the way he gave me the creeps even before the first time he hit on me, zips shivers down my spine, turns my breakfast sour in my stomach. His wrongness is more than being an arrogant cheater, or even the kind of guy who would press an advantage, and it seems impossible to believe he's never shown that side to my cousin during the five years they've been married.

The sound of Beau's Styrofoam container popping closed brings me back to the present, and to the man in front of me—who must have secrets, but it would surprise me to find out they are sinister.

"So, are you going to tell me what's in that box you made me fetch? Or am I going to have to pry it out of you with my considerable tactics?"

The way he waggles his eyebrows encourages me to consider what kinds of tactics a man like him might employ in order to get his information. There is heat in places that have gone cold, including my heart, and it makes me want to hate him and jump him at the same time. It's safer the way I am, playing dead behind poorly constructed but determined walls, but he's determined to poke until he finds a weak spot.

Which is apparently in my pants.

Now that the moment of truth has arrived, at least as far as where I was the morning Gramps got sick—including how I got there and what I found—hesitation stills my tongue. For the millionth time since Anne's ghost appeared to me, I consider the fact that I'm crazy. That all of this is in my head.

Except if that's true, what are the chances I stumbled on that journal by happenstance?

No. And I have to tell someone. I don't have the energy to handle losing Gramps, worry about Amelia, be haunted by a ghost, terrorized by Mrs. LaBadie, and figure out what the heck to do with the diary all by myself.

"Okay, but you're going to have to suspend disbelief for a few minutes."

"I think I've proven myself capable in that arena."

I have a feeling he'd prove himself capable in most arenas. I don't even realize the thought has put a wicked smile on my face until Beau cocks his head to one side in a silent question.

"Nothing. Never mind."

"Graciela, I've said this a few times already, but if it helps, I'll say it again. I don't think you're crazy. Impulsive, perhaps, and bullheaded. Interesting. Speak."

My cheeks heat up even more at the compliment, which is better than telling me I'm pretty. Interesting is far more useful, and it lasts longer, too.

"Anne showed up the night before last, waiting for me when I got into my room."

"I'd think you'd be used to her by now." The twinkle in Beau's eyes makes me wonder whether or not he really believes I'm seeing a ghost, or is humoring me.

Until now, I've pretty much humored anyone who claimed to see spirits, but I'll have to reconsider my reactions in the future. "Oh, I am. She and I are besties now, usually sit around painting each other's toenails and gossiping about the cleanest way to slit a throat." I roll my eyes. "She was different the other night. Insistent."

"How so?"

"She ran off with my car keys."

His lips had pulled down, the lines around his mouth signaling concern, but now they tip up, a deep chuckle rumbling from his chest across the space between us. It makes me roll my eyes again.

"It's not funny, okay? I followed her out to the car and she insisted I chauffeur her around until she pointed me toward the land that used to belong to her father. She's a *big* fan of pointing."

No point in mentioning that the borrowed archive documents had helped us figure out where to go. It wouldn't look good for the mayor to have knowledge of a breaking and entering when Mrs. LaBadie finds out and calls the cops. Or kills me and drinks my blood, then makes a stick doll out of my dry bones.

"Where was it? What did she show you?"

"It's a plantation museum house, now. We parked, Anne prodded me out of the car and off the path, and we traipsed through trees and clearings until she found the one she was looking for, then she disappeared."

"Then what?"

"I tripped, which accounts for most of the scrapes and the tweaked ankle, and while I was on the ground found a bunch of white rocks in the shape of an X."

His expression turns skeptical now, eyebrows raised and chin tipped to one side. "Seriously? Come on."

"It's cheesy, I know, but when I dug in the middle I found that box." I mentally dare him to argue with that, or say I'm making it all up, with physical evidence on the table between us.

"Okay, but why did you stay out there all night and half the next day?"

"I told you the truth about that already. It was pouring, and I followed Anne out there like a blind lady. Once she disappeared, there was no way I could find the damn car without sunlight, and even then it took me until lunch."

"Not much of an outdoorsy girl, eh?"

"No, not exactly, Mr. Mayor," I snap, unwilling to check my sarcasm. It does nothing but make his eyes dance. "Anyway, I've been here ever since."

"I meant to ask how your discussion went with Martin went this morning, but your face when I first arrived said it all." He's not smiling now, genuine sorrow chasing away the amusement in his gaze.

The lump is back in my throat, but it's been such a constant companion that talking around it is getting to be a special skill. Maybe I can put it on my résumé. "I'm going to lose him, Beau. The doctor says he should think about it, but I doubt Gramps will change his mind. And I can't be the selfish one to ask him to do that."

"You think he's ready."

I nod. "How can I love him and ask him to keep suffering, and probably lose his dignity along the way? He's old, but his identity is rooted in his independence and the relationships he's formed. All that would go away if he spent his last months in and out of the hospital. It would be for me, not him."

The tears break loose again, plopping from my chin onto the lid of my container. Beau's fingers curl around mine in an attempt to hold me up while imaginary, muddy earth slips between my toes, disappears as I scrabble for purchase and for the strength to stand up. I fail miserably, the slop smearing my face and clogging my lungs.

A million wishes tear loose from my insides and float away like balloons on the wind—that Gramps had more time, that I was a better person. That Amelia could be here and our relationship could be the way it was. I'm spiraling downward so fast it makes me nauseous, until a thought pops into my mind and surprises a wet giggle from my pinched windpipe.

"What?" The question comes in tandem with a light touch on my forehead, the gentle sweep of loose hairs back over my shoulder.

"I just remembered something Gramps always said when we were young and wishing for something. He'd tell us that we should take a crap in one hand and wish in the other and see which fills up faster." My smile wobbles. "His way of telling us to work hard for the things we wanted, not wish for them."

"He's a smart man, your Gramps. I'm quite fond of him."

"Everyone is."

A sigh bubbles past my lips. I sit up straighter, stretching the kinks out of my back while the rest of my tears dry up. This isn't the time to feel sorry for myself, There will be time for grief once Gramps is gone. For now, he's still here, and so am I.

"So, don't you want to know what's in the box?"

Chapter Sixteen

"So, there's another diary out there somewhere with the rest of the story, and what Anne believes is the answer to the curse this Caribbean woman put on her son?"

"I suppose. If she ever got the chance to write it, if Jack Jr. delivered it, and if the relative hung on to it and passed it down, if, if, if. It's just as likely the cousin tossed it away, thinking to protect her niece and even Jack from the world of his mother."

He clears the table, tossing our trash into the nearest army green receptacle. "Well, I definitely can't think you're crazy now. It'd be harder to believe that you came across that diary on accident. Something out there—something we don't understand—led you there because it believes you can do what needs to be done."

"That would involve actually knowing what that is, I assume."

"Isn't it obvious? We have to find the second journal."

"Why? Why do I care about Anne and Jack's descendants? I don't have time for this shit." And why does he keep saying *we*?

"Because you're a historian, Gracie. Don't try to tell me your brain hasn't been working a mile a minute, wondering if you can hunt down Mary Read's daughter's progeny, or the kids running around with Anne Bonny and Calico Jack blood in their veins. It's the kind of unique contribution to history that comes around once in a lifetime, and you know it." The expression on his face dares me to disagree. "You still work at the library, right?"

"I doubt it. Mrs. LaBadie can't wait to fire me, and I haven't shown up for two days."

"You are terrible to that poor woman. I stopped by this morning and spoke with her, but the Freedmans had already informed her of Gramps' situation."

He talked to Mrs. LaBadie for me? I didn't ask him to do that, and besides, maybe I *wanted* to get fired.

The frown on his face says he can tell he's done something wrong, but he can't figure out exactly what. "I didn't mean to step on any toes, but it seemed like you had your hands full and I was stopping by to speak with Ralph anyway."

"Job or not, she's not going to let me anywhere near those archives," I comment, ignoring his explanation. "She guards them like a rat with a chunk of cheese." I bite my lip, mind reeling. "It would probably be as easy to track down Mary Read's family online, with all the genealogy records available now."

"You'd better do something," he comments as he wheels me inside. I don't have to turn around to know there's some kind of jab he finds amusing coming next—the smile in his voice gives it away. "I doubt Anne's going to leave you alone until you do what she wants.

The memory of her in my room last night, her focus not only undeterred but increased, tells me he's not wrong.

Aside from the draw of the historical contribution, getting that pushy, reeking ghost to leave me alone might be prize enough.

"Why do you think she chose me, though? Am I just gullible? Did she know I'm a loser with no life who had time to spare? Did she think I drank enough to not question the appearance of a dead pirate in my life?"

"Can't say. Maybe she knew you'd care enough to follow her, or there's some other reason that's still a mystery—something we might learn later."

"You know, that's the second time you've used the word *we*." I angle my neck around but still can't quite see him. A cramp seizes my muscle and forces my face forward again.

There's something about having another person on my side without having to ask them to be there that makes my heart feel squishy. It's a strange feeling, one that hasn't been around since my romance ended with Will. That light hope that accompanies a brand-new friendship-maybe-more. I'd never realized David and I missed that stage until things were over. Our relationship was heavy from the start.

"I have to admit, my curiosity is piqued over this whole thing. Not to mention that, even though you don't need anyone looking out for you, I don't mind volunteering."

"Oh, yeah?"

"I'm trying to decide whether looking from the front or behind is more preferable."

That makes me laugh, and some of my depression and lethargy might have dried up had the sound of Melanie's tinkling laugh not squirmed underneath Gramps's door. It reminds me that now is not the time for laughing or letting my guard down.

It does also remind me that Beau may not be the only person on my side.

Mayor Beau spins me around so he can look into my face, and gathers my hands in his to haul me to my feet. I end up pressed against his chest, strong arms helping support me and my bum foot. My mouth goes dry, and my heart tries its best to crack its way out of my ribs.

His fingers slip under my chin and tip my face up, where my lips meet his. They're as soft as they were last night but taste like hash browns instead of syrup. The kiss doesn't last as long, but that doesn't make it any less exciting, and by the time we pull away I have to lay my head on his chest to catch my breath.

"Graciela, when things get back to normal I really hope you'll find time in your ghost-chasing schedule to let me cook you dinner at my place."

I manage a nod, and then stand on my own two feet. He's halfway down the hall before I find my tongue. "Beau?"

He turns, and the flash of dimples almost dumps me onto the linoleum. "Yes?"

"Could you come back after work tonight and drive me home to get some things?"

"It would be my pleasure. I'll be back around six."

His smile encourages my own, and gives me the strength to keep it in place as I open the door to face my past. And also my family.

ଓ

Aunt Karen and Uncle Wally left right after I returned from breakfast. She wanted to get some rest, and probably go back and hit the antique store she'd missed that morning. It's good news, and the serenity of last night returns to Gramps's hospital room. The fact that she's going to see the hot mess that is my bedroom, and also the laundry room, gives me slight anxiety. Then again, it'll drive her nuts, so maybe it's a win.

Mel and Will are still here, and her parents are watching Grant so they don't have to leave. It surprises me to find that hours have passed without me wishing that they would go, even though a nap wouldn't kill me. It's late afternoon now, the sun bleeding red through the flimsy curtains and Gramps awake for the first time since lunch. We've set up a game of euchre on his tray table, and as usual, Melanie's getting the brunt of everyone's frustration because she is the slowest card player in the history of the universe.

"For heaven's sake, Mel, you've only got three cards in your hand. Pick one and play it before I die waiting."

"Gramps, don't say things like that. And be nice," I chastise, hiding my smile behind my own three cards. If Gramps says no to the feeding tube, it's going to be a blessing and a curse, these last days. *Knowing* they're the last days.

Mel ignores us both, like she's been doing for over half her life now, and after another thirty or forty-five seconds grabs a ten of spades and tosses it on my ace of hearts. Her gaze turns to Gramps, lit with a typical Melanie challenge, but even I recognize her mistake.

Mel's not only the slowest, but also the *worst* card player in the history of the universe.

"Melanie, Melanie, Melanie. How many years have we been playing cards? Ten? Twenty? I can't remember how old y'all are anymore, and you still seem to be fifteen to these old eyes. They're not too old to miss the trick you just laid out for me, though, sending a boy to do a man's job."

He tosses a queen of spades on top of her ten, which is what's known as out-trumping. Will, her partner, gives an exaggerated sigh and throws a low heart, which gives Gramps and I the trick.

Melanie turns a glare on her husband, one that we've all had years of practice avoiding. "I didn't have another spade, William."

"And now they know that, too." He grins and shakes his head, giving her a wink. "It's okay. I didn't marry you because you'd be a good euchre partner. Or a good spades partner, or hearts, or--"

"I think we get the point," she snaps, but there's no hiding the fact that her glare has turned into a smile before it could slice him open.

Will and Mel are spared the embarrassment of losing when a nurse—a new one—comes in to check Gramps's vitals and give him another round of antibiotics and painkillers. They stand up and pull their chairs out of the way, then Will reaches down to help me up and onto the still-unoccupied second bed.

"We should get going, Martin. I promised my mom we'd be back before dinner—Grant's a messy eater and you know she's always had a touch of the OCD when it comes to her kitchen." Will shakes Gramps's hand, holding on for a couple extra seconds. His blue eyes shine when he turns away but he blinks them clear in half a heartbeat.

Our gazes meet and his sadness meshes with mine. We share a melancholy smile, and doing things with Will hurts a little bit less than it did the last time. Maybe it will continue to lessen if we keep practicing being friends again. Melanie kisses Gramps's cheek before they leave, and squeezes my hand on the way out the door.

Despite the shitty nature of the news over the past day, my heart is full and warm. There are people who care about me, even when I've done my best to make sure they shouldn't.

When the nurse leaves, Gramps turns a tired but satisfied gaze my direction. "That William's a nice boy. Always has been, but he's not the one for you, Gracie-baby. Don't go wasting your time regretting your decision there. It was a good one. Can't take back the choices we done made, anyhow."

"I know that, Gramps."

"You've got to be patient. It's not one of your strongest qualities, so you'll have to work on it."

I shake my head, and give him the smile he wants. "I'll do that. No more Davids."

"Good girl. I'm not worried about you, you know. You'll figure it out." He looks me up and down, wild eyebrows knitting into a single caterpillar before he finishes.

"You need to get home and shower. Get some fresh clothes and such."

"Thanks, Gramps. I'm planning on it. Mayor Drayton will be back soon to grab me."

"Never doubted he'd be back around, sweet girl."

I ignore the implications of his statement. "Aunt Karen and Uncle Wally should be here anytime. I thought they'd be back already or I would've told Beau later. Make sure to ring the call button if you need anything."

He avoids my stern look, because we both know he has a problem asking for help. "Bothering" people, he claims, even if he's uncomfortable or sick. It's the reason he didn't complain about how bad his cough hurt until he collapsed on the living room floor, and I should have realized it days ago. I was too focused on my own dissolving life, my attraction to Beau, even Anne and her problems.

Which are my problems now, apparently.

"Seriously, Gramps," I follow up when he finally meets my eye. "It's their job to take care of you. Whatever else they're doing to kill time in between rings isn't more important."

"Okay, yes. You've always been such a pushy girl. Like your grandmother."

I kiss him on the cheek and take off, wanting to be outside and ready to go when Beau gets here. It's weird, but a shower actually sounds amazing, and I've been wearing the same clothes for three days now.

I realize before we even leave the parking lot that Beau's concentration on driving gives me a good opportunity to get the jump on learning more about him, instead of the other way around.

After the third question, about what he studied in college and whether or not he always aspired to political office, he shoots me a bemused glance. "Are you pumping me for information? You're about as subtle as the Spanish during the Inquisition."

"That wasn't actually a questioning so much as an excuse to burn heretics at the stake."

"Exactly my point."

"Do you not want to reveal your secrets, Mr. Mayor?" The intention behind the question is innocent, but it sounds accusatory when it falls from my lips. It gives me a start, to realize that I've become the kind of person who assumes other people have secrets they'd rather keep—especially men.

"I'll answer anything you'd like." His response feels cool, like a brush of Iowa winter in this Southern summer.

"I'm sure you don't have anything good and juicy hidden in your closets. People with the bad kind of secrets don't get elected to political office."

"Gracie, for Pete's sake. Just because there are things you don't know about me doesn't mean I have secrets. The things you're embarrassed about in your past aren't dirty secrets, either, no matter what you've somehow started to believe in that maddening, pretty head. Everyone has a past." His tone warms during the speech, which irritates me with its accuracy. "Even me."

"Fine."

"No more questions?" He queries after a couple blocks of silence.

We're going to be at Gramps' house inside of a minute, and all of a sudden I'm too tired to think. Too exhausted to come up with anything interesting, or even coherent. "Not today."

"Would you like me to take you for dinner before we go back to the hospital?"

I shake my head, pushing the door of his SUV open and landing on the familiar, cracked concrete of their driveway. "No. I don't . . . there's not much time left, before. I just want to be with Gramps."

It's probably not healthy that I can't say that Gramps is going to die. Then I decide it doesn't matter one way or another. Soon, I'll be face-to-face with the reality.

Chapter Seventeen

Gramps has been home a week and a half, and since he refused the feeding tube and therapy, time is running out. He sleeps away most of every day and hardly anything but loose skin covers his bones. He's eaten, of course, when he gets too hungry, but his cough is terrible afterward and he does it only when the pain in his gut becomes unbearable.

Not that he's shared any of this, or complained much at all, but I'm not blind. Aunt Karen sees, and so do Will and Melanie when they stop by once a day to say hi. There's a hospice nurse living in the main floor guest suite, a sweet old black woman named Lynette, and she says it won't be much longer.

I'm lying in bed, trying to sleep even though the first streaks of dawn lighten the sky. Amelia hasn't come, but Aunt Karen swears every day that she'll be here soon. Each one that passes without her pulling up in the driveway increases my anxiety over what's happening in her life, because she can't have changed that much. We both love Gramps with such endless ferocity that she wouldn't miss this, not by her own choice.

If she *is* willingly missing the last couple of days with Gramps, then she's no longer the girl I knew. She's someone else entirely, and it's going to turn my world upside down all over again to realize that not only have I lost her, I'll never get her back. Not the way she was. The way we were.

Anne has been a daily visitor, and though it's not exactly a comfort when she shows up, the day has started to feel incomplete, somehow, without her. She's an anchor, a constant, which is a pretty weird thing to say considering she shouldn't be here at all. She still wears her impatience like a second set of clothes, but pulls it tight around herself now instead of trying to fling it onto me.

Gramps's hospital stay sobered Anne, too. I'm not silly enough to think she's worried, or cares about how I feel, but she might realize that she's not going to budge me from Gramps' side again. I'm not sure how much dead people know, but it doesn't take a trained eye to know she won't have to wait long.

The thought fills me with self-pity so I sit up, grabbing my laptop from beside my bed in an attempt to do something other than think about myself. The clock on my phone says it's only six in the morning, and no one's arriving for the picnic until eleven. Lynette and I made all of the food last night, so there's plenty of time to poke around the genealogy site I signed up for the other day.

Beau has been around as often as Will and Melanie, quiet but supportive. In the background. There haven't been any more kisses, but the mayor's ever-present sexiness manages to distract me, anyhow. He's doing exactly what I asked him to the first time we went out to dinner—be my friend. It's making me love him.

The way family history websites are set up is giving me trouble, since they're designed to work from the present generation backward, not the other way around. It's harder, even, since Mary was a woman. Her last name wouldn't have survived, and there's a good chance Read wasn't the surname of the cousin that took in the baby girl, since Anne's diary suggests it was a woman, and she was probably married.

I give up after another unsuccessful hour and a half of scouring birth and death records in the state of Virginia during the appropriate time frame. There are simply too many to make it a simple task, but slow and steady wins the race, I suppose. Anne Bonny's not going anywhere.

The dead joke only plays in my mind, but it makes me snicker at the old pirate's expense. I'm still too chicken to be a smart-ass to her face.

In the shower, which I've been visiting at least every other day now, I decide it might behoove me to reach out to a professional, since genealogical research isn't my forte. There are several professors at the University of Iowa who might be able to help, but it's best to go local when the history is region-specific. There might be someone at the College of Charleston, or maybe one of the big North Carolina schools who specializes in this sort of thing.

By the time I've toweled off and picked out a comfortable pair of shorts and long tank top to wear out to the docks, the search for Mary Read's family has fallen to the back of my mind. It's after nine, and the smell of sizzling breakfast announced Aunt Karen's presence an hour and a half ago. It took all of my willpower to not succumb to the siren call of bacon, but sitting down at a table with my aunt kills my appetite, anyway. It's strange, but as relieved as it makes me to not be doing this alone, I miss my mornings and evenings on the couch, just me and Gramps.

We're easy together. Quiet, but companionable. Now, it seems as though someone's always shouting, and underneath all of the noise, Gramps fades further and further away.

Today is my idea, because there was a time when Gramps loved nothing better than taking the boat out fishing in the morning and coming home to a picnic and his girls on the docks. Aunt Karen bitched about the logistics at first, but settled down once Gramps said he'd like to at least try. Will's coming a little early and bringing his parents' smart car, which should get us close enough to help Gramps the rest of the way.

Beau will be here, and so will Melanie and Grant. My aunt and uncle, of course. It's going to be as happy as we can all make it, around the Amelia-sized hole. I never noticed it before, because when we were kids it was always the four of us, never one less, but our group feels incomplete without my cousin. Would it be the same without any one of us, such as a square that's missing a side, or does Amelia's specific energy form some kind of adhesive?

Gramps is alone in the living room, staring at the television with his headphones on and shivering under his fleece blanket. It's ninety degrees outside at 10:00 a.m., and the house feels like a sauna, but I tug the blanket closer to his chin and plant a kiss on his cheek.

"Morning, Gracie-baby."

"Where's Aunt Karen?"

"Ran out to the store. Don't know what for, got enough food in the kitchen to feed the whole town." He grins, but it takes effort. "Not much like how our fishing days used to start, but it'll have to do."

I flop on the couch, loving the smell of summer in the room. "I know. I didn't have to wake up before the sun, and no one pulled me out of bed by my big toe." Even in my teens, I hadn't minded getting up early. Amelia never wanted to go fishing, so I'd have Gramps to myself the whole morning. We never talked much as the sun rose over the horizon, painting the river with pinks and purples, then oranges and reds, his pole in the water, my nose in a book. We'd just been. Together.

"You know people have commented on how one of my toes is too long. I blame you."

He shrugs. "Feet are feet. Be glad yours work."

We pass the rest of the time quietly, him napping and me back on the laptop, trying to track down the best person to ask for help regarding local ancestry. I end up with two possible names, one at Clemson and the other at UNC Wilmington. I shoot them both an e-mail and close my computer the same moment the doorbell rings, startling Gramps awake.

It's Will, with the smart car. Aunt Karen and Uncle Wally arrive right behind him, and the men wrestle Gramps into the front seat of the car then start down toward the dock. There's a path that runs out the last twenty feet or so, but they'll take good care of him.

Aunt Karen helps me gather the food, and when the smart car returns bearing just Will, we load it up with casserole dishes and sandwiches and coolers filled with desserts and drinks. Sunlight winks through the gently swaying fronds of the palmettos and magnolias, the live oaks draped with their Spanish moss until it skips and dances along the wooded ground like fairies. It's hot but there's a breeze, and the bumpy path down to the river smells like moss and salt water.

It takes us a few minutes to get everything unloaded and down the twenty-foot ramp to the open, square wooden platform that we call the dock. Melanie and Grant are here, and so is Beau, and with all of the hands the food's set up on the long picnic table, and a canopy set up to shade Gramps and Aunt Karen, in no time at all.

"You look beautiful, Graciela."

Beau leans over and kisses my temple as we're unloading the last cooler from the smart car. No one is around to see, and for more than a couple of seconds I struggle against the desire to drag him into the bushes.

"Thank you."

"How's Gramps today?"

"He seems good this morning." I grab the handle on one side and Beau snags the other. "Oh! I'm not having much luck with the whole genealogy research thing, but I did find a couple of local college professors who might be willing to help out, or at least point me in the right direction."

"I imagine dangling the journal in front of their noses and offering to give them a piece of the discovery pie will help grease the wheels."

"Yeah. Anyway, I e-mailed them. We'll see what they say."

The chatter on the dock, punctuated by splashes into the water by Grant, who is a thin, pale wisp in his swim trunks and water wings, does its best to fill the empty caverns inside me. Even Aunt Karen seems content, and except for near-constant bitching about the heat, even manages a few chuckles while discussing child rearing with Mel. I'll have to remember to thank my old friend for taking one for the team.

Beau sits beside me, his long legs tan beneath his shorts and his bare feet driving me to distraction. Will goes back and forth between joking around with Gramps and playing with Grant in and around the water, while Uncle Wally tries his best to convince the fish they'd like to gobble his lure despite the melee.

Gramps surveys us—what's left of his family, for all intents and purposes, save Amelia—wearing a tired, satisfied smile. He drops down a hand, a wrinkled, age-spotted remnant of the strong paw that used to grab my knee under the dining room table during prayers, pinching hard to see if I could hold back my squeals until Grams finished pontificating. I capture it and give it a squeeze. He squeezes back.

"Good day, girl. That death nurse makes some excellent fried chicken."

My lips twitch despite the horrible backbone of his statement. "She doesn't like when you call her that."

"Why do you think I do it?"

Beau chuckles next to me, vibrating the dock under my legs. It's getting hotter by the minute, and the sweat shining on Gramps' brow means we've got to end this little party sooner than later, even if his being warm seems preferable to watching him shiver in the house.

I don't want to be the one to call it, though, because the end of today feels like the end of everything. Nothing to look forward to, only the expectation of looming loss to fill the hours. Beau's hand covers mine on the warm wooden slats, Will turns around to smile at Gramps, Grant runs over to see the little sunfish Uncle Wally has managed to snag, and I take it in, letting the moment paint broad strokes of beauty in my memory.

Then Aunt Karen does my dirty work, which doesn't make me feel grown-up, but *does* grow my affection for her more than it has since she bought me an American Girl doll that matched Amelia's in the fourth grade.

We pack it in and haul back to the house, Will and Mel helping Gramps inside and then saying good-bye, Grant snoring and tossed over his daddy's shoulder. For the first time, looking at them, I know for a fact that what they have is not what I want—at least not right now. I thought I did, or I'd let myself believe it when I'd gotten so obsessed with David, but a desire for adventure, for a different kind of experience, is the reason I left Will behind in the first place.

I wouldn't be happy married with a little boy, every day of my life mapped out for me, a copy of the one that came before it. The living in Heron Creek part feels right, because it's starting to seem as though places are places—each is the same, if you call it home. There are adventures waiting for me here, if I count Anne, and the archives, and getting to know Mayor Beau.

I sneak a sidelong glance at him as we sit on the front porch swing. He's a little older than me, closer to thirty than twenty, and has never been married. That I know of, anyway. Add that to the list of questions to ask next time I get him alone. If we're talking.

The point demanding attention is that it's possible *he's* looking for someone to settle down with—to give him the home and the marriage and the babies. It might change the way he thinks about me, or make him less interested in coming around, if he knows I'm not ready for any of that.

Then again, I told him I'm not ready for a relationship. One would think a lifetime commitment would fall under the purview of "relationship." He catches me watching him and smiles, but it's a small one that says the same feeling I've had all day—that we're here to say good-bye. I'm overthinking things, as usual. He knows I'm a hot mess who's only in Heron Creek because she was running from her old life. One that goes chasing after dead people, gets caught in storms, and every other example of immaturity I've displayed in the past month.

We haven't even made out. The marriage discussion can wait.

And it's not that I never want those kinds of things. It's just that the thought of giving myself away, after almost losing it to David, after working so hard to get back—even just this far—to good, makes my legs tingle with the desire to take off running.

He kisses me lightly on the lips, lingering long enough for me to taste sunshine and syrup, long enough to promise the desire for more remains, and takes his leave.

Then everyone's gone, and Aunt Karen and Uncle Wally are in their room. It's Gramps and me in the living room, the way the day began, with him snoring and me reading. And even though I know this moment can't last, isn't meant to tarry, I dig in, determined to hold on for as long as the world will let me.

☙

It's early again, just before dawn, but my eyes are stubborn and open. I'm thinking about Anne, about the e-mail the UNC Wilmington professor returned a few days ago offering to look into eighteenth-century records regarding Mary Read to see if there are any aunts or uncles mentioned anywhere. He hasn't written again, but he didn't sound as though it was the dumbest request he'd ever gotten, either.

His specialty is maritime history local to the British Navy, which turns out to be where Mary got her start, so if anyone can get their hands on great primary-source material, he's the guy.

I feel privileged by Anne Bonny's trust, in some ways. She led me to that diary. *Me,* after two hundred years. Despite my complaints to Beau that I don't have the time to deal with her drama and mine, too, a sense of responsibility has wormed its way inside me. It glows, insisting on not being forgotten, but because of Gramps, the mystery remains relegated to the backseat of my life. Which is, of course where Anne and I first met.

As though she hears my thoughts, the ghostly figure climbs over my open windowsill and takes a seat, dirty boots resting on the arm of a wingback chair. The moonlight illuminates the lines on her face, carved by years or grief, more likely both. She's beautiful by anyone's standards, a woman who could have fit into Charleston society despite the circumstances of her birth, should she have wanted that life. But her rough personality shows in the set of her jaw, the tightness of her gait, and the way she holds her shoulders back as though she's ready for a fight. Anne Bonny has zero reputation for being soft or pliant, and the ghostly version of her has never been any different. There's a wildness about her that's fused with her essence that could never have blended in or been smoothed over, no matter how hard she tried.

The circumstances of her life have turned over and over in my mind during my recent bevy of sleepless hours, and I've considered what it means to embrace who we truly are, even when other people don't like it. Don't understand it. To do what our hearts desire, even when it's not what the world expects—that maybe the mistake most people make is thinking that our lives are made to please anyone other than ourselves.

What a pickle she'd been in, all those years ago. With the exception of the few short months she spent at sea with Jack, she never knew happiness. Had never been able to lay down the fight, to let her true self rule on a daily basis. First it had been her father trapping her, and then James Bonny.

Later, Joseph Burleigh. Even her son, though clearly one of the greatest loves of her life, had forced her to live a life she hated. She loved him because she recognized that, much like her, he was a victim of his circumstances more than anything.

It makes me sure that, at least for now, my feeling that I need time alone should be honored.

Anne's ghost watches me while all these thoughts and more swirl through my overwrought brain, her typical, heartbreaking expression still able to sucker punch me.

"I haven't forgotten you, Anne. I promise."

I wouldn't promise her lightly, and the slight upturn of her lips says she knows it. Then she sits up abruptly, cocks an ear toward the door, and dissolves before my eyes. The sound of footsteps at this hour can only mean one thing, and every single cell in my body blackens with dread.

"Come in," I croak in answer to the light knock at my door.

The whites of Lynette's eyes shine in the filmy light streaming through my windows. Even in the dark they look sad, and the words that drip from her lips like tears don't come as a surprise. "Miss Graciela, you'd better come on down. He's not going to make it until morning."

"I'll be right there." I lick my lips, mouth too dry. "Have you woken my aunt?"

"Not yet. I'm headed to their room now. Unless you'd like me to wait."

Aunt Karen and I are splitting the cost of the at-home care, so maybe it's not fair that Lynette's asking, or giving me the ability to keep daughter from father, but I don't think she'd offer if ten extra minutes meant Aunt Karen wouldn't get some time, too.

"Maybe just wait ten or fifteen minutes? I'd like to have some time alone with him, if it's okay."

She nods and turns away, leaving me to appreciate again her ability to read people. I take a deep breath, then another, and close my eyes, taking a moment to wrap my heart up in that stretchy kind of stuff that's holding my ankle together at the moment. It's flesh colored, so Gramps won't be able to see it. I've never done this before—been there to say good-bye—but blubbering all over him can't be the best use of the gift.

There's time for that later. For this morning, I'll smile even though it hurts.

I swing my bare legs from underneath the piles of quilted comfort, take the time to put on a bra under my sleep shorts and tank top, and grab a long-sleeved house sweater, along with Anne's journal, before padding down the hall. She didn't say whether or not Gramps is awake. If he's sleeping, I'm going to need something to occupy my hands and mind.

My grandparents' room has changed so much from the space lingering in my past. The light beside the hospital bed, which we swapped for their old queen-size when we brought Gramps home—is on its lowest setting, casting a golden ring in a four-foot arc. It smells like a hospital in here, too, with the odor of antiseptic and disease smothering the more familiar scent of my grandmother's floral perfume, the salty reek of Gramps's fishing clothes festering in the hamper. It's been a long time since this room smelled of either of those things, but it doesn't stop my brain from expecting them, from being offended by what it finds in their place.

Gramps' withered arms tremble at his sides. He opens his eyes as I pile extra blankets on top of him, but it takes several seconds for him to recognize me through the pain, and worse than that is the heartbreaking fear casting shadows in the hollows of his face. It scares me, but before I can open my mouth to call for Lynette, recognition switches on in his gaze.

A million thoughts try to form into words, into something that might help, but nothing is good enough for my gramps. It's been too long since I've believed in God with any real conviction. I'm the wrong person to go to for reassurances about how everything will be fine, because it feels like empty promises.

I wrap my hands around one of his and hold on tight, my heart aching at my total failure to be a good person in this moment. He moves, with effort, and reaches his other hand around to cup my face. The gesture is familiar, and time-tested, and comforts me. The muscles in his face relax a smidge, as though it comforts him, too.

They scare me, his fear and his pain, and the fact that he doesn't have much strength left.

I swallow hard, reach down inside myself, and come up with little wisps of bravery. Light, nearly insubstantial, like feathers. Cupped in my mind's palm, they seem pathetic. They'll have to do. "How's your faith?"

"It's all I have now, Gracie-baby. I'm counting on it."

"You've always seen a better person inside me than I've seen in myself, Gramps. Treated me like I'm something special. I wouldn't be half as good without you." I take another breath, hoping that he can't hear how it shakes. "I'm going to miss you so much, Gramps, but I know you're ready. We'll all be okay."

"I know you will, darling. You'll always find your way. It's never been the same path as everyone else's." He swallows, wincing, and squeezes my hand harder. "Don't give up on your cousin. She needs you, whether she'll ever say it out loud or not."

"Okay, Gramps." The mention of Amelia makes it hard to breathe. I'm so angry at her for not being here, but looking at our grandfather, it's clear he's already forgiven her. It might take some time for me to do the same, but for him, anything.

For her, anything. Bottom line.

"Is Karen coming down?"

"Yes, she should be here soon. Do you want me to go get her?" I start to stand up, worried my selfishness is going to cost my aunt her good-bye, but he hangs on to my hand and shakes his head.

"No, I want to tell you something. You can't think I'm talking crazy because I'm dying, either."

"I've never thought you talked crazy, Gramps." The protest that he's not dying withers on my tongue. It's a knee-jerk reaction, a comment that's made me smile since I've been back, but now seems kind of macabre.

"It's about your ghost."

"Anne Bonny?"

He nods and struggles to catch his breath for a moment, a weak cough rattling his chest. It sounds as though his ribs are clacking together. "She still bothering you?"

I nod, feeling silly all over again. Trust me to pick up a damn ghost when all I wanted was solitude and a proper drinking problem.

"Thought so. Should have said something when you first brought it up, but you were in bad shape, drinking yourself to sleep at night and stinking up the house with your moods. Not that you didn't deserve at least a little bit of wallowing, after losing your momma and your grams, then David treating you like that. But you always did have trouble knowing when to quit."

It makes me smile, the way he doesn't admit to being aware of what a mess I'd been when I'd first come back to town until he's sure it's in the past. Or he's run out of time. "Should have told me what?"

"Anny Bonny's your ancestor. Your grams' great-grandmother times four or five generations." He closes his eyes for a second, then two. It might be longer, because it's as though time has stopped.

That's why me, I realize. It doesn't have anything to do with me barely clinging to my rocker—Anne thinks that if I'm inclined to believe in things like voodoo curses, it affects me, too.

My mouth has been open this whole time. Ready for fly-catching, Grams would have said, but no response formulates before Aunt Karen rushes in. Her pink bathrobe streams behind her like a five-year-old's princess cape, hair in curlers, face naked and lined with worry. Uncle Wally lurks inside the door, his expression pained.

I kiss Gramps, then move out of the way and give her the bedside. My good-byes have been said and, for all of my disagreements with my aunt, for all the things we each think the other could have done better, she's his daughter. Her lips move against his ear, whispering words too quiet, or too private, to reach our ears. It's like they refuse, on principle, to lift to a normal decibel, and even though it's hard to believe, Gramps hears. At least, I think he does because he smiles slightly and pats her cheek the way he patted mine.

Tears shine on her cheeks and wash onto his, and she clings to him for another few seconds before standing up and finding Lynette, who's near Uncle Wally. "Is he comfortable?"

"I wouldn't let him suffer, Ms. Karen."

Aunt Karen's wet gaze meets mine and she softens, motioning me toward the bed. We stand there together, her hand wrapped around his, my fingertips squeezing his arm. Lynette moves to the other side, fluttering around the machines and IV, checking things for the last time. Gramps catches her hand as she moves away and she turns, looking down into his face with brave compassion that humbles me. *What an impossible job.*

"Thank you."

Tears glisten in her dark eyes but she gives him a winning smile, then pats his hand. "You've made it hard on me, Martin. I appreciate that in a patient."

His chuckle turns into a cough, and then he closes his eyes. Uncle Wally takes Lynette's place on the other side of the bed, arms crossed over his belly and sorrow etched deep on his face. He loves my gramps as well as anyone else, which is a lot. Gramps nods off, his breathing steady but shallow, as we all hold our breath and wait. Lynette sits in a chair by the door and picks up some knitting, present but affording us privacy.

It's not long before his breaths space out, until I can count five or ten seconds in between, then twenty. Then one final gasp before they stop altogether.

Even though I don't have Gramps' faith, in that moment, I pray through my tears that if we have something more inside us than flesh and blood, and Gramps' soul is leaving his body, that there's someone out there to gather it up. Take care of him. Love him the way we do.

Then I unbind my heart, and cry.

Chapter Eighteen

The house's seams struggle to hold the friends, family, neighbors, old employees, and strangers bloating the rooms and hallways after Gramps' funeral. Many of the faces are foreign, but they regale me with stories that are vintage Gramps. It makes me feel inflated, too, ready to burst from the grief and happiness and celebration lining the walls and dusting the carpet. As good as solitude sounds, I also have a desperate desire to keep these people around me indefinitely, because it feels like my grandfather isn't gone.

He'll never be gone from Heron Creek. I know that.

Aunt Karen took charge of organizing today, which is fine with me. I'm exhausted from crying, from the endless decisions about food and times and programs, not to mention the question of what I'm going to do next. The house will probably belong to the Coopers now, but I'm holding on to the smallest sliver of hope that my aunt will be gracious and let me stay, at least for a while.

It will kill me if she wants to sell it, but there won't be anything I can do to stop her.

I wander from room to room with a giant yellow trash bag, snagging stray paper plates and balled-up napkins, funeral programs that have been discarded on end tables, content to be among the mourners but, for a few precious moments, fade into the background.

"Hey, Grace."

My shoulders tense at the familiar face, heart still struggling with my mixed-feelings over Gramps' last request. I know my instant reaction of ire has more to do with my own sorrow than anything she's done, but recognizing that and controlling my reaction are two different things. The whole maturing plan is a work in progress.

"Amelia. It's nice that you were able to make it today. Have you tried the punch?"

She closes her eyes for a second, and I take the opportunity to study her. Amelia's always been the prettier of the two of us, and though we share the same green eyes—handed down from Grams—she's got her mother's blond pixie looks as opposed to the dusky brown hues that darken my features. Her skin glows today, peachy and dewy, and even though she's barley showing, that she's pregnant seems written all over her.

Her bright green eyes flutter open, and they're guarded in a way that never would have seemed possible ten years ago. She doesn't trust me, and even her sorrow is masked by a cool facade designed to keep me at bay. "I meant to come sooner, Grace, I did. Can I help?"

The weakness of her apology kills what little energy I have left. We're both reeling from the loss of Gramps, whether she thought it was important to show up before the fact or not. This isn't the time to revisit our personal war, and a tired sigh wriggles loose from my chest. "Sure. I was going to wash up the coffee cups and silverware. Your mom is going to want to drop once everyone leaves. Are you staying tonight?"

"Yes, I'd planned on it. I'll get those dishes."

My cousin heads off toward the kitchen, having done the impossible—made me feel guilty for treating her coolly, when she's the one who should feel badly. She'd only driven into town this morning, in time to change clothes and go with us to the church, then the graveside, and I'd avoided talking to her until now. The thought of seeing her pig husband had twisted my guts into hopeless tangles all day, but he didn't made an appearance. Now, I'm not sure why I expected him to be here at all.

I follow her into the kitchen after cleaning the trash out of the music room, and stuff everything disposable on the counters into the bag before tying it closed. She washes dishes, a disquiet about her that sets my nerves on edge. No matter what else is going on, I'm not going to miss out on the opportunity to talk with her while she's in town—really talk, and see if she can convince me the thrum of dread I feel is unfounded.

The bag weighs a ton, scraping the ground as I hoist it and lurch toward the back door. It tumbles out of my grasp during a superhuman attempt to kick the waist-high handle, but a strong, tanned hand reaches out and retrieves it.

I look up into golden eyes, sober but clear. A lifeline. "Hi, Mr. Mayor. Thanks for coming."

It's an automatic response after so many of the same, but inside it makes me wince. No irritation crosses his face, though, as he holds open the door. "I'll carry this out to the Dumpster. Would you fancy a walk?"

The Dumpster is at the end of the block, behind a bait-and-tackle shop. I wasn't going to make the trip until everyone leaves, but now the idea of fresh air and silence tugs me outside without another thought.

Beau's been around over the past three days, a silent, supportive, gorgeous piece of scenery. Aunt Karen has gotten used to him, even though she still thanks him fifteen times a day for basically just breathing. He and I haven't had much time alone, but his presence alone bolsters my resolve when it seems impossible to walk through another minute. It surprises me how easily he's slipped into my life, and how wrong it would feel if he disappeared.

Surprises, terrifies. Potato, pohtahto.

Once the numbness that's accompanied the planning phase of Gramps' death wears off, I'll have to face what's going on between the mayor and me, along with what I *want* to be going on between the two of us. Right now, I'm thankful he's here.

He takes my hand in his halfway down the block, holding it lightly as though it might break. Or he's afraid I'm going to pull away. "You're doing fine, Gracie. Keep smiling. People will start leaving soon."

Tears gather in my eyes but I blink them away. Keep smiling. We make it to the end of the block in silence, but it's not strained or empty. Not missing words, but fine without them. Beau tosses the heavy bag into the green Dumpster while I hold up the lid, then we turn and head back.

"I don't know if this appeals to you, but if you'd like to get out of the house this evening, I'd be happy to cook you dinner at my place. If you'd rather stay with your family, that's fine, but I wanted you to know the offer's out there. I know sometimes it's good to change up the scenery."

I should say no because Amelia and I have things to discuss and I don't know how long she's going to stay. I should say no because my grandfather just died, and the idea of spending the evening with a handsome man who makes me feel good shouldn't be so appealing. I should say no, but the idea of being able to breathe in air, to exist in rooms that don't remind me of Gramps sounds like a life preserver in a choppy sea.

"I'd like that."

Pleasure lights his face, turns his eyes amber in the afternoon light. "Is eight o'clock okay? That should give you plenty of time to wind things down here and head over. But I have one condition—keep it casual."

A faint smile, the first one in days that doesn't wobble and isn't brought on by a Gramps memory, feels strange on my lips. It's as though I thought it would never happen again, but here it is, only three days later. "What, no demands to wear a dress this time?"

"Heck, no. Come in your pajamas if you want."

The house looms ahead before I'm ready to see it, which is the strangest feeling of all. I wonder if it will always be a sad place now, or if all of the laughter and pranks, nights spent playing cards or whispering after bedtime, will wash away the briefer moments of loss. They have to.

The sight of Amelia at the sink helps, in some strange way. Her arms are submerged in soapy water and she hums a quiet song. It's sad, but familiar in a way that tugs on my heart. She hears us and turns, leaving me no alternative but to introduce the two of them. Given her perfect looks and even more perfect manners, introducing boys to my cousin has never been my favorite thing to do. Next to her, I feel a little like Anne Bonny must have felt—wild and awkward.

"Mayor Drayton, this is my cousin, Amelia Cooper Middleton."

"A pleasure." Amelia wipes her hand on the sunny yellow apron, faded from years of protecting my Grams from jams and piecrusts and applesauce.

Beau smiles at her, dimples in full force. "Mine. You can call me Beau, as I've asked Gracie to do on many occasions."

She laughs, a pretty, tinkling sound that's never been a true indication of how evil her sense of humor really is, and extends a hand to Beau. "Grace can be stubborn."

My gasp startles them both, and I can't tear my eyes away from their joined hands. "Millie, Jesus, what happened to your arm?"

Bruises—purple and black, some greenish yellow—loop her wrist and forearm, some closer to her elbow. She pulls her hand from Beau's and rolls her sleeve back down to her wrist, pink clouds blossoming in her cheeks. I grab her hand and yank it toward me before she can hide it, but drop it like it's on fire when she yelps in pain.

"It's nothing, just an accident. I was w-walking the dogs the other day and a f-fox ran across the street. Their leashes got tangled up around my arm."

"You're lying." Millie's stutter had disappeared before we hit junior high—Aunt Karen had seen to that—except when she wasn't being truthful. Sometimes I thought her mother had paid the speech therapist so it turned out that way. "Why would you lie to me?"

The fear and humiliation pinching her features transforms back into the cool mask, and she pins me with a gaze that backs me up two or three steps with the force of its contempt. "I think you know very well why I wouldn't trust you."

Venom hits me, burns. Eats at my resolve.

Beau steps up, the heat of his body radiating into my back, and presses a warm hand to my waist. "Would you walk me out, Graciela? I'm afraid I need to get going. It was very nice to meet you, Amelia."

She doesn't respond, just turns back to the sink and plunges her hands into the soapy water with so much force that a bunch sloshes onto the floor. Protests and emotions clog my throat, slow my thoughts and my feet, but Beau grabs my hand and tugs me out of the kitchen, through the music room, and into the foyer.

His arms go around me and, without thinking, I squeeze his hard body with everything I've got. The ground is shifting again, rocks tumbling under my toes, but Beau won't let me fall.

"Don't let it go, Gracie." His soft breath tickles the skin under my ear. "She's scared and embarrassed, but you might be the one she'll talk to. Get her alone, and don't let her lie anymore." He pulls back, brushing a kiss at my hairline. "I'll see you tonight, okay? Keep your chin up."

He leaves after typing his address into my phone, letting the screen door slam behind him. I spend the rest of the afternoon on autopilot—cleaning, thanking people for coming, walking them to the door. Aunt Karen seems to have aged ten years in the past couple of weeks, and Uncle Wally feet are dragging, too. Amelia and I pick up the slack, in silent agreement that it's our turn to take charge, and send her parents out to dinner since none of us managed to choke down anything during the reception.

It's seven before my cousin finishes the last of the dishes, and I've hauled four more giant trash bags down the street to the Dumpster. I take a quick shower, then choose a pair of jeans and a yellow tank top, add my favorite pair of flat sandals, and put my hair up in a bun once it's dry. He did say come casual, but even so I stand in front of the mirror, staring blankly at my straightener before giving up on the idea of fixing my hair.

I almost trip twice on my way down the stairs, even though there's still time to get to the mayor's house. Uncle Wally's in the living room, his feet up on the coffee table and a newspaper in hand.

He raises an eyebrow at my appearance. "Where ya going?"

"To the mayor's house for dinner. I won't be late." I avoid looking at Gramps's empty chair, as I have since he passed. "Where's Millie?"

"In the kitchen, I think."

Amelia's slumped over in a kitchen chair, a cool, evening breeze ruffling the hem of her navy blue skirt. I gird myself for another attack, but her eyes are red, defeated, when she raises her head from her hands. "Hey."

"Hey. I'm going over to Mayor Drayton's for a little while, but . . . don't leave, Millie. I want to talk to you while you're here."

She seems to consider, her lips pressed in a tight line. "I won't leave, Grace," she finally replies. "Not tonight. Have fun."

I back out of the room before she changes her mind, then scoot out the front door before Aunt Karen accosts me with a hundred more questions about my relationship with the mayor.

Despite the fact that it's ten minutes until eight, I decide to walk. The sun hovers just above the horizon, content to show off the beauty of its rays but release us from the brunt of its heat. The air smells like salt and moss as it fills my lungs, and being outside the house slips energy and excitement into my blood. I set off down the sidewalk, content to let my mind switch into an "off" position for the first time in days. No Anne Bonny, no grief. No worry over Amelia or constantly being picked at by Aunt Karen. The town passes by, a place that still feels like home, despite the loss of my grandfather.

Beau's house peers out over the riverfront, with a half-acre or so separating the three-story turn-of-the-century home from the marsh that turns into water. It's quiet, with no neighbors on either side. Giant live oaks dot the expanse of grass, heavy branches twisting down into the water, their moss trailing across the surface. It's beautiful, and I take a moment to breathe it in before heading up onto the white-painted wraparound porch.

I use the ornate door knocker just for the hell of it, then bare my teeth at the bronze lion's head. Footsteps approach from inside and I rearrange my face into something less insane—at least marginally. Nerves get to work on my stomach, tangoing and salsaing up a storm.

They're Latin, my nerves. I wonder if they'd settle down if I spoke to them in Spanish. Which would, of course, mean learning Spanish.

They seem intent on forcing me to hurl all over the threshold, even though there's almost nothing in my stomach. It would be mortifying to puke on the mayor. Typical, for the current state of my life, but mortifying all the same.

I manage to not heave as he opens the door, wearing a soft smile that for some reason looks as though he's been waiting all day just to give it to me. It steals what's left of my breath, and makes my Latin nerves shimmy into overdrive, until the world spins a bit on the edges. He holds out a hand and pulls me into the foyer.

"Hasn't anyone ever told you it's rude to lurk in doorways?" He grins wider, then takes a deep breath through his nose. "Mmm. You smell fantastic."

Now, *that's* a reason to shower more often. My heart speeds up, and even though I'm a twenty-five-year-old woman who has been engaged, I feel for all the world like a fifteen-year-old girl on her first date. It's amazing to realize that I can still get excited, feel things other than cynicism and distrust, but more than that, it keeps at bay the pain of the past several days.

Weeks. Months.

I follow Beau through the foyer and a proper dining room, then into the kitchen. It's masculine and modern, with dark hardwood floors, matching cabinets, granite countertops, and stainless-steel appliances. It surprises me that he'd want an updated kitchen, since most bachelors I know aren't very into cooking, but I've been realizing—slowly—that maybe Beau's not like other single guys.

He motions me to a stool on the outside edge of a good-sized island, then returns his attention to one skillet full of sizzling mushrooms, onions, and red peppers, another browning chicken, on the stove between us. The cookware suspended from a rack on the ceiling gives me pause—with my luck, there's an excellent chance it'll brain me.

Mayor Beau catches the direction of my gaze and chuckles, flipping some chicken and then checking on a boiling pot of pasta. "I think you'll be fine, Graciela. That stuff's been hanging there all three years I've been in the house, and hasn't killed a guest yet."

The comment makes me wonder how many other girls have sat on this stool, but even though he knows more about my past relationships than I do about his, getting the answer doesn't appeal to me. While details about exes have never been interesting to me, a little more about his dating history would be welcome information. But kicking loose from warmth of the moment, like an insulting cocoon, sounds like the worst idea ever.

He turns around to grab more items out of the fridge, giving me a nice view of his backside in the process. Jeans so faded the pockets are tearing loose, paired with a soft-looking Gamecocks T-shirt say he took his own advice to keep the evening casual. He's barefoot, and while I've never considered it before now, the sight of him cooking for me this way makes me think I might have a bit of a foot fetish. If I were a different person I'd rip my clothes off and hop on the counter.

His eyebrows pop upward when he turns and catches me staring, those eyes drinking in my expression until they flash with hunger. "Gracie . . ."

I shake my head, struggling to breathe. "What are you cooking?"

The question lets the air out of the heat between us, enough that it's not going to ignite right away, but not for it to vacate the room entirely.

He steps back to the stove, slicing off some butter into the skillet, then adding chunks of garlic and a few tablespoons of lemon juice. Avoiding looking at me. "I hope pasta's okay. To be honest, my repertoire of recipes isn't all that vast."

"It smells good. I think I'm hungry, actually."

"When's the last time you ate something?"

It takes me a full minute to figure out it's Thursday, and another to think back to the last meal I actually sat down and ate. "Tuesday night?"

"For heaven's sake. Hasn't anyone been looking out for you?"

"I'm a grown woman, Beau. I can take care of myself. None of us have felt much like eating, I guess, and there's been plenty to do."

"I'm aware that you're a grown woman, Graciela. Trust me. But everyone can use some help now and again."

I shrug, dismissing the lecture, and he frowns into his melting butter concoction.

"See, watch me." He clears his throat as though he's about to give a demonstration in front of the Chamber of Commerce. "Would you please grab some garlic bread from the freezer and pop it in the oven while I finish up the sauce?"

"Sure." I slide off the stool, slipping off my sandals and leaving them under the bar. Maybe he's one of those people who doesn't like shoes in the house but didn't want to embarrass me.

There are two boxes of bread in the freezer, one with cheese and the other with plain breadsticks. I choose the cheesy option, deciding that I should enjoy this rare and probably never-to-come-again opportunity to need to put *on* weight instead of the other way around. Once the bread is in the oven I lean back against the counter, watching Beau combine his thin spaghetti noodles with his buttery lemon sauce, chicken, and vegetables. He tosses it together in the bigger pot, then dumps it into a big serving bowl and sets it between the stools.

"Four minutes until the bread's done," I tell him.

He's in front of me then, hands on my waist, before I know what happened. "I think I know how to kill that time," he murmurs.

His lips brush mine, as soft as ever, but that's not going to do it for me. For everything Beau has the potential to be in my life, tonight he's a sexy, welcome distraction. I crush my mouth against his, opening my lips for him, find his tongue hot and willing as it toys with mine. My hands grasp his neck, one sliding higher until it twists in his hair, the combined motion pulling his body tight against mine. It's hard and hot, molding his hips against mine, pressing my back into the countertop before he lifts me up by my ass and my feet lock behind his back.

A growl rumbles from his throat and he nips my bottom lip, diving back in for more. The way he tastes me, as though he's dying of thirst and I'm the only one who can save him, drips sizzling heat into my belly, spills it down between my legs. I'm lost in the moment, in the feeling of his wanting me, and it's exactly what I need because there's no room for anything else in my head.

Then the timer goes off, a loud, insistent beep that urges another growl from Beau—more annoyed than impatient and needy this time. We break apart and he grabs the tray of bread from the oven while I wait for the kitchen to reemerge from the hazy mist hovering around the edges of my vision.

My legs are numb but manage to deliver me back to my stool. I use a pair of tongs to scatter the pasta into the two waiting bowls, and then Beau sits next to me with a plate of garlic bread and a bottle of wine. My stomach growls, which is odd because I can't feel anything except a rampant need to keep touching the man beside me, to let him make me feel good instead of bad.

The silence between us is different, as though there are things we'd both like to say but are keeping to ourselves. I need to eat, though, and the food is hot.

He chuckles the second time my stomach protests how empty it is, pouring generous amounts of wine into both glasses. "Let's not argue with your stomach, no matter how much I'd like to."

"I normally wouldn't argue, but . . ."

His hand covers mine, and I look up to find desire, heady and strong, oozing from his gorgeous eyes. "That isn't why I invited you over tonight, Graciela. Not that I'm complaining."

"I know. It's just . . . nice. To not think about everything else."

"I don't mind being a distraction when you need it, but I hope that's not all I am to you."

"No." I pick up my fork, ignoring the way it shakes in my hand. "I don't know what you are, Beau, or what I want you to be, or what I can handle. But you're not only one thing to me. I like having you in my life."

"That's a good start." He smiles, and the air between us relaxes, as though it exhales, too. "Now, eat."

The pasta is delicious, with flavors that wake up my mouth in a different way, and I feel better—stronger—almost as soon as it hits my belly. We eat in silence for a while, but when I take a break for a few sips of wine, he asks about the e-mails I sent the professors.

"I never heard back from the guy at Clemson, but the local history guy at UNC Wilmington, Dr. Flannigan, said he would do some checking for me. I haven't heard back yet, but it's only been about a week."

"Has Anne been around?"

"Yes, but not as often, and she hasn't been demanding at all."

"She's waited over two centuries. I'm sure she's smart enough to know a couple more weeks aren't going to matter."

"Yeah." I think about what Gramps said before he died. I haven't told anyone, or thought about it much at all, but now I realize that I should be looking into my own family tree. If it's true that we're descended from Anne—and Jack Jr.—then the answers to the Mary Read question might be closer than I think.

"What is it? You're a million miles away right now." He reaches over and swipes the corner of my lips. It takes everything in my willpower not to lick his finger.

"Gramps told me that my grandmother is descended from Anne Bonny."

"What? How could he know that when her survival after Port Royal has always been in question?"

"I don't know. He didn't have time to say any more about it, but it makes sense that Anne confided in her son, and he in his children, and so on. Oral history seems more likely than written in this case." I pause, crunching a bite of garlic bread. "And it explains why she's so intent on haunting me for the rest of my natural born days. Or longer."

"That's true. And it's not like Gramps would make that up. But your mother never said anything?"

"No. But her death was sudden. I could ask Aunt Karen, I guess."

I wipe the last bite of bread through the remainder of my lemon-butter sauce, then hop off my stool. Beau starts to get up, leaving five bites of pasta on his plate, but I shake my head. "I can rinse my plate. You finish."

He's done eating by the time I have my plate, the skillets, and the pot rinsed and settled in the dishwasher. Beau adds his to the mix, a thoughtful expression his face. "Is Amelia your only cousin?"

"Yes. She had a younger brother, but he was hit by a car on his bike when he was five."

"And your mother and Karen don't have brothers?"

"No. Grams had a couple of miscarriages, and a toddler that drowned in the river." His questions give me pause. It is weird that there aren't any boys in our family. "I've never thought about it before, but there aren't any boys descended from Grams' side of the family."

"Agreed. I'm not sure it means anything, but it's definitely intriguing. Would you like coffee?"

I'm kind of tired, but shake my head no. Bad breath. He doesn't make any for himself, either, and tips his head toward the doorway. "Would you like to stay awhile?"

"Sure."

He leads me down the hall, into a study that's as immaculate and masculine as the kitchen. Bookshelves cover the walls, the shelves heavy with spines of all sizes and colors. Some are faded and others are bright, embossed words begging to be touched, but I refrain. For today.

A gigantic television and sound system dominate the space, complemented by luxurious, deep brown leather theater seating that begs for a good snuggle. A desk takes up the space under the big bay window, but it's too tidy to double as Beau's home office. It's likely for guests, whoever they may be, and the total effect of the room tugs my eyebrows toward my hairline.

"Wow. And you came to Gramps' to watch baseball games?"

"There's something to be said for excellent company." He sits, and pats the space next to him.

My body obeys without asking me first, and I'm curled up into his side, head on his shoulder, a moment later. He's strong but soft, the way the angles of his face are gentled by his eyes, and how the edges of his personality soften around his willingness to be open and sweet.

An arm snakes around my waist and pulls me tight against him, and the slight weight of his chin on top of my head makes me feel cared for, which is not something I'm used to, or even anything I think I want. *I* want to take care of me. My body ignores the panic in my brain, shushing the need to analyze, and snuggles closer. The spicy scent of his cologne, the clean smell of his shampoo, wind around me and I breathe in. Breathe out.

Beau flicks on the television with his other hand, flipping channels lazily. It feels strangely as though we've done this a million times before, not as though it's the first time we've really been alone together. The Braves game flashes on the screen but he passes it without pause, allowing me to keep my shit together a little longer.

I'm sure there will come a time when the sight of their blue and red uniforms on the field won't hurt my soul, but that day is not today.

My insides rumble and toss, like the sea before a storm. There are flashes of lust and waves of hot desire, but they're tempered by the pulling tide of exhaustion that's plagued me for days, even before Gramps left us. In the kitchen, when I almost jumped him on the countertop, I'd thought to use him to distract me from my pain. Now, touching him gives me a release from the grief without forcing me to pretend it's not there.

Not quite as easy, but it's more honest. If Beau and I are going to move from friends that sometimes kiss into more, into the bedroom—and we want it to mean more than comfort or a distraction—tonight isn't the night.

He seems reconciled to that fact, too, settling on the History Channel and pushing farther back into the cushions. "Have you had a chance to talk to Amelia?"

"No. She's going to stay overnight, though, so I'm hoping to when I get home, or in the morning. I want to be able to talk about all of this Anne stuff with her, and I'm worried about what's going on in her life."

"What happened before between the two of you isn't important. I mean, it *is,* but you know . . . maybe focus on how you can repair your relationship going forward." Beau's fingers trail up and down my arm, leaving electricity and goose bumps in their wake. "I saw her face today, Gracie. She misses you as much as you miss her."

"Maybe." I had the same feeling, that the emptiness between us begged to be filled with laughter and secrets, but if I'm stubborn, there needs to be a different word altogether for my cousin. "I'm going to try."

Sleep almost catches me half a dozen times before I sit up and stretch, admitting that as safe and content as I am right now, it's time to leave. "Thank you for listening, and for making me feel better."

His palm caresses my cheek, sweet and full of fire, as he pulls my lips against his. The kiss stays somewhere between the simmering heat of the hospital and the clawing bonfire we ignited in the kitchen. There's need, evident in the way neither of us pulls back, our tongues not content unless they're exploring each other, and the certainty that this is a preview excites me like nothing else.

"Thank you for letting me, Graciela Harper," he murmurs as we pull back. Beau stands in a little bit of a rush, making me think his brain keeps wandering to what might happen between us the next time, too, and then reaches down to pull me to my feet. "I'm happy to oblige any time."

I can't help it. He's too adorable, too unsure of the moment, and I wrap my arms around his neck and drag him close for another kiss. Our lips are like magnets, and I'm powerless to pull away after one or two. It's been years since I've had so much fun kissing someone—David wasn't interested in affection that didn't end in bed, and it's strange but I hadn't thought to miss it. As though maybe making out with no other end had to be left behind in my youth, like everything else worth keeping.

If nothing else, coming back to Heron Creek has shown me that I don't have to grow up until I'm ready, not on the inside, and also that there are things about my past that deserve to be cherished. Repeated. The time with Gramps was too short, but still a reminder of how I'd been once, what I'd dreamed. How I'd loved.

Beau nips my bottom lip and eases back, his eyes hungry on mine. "If you're going, you'd better go."

"Agreed."

He swats my butt as I leave the room, and along with showing me an endearing playful side, leaves me wondering if he might be a little demanding in the bedroom. The idea sends a million shivers of expectation down my spine; the image of him in control does delicious things to my body.

I don't have a ton of experience in the area—Will and I both bumbled along during our first time and most times afterward, and in my memory the sex is sweet and filled with laughter. A one-night stand that is more hazy than anything, and then David. Sex with him had been perfunctory at best, and felt like obligation more than fun.

A sidelong glance at Beau as he walks me out the front door leaves me hot all over, and sure that something different, new—and yes, better—waits beneath his polished exterior. It makes me smile, and I have a sense that it's a little bit wicked.

He groans, his eyes hungry on my face. "Good night, Gracie."

"Good night, Mr. Mayor."

My step is lighter on the way home than it had been on the way to his house, and I think again that maybe, just maybe, my future in Heron Creek could be as wonderful as my past.

Chapter Nineteen

It's not that late when I get home, a little before midnight, but the lights are off. Nothing but dark silence greets me at the front door, not even Anne. We've been going to bed early, and clearly the events of the past couple of weeks have taken toll on my aunt and uncle. I decide to change into pajamas before confronting Amelia, but stop and stare at the sight of her slight form curled under the covers on my bed.

She's breathing deep, on the side of the bed nearest the windows— that's always been her side—but she's not asleep. We've spent way too many nights pretending to snooze away before sneaking out to meet Will and Mel for her to fool me, but I let her fake it while I swap my jeans for shorts and wash my face.

In bed next to her, the comforter tucked under my chin, the way to start the conversation slides through my fingers like river water. My soul remains calm from the evening at Beau's, though, and his advice to not rehash the past rings in my ears. There's no way to change what tore us apart. I can't take back the way I feel about Jake—wouldn't, even if I could—but maybe there's a way for me to keep my cousin, regardless of who she's married to. Her betrayal, the fact that she believed him and cut me loose, left me dangling in the wind that became a gale when my mother died, a hurricane when my relationship imploded, still cuts like a hot knife through butter.

But if I can find the way to forgiveness, maybe there's a way to keep her.

It's not ideal, not what we planned, but after the past five years of silence, the thought of even being able to share her makes my heart hurt. Hope is as painful as anything else, in the right dosage.

"Millie, are you awake?"

No response breaks the night's quiet, but I wait her out. She's deciding, and if she suspects I'm aware she's been awake this whole time she'll just get stubborn. Other than marrying Jacob Middleton, my cousin has never made a rash decision in her life. To my surprise—shock, even—her shoulders start to tremble. A small whimper, then a sniffle convince me she's crying, but I still can't believe it.

"What is it? You can tell me anything, I swear." I put a hand on her bare arm, hesitant, terrified she'll shrink away.

She doesn't, but a little laugh joins her soft tears. "You sound exactly like you did when we were twelve and you begged for ten minutes straight for all the details of my first kiss."

"Maybe things haven't changed as much as we think."

That makes her cry harder, but she rolls toward me in the process. Desperation, fierce enough that it reminds me of Anne's face when she gets super worked up, bunches her features. "It's just the pregnancy hormones. I'm such a bawl-baby now, you wouldn't believe it."

The lie blubbers out with as much gusto as she can muster, which isn't a whole lot. I let it go, walking beside her to see where she'll lead me instead of trying to drag her along where I think we should go.

I feel my way, blind after being out of her life for the past five years. "Tell me about being pregnant, Millie. How far along?"

"Eighteen weeks now."

"Farther than I thought. You're barely showing."

"It's halfway gone. My time alone with him."

"Him?" The revelation crumples the sheet inside my fists. After my conversation with Beau over dinner, the baby being a boy seems like an omen, and not the good kind.

"I don't know. I don't *want* to know, for some reason, but in my mind it's a boy."

The other part of her previous statement strikes me as odd, too. "You sound so sad about not having more time alone with him. Won't it be exciting to meet him?"

"I won't be able to keep him safe then." She shakes her head, eyes still brimming with water. "I'm scared, Grace."

It's a normal new-mother worry, probably, the terror that all of your efforts and love won't be enough to keep your child safe and healthy and alive. Because no one can see the future, or watch every minute. Even as I tell myself that, though, I'm convinced there's more to it. Trepidation stutters through me like a hot wind, as though the devil himself is panting in anticipation.

"Have you and Jake thought of any names?" I hate uttering his name aloud, how it tastes like rotten fish scales slathered on my tongue. It's my first concession to her, my olive branch. A promise that there aren't taboo topics between us.

She hesitates again, so long this time that it feels more like a refusal to answer. My fists curl tighter, the pain in my stomach sharper. Amelia-that-was would be dying to discuss every detail of her pregnancy, bubbling with excitement and uncaring whether everyone else in the room got bored with her or not.

This Amelia, considering the impact of every single word, afraid, is someone else.

"Millie? Is something wrong with the baby?" I whisper, reaching out to touch her.

"No. He's perfect." She smiles now, more like the expectant mother in my mind.

I believe her about this, and she caresses her belly lightly, as though in her mind she's running a finger over the soft hair on his newborn head. Whatever her concern, it's not his health. I guess at what's bothering her, but I can't go there. She has to take me.

"How can you just say his name like that? After everything?"

My stomach sinks. Here we go. "Whose name?"

"Jake's."

"Millie . . . he's your husband. You guys are having a baby. It's over and done. I'll never . . . I can't take back what I said all those years ago, because it's the truth. As I see it. But I miss you so much, and the fact that I love you more than anyone else in this entire world means I'd do about anything to have you in my life."

Her sniffles turn into sobs and her thin arms fly around my waist. We're hugging so tightly my bones hurt, but there's no way I'm letting go.

Tears wet the front of my tank top, and through her tears she mumbles, "I miss you, too."

Her strains of sadness fade to hiccups, then finally sighs as she relaxes next to me. We sink into the pillows and let the reconciliation blanket the room where we grew up, now just another in a long line of arguments and slights that we can, at last, relegate to the past. I think she's asleep, but a while later she kicks loose the covers and gets up to head into the bathroom, muttering something about loss of bladder control.

When she flicks on the bathroom light it illuminates her china doll skin—and the giant purple bruise dipping along the part of her spine exposed by her hip hugging pants. It looks like an inkblot test, but if I'm taking that quiz, my guess would be a hand.

A handprint.

"Amelia." It's not a gasp as much as my lungs deflating into pancakes.

Her body goes rigid and she slams the bathroom door. "It's nothing, Grace! Drop it!"

My muscles tense in response to her muffled shout, anger over her intentional blindness bubbling back to the surface. She's got a baby to think about—one she's more than a little worried about, it seems, yet she stays with a man who hurts her. There's not a doubt in my mind that it's Jake's hand. Jake's abuse. The guy is a menace.

I'm torn, because confronting her could send her running straight back to the problem because she's not ready to face it. There must be websites and books and articles written about how to handle someone in this situation, and the academic in me longs to read every single one of them before tackling her with knowledge. But there isn't time. She's going to come out of that bathroom, and that's going to be the moment.

Her believing Jake, not coming when my mother died, or when Gramps got sick the last time all seemed so important a week ago. Three days ago. But Amelia is all I have left, and she's going to have a baby.

The rest feels as insignificant as the specks of dust waltzing in the moonlight.

Anne's scent, followed immediately by her arrival, surprises me for the first time in days. She sits in her favorite place in this room, butt on the windowsill so her sword has room to hang, boots up on the arm of the chair positioned perfectly for a day of reading in the sunlight. She's got her elbows on her knees, chin in her hands, and watches me with a new kind of interest. Still sad, but also expectant. Her gaze trains on the bathroom.

"Are you going to stay?"

She nods, desire brightening her face.

"Great. Maybe Amelia will stick around and help me get rid of your stinky ass instead of going home."

The ghost nods more vigorously, making me glad she's not completely corporeal. She'd smell even worse, and her head would probably flop right off her rotted shoulders. Before I can make any decisions about Amelia, aside from hoping she'll be able to see Anne, too, the bathroom door swings open. The light flicks off, dousing the room in its previous darkness.

"I know what you're going to say, Grace, and I . . . wait, is that you? What did the mayor *make* you for dinner?"

"Um, well . . ."

"Seriously, what is that stench?"

I stare at Anne's ghost, and Amelia follows my gaze. There's no way to prepare her, but between the two of us, she's always been less of a scaredy-cat.

But I've been better at taking things in stride.

Amelia sees Anne perched on the windowsill and jumps backward over the threshold into the bathroom. She peers around the jamb, her green eyes huge. "Holy shit. What is that?"

Her reaction makes me laugh, mostly because she never uses curse words stronger than *crap,* but also because of the relief. I'm not alone. I'm not crazy. Someone else can see her.

Without taking her eyes off my ghost—maybe our ghost now—Amelia creeps over to the bed and climbs in, pressing her back against me. She trembles slightly, but in true Amelia form, seems more curious than frightened.

"You don't have to be afraid of her, I don't think." Anne makes a face at the doubtful way I end my statement, then rolls her eyes. "Don't let her touch you, though. It sucks."

"Who is she?"

"Anne Bonny. She's been coming around since I've been back in Heron Creek."

My cousin turns her skeptical gaze on me. "Anne Bonny? Et tu, cousin?"

"Amelia. There's a lady ghost in boots, pants, and carrying a cutlass in our room. Who on earth do you think she is?"

"Fine."

"Gramps told me before he died that we're related to her. That Grams was her descendant."

"Didn't she die before she had children? Or maybe it was after . . ." She trails off, her brain trying to recall the same history that escaped me at first. In Heron Creek, tales of Anne are so common you hardly remember them, because you don't have to. You'll hear them again.

"According to her diary, she had her son and moved back to Charleston. It's reasonable." I pause, licking my lips and saying a quick prayer. "She wants us to do something for her, but I'm only half sure what."

"Wait, her diary? And what do you mean, *us*?"

"She's never stuck around to meet anyone else before, so welcome to the Unwilling Friends of the Dead Club." Amelia snorts, but she's relaxed now, and even scoots to the edge of the bed, nearer our smelly friend. "You, me, and your mom are her only remaining descendants, I guess. And the little one you're baking."

Anne perks up at my statement and clomps silently toward the bed. She drops to her knees in front of Amelia, staring intently at her belly, but when she reaches out to touch it, my cousin shrinks away. It's a good decision on her part, but Anne's face falls, wrenching more of me apart.

"I'm sorry. I don't think . . . you can't touch him. But you can look." Amelia's voice shakes, telling me that Anne's sorrowful countenance affects her, too.

Despite the suffocating air of grief in the room, I'm glad both Anne and Amelia are here.

Anne doesn't move for a long time, and I have to remind myself to breathe every once in a while. Finally she stands up, extending one hand toward Amelia and the other toward me, then bringing them together. The hard expression in her eyes leaves no doubt of her meaning—we're in this together.

ଔ

Talking Amelia into staying an extra week after her parents leave turns out to be easier than I imagined. Jake's out of town—Europe, this time—doing some kind of work that he hopes will land him an ambassadorship one day soon. Lord knows they donate enough money to political campaigns. All that's left is for him to suck up to the right candidate at the most fortuitous time and voila. Washington.

I've been back at work for a few days, catching hell for my "unscheduled absence" whenever Mr. Freedman Part Deux isn't around to overhear. Mrs. LaBadie hasn't grown any manners where I'm concerned, but she does seem slightly less querulous when her boss is within hearing distance. I haven't had a chance to get into the archives to check on Mary Read, but I'm not expecting there to be anything there. She didn't grow up in the area, but Amelia's going to come in later and ask to poke around just in case.

She's spent the past three days helping Aunt Karen inventory and clean out Grams and Gramps' bedroom, and now it's a guest room that still reminds me of them but isn't theirs. It's for the best, and I'm glad the task didn't fall to me. They changed out most of the living room furniture, too, moving the recliner we all thought of as Gramps's chair into his old room and replacing it with a leather one that looks out of place. It's still weird, but I'm sure we'll get used to it.

We've put off the discussion about what will happen to the house, whether or not they'll let me stay, until the will is read in a couple of weeks. I'd like to put it off longer.

I'm about to be late for work, which will do nothing but make my professional life descend into the sixth circle of hell, but take a minute to pop my head into the kitchen to say good-bye to my cousin. My heart stops at the sight of the phone in her hand, and the ashen state of her face. "What's wrong?"

She shakes off her fog. "What? Nothing. It's just that I might not be able to stay the whole week. Jake's going to be home a few days earlier than planned."

That only leaves one or two more days to find the other half of Anne's diary. Worry lines Amelia's face, chased by fear.

It makes me mad, but there's nothing to be gained from making her feel even worse. "Oh. Well, we'll make the most of it. Are you still coming by the library today? I need you to put those documents back in Anne's file, and then check and see if—"

"There's anything on Mary Read. I know, Grace."

"Don't forget to act like you don't know me."

"No problem. Plenty of practice."

I shrug. "Hanging in there. I get the feeling she's considering making a move but hasn't gotten there yet. I plan to make it clear before she leaves that she can always stay with me if she leaves Jake."

"Do you think she could spare you for dinner tonight?"

"I told her we could eat after I got off work, so maybe tomorrow?"

"Breakfast?" He grins, a little sheepish, as though a whole extra day is too long to wait.

"That would be okay, I guess." Except for the getting up early and looking nice, besides. "What time?"

"Eight thirty? That gives us an hour before you have to leave for work."

The car pulls up in front of the library steps, putting an end to our brief alone time. I agree to be at his house at the ungodly hour of eight thirty, then snag another kiss and hop out to face the day. I trudge up the steps and in the front door, bidding Mrs. LaBadie a good morning with as much good cheer as I can muster. Beating her crankiness with kindness isn't working any better than ignoring her, but it seems to annoy her more, so points for that. She grunts and points me toward three carts of books that need to be reshelved. There's no way that many books have been returned since yesterday, so I'm pretty sure she's spent the hour before my arrival pulling random volumes down to thwart any idle time I might use to get into the archives.

It's busywork, but it keeps my hands occupied and my brain free to storm away. I'm almost through the first cart when the sound of the front door opening and Amelia's tinkling laugh hitches my progress.

"Good morning! I'm in town visiting an old friend and heard you have some fantastic local archives here. I'm thinking of giving my husband a family tree for his birthday; he's from the area."

"What's your husband's name?"

"Middleton."

"Lots of those running around the area. I'm not sure we're going to have anything extensive enough for the kind of project you're describing." The grumpy response baffles me, because I've been operating under the assumption that her prejudice is Gracie-specific.

Beau's just wrong about that woman, bottom line—it's not just me.

"Even so, I'd love to take a look. Just to be sure." Amelia's insistent but sweet, donning the entitled society-lady voice that she used to put on to imitate her mother.

"I'll have to go in and see if they're available for access today. We keep strict track of the humidity in the room and other factors." My boss isn't backing down. Frustration tightens my hand around a musty red book.

"Mrs. LaBadie, you're being overcautious. If Mrs. Middleton wishes to peruse our local archives, she's more than welcome to do so, and for as long as she likes." Mr. Freedman's stern voice makes me want to cheer.

Maybe do a little dance.

I haven't asked him for access to the room since I've already stolen what I want and it would give the wicked woman more of a reason to treat me like a serf. There's no more discussion from the front, and I remove myself from the path they'll take back into the archives. The building goes quiet again, and I return to shelving, at least until the craggy, missing-toothed face of Mrs. LaBadie pops up over my shoulder.

"Shit!"

"You'd better watch that filthy mouth, or I'm gonna haveta write you up. You're all the same."

"*Who's* all the same? People you scare the crap out of? Why are you sneaking around like that?"

"Sneaking? The only people that accuse others of sneaking around are sneaks. I didn't hear ya working so I thought I'd come back and make sure ya din't fall asleep." The more upset she gets, the more her accent comes out. It's still hard to place, but I'm starting to think Caribbean.

That, and the fact that she's pure evil, makes me think of Anne's voodoo woman.

"No, I didn't fall asleep." My heart keeps pounding, even though it should have calmed from the scare by now. It's racing as hard as Beau has ever made it, and I realize that she scares me. Which juts out my chin. "Why are you so mean to me? I mean, what did I ever do to you?"

A storm gathers in her obsidian gaze, flashing with a truth that's evident but impossible to read. "You have your role, and I have mine, Graciela Anne Harper. They were cast long ago, and neither you nor I can change them. Not that I'd want to, because you're the kind of girl who refuses to accept things the way they are."

"And how's that?" My teeth chatter, and tingles zap my spine. It's not cold in here but she's freaking me out. Everything she's said is nonsense, yet the corners of my brain insist they have a order that's eluding me.

Mrs. LaBadie glances down at my second cart, half emptied, and ignores the question. "Hurry up with that, the front windows need to be washed today."

She stalks off, but it takes a good ten minutes before I warm up, before I stop glancing over my shoulder. I've got the last bundle of books in my arms an hour later when Amelia pops around the corner with a grin.

"Boo!" After Mrs. LaBadie's weirdness and weeks of dead Anne Bonny, Amelia doesn't make me flinch.

"What is it?" I hiss, annoyed she can't remember that we're supposed to be pretending we're strangers.

"Oh, Grace, come on. That woman is eight hundred years old. She can't hear us talking all the way back here." She rolls her eyes, then reaches into her purse. Her fingers come out covered in what looks like black dirt, and her face dissolves into confusion.

"What's that?"

"I don't know." She brings her hand to her nose and breathes in, then gags. "Good Lord, that smells like death."

"Did you find anything?"

"What? No. There's nothing about Mary Read. But I did put your contraband back where it belongs."

"And she didn't see you?"

"No, she checked on me about a hundred times, though, and brought some herbal tea that was quite tasty." She pauses, wiping the black gunk onto her jeans and grabbing a tissue from a front pocket of her purse to clean out the rest of the . . . whatever it is. "There seem to be files missing. We'd need more time alone in there to figure out any rhyme or reason."

"Okay. Get out of here. I'll meet you at the Wreck after work."

I don't bother telling her not to assume anything about Mrs. LaBadie, or that she's not as old and harmless as she appears to the untrained eye. We can dissect the weird shit she said to me later. My cousin flounces out the front door and a half hour later I stand up, stretch my shoulders, and tell Mrs. LaBadie I'm going to lunch.

And that I just can't *wait* to wash the windows afterward.

Chapter Twenty

The coffee shop is packed, as usual. Leo's nowhere to be seen outside, which disappoints me. I kind of wanted to see how he's doing, and ask about getting together before Amelia goes back to Charleston. She'll be delighted at us starting a friendship now, after all those years pretending to battle 24-7.

The sight of the two of them at a table in front of the windows ruins the surprise, but gives me pleasure all the same.

"Hey."

They look up, Amelia's green eyes sparkling and Leo breaking into a smile.

"Hey, Graciela. Why didn't you tell me your beautiful and much-more-charming cousin was visiting?"

"I've been a little busy, Leo."

I don't mean it to come off rude, but his expression sobers in the blink of an eye. "I'm sorry about your Gramps. It was a great funeral. Exactly the way I'd want to go out, with a bunch of people talking about how much better I made their lives."

"Thanks." It's amazing that even though it's only been a week I can already accept those kinds of condolences without choking up. "I'm going to get a sandwich. Be right back."

The line moves quickly since the staff has plenty of practice catering to the crush of hungry people on their lunch breaks, and I'm back at the table with chicken salad on a croissant in fewer than ten minutes. I set down my raspberry iced tea and slide into the seat between Amelia and Leo, digging in while the sound of their catching up blends in with the twenty-three other conversations bouncing off the walls.

Leo stands up before my sandwich is half gone, offering an apologetic smile. "I've got to get back to work, I'm afraid, and then bring Marcella to story time. But let's get dinner before you leave, Amelia."

"Maybe we can join Grace on one of her dates with the mayor."

The pause grows uncomfortable, and Millie shoots me a glance that says she has no idea what she said wrong. I don't, either, but it's been clear since the first day I saw Leo and Beau interact that there's some sort of weirdness between them.

"Maybe just the three of us," he amends finally, a small smile trying to undo the avoidance in his response.

He exits after gathering up assenting nods from Amelia and me, then she makes an awkward face in my direction. "What was that about?"

"I don't know. They don't like each other or something, but I keep forgetting to ask about it."

"Probably because you're too busy doing *other* things." Her teasing tone makes me snort, mostly because she sounds as though we're back in high school.

"It's not like that, at least not right now. I don't really know what he wants from me at the moment."

"I can tell you what he wants." She waggles her eyebrows and takes a bite of coleslaw. "Things have been awkward because of Gramps being sick and then passing. Mayor Drayton's had to play the supportive friend part, but the guy wants the starring role. I'm positive."

"I don't know."

Beau likes me, and he's attracted to me—I haven't been out of the game long enough to argue against either of those statements. But whether or not I'm the kind of girl he could ever take public remains to be seen.

"I saw him pick you up on the street this morning. Why don't you let him get you at the house instead of sneaking around?"

It's the second time today someone's accused me of sneaking around. Sheesh. "I'm not *asking* him for rides. He kind of keeps appearing out of thin air."

"Poor, poor Grace. I can see how inconvenient and annoying it would be to have handsome, well-connected, grown-up men offering you rides around town." She pats my hand sympathetically.

I swat her away and we both laugh. I'm probably being silly, she's right. As usual.

"I can't believe there's nothing in the archives about Mary Read."

"She's not even from here, though, right? The journal makes it sound like her family was from Virginia," Amelia sits back, rubbing her stomach.

"I know. It was a long shot. I'm not sure she ever lived in the colonies, even."

"So, if that professor doesn't come through for you, we're back at square one."

"I can't believe they let the two of you in here, after that incident with the lemonade machine in seventh grade." It's Mel's voice that interrupts, and she bends down to pull Amelia into a hug. "How are you feeling?"

"Good, mostly. You?"

"Constantly sick to my stomach."

"Well, sit and have lunch with us! We were just lamenting the sorry state of the local archives, and also the impressive bitchiness of Grace's boss."

"*You* were in the archives?" Mel sits, opening the lid to her just-purchased soup, which looks like potato. She takes a whiff and blanches, then sits back and contents herself with water. Pregnancy is weird. "Amelia Cooper, pretending interest in historical documents. That I would have loved to see. Are you sure you didn't just miss it?"

"Very funny. But, no. I mean yes, I'm sure."

"She was helping me with some research on local history to pass the time. No big deal." I ignore the look Amelia shoots me. It's not that I don't trust Mel, but Anne didn't come to her. She came to us.

"Was that Leo Boone eating with you guys when I came in?" Mel changes the subject, which doesn't surprise me. She and Amelia had never shared my love of the past, scary stories aside.

"Yeah. I ran into him a few weeks ago, and he brings his niece into the library for story time every week. She's adorable."

"Yeah. Too bad about her mom, though."

"What happened to her?"

"She got arrested for drugs and prostitution, and even though there seemed to be a case for coercion—there was this horrible dealer-pimp kind of guy lurking around Charleston a few years back—they threw the book at her for the amount of heroin she had in her possession. She's in jail for twenty years, and Leo's raising Marcella."

"That's terrible."

"Yeah. The Boones fought the conviction hard, but the cop was new and determined to make a name for himself. See, your Mayor Drayton isn't loved by everyone in Heron Creek, Gracie."

"Beau's the one who put her away?" That explains the bad blood between the two of them, and I'm not sure how hard-ass-lawyer Beau reconciles with the guy I'm slowly getting to know. I can see it, I suppose. Underneath his gentle exterior runs a man who knows exactly how to get what he wants.

"Yep."

I cast a glance at Amelia, waiting for her to make some kind of quip about the mayor's hard ass, but she's not paying attention. Her hands rub her stomach and her eyes are fixed on the table. Something's wrong, and when she feels my gaze, she looks up.

The fear in her eyes seizes my heart, and I fly to my feet. "What is it?"

"I don't know. I'm . . . something's wrong with the baby."

ଓ

Being back in Heron Creek General Hospital does not amuse me in the slightest. Reminders of Gramps lurk around every corner, not to mention that they still employ my least favorite people ever—doctors. They've been monitoring Amelia and the baby for three hours now, and her contractions have stopped. The doctors don't know what caused them yet, and until they figure it out there isn't any way to be sure they won't happen again. Amelia's feeling better, and has convinced me not to call her mother or Jake because they'll make a big deal out of it.

I'm not convinced it's *not* a big deal, but it's her body and her baby, so I keep my mouth shut and my itchy fingers off my cell phone. I don't blame her for not wanting to call Jake, but I would have done it if she'd asked. Aunt Karen, for all of her faults, loves her daughter, and she should be here.

She's going to take it out on me, no doubt, when she finds out she wasn't.

I called the library once they ran the initial tests on Amelia. Mrs. LaBadie put me through to Mr. Freedman on my fourth request, which means I still have a job, even if there's hardly time to work around all of the drama in my life.

My cousin dozes in the bed under the windows, which gives me hope that her pain has eased altogether. The test results aren't back yet. Beau's texted me once after the news of the coffee shop excitement spread to his office, asking what's going on, and I assured him he does not need to stop what he's doing and rush over here. Melanie had to leave a little while ago to pick up Grant, but she'll call or be back as soon as she's free.

I'm struggling not to nod off, despite an awkward attempt to cram the angles of my body into the plastic bedside chair, when my phone dings with an e-mail. Based on my unofficial study, there's a 267 percent chance it's spam, either from a lingerie company that refuses to take me off their list or one of the seven workout programs that kept my attention for approximately three days.

No one—not one single person—in Iowa City has contacted me since I left. They were always David's friends, as opposed to mine, and even though there aren't any of them that I miss, their total lack of interest in my well-being kind of stings. No one in Heron Creek uses e-mail, probably because all one has to do is wander down the street to connect with anyone they'd like.

This e-mail isn't spam, though, and straightens my spine so quickly I almost topple onto the floor. It's from the UNC Wilmington professor, and my thumbs manage to click it open without accidentally deleting anything.

Ms. Harper,

I must admit my surprise at finding answers to your query about genealogical information relating to Mary Read. I'm pleased to tell you that I did track down two aunts living at the time of her death, both on her paternal side. I've enclosed a document that outlines what little is known of her life prior to joining Jack Rackham's crew, and another that traces what lineage we've been able to find following her death. It's unclear, as you know, whether she has any direct descendants, since the disposition of her child after her death is a matter of contention. The names listed are the progeny of the aunts on the Read side of the family.

Please let me know if I can be of any further assistance, and of course, I would love to hear more about this line of research when you've completed it and have the time.

He signs off in a professional manner and I click on the attachments, impatience almost making me growl. The only reason he agreed to help was because he had read my master's thesis and thought it showed promise, but I'm not complaining. Help is help, and this is free.

I skip the first attachment, because obliviously I've read everything I can easily find on Mary's life before piracy—there isn't much known for sure, other than that her father, a sea captain, died before she was born and that the first person to dress her like a boy had been her mother. Later she'd been married, he died, too, and she ended up making a living for herself at sea. Short and not very sweet, had been Mary's story before the *Revenge*.

Come to think of it, her life had been short *after* meeting Anne and Jack, too, but if Anne's diary is as true as it seems, at least the woman had some sweetness at the end. Her friendship with Anne, and presumably making the baby, at least, had been fun.

The second attachment begins with the two aunts, one who had been living in England still, and the other—to my delight—residing in Virginia. The second's name was Eliza Goode, and her known descendants run out with a woman and a man, both still living. And I know them.

I have to blink a half-dozen times to convince myself I didn't fall asleep after all.

Melanie Massie.

My Mel, and her younger brother, Jonah, are the final two descendants of Mary Read's aunt Eliza—from a girl-child, also Mary, whose eldest daughter was born almost seven years after her sons. If she's the one who took in her baby cousin, Melanie could be Mary Read's great-granddaughter times however many generations that makes.

It blows my mind. It doesn't seem possible that the answer could have been under my nose not only the past month, but my entire life. Melanie never mentioned it, but then again, my own mother and grandmother never mentioned my relation to Anne Bonny, either.

I wish there had been more time to ask Gramps why. Why no one said anything to me, or to Amelia. Were they embarrassed, or maybe no one wanted to believe it? Neither of those things seems like something that would affect the decisions made by the women who had raised me.

The only thing that might have convinced them to keep their mouths shut is that making our heritage common knowledge would have made certain people in Heron Creek look at our family differently. Whether or not the residents claim to believe in ghosts, everyone knows the story, and no little girl wants to grow up with everyone asking about her pirate blood, or whether or not the ghost lives in the guest room.

And they didn't know about the diary, I remind myself. Neither my mother nor grandmother could have known there is more to the story, perhaps more of a reason for us to learn everything we can about our history. Maybe they weren't even sure they believed it.

Amelia's still asleep when the doctor, a female ob-gyn whose name isn't familiar, strides in a few seconds later. Every thought of Anne and Melanie and Mary Read flees my head as she nudges my cousin awake, a serious expression on her pretty, middle-aged face.

"Mrs. Middleton?"

It takes Millie a minute to come fully awake, but the way she scrambles into a seated position tells me she's more worried about the baby than she's letting on. The drive to the hospital was endless, with sweat and tears mingling on her cheeks, panted breaths punching me in the stomach, her hands clutched over the baby.

Melanie was a huge help, much calmer than either Amelia or me, and we fell back into old roles and friendships that might turn out to be timeless after all without a second thought.

"Yes? Is he okay?"

The doctor gives my cousin a tight smile, but it's enough to unknot the ball twisted between my shoulders. "As far as we can tell, he's doing fine. There was some stress due to those contractions, but we've got that under control and it doesn't seem as though your body is determined to continue."

"That's good, right?"

"Yes." She studies Amelia for a moment before saying more. "Are you familiar with black and blue cohosh?"

"No."

"It's sometimes called Callphyllum or Cimicifuga." My cousin shakes her head again, and the words are foreign to me, too. She might as well be reciting *Oedipus* in the original Greek. "They're herbs, the natural equivalent of Pitocin. Given in the right dosage, they can induce labor at any stage of pregnancy."

"What? I haven't taken any herbs, or eaten anything odd."

"Did you find traces in her blood?"

"Yes, we did. Significant amounts." Her eyes flick to me before landing back on her patient.

It crosses my mind that she's evaluating Millie's mental health. As though she thinks my cousin could have done this on purpose, tried to abort her baby.

"Is it possible to ingest or . . . breathe them in or something and not know?" Amelia's confusion thickens the question, as though she's not sure exactly why this is happening.

"They have a pretty intense scent and taste, and they're not terribly common, so I'd say it's unlikely." The doctor snaps closed her pad and pins my cousin with a look. "We're going to keep you here overnight to make sure everything flushes out of your system properly, but then you're free to go. I'd advise you to be more careful with unknown food and drink during your pregnancy."

Her patient swallows and nods, a little too meek for my tastes. I want her to yell at that doctor, tell her no way that's right, or if it is, it has to be an accident, but the fear glistening in Millie's eyes stills my tongue.

"I will. And ma'am?"

"Doctor Lyons."

"Doctor Lyons . . . did you call the baby a him?" Amelia holds her breath, eyes huge and full of expectation. It's not clear whether she wants to know or doesn't want to know.

"It's a boy. I'm sorry. I thought you knew because you referred to him that way first."

Tears spill over now, and the smile that lights up Millie's face can't fail to convince the doctor that she would never, ever do anything to harm the little guy growing inside her. It seems to relax the entire room, like the ceiling and doorframe and the tops of the windows all sag with certainty.

Then we're alone. I sit on the edge of the bed and fold my cousin in a hug, careful to avoid the wires attached to her arms and hand and belly, but holding on tight. "It's going to be okay. He's going to be okay."

She nods, and once her heartbeat stops fluttering like a pent-up bird, she lays back on the pillows, hands brushing her belly with light strokes. A soft smile paints her face with the kind of beauty that exceeds even her typical blinding fare. "A boy. I knew it."

Remember my conversation with Beau about the lack of boys in our family, the confirmation makes me sure time is running out.

Chapter Twenty-One

There doesn't seem to be any point in hanging around the hospital after Amelia falls asleep. She makes me promise to come back for dinner, and to bring her something that's not hospital food—she and I share an aversion to Jell-O that neither of our grandparents ever understood. I agree before heading out to the parking lot and then taking a right to hike back toward the center of town.

My phone's in my hand, Melanie's number punched in, the moment I'm free of the doors.

"Hello? Gracie? Is everything okay with Amelia and the baby?"

"Yes, at least for now. They've stopped the contractions and don't foresee a repeat."

"Did they find out why it happened?" The edge in her voice makes me smile. Mama Bear Mel.

"They said she somehow ingested some kind of herbs that can induce labor."

"How?"

"We don't know. The stupid doctor was acting like she might have done it on purpose, but obviously that's not the case." Even though things are bad at home, and Jake is not going to make a gold-star father, I have to believe Millie would leave him before harming her child. Have to.

"Okay, well, I guess that's good news. Maybe later we can help her go over everything she ate or drank today and figure out where she got into it. We definitely don't want to go through that again."

"Sure. I told her I'd be back with dinner by six thirty. We could grab takeout from the Wreck and eat with her."

"Sounds good." A squeal in the background shatters my eardrum. Grant is going to steal her attention sooner than later. "I need a favor, Mel."

"Okay . . ." Her hesitation is warranted, knowing the kind of favors I've asked her for over the years.

At least this one's legal.

"I'm running back to the library to grab my purse and keys—is there any way you could meet me there? I have something to tell you and it can't wait."

"Sure, I think that can work. Will should be home any time, so I can leave Grant. Fifteen minutes?"

"See you then."

☙

Melanie rushes into the library a mere ten minutes later, red-cheeked and sweaty. I sit on one side of a table made for first-graders, because it's the farthest from the front desk. She sits on the other side, and no doubt the two of us look pretty funny. Like giants.

It's not even that Anne's diaries are a secret, at least they won't be for much longer, but Mrs. LaBadie has done everything in her power to make my life more difficult, and after she creeped me out earlier, I've never wanted less for her to overhear. If it weren't nine hundred degrees outside I would have waited on the steps.

"Hey, sorry. Will was running late." She sucks more air, pressing her palms against the table. "Man. I've got to get in better shape. What's up?"

"Okay, so you know how Amelia was in the archives earlier today looking for something for me?"

"Yeah . . ."

"Well, it turns out you might have the answer. I'm looking for genealogical information on the family of Mary Read. The pirate."

"I know who she is, Gracie. She's a relation. My granny's side."

Mel says this as if it's no big deal, as though she's commenting on my dress or the fact that it's still a bazillion degrees outside. My mouth falls open, but in the back of my mind, I'm not sure why it surprises me. It's exactly the kind of information that wouldn't impress her.

"How have you never mentioned this before now? Have you always known?"

"Um, I guess? I wasn't really interested in any of that crap as a kid, you know, and besides, she's not really the kind of woman a respectable family wants to claim." She pauses, then grins at me. "I mean, she's probably the kind of ancestor *you* would like to claim, but not me."

"Thanks," I say dryly.

"Anyway, when Granny was dying a few years ago I spent time with her and she talked a lot about it—how we're actually Mary's 'lost' descendants since the history books don't record her child living. It's sort of interesting, I guess." She pauses, her lips pulling down into a frown. "But how do you know about it?"

Melanie's always been sharp, and I'm hoping she paid more than passing attention to her Granny's stories.

"I came across a diary written by a woman who claims to be Anne Bonny, and there's a bit in it about Mary Read. Anne claims to have brought Mary's baby back to the mainland when her father secretly sprung her from jail, and that a cousin or aunt—she's not clear on that—in Virginia took the baby in."

"That's pretty much the story I heard. It was a cousin."

"It also says that later in her life, Anne's husband forced her to send her son to live with that same family, when he was a teenager. He took the other half of her journal with him." Mel sits up, her chocolate eyes sparkling. It's a mystery, she can smell it. Her eager-beaver face fills my heart with hope, because once Mel gets her teeth into something, she won't let go.

"I need the other half of the journal. If Jack Jr. made it to Virginia, he was supposed to entrust it to Mary's family for safekeeping."

"Her son's name was Jack?"

"Yes. After her husband. He went to Virginia as Jack Cormac, her maiden name."

"Granny talked about him, too, like he was Mary's brother. One of us."

"They took him in."

"Yes. It seems he was quite charming. For what it's worth, he made quite a lot of his life, stirring up a good amount of trouble in local politics, if Granny's to be believed."

I'm grinning from ear to ear before I realize what's happening, and my first, disturbing thought is to wonder if Anne knows her son lived. Flourished. She must be thrilled.

"If the entire *story* is to believed, it makes sense that any child of Anne Bonny and Calico Jack Rackham wouldn't be much for blending into the background." My smile fades with the memory of why I came here to begin with—to find the other half of the diary, learn what Anne discovered about the curse on her son, and somehow make her feel better about the whole thing. "Do you know anything about the journal?"

Mel eyes me, sniffing out not only the mystery, but the fact that she's not being told the whole of it. My breath catches, because along with the excitement spawned by my discovery, an unexpected fear douses me.

Someone in Heron Creek isn't keen on my uncovering anything that might be hidden in those archives, which is exactly where Anne wanted me to go, and the idea of involving Mel makes me uncomfortable, at best.

"What aren't you telling me? What's so important about this diary?"

"I won't know until I read the other half, but it means a lot that I do."

Her gaze sharpens, clings to my response with invisible talons. "Means a lot to whom?"

"Me, maybe Amelia." I swallow hard. "Anne Bonny."

"Anne Bonny?" she says, too loudly for my taste, then glances over her shoulder at my obvious wince. She lowers her voice. "Don't you think she's a little, you know, *dead* to be worried about what became of her old diary?"

"Probably."

"Are you being haunted, Gracie? Have you gone mad, is that what this is about?" She's full of giggles. They pry open her lips and spill out all over the kiddie table.

"Would you lower your voice?" I hiss, wanting to smash them. "Yes, okay, I've been seeing her ghost and that's how I found the diary. Amelia saw her, too. You can ask her."

The mention of my cousin being willing to back me up slays the giggles where they writhe in delight, and her expression turns skeptical. Questioning. Amelia is historically less prone to nonsense and theatrics than yours truly. "I can go through Granny's things before I come to the hospital. She only had a couple boxes when she died in the nursing home, and there are a few books. I'll check."

I cover her hands with mine, the gesture of warmth surprising us both. Impulsive affection has almost disappeared completely from my life, aside from the mayor, and the fact that it feels good needles me with discomfort. When I left Iowa City, it was with determination—mostly to not put myself in the position of depending on anyone else again.

Ever.

Yet here I am, needing Mel's help. Accepting Beau's support, in more ways than one. It feels like an old sweater, maybe even one that had once been well loved, but shrunk along the way until it doesn't fit. It could be that it'll stretch back out, with some love and time.

If I want it to.

"I think the words you're looking for are 'Thank you, Mel,'" she says, her tone soft, eyes careful.

"You always did say things better than me," I quip in return, breaking the tension but not the feeling of friendship between us. "I'm going to grab dinner and head to the hospital. You see what you can find in those boxes and join us, if you can get away."

"Will's home all night. He won't mind."

Will never minded girl time, or being on his own for a few hours or even a weekend. One of his better qualities, though he'd had more than a few.

"Okay." I stand up and snag my purse from the back of the miniature chair. "What do you want for dinner?"

"Fish tacos, duh. Nothing to drink." She sighs. "I miss wine already."

We step into the stacks and nearly run down Mrs. LaBadie. A scowl twists her face, one that makes her resemble a rabid raccoon or and angry crocodile—she's all teeth and crazed black eyes. Even Mel starts and takes a step back. The old woman makes no excuse for hovering so close, and there's no cart of books or other reason for her to be back here. The library closes in five minutes; she's always ready to go the moment clock ticks to five thirty. She was spying on us.

When she whirls away without a word, something oily and unsavory clings to the air. Mel raises her eyebrows, one hand pressed to her chest, and I shrug. "I don't know. She's a freak."

"She was listening to us."

"I know."

Chapter Twenty-Two

Melanie, Amelia, and I had a great time at the hospital last night, despite the circumstances. We all love the 4th of July, and being together again, the sound of fireworks booming and crackling and popping outside the windows, provides a kind of magic even though our conversations are less than helpful. Mel hadn't realized her Granny's boxes were in storage, so she'd have to wait until morning to get to them, and Amelia couldn't remember drinking or eating anything that would have contained those random herbs. Even so, the three of us gossiped, caught up on the past five-plus years, and even though rekindling their friendships hadn't been part of my plan when returning here, it's starting to feel as though it's just what I need.

Between the two of them, Anne, and Beau, I might as well give up on a damn thing going as planned.

I'm up by seven thirty, which is obscene even considering my bedtime of 10:00 p.m., but stumbling half blind into the bathroom to find Anne sitting on the closed toilet seat startles me fully awake, nose first. I clap my hands over my mouth to muffle my shriek, even though there isn't anyone else around to hear now.

"Do you pick the places you show up based on which will be most likely to make me shit my pants?" I growl at her, still trying to coax my heart out of my ass. She doesn't reply, per usual, but the sparkle in her typically pissy gaze confirms my suspicions. "I can't say I approve, since it's my shit, but I suppose there isn't a whole lot that amuses you these days."

I turn on the shower, then eye her. "Are you going to watch?"

She cocks an eyebrow but doesn't move, crossing her arms over her chest.

"Making me uncomfortable isn't going to make Mel find the other half of your diary any faster. Did you know your son became a politician? I would love to have heard what he had to say about the Civil War." Her expression changes from one of mild interest to rapt attention, and guilt at my scant details pinches my cheeks until they burn. I should have thought to research him further. "I don't know details, but I can look them up if you want and tell you later."

She looks satisfied, at least for now, and when I check on her again after testing the water temperature, she's nowhere to be seen. Which is good, because I'd love to not smell like rotting wood during breakfast with Beau.

A shower, makeup, and fresh clothes—Amelia did my laundry—help me achieve that goal, and the cool morning air puts a smile on my face when I step out the front door, locking it behind me. If reasons exist to get up early, sunrise might be one of them.

"Where's Miss Amelia?" Mrs. Walters rocks on her front porch, two houses down, and squints as though the sun ought to slink away because it's inconveniencing her.

The reply that it's none of her damn business shoots onto my tongue, but I bite it back at the last second. It's not the way people respond to prying conversation, not in Iowa and not in Heron Creek. "She'll be along soon, Mrs. Walters. I'll be sure and tell her you were worried about her. So kind of you."

"Humph. And your aunt and uncle, they going to sell the house now that Martin's passed on?"

"I don't know, but I'm sure they'll want to do what's best for the community when the time comes." My steps take me past her porch and I force a smile, too bright and perhaps a little on the sneery side. "I hope you have a lovely day, ma'am."

She *humph*s again, but it's almost not strong enough to follow me. The sun climbs higher in the sky, which abandons its pastel hues for a bright, cloudless blue. The walk to Beau's takes about fifteen minutes, and it's a pleasant one, with the scent of salt on the air. I take a path that trails along the marshy portion of the riverfront, deciding to carry my shoes so they won't get muddy. It's a toss-up, muddy feet or muddy shoes, but if Beau doesn't like me with dirty toes, we were never going to work out, anyway.

The feeling of the squishy ground relaxes my soul. The sound of a car creeps up the street behind me, but I don't turn around. I'm twenty feet off the sidewalk, so no need to worry, and I'm simply not concerned with the humans that live in Heron Creek this morning. Right now, the blue herons, great egrets, and hawks command my attention and hold it captive with their elegance and chatter.

They take flight all at once, the birds gathered nearest to me in the trees and along the marshy bank, at the same moment that the sound of footsteps registers, followed by an impossibly strong grip that pinches my elbows together behind my back. I get an impression of a smallish, black-clad figure before it twists my arm, hard, and kicks my legs out from underneath me. The scream that gathered in my chest wheezes out in a pointless gasp as my face hits the marshy ground. The weight on top of me seems far too much, the strength an insane impossibility for how small the figure seems.

I'm not much of a fighter, but my assailant blocks every attempt at bucking him off, thwarting twists by delivering a crazy amount of pain to my twisted shoulder, and I give up and lie still, listening to the sound of my breaths fill the quiet morning.

"What do you want?" I manage to gasp between stabs of pain.

The person doesn't answer, and my heart accelerates. Sweat drips down my temples and into my hair, dampens my armpits and pools between my breasts. There's dirt and moss on my lips. It tastes earthy as I lick it away, then bite down to manage the pain. I could scream, but if no one's close enough to see what's going on, no one's close enough to hear.

The ninja-person must decide he doesn't want to chance being seen, because he drags me into the waist-high grasses closer to the river. Every lecture my mother ever gave me about paying attention to my surroundings plays in my ears, and I have a feeling now that she didn't mean watching birds. I whimper as the person wrenches my arms again, then kicks my ribs when my noise level raises toward a shriek.

Waves of pain shoot out from my center, jangling all the way to my fingertips. At first, I think the sound of voices must be coming from my own mind, but when the black figure jerks up and listens like a dog in the dark, I know they're not. He stops moving me, and in one swift movement, reels back and cracks me in the face.

☙

I'm a puddle of sweat and pain when my eyes peel back again, starting in my face and ending in my midsection. Nothing hurts worse than my shoulder, a fact that presents itself when I attempt to move and find it tied behind me, my back pressed against something warm.

My arm throbs, making my stomach sour, and I gag on the meager remnants of last night's dinner. This is the second time in a few weeks that I've cracked my face—or had it cracked for me—and I'm sure now that professional boxing is not a missed career opportunity.

I don't know who happened by and startled off my assailant, but I know in the pit of my stomach, without the shadow of a doubt, that, uninterrupted, they would have killed me.

I bite back a groan and try wriggling, anything to readjust my position to relieve the pressure on my arm, but freeze when something soft and silky tickles my cheek.

It's followed by something heavy flopping onto my shoulder, and I manage to crane my neck enough to discover a head attached to light blond hair. We're tied together, sitting up on the floor of a room that looks familiar but I can't quite place because the room is so damn dark.

Wait. Why is the room dark? It's morning, or at least it was, but the complete blackness suggests the entire day has come and gone. It doesn't seem possible that a punch to the face could have knocked me out for so long, or that there's anywhere in Heron Creek that could hide me for hours when Beau surely called out the dogs after I didn't show up for breakfast.

Anger lights a hot, quick fire in my belly. Someone felt as though they had the right to put their fucking hands on me, and I don't know who is tied behind me, but I bet they don't deserve to be here, either. My fight response kicks in, along with more fear than anything, because as hard as I try to act as though I'm handling this shit, I'm so not. I've been attacked. Kidnapped. Tied up. No one but the kind of psychos in the movies does things like that, and from what I can recall, they're not much for letting people go.

I work harder at getting loose, until I've worked up a sweat and bloodied my wrists, but make no measurable progress aside from earning a harder throb in my shoulder. The form bound to my back groans and shifts, coming awake. I'm not sure if that counts as progress.

"Gracie?" The voice is groggy, confused, and shakes its head a couple of times, which is as long as it takes me to place it.

"Mel? What are you doing here?"

"I got a text around nine p.m. on my way out of class, asking me to meet you at the library. You said it was a matter of life and death, then didn't answer when I tried to call."

"I didn't text you."

"Well your phone did, then. Maybe it was Anne Bonny's ghost."

It's good she can joke, even if her voice is a mass of broken crystals. Someone, most likely the person who attacked me, and the two of us lapse into silence as we consider our own failures, lured her here. It's not my fault, or hers, except it's kind of more mine. I didn't tell her that getting involved in this whole historical hide-and-seek seems to be hazardous to health and property. After the warnings I've gotten, and the mysterious circumstances surrounding Amelia's contractions, I'm almost convinced of the curse in Anne's journal.

"Are you okay?" My own voice trembles, skitters. She's got to be okay.

"My head's killing me and I'm tied to your dumb ass in the dark, but other than that, yes."

The darkness has faded to shades of gray punctuated by shadows, and I realize why the room looks familiar. "We're in Mr. Freedman's office."

"At the library?"

"Yeah." Something about this doesn't add up. I mean, several somethings, but one in particular. "Didn't you know I was missing?"

"You were missing?"

"I got jumped on the way to Beau's house this morning, around eight thirty. I've been gone all day. He didn't report it?" Because of the situation, my brain comes up with a million reasons why, but not one that doesn't include him being involved somehow.

"Not that I know of, and I can't imagine not hearing about it all day." She slumps against me. "If whoever did this texted me, Gracie, who's to say they didn't send the mayor a message, too?"

It's possible, but no one knew about our breakfast date except Amelia and Mel. I don't think.

"Who wanted us here together?" Mel's mind seems to be fine, at any rate.

"I don't know, but I wish they'd stop acting like a cowardly shithead, playing the note-leaving, smack-me-in-the-face game, and tell me what in the hell they want. So I can spit in their face and tell them to go to hell."

"I'm not sure that's the best course of action," she replies, sounding more like the dry Melanie I know and might still love. "Did you see their face?"

I shake my head. "No. Whoever it is wears a mask, anyway. Like the lily-livered oaf he is."

"I didn't, either. I was on the phone with Will, waiting for you when someone got in the passenger door. I thought it was you, but they thunked me before I could turn and look."

I remember the softness of the person's chest, combine it with the small stature. The only thing that seems off is the strength, but what kind of feminist am I, assuming it's a man? "I think it might be a woman."

"Let's get the hell out of here and discuss later."

We work together on the bindings around our wrists, but all we do is cut more of our flesh until hot blood smears us both. We could try scooting toward the door, but we can't get all the way out of the locked library that way, and every time we move the pounding in my head makes me retch.

Mel sits up straighter, her fingers tightening around mine. "Do you hear that?"

I turn off my racing thoughts and focus, picking up the sound of approaching footsteps. They're shuffling along the thin carpet in the corridor, then the lock snicks open and they cross the threshold. It's the same dark clad figure, small and wiry, and—– close—definitely a woman. It rounds us and bends down, looking into my face, and even though my anger doesn't leave, my fear burns far hotter.

This isn't real life, being attacked and bound and threatened by ninja women. I'm a recently dumped archivist from Iowa, not a super sleuth ghost hunter. I don't think.

Despite my trembling limbs I don't blink. "Listen, asshole, what do you want? And you can let her go, she has nothing to do with anything."

"You haven't the slightest idea whether or not your friend is important, just as you haven't the slightest idea why you've been caught in the snare, either. You're a disgrace to your heritage, and that's pretty pockmarked to start with." The accent is familiar to me, in the way that Shakespeare makes sense if you don't listen too hard.

I've heard a version of it before, but not so thick and lilting. It leaps over rolling hills and tumbles into deep valleys—too pleasant of tone to forget. Maybe I am a disgrace. All signs point to yes.

I wish Anne would show up. The sight of her might give this bitch a good scare, at the least. A solid heart attack at most.

"No use wishing for Anne Bonny to help you. Getting you to see her takes all of the energy she can muster in this world. She can do no more."

Shit, she's some kind of mind reader.

Melanie tenses but stays silent. The woman wanders into the shadows over by Mr. Freedman's desk. She pulls off the mask and stretches, too much in the darkness to be identified. My mind races, trying to put the pieces together, to figure out for the hundredth time what any of this has to do with Anne.

"It *all* has to do with Anne Bonny, daft child. Have you not realized that none of your troubles began until she started to plague you? The fruits of her womb must never be allowed to multiply, not as long as me and my kind are around to ensure the curse. I tried to warn you to stop looking. But you convinced your poor little friend to find the other half of that journal. And now we're here."

The journal?

"You're talking about the curse on Anne and Jack's lineage," Melanie supplies, her shoulders still tight.

Mel must have read the other part of the diary. She knows what Anne found out about her husband's mistress before Jack Jr. left for Virginia. Which apparently concerns her worst fears—an island curse.

Come to think of it, this woman's accent sounds suspiciously like one from the Caribbean.

Kind of like a full-blown version of Mrs. LaBadie's thin trace.

"Mrs. LaBadie?" Her name slips off my tongue before I can check it, but there's too much going through my mind—not the least of which is that I've been right about her this entire time.

If I get out of here alive, Beau is so going to eat his words.

She steps into the small patch of moonlight coming from the tiny window near the ceiling. It illuminates the whites of her eyes, her bared teeth, but leaves the rest of her in shadows—a ghostly figure more terrifying than Anne ever dreamed of being.

It all clicks into place—the reasons she didn't want me near the archives, the foul-smelling dirt in Amelia's purse after she spent twenty minutes researching, her eavesdropping on Mel and I discussing the diary. The one thing that doesn't make sense is why she cares about Anne Bonny or some made-up curse from two hundred years ago.

"Think harder." The creepy old librarian smirks, and pulls a long knife from a sheath on her belt. It's a dagger, maybe, and the edges glint in the soft moonlight.

Mel gasps, but as I twist my head to reassure her with words that don't mean dick in the face of our imminent death, I see that she's not afraid. She's surprised.

A figure that I would recognize anywhere slides through the door, still ajar, on his belly. It's Will. It makes sense, since his wife was talking to him in the parking lot when she got knocked out.

We need to distract the crazy lady.

The thought stutters through my head as Mel starts talking. "So, you're, like, related to the mistress? The voodoo priestess from the kitchens on the plantation or whatever?"

"I am part of her line, yes. Not blood of the body, but of the soul. We are bound to the curse."

Zaierra. Her strange name snaps into place, similar to the one Anne wrote in her journal. I keep Will in my peripheral vision and work on my bonds, ignoring the chafing pain, as Mel keeps chattering.

"I don't believe in that crap, personally. Curses and the like. Bunch of nonsense if you ask me."

"Yeah, and you've been mean to me since before Anne even visited me the first time," I add, trying to keep her attention. "You didn't know I'd listen to her."

"I have been charged with keeping this curse. It is my duty to watch over your family in this town, and when you returned, that included you." She frowns. "Along with the curse, the hatred continues, undiluted. Zolarra called on great power, and the strength with which she despised Anne for tossing away all Zolarra ever wanted formed a curious but unbreakable line."

"That's what you meant the other day in the library? About our roles being cast?" It takes all of my willpower not to check on Will's progress.

"Yes. The nature of the curse is binding, passing from true witch's blood to true witch's blood. We can never be released, not while the combination of Anne and Jack's blood runs in living veins." She sounds tired, so tired, raising the question of her age in my mind once again. "When I heard the two of you talking, it became clear you'd found the diaries, or were about to find them. We've searched through generations on the spirits' insistence they be destroyed."

"You've never read them?"

"Anne might have been a murderer and a whore, but no one can claim she wasn't clever. Especially so when it came to protecting her heathen child."

More clever than you, by half, I think, just to watch her snarl.

It's a duty, she said, but also that it's unbreakable. Binding. What if she's helpless but to carry it out?

I decide I don't give a shit. She doesn't have to be so mean, and she certainly has no right to assault me or my pregnant friend. The memory of Amelia's hand covered in stinky dirt after coming out of the archives—where Mrs. LaBadie served her herbal tea—makes it clear the crazy witch is behind the almost-miscarriage, too.

"So, you're a baby killer?" I spit at her.

"I do what must be done."

"And you call Anne heartless," Mel scoffs. "Doctor Pot, paging Doctor Kettle!"

"The witches are tools, no more. The spirits ensure the curse stays intact, and use earthly servants of their choosing, willing and unwilling alike."

She is creeping me the fuck out, but I also feel as though she's on the verge of revealing a detail that can help us make sense of her crazy. Whether or not there's an actual curse, we're dealing with an actual insane person who believes there is, one who's already tried to kill Amelia's baby.

Before she can say any more, Will misjudges the space between a chair and the bookcases. His toe catches on the foot of the wingback, sending it toppling over, and a smattering of books crash to the ground.

Mrs. LaBadie—or whoever she really is—whirls as he bursts from his compromised hiding place. They crash into each other, but whether Will never saw the dagger, or noticed it too late, I don't know. It disappears into his midsection to the sound of Mel and me screaming bloody murder.

"Will! Oh my god, Will!"

Mel's desperate shrieks pierce my heart as surely as that blade just sliced through my first love. My entire body feels cold, numb, unattached to my brain, this situation. As though I float above the room, taking it all in as a passive observer.

That changes as Mrs. LaBadie jerks her blade free and whirls on Mel. Her eyes are crazed, burning with a strange fire as she advances, blood dripping from the dagger onto the carpet. My friend sobs, sagging against our bonds, all the fight gone out of her even though she has so much to live for.

Not Will, something evil whispers in my ear.

I snarl, push it away. Will's not gone. It's not possible.

Yet it is, and Grant's going to be an orphan if Melanie and I don't pull our heads out of our asses and do something about it. I tear my eyes from the growing black stain surrounding Will's guts and focus on the voodoo woman. She makes a mistake in the final moment before she's close enough to slice Mel open, when she steps too close.

The pain in my shoulder tears a scream from my lips as I jerk forward, hooking my bound feet around her leg and toppling her to the ground. She lands with a heap and grunt, but like a wildcat taken down by a bigger beast, she scrabbles for her weapon, snarling as I kick it farther away from her grasp and then land a good whack in her stomach.

She forgets the weapon and turns on me, tearing at my face with her nails. It's all happening in slow motion to the sound of Melanie's shouted sobs, but somehow I get my knees against my chest and shove.

The tiny woman flies away from me and into Mr. Freedman's desk, slumping onto the floor in a heap. My ragged breaths turn into torn sobs as terror joins my adrenaline rush, leaving my body shaking like a leaf in a twister. I watch Mrs. LaBadie for several seconds, until the movement of her chest up and down, in and out, catches a beam of moonlight.

She's not dead, which means we don't have much time to get the hell out of here.

"Melanie." She doesn't stop crying, or shaking. "Melanie!"

"Wha . . . what?"

"We need to scoot over to Will. He's probably got a cell phone in his pocket, right?"

"His back one," she manages, her whisper as broken as my body, as her soul, as both of our hearts.

"Okay. On three, okay, we scoot."

It takes four tries to get it right, and at least ten minutes for us to get across the room. Another five elapse, and my nerves jangle like sleigh bells by the time we manage to maneuver the phone loose and work together to dial 911.

By then, Mel's gone into shock, a silent, pale ghost. Her tears make no noise as she leans over, pulling me with her as she lays her head on Will's chest.

The operator comes on, and in a voice so calm it can't possibly belong to me, I tell her we need help in the library director's office, that someone's been stabbed, and we're still in danger.

Then I lay down next to Mel, our backs pressed together, our heads resting on the boy we've both loved.

Chapter Twenty-Three

It seems like half the town mills around the waiting room in the damn hospital, a place that I would prefer never to set foot in again for my entire life. The doctor's bandaged my wrists and my forehead from the struggle along the river, then tended to Mel even though she told them a hundred times she wanted to be with Will.

Will's in surgery, and they haven't been out to update us yet. Will's parents are here, and so are Mel's. Grant's with one of his great-grandparents, and the rest of the people sitting or lounging or pacing are concerned friends. I spot Leo and give him a tight smile.

Beau's next to me, hasn't left my side, and his hands have hardly left my body. They wanted to admit me, give me a bed, but even though I refused, it doesn't stop the mayor from hovering. He shifts so we're facing each other, concern and anger swirling into dark clouds in his eyes, then runs rough fingertips over my cheeks. "What hurts?"

"I'm fine, Beau." When he refuses to accept that answer again, I give in. "Shoulder hurts. Face."

"Yeah, you've looked better." He sets one hand on my waist and uses the other to swipe filthy hair off my forehead, the grimaces. "Don't move."

I'm not going anywhere, and not just because the cops haven't been around to take my statement yet.

Beau returns with two ice packs and a fistful of ibuprofen at the same time as two identical police officers stride toward me. Their nametags declare them Officer Ryan and Officer Ryan, which makes my eyes pop painfully wide.

"Tom and Ted Ryan? You're *cops*?" The idea strikes me as hilarious—the only kids to land in hot water more often as kids than Leo Boone and me are policemen. If it wouldn't have hurt like the dickens, I would have laughed until I peed myself.

They grin, twin pictures of Irish heritage, right down to their whiskey-loving bellies. "I know. It's like the biggest finger ever to that old prick sheriff, right?"

I have no idea which one of them speaks. I never could tell them apart, and never had any desire to try once they told me the only sure way was to check out the birthmark on Tom's ass.

"You've got that right."

The old sheriff had been ancient, and his face would turn the color of an eggplant when we got him going. Their smiles fall away as they study my injuries, and eyebrows go up when Beau snags my hand.

"We've got to ask you what happened, Graciela. We've talked to Melanie already."

"Fine."

The Ryan twins grow more serious than I've ever believed possible, pulling out a recorder and a pad to take notes, then asking me to recount the events of the day, starting with the attack that morning. I tell them everything, distracted more than once by Beau's face in the corner of my eye. It appears to be carved from stone, with the exception of his eyes, which glitter with something fierce. Determined. Fiery.

It reminds me of the story Mel told about Leo's sister, and distracts me from one of the cops' questions. "What?"

"I asked why you didn't report the threats you received."

"I don't know. It seemed like some kind of teenage prank."

"Kids breaking out car windows? That's pretty extreme," one of them comments, skepticism plain in the twist of his lips. If anyone would know, the two of them would.

"It didn't seem possible that anyone was after me in particular--I'd been gone for years, and back only a couple of days when it started." At the time, I wasn't aware of the centuries-old hex on my family that lived on in the form of a deceptively strong voodoo witch.

"You always were a pain in the ass. Surprised you haven't kept a list of people you've annoyed in town, just in case."

"Hilarious," I reply, not really in the mood.

They stow their equipment and leave, exchanging looks that say the Ryan twins have heard the rumors about my sanity—or lack thereof—and are less than impressed with my tale. In fact, no one seems to really believe us about Mrs. LaBadie—we stuck with the story that she went crazy, not mentioning anything that sounds insane or impossible—but she disappeared from the scene without a sound.

My exhausted, throbbing body thrums with nerves, knowing she's still out there. Based on everything she said in the office about duty and witch's blood and curses, it's clear that *she* believes in it. Which means she's not just going to pack up and leave town.

Despite the pain and the fatigue, the shock, sitting still feels like too much to ask. I disentangle from Mayor Beau with the excuse of needing a moment alone, then cross the waiting room.

"I'm going to find Amelia and tell her what's going on," I tell Melanie. Me sitting here isn't going to make Will okay, and I'm not the one they'll come looking for when there's news, anyway. Maybe I could have been, maybe I even *would* have been, but I'm not.

Her eyes struggle to focus, then to comprehend English, but eventually she nods. "Okay."

"I'll be back."

I squeeze her hand and she holds on, crushing my fingers together for a solid thirty seconds before letting go and reaching into her purse to drag out a plastic bag containing a book identical to the one I dug out of the ground, though not nearly as worn.

"Here. My mom brought my purse. I was going to give this to you last night. Stupid evil bitch didn't realize it was in my trunk the whole time."

It sounds wrong, curse words on Mel's tongue. I hate that they're there, that something so upsetting has knocked her life off-kilter, and guilt puddles in my knees. There's nothing to do but take the book, and say another prayer that Will will be fine. That things will go back to the new normal.

Amelia's room is on the third floor, one flight of stairs up from where we've been waiting for news. I take the elevator instead of the steps, because I'd be lying if I said my heart didn't leap into my mouth at every movement in the corner of my eye.

The sight of her empty bed stops me short, but given the couple of days I've had, it seems more likely that I've walked into the wrong room than that she's not here. I double check the room number, which seems right, then backtrack to the nurse's station, swallowing bubbles of panic. "Hi, I'm Graciela Harper. My cousin Amelia Cooper, er, Middleton was here. Was she moved?"

It seems wrong that she wouldn't text or call if they moved her, or that she didn't try to get ahold of me when she was supposed to be released earlier today, and the wrongness gathers into a storm as the nurse checks her computer.

"No, we released her this afternoon."

"What?"

"The doctor advised against it, actually, but her husband was quite insistent."

Jake was here. Everything makes sense, now, especially that she didn't call, but it hurts that she didn't even think to leave me a message. I'm worried about her, a mess emotionally from the entire day, and I need more than anything a dark room to curl up in until everything is magically okay.

The nurse must sense my imminent implosion, because the way she's looking at me changes from cursory, maybe curious, to concern. Maybe she thinks I'm going to collapse on her desk.

"There's a chapel on the second floor. It's usually pretty empty and quiet if you need a moment."

I manage a nod, and somehow get down the stairs and into the chapel, which is thankfully, blessedly silent. I drop into a pew in the back corner, where no one will see me if they come in. Where it's dark, with only the light of a few candles flickering off the wall.

For the first time since I woke up this morning, I feel like I can breathe. The longer I sit and stare, sucking in oxygen and blowing it out, the more weight falls away from my shoulders. It'll never be gone, not until I hear about Will, until I check on Amelia and make sure everything's as fine as it can be in that situation.

Until I can find what Anne needs and finish what she started.

But the weight is bearable now, and after almost an hour I find the strength to pull the other half of the diary out of the plastic and crack it open, to face whatever demons, or curses, or consequences lie within its pages.

ↄƦ

February, 1733

I can't avoid it another day. Jack has reached his thirteenth year, and Joseph loses patience with every breath my son draws inside the walls of his house. My solace, at least in knowledge, comes in the form of a pliable young kitchen girl. Our conversations have made it clear that Jack is no longer safe here, and I'm most frightened of what might happen to him if he stays. There may be no way to prevent the loss of everything dear to me in the world, but I know that keeping Jack here will accomplish nothing toward that end.

Over a decade ago, my father and husband conspired to bring me home from Port Royal, and I am honestly thankful to have been able to hold on to Jack Jr., the last link between my love and myself, for this long.

I've tried over the past several months, since I learned of the trysts between Zolarra and Joseph and began to suspect her ill intentions toward my son and me, to discover what black, evil magic she might have worked. Until a few days ago, I have been unable to pry any details from the rest of the staff, who all fear her with a completeness I now know is warranted. Earned.

The kitchen girl, Melaine, who finally revealed what she's heard around corners and in the latrine, is too young to be of much use, and not quite all there in the head to begin with. It's unfair of me to take advantage of these things, but Jack must come first. Before the girl, and before my own soul, if it ever had a chance of being saved in the first place.

Melaine also hails from the Caribbean, but I'm not aware of the circumstances that brought her into the employ of the Burleigh family. She's not well liked among the staff, slaves, or other children—has a reputation for being a snoop and an eavesdropper, which is exactly what made her invaluable to me. She gets slighted as far as meals, since being underfoot angers the cooks, so I've been slipping her food and toys whenever I can, and Jack's befriended her at my request as well.

She's smart enough to fear Zolarra, but she's young and daft enough to be swayed by gifts and her own natural curiosity.

I found her two nights ago in the barn's hayloft, buried in the scratchy golden stalks and singing softly in a language I haven't heard since returning from the sea. She watched me with big eyes, then said plainly that she'd been expecting that I'd want something from her, and for me to just tell her straight what it might be.

Her perception surprised me, though I don't know why. There are so many kinds of intelligence in the world, and among thieves and criminals and pirates and Charleston society, I've met all kinds—intuitive, actual smarts, intelligence that came in the form of the ability to pick up fighting from the first touch of a weapon—all useful, in the right situation. This girl, Melaine, had the ability to read people, and I can tell you that it endeared her to me.

She scooted close, not near enough to touch but to share my heat. It made me wonder again where she came from, why or when she was separated from her own parents. Being a pirate, embracing the idea that every person has the right to live the kind of life they choose as long as they're willing to accept the consequences, means slavery's never sat well with me. But Joseph, like my father, never asks my opinion and so I do what I can for the slaves, when I am able. I will take more care with Melaine, for she's become a little friend.

I talked to her about Jack Jr., told her how he said she'd been good at learning to swim and that he'd had fun fighting with wooden swords with her. The compliments, and the mention of my son, lit up her face like a hundred candles. I knew then that I had her, that she would tell me what I wanted to know, and even though it took me another fifteen minutes of soothing her fears regarding the devil woman, she spilled her secrets.

It was asking her about her native land, and her mother, and her religion that opened the door. She felt comfortable sharing stories of curses, and hexes, and spells with me in a general sense, and there we began. Melaine informed me that in voodoo curses can be placed with the assistance of a witch doctor, and the use of certain herbs and bones, but never without the acquiescence of the spirits, dark or light.

When I asked her if it would make her sad to know someone put a curse on Jack Jr., her eyes filled with tears and she nodded. When I asked her if she knew about any such thing, she nodded again, and provided these details:

Joseph asked Zolarra to place a curse, a hex, on not only my son but the entirety of my lineage through him. That Joseph wants his own line to exceed anything begot by the likes of Jack Rackham, and in the end, the curse will leave my son with no male descendants. No one will ever again be called Cormac, or Rackham, once his beautiful soul leaves this earth.

The girl said that because my Jack is nearly a man grown, there isn't anything Zolarra can do to stop his seed from planting in a wife one day, but if they produce children, no boy will outlive his twelfth birthday. None will be older than he is now, and heartache and death will plague my family, and Jack Rackham's, as long as the curse remains strong.

I asked her about that, too, even though I'm not sure I believe it's possible, what she says. Not sure chanting and herbs can affect the lives of people born tens and hundreds of years in the future, but my mind conjures the fear I felt in those Caribbean alleyways, and my guts twist into knots, full of the question of what-if.

Melaine says that in voodoo, curses can be nullified if the hexed finds a way to make it not come true. It's that simple, she believes, and gave an example of a woman cursed by an old lover to never marry. She paid a man to marry her, a situation not foreseen by the witch doctor or the spirits, and the curse ceased to be.

This is what I hope to accomplish with these diaries. Should the curse be real, not an idle threat, and should Jack's male children and grandchildren be plagued by tragedy, perhaps it can be altered with the knowledge of these details.

I'll not tell my son about this, because at his age, there will be no fear of things that cannot be seen, and he will not take it seriously. I hope the note I send along to Mary's cousin will be handled with care, and that she will see to the journal's safekeeping and speak with Jack Jr. about the contents when he is old enough, or it becomes tragically relevant.

A letter falls from between the final pages, threadbare, faded, but readable. I hold my breath and read it, too, my heart in my throat. It details the fact that a week after her discussion with the girl called Melaine, Anne found her body in the hayloft, completely devoid of blood. Someone had cut out her eyes, lopped off her ears, and peeled her lips from her face. Anne was sure no one could have overheard their discussion, and she spoke of it not at all, save in the diary. The girl, she felt certain, had too much fear of both Zolarra and voodoo to have breathed a word, yet the events had to be connected.

She herself fell ill at the same time, and the page leaves little doubt that Anne Bonny didn't long survive losing her son, if only to another state.

I think of how Mrs. LaBadie seemed to know every time I made a move, took a breath. How she knew who Amelia was when she came to the library, how we're connected. And in the office tonight, how she heard my thoughts, at least when they related to Anne Bonny.

My next thought is of my cousin, back in Charleston with an abusive husband, one of the last in the line of Anne Bonny and Calico Jack Rackham.

And pregnant with a boy.

Chapter Twenty-Four

Beau finds me in the chapel, the journal open on my lap and my cell phone to my ear. He sits in silence, hand over mine, until I put down the phone. I've called Amelia seven times and left as many messages, twice as many texts, all without a response.

My storm of worry has churned into a hurricane of panic with the absolute certainty that she's in trouble.

"Hey," Beau says, softly rubbing my knuckles. "How are you doing?"

"I've been better."

"We're going to find that woman, Gracie. She's not going to hurt you again."

I wave him away, my own safety the least of my concerns. I'd be happy if she'd never hurt any of my friends again. "Have the doctors been back?"

"Will's out of surgery but he's in a coma. They're concerned about blood loss and internal bleeding. It's still . . . it could be better news, sweetheart."

The news hits me with more force than expected, given everything I've just learned about my family, about Jake taking Millie away from me again, not to mention that I've managed to get my ass kicked in one of the safest towns in the country.

Beau's arms go around me. His fingertips trail over my arms and neck, across my cheeks, as gentle as feathers, giving me a moment of peace to utter another silent prayer for the boy who meant everything to me once. Who still does, in his way.

Then I locate my nerve, sit up, stand up. There's only one thing I can actually *do* right now. "I have to go to Charleston. Amelia needs me."

"What? Isn't she here?"

"No. Jake came and checked her out, and now she won't answer her phone or respond to any texts." I glance down at the diary in my lap, the product of Anne's paranoia, maybe, but after everything Mrs. LaBadie has subjected me to, I'm not willing to write it off as nonsense.

Not to mention that, to my knowledge, a boy has never survived past the age of twelve in our family. Ever.

"Here. Read this if you want. It's the other half of Anne's diary, and I know something's wrong." I step past him but he's on his feet fast, a strong hand circled around my wrist.

"Stop, Gracie. I'll go with you to check on your cousin if you want, but after everything that's happened, I'm not letting you out of my sight until they find Zaierra."

I'm not sure they'll find her, if they're even looking. Not if she doesn't want to be found. If Anne was right, and if one believes in voodoo, maybe she's not even wholly human. The idea of being alone makes me shake all over, and his offer to come along steadies me. It's more than comfort, or protection. It's as though maybe, with him by my side, Amelia might have a chance at being okay.

Mrs. LaBadie's words from the library dance in my mind, the ones she uttered when Melanie accused her of being no better than Anne herself—that she had no control over how the spirits ensured the survival of the curse. That they used "servants."

An abusive, controlling husband seems like a likely candidate for brainwashing.

"Gracie. I'm not taking no for an answer."

"That's okay. I was going to say yes."

We head back down to the waiting area, which has largely cleared out after the news of Will's condition. His and Mel's parents are still there, and my friend sits curled in a chair, watching her hands.

"Mel?"

She looks up, her dark eyes rimmed by red circles and cracked with crimson veins. "Gracie."

My name dissolves into sobs and I fall to my knees, gathering her slight frame in my arms. Guilt makes me want to die, because if she loses Will, nothing will absolve me.

"I know." I pat her back, letting her loose her tears into my neck until she's finished, and pulls away. "I'm going to Charleston to check on Amelia, but I'll call for updates."

"Don't let it be for nothing, Gracie. All of this. Get her out."

Her words harpoon me through the middle, barbs snagged tight in essential organs. Even now, with her husband fighting what sounds like a losing battle for his life, she's concerned about Amelia, too.

Mel read the diary. Fear crackles in her gaze, unable to hide completely behind her grief.

I squeeze her hand, taking one more moment even though the atoms that make up my muscles beg me to sprint all the way to Charleston. "Will's a fighter, Mel, and the only person on this planet more stubborn than Millie. We can't give up on him."

"Never, Gracie. We stick together."

"Until the end."

"Until the end."

☙

Beau's face has settled into hard lines by the time I throw myself into his passenger seat and buckle myself in. It crosses my mind that all of this drama and pain is going to hamper, even kill, our new relationship, but my loyalty lies with others first. My ties to Will and Mel, to Amelia, run so much deeper than any others in my life, and as much as I like Beau and would like to get to know him better, whether or not we'll survive whatever we find in Charleston and emerge with our potential still intact has to take a backseat.

"Hey. Where's your driver? I didn't know you could drive, should I be worried? Do you even have a license?" My lame attempt at teasing relaxes him slightly, twitching a smile from the corners of his lips as he pulls onto the street, squinting into the early morning sunshine.

"Where are your sunglasses?" I ask.

"What?"

"Your sunglasses. You'll get wrinkles, squinting like that."

He slides a bemused gaze my direction, before returning to his squinting. "Wrinkles, huh? Well, if you must know, I left them in my other car."

I laugh without a second thought, then jerk with the realization that I can laugh, after everything. Maybe I'm not damaged for good this time.

"What are you laughing at, you terrible woman?"

"Your 'other' car," I drawl, putting air quotes around the word *other*. "Sheesh. Spoiled much?"

"How can you say that?" The tinge of mock outrage in this voice makes me snort. "I just told you I only have one pair of sunglasses."

I nod, rearranging my face into a serious expression. "That's true. Very frugal of you."

"Tell me about the diary," he says, sobering again as we turn onto the highway.

I do, leaving nothing out, even the parts that seem insane. My tongue trips over words like *curse, witch,* and *voodoo,* wondering when in the world those became concepts normal people talk about in real life.

There's no denying Anne's fear, though. It soaks every page, and the air of anguish that fills the space around her spirit doesn't lie. She thinks this is real. The fact that there's not a single boy in my entire family makes me not want to dismiss it, either.

Beau's quiet when I finish, watching the road and asking me which exit to take to get to Jake and Amelia's huge antebellum home on an Ashley River tributary. The property has been around forever, but the original house was a casualty during the Union army's march toward the coast.

Jake's family purchased the land soon after, and the house standing now had been built around the turn of the century, but in a colonial style.

It's beautiful architecture, but true to the time period, it's separated from the main thoroughfare by a long, winding, oak-lined drive. There aren't other houses nearby, but thank goodness it's not as isolated as it once was.

I put my hand on Beau's arm while we're still on the main road. "Wait, stop."

"Here?" He glances around but there's nothing to see but a grocery store and a few small restaurants. "Why?"

My brain trips and falls, urged by fear and an instinct I can't explain. "I think we should walk the rest of the way. Just in case."

"Just in case of what?" He sounds a little exasperated, and it's hard to blame him.

I'm not making much sense, but all I know is that giving Jake any kind of warning that he's going to have guests could be a mistake. "I don't know. What if he's hurt her, or forbidden her to contact me? If he sees us drive up, he'll be able to hide or think up some story."

Beau flips his hand under mine, tugging my fingers between his. Calm flows across my skin, crawls underneath, until the manic nature of my thoughts slows to a manageable pace. It doesn't change my mind about the best course of action, but now it seems as though walking on my own scratched-up legs might be possible.

His touch is so soft, so reassuring, and in that moment I realize that Amelia's safety isn't the only reason for my nerves. The thought of seeing Jake again, of being reminded of everything he did to me, sets me to shaking.

"Gracie, you don't have to go anywhere near that man. I can go and check on Amelia."

I shake my head, even though laying eyes on Jacob Middleton is about the last thing I ever want to do. Having tea with David and his busty coed holds more appeal than being in a room with Jake. Refraining from scratching his eyes out not only for what he did to me or what he's doing to Amelia, but also what he did to us.

"I'm going. He's not winning."

Also, Amelia will believe me about Anne's diary. She might like Beau, but she doesn't know him well enough to trust him in a situation like his.

Beau doesn't argue, just puts the SUV in park and climbs out, walking around to open my door. I take a few seconds to compose myself, because me flying off the handle or completely losing my shit isn't going to help anyone. He grabs me out of the car, wrapping me against his chest with gentle arms, and plants a hard kiss right on my mouth.

I relax into his lips in spite of my surprise, letting their warmth and insistent prying settle my nerves even further. When he lowers me back onto my feet with a satisfied smile, I'm as loose as a goose on a bed of clovers.

"What was that for?"

"I wanted to get our first middle-of-the-day, for-no-reason kiss out of the way. Now I can kiss you whenever I want."

"Is that right?"

He smiles, all dimples, and grabs my hand. I lead him toward the driveway that runs up to the Middleton residence. We move fast, because once we leave the cover of the trees, they only have to glance out the front window to glimpse us stealing across the expanse of naked cut grass toward the garage. Every bruise and scrape screams in protest but I don't slow down. Can't.

The home is three stories and a pretty, burnt brick. Wide white-painted columns support two large decks on the front. The garage stands off to one side, built in the style that would have been called a flanker in the seventeen hundreds, and matches the main house perfectly.

The closer we get, the more repulsion churns my stomach. It's as though the proximity to Jake soils my soul.

I stand on my tiptoes and peer into the garage, seeing Amelia's silver BMW and Jake's black Escalade parked next to each other, as though this is the most normal of normal days.

"What are we hiding for, Gracie? Let's go ring the damn doorbell."

"I have a bad feeling, that's all." *I'm scared. Help me.*

"It's so quiet," he comments. "Too quiet, don't you think?"

It is, and the observation is part of what's reigniting my panic. What if I'm too late? What if he's stolen her away, and I'll never see her again? What if he's hurt her, or worse?

"Gracie, there's no way to find out the truth unless we knock on that door."

I nod, stepping out from the shadows and stretching the kinks from my muscles. They're tight from the drive, from last night's bonds and the morning beating. Beau copies me, walking at my side the short distance through the summer browned grass and up the creaking front porch.

A light flips on in the foyer and my every muscle snaps like a rubber band. I hold my breath as the locks disengage, holding onto Beau's hand for dear life.

The sight of Jake impacts me even more than I expect. He fills up the doorframe, buckling my knees with his presence, and a sneer twists his handsome face into a monster's mask.

"Well, well, well, if it isn't little Graciela Harper. Guess you're still going by Harper, given that your man finally wised up and found something warmer for his bed."

I can almost hear Beau's teeth grinding together, but Jake's meanness helps me recover from my terror. He's a little boy with nothing that can hurt me, and his words strike me as stupid pebbles tossed by a child. They hit me, doing little more than causing an annoying shower of dust.

He doesn't see it, of course, and takes my silence for shock. He turns to Beau, a self-satisfied smile painted on his lips. "And you are?"

Beau must have reserves of patience and resolve I've only guessed at, because he shakes the devil's hand. "Mayor Beauregard Drayton."

We need to get inside. I need to see Amelia. We can't do that unless Jake lets us in.

"Jacob Middleton, no title. Yet." His ravenous gaze prowls back to me, where he senses weakness. He never was very bright. "What are you doing here?"

"I want to see Millie."

"*Amelia* doesn't want to talk to you."

"That's fine. She doesn't have to say a word. But I've been trying to get ahold of her all day and I'm not leaving until I see her."

The three of us stand in silence, a quiet face-off that ends when Jake's grin widens and he opens the door to allow us entrance. "You know I'm only kidding, Graciela. What kind of husband would I be, speaking for my wife? You know me better than that. Please, come in."

His pleasant host-with-the-most mask unnerves me more than his hostility. It reminds me of a predator, a giant cat hunched in the bushes, perfectly still and unthreatening.

Until its prey wanders close enough, and then it pounces.

"Amelia's in the kitchen," he offers.

Beau moves between Jake and me, putting a hand on the small of my back. For once, I appreciate his desire to do something for me without being asked, because even accidentally brushing against that man might make me blow chunks.

My cousin stands over the stove, stirring what might be some kind of pasta or rice that steams toward her face. Her shoulders tense but she makes no greeting as Jake motions us toward the table in the breakfast nook, then offers us something to drink.

I ignore him, moving toward the stove with slow steps as though approaching a terrified, beaten, feral cat.

"What's going on, Millie?"

She shakes her head without turning around, and from across the room, the tremble in her shoulders is painfully obvious. Once at her side, I put a hand on Millie's shoulder, feeling it shudder under my touch.

Without warning she turns, throwing herself into my arms and squeezing so hard my bruised ribs scream in protest. I watch spaghetti sauce bubble on the stove behind her, popping little red dots onto the stainless steel. She smells dirty, as though she hasn't washed off any of the antiseptic or cleaned her hair since Jake checked her out of the hospital yesterday. When she pulls back, revealing a massive ring of black and purple around her eye., It makes me gasp.

She whirls, putting her back to me, and starts wiping at the sauce.

"Are you okay?" I whisper, even though the lowest voice possible isn't quiet enough to go unheard. "Talk to me."

Her laugh is an ugly, forced thing that sounds more like a child choking. "I'm fine. Walked right into the door on my way inside yesterday, is all. I'm glad that you're all right. I was worried when I didn't hear from you sooner." When I don't answer, guilt slashes her face open until it weeps. "You shouldn't have come, Grace."

"Can we talk in private, Amelia? I have something to tell you."

"Whatever you have to say to my wife, you can say in front of me. Isn't that right, dear?" Jake is at Amelia's elbow, grasping her arm hard enough to make her wince. She nods, her eyes on the floor. "What exactly did you come all this way to say? It must be awfully important."

My brain races, trying to claw through the worry and panic, through the knowledge that none of this is helping Millie, and Beau comes to my rescue.

"She thought Amelia would like to know what happened to William."

Her eyes snap to mine, and I don't have to fake agony over this news. All of the color drains from her face and she reaches out, grasping my hands. "What happened to Will?"

"He was stabbed. The doctors don't know if he's going to make it."

"What? How?"

Jake plucks a strand of spaghetti from the pot, chewing on it as he leans against the sink, studying his wife's horror with a distant look of annoyance.

"Mrs. LaBadie, from the library. It's kind of a long story, but she kidnapped Mel and me, and when Will tried to free us they struggled." I swallow. "She was going to kill us. Because of Anne's diary. The second half."

"You found it?"

"Mel did. That's a long story." Impotence rages in my blood, bites my fingernails into my palm. I can't leave without telling Amelia about the curse, and letting her decide for herself whether or not she and the baby are in real danger.

The sight of her marred face, and the evil glint in Jake's eye, screams that it's not a matter of opinion.

Bu there's no way to say more without Jake overhearing, and when our silence has gone on long enough to his mind, he pushes away from the counter and wraps an arm around Millie.

"Well, I can't tell you how nice it's been seeing you again, Graciela. As you can see, my wife has had a rough couple of days and we're about to have dinner and retire for the evening. I think you should go, if you're convinced she's alive and well."

Alive, maybe.

"A pleasure to meet you, Mr. Mayor." Jake's smooth voice smothers my hope, presses all of the light from the room. From the world. His dismissal is impossible to miss, even more so to ignore. We're on his property. "A piece of advice, if you're interested. Stay away from that one. She's crazy as a loon and a prude, to boot."

Beau's fist smashes into Jake's nose before the last word falls off his lips. It snaps his head backward and sends him crashing into one of the barstools against the marble-topped island. He cups a hand around his gushing nose, eyes full of more hatred than any human should possess as they fix on Beau.

For his part, the mayor does not seem concerned. He steps forward until their faces are inches apart as Amelia and I stare. My feet are fused to the spot, and Millie's fingers twist a strawberry-printed dish towel into a knot.

"Let's get one thing straight, dirtbag. You don't fool me. Don't ever speak Graciela's name again or you'll get worse. And I know what you're doing to your wife. It's despicable." His eyes slide to Amelia. "You're welcome to come with us."

"You're not taking her anywhere, dickhead."

"I'm fine," comes Millie's automatic response.

"Millie, you're not fine and everyone in this room knows it. Come."

"No. I belong here. I don't want to leave my husband."

She does want to leave; it's written all over her face, in ink forged by the kind of stress and despair that will be part of her for the rest of her life. I can't understand why, even if she's scared, she's not more terrified for her child. I've never been in her shoes, though, and judging her isn't going to help anyone.

"I believe my wife said she's fine, and I've asked you both to leave." He glares at Beau. "Consider yourself lucky that I don't call the police and file assault charges. Get out of my house."

"We can't make her come, Graciela. Let's go."

I jerk my arm away when Beau places a hand on my elbow, turning to my cousin and snatching her into a fierce hug. With my face buried in her filthy blond hair I whisper, "It's the baby, Millie. He's still not safe. Find a way to call me."

I'd leave her the diary, but I don't trust Jake not to destroy it, and there's no way to slip it to her or hide it without his seeing. She tries hard for a neutral expression as we pull away, our matching green eyes holding on for dear life. I have no idea why she won't come with us now, except I know Jake as well as she does, and it won't be over. He'll come for her, and if he thinks he's lost her, I can't imagine any limit to what he might do.

I walk out without another word, ignoring Jake and pushing past Beau, bursting past the heavy wooden front door and onto the creaking porch. The mayor's footsteps thud behind me, catching up by the time we hit the grass. The world, reality, slides from under my feet. It slips away until I'm spinning my wheels, falling through darkness and strange worlds where everyone that loves me, that made me, is gone. Beau tries to grab my hand but I jerk away, walking as fast as I can down the lane and toward the car. Tears roll down my cheeks and I want to scream, but directing my anger at him helps a little bit.

"Keep walking, Gracie. He's standing on the porch watching us."

Beau shakes with rage at my side, so palpable I can taste it, like sour candy. Every fiber in my body throbs with the need to turn back, to grab Amelia and run. Whether it's the curse or not, this is going to end badly.

The seven or eight minutes back to the car feels endless. I slam the door behind me as I climb in, then sit shuddering with rage in the passenger seat. Helpless.

Beau puts the car into drive and peels out, but not the direction we drove in from earlier. My heart seizes. "Where are we going?"

"Back to their house. I shouldn't have hit him. He's going to take out his frustration on her, I'd bet my very last pair of socks. If we catch him in the act, we've got grounds for an arrest."

"He deserved it. The punch."

"Yes, and it felt good. But he's going to be anxious to recoup his pride."

Something about the way he bites off his words sinks my heart into my gut. "You sound like you know something about that."

He flies up the driveway, dust kicking up behind the SUV. The smile on his face is ugly, sardonic. Hateful. "My family is one of the most powerful and influential in the state, Graciela. Those things don't come without sacrifices. Family is usually the first thing to go."

He doesn't elaborate and I don't ask him to. It's not the time to swap family histories, and despite his family's money and power and influence, I've always felt lucky to have been born into mine.

The car jerks to a stop in front of the house and we fly out the doors. The first crash explodes in my ears as my foot hits the front steps, and the sound of Amelia's scream pierces the day.

Chapter Twenty-Five

Beau grabs my hand and hauls me the rest of the way up the steps. We press against the house to one side of the front door. I'm numb, in shock, but struggling to find a way to help my cousin.

Jake's voice booms from inside, loud enough I'm surprised the bricks don't rattle against my back.

"When did you sneak away and call her, tell her to come?"

More banging, punctuated by what sounds like china smashing into the floor or walls. Each shattering thud makes me jump, and my heart stumbles loose from my chest at what sounds like an overturned table. Amelia's sobs rip out pieces of my soul. The wind sucks them away.

"What are we going to do?" I whisper to Beau.

He doesn't answer, but he does pull out his phone and dial, pressing it to his ear. "Hello. Yes, I'd like to report a domestic disturbance. The address is . . ." He raises his eyebrows at me, then repeats what I rattle off from memory before disconnecting.

"You don't deserve to have my baby! You're nothing but a whore. It's probably not even mine, the way you run around like the little slut you used to be whenever I'm out of town—don't think I haven't been watching you." Another sickening thump and crack leap through the walls, and Amelia shrieks again.

We can't wait.

"You're lucky I married you in the first place. You played such an innocent little goody-goody, little Millie Cooper from one of the most worthless families in Charleston. But I chose you. Raised you up. And this is how you repay me. Telling lies to your bitch cousin, inviting her here without permission."

"I didn't invite her, Jake, I swear. I don't want anyone but you," Amelia begs, sobbing so hard the words are hard to understand.

"You can't go back to your old life, Amelia. I won't let you leave."

"I won't say a word, Jake, and I'll never talk to Gracie again, I swear. I only want you. You, me, and the baby."

It's hard to know what effect she expects her words to have, but their impact seems lost on Jake, who's worked himself into the kind of rage that's blind, deaf, and dumb, to boot.

The police aren't going to make it in time, and as the sickening sound of flesh hitting flesh pummels my ears, combining with my cousin's pathetic mewls, Beau puts his hand on the doorknob. It turns under the pressure, surprising us both. Jake doesn't seem like the careless type, but if he was in as big a hurry as Beau guessed, it makes sense.

There's no way they can hear us creeping on the hardwood floors over the ruckus of their fight. We pause outside the kitchen threshold, Beau checking his watch with an impatient expression. It would be best, and smartest, to wait for the police. Nothing good can come of us barging in playing the vigilante heroes, but I'm not going to stand here and let him kill her.

"Let go, Jake, you're hurting me. Think about the baby." Her voice is a sliver, barely audible through the razor wire of pain.

Jake's voice drops, too, barely above a whisper now. "I'm going to kill you, Amelia. Do you want to know how?"

She sobs almost silently, and Beau's eyes meet mine. They say we won't let that happen, not without a fight. *Talk to him,* I mentally urge my cousin. *Buy us some time.*

"Your stupid, meddlesome cousin and that fancy boy she's spreading her legs for will come sniffing around, so we've got to have a good story. Here's what I think. You'll kill yourself. It's believable after that pathetic display you put on for them tonight."

"Thi . . . think about it, Jake." Her voice trembles, but works at being conversational. "Why would I kill myself?"

"You won't want to live after you lose another baby, sweetheart."

His words, so calm and sure, leave no room for doubt that he would do it. Kill his own child. Whether he's convinced himself that it might not be his, or he's so insane that getting rid of Amelia takes precedence over everything else, or voodoo spirits have taken over his body, it doesn't matter.

He's going to kill them both.

"What do you mean, lose the baby?" She's keeping him talking now, which means he's not hurting her, at least not at the moment. I wonder if she heard me.

"You're so clumsy, lovebug. A fall down the stairs should do it. Or some more of those herbs. Everyone, including Graciela, knows that nothing means as much to you as being a mother. You've failed at that, too. Like everything else."

Beau tenses beside me, a frown making use of every muscle in his face. I can tell it really chaps his ass that Jake ignored his warning about mentioning my name, even though he can't know we're listening.

Without warning, a hard slap echoes off the walls, rattles my skeleton. It's followed by the spine-chilling sound of fingernails scrabbling against the floor, or maybe the drywall, and without warning, Beau rushes into the kitchen.

I follow, almost skidding into him where he's stopped just inside the room. Around his bulky form, I see Amelia crumpled on the floor, curled protectively around her belly. The hardwood and wall behind her are spattered with bright red blood, bringing to mind the splattered spaghetti sauce on the stove.

Jake whirls at the sound of our entrance, his eyes gleaming almost yellow, giving his whole face an otherworldly appearance. I'm sure it's the words from the diary swirling thoughts of curses and witches through my mind, but holy shit the guy looks possessed. Even for him.

My gaze falls to my cousin, who pants hard, watching us from the floor. Her face is a mass of flesh and blood, her eyes swollen like muffins bursting from a pan. Blood cakes her hair and face, and the nose that had been slightly cracked earlier now sits off to one side of her face. A gasp sucks the air from my lungs, but Beau puts out an arm, stopping me from going to her.

I look up in anger, ready to shove him out of the way, but his eyes are locked on Jake. The two men stare each other down but Beau puts his hands up, showing that we don't have a weapon. I get the sense that the otherness of Jake unnerves him, too, and we don't have to fight. Help is coming.

"We called the police. They're going to be here any minute, and Gracie and I heard everything you just said. Give it up, man."

Jake wanders toward the counter, then puts it at his back, looking as though he hasn't a care in the world. From the corner of my eye, I see Amelia drag herself toward the other doorway, the one that leads into the formal dining room. With Beau blocking one exit, it's as though she means to block the other. Her fight impresses me, but she won't be able to stop him.

Now that Jake's picked a side of the room, I duck under Beau's arm and skitter across the floor to my cousin, holding on to her as tight as I dare. Together, we'll at least be able to slow him down.

"You're a Drayton," Jake comments. "You know how this works. No one's going to believe you, and even if they do, me going to jail is a laughable prospect. You can't win. She's my wife, and she's mine to dispose of as I see fit."

He leans forward, and reveals an open drawer behind his waist.

And a gun. In his hand.

It glints under the kitchen lights as he taps it lightly against his thigh. Beau starts, backing up and keeping his hands up in front of his chest.

"Are you going to play the tragic hero, tough guy? I'll be more than happy to explain to the cops how you and your little slut invaded my property after I asked you nicely to leave."

Beau's gaze slides to me, and in that split second, Jake yanks up the gun and pulls the trigger.

The sharp report deafens me, muffles the scream that rips from my lips. A red splotch blooms on the mayor's arm, up near his shoulder, and the look of surprise on his face is anything but comical.

Jake goes pale, making me think it was an accident, but takes advantage of the moment of confusion to bolt into the foyer, toward the front door.

"Beau! Oh my god. Oh my god." I leave Amelia and fly across the kitchen, dropping to my knees at his side and pressing a hand to the side of his face. There's a towel beside the island, the strawberry-printed one Amelia had been holding when we left, and I press it to his wound, babbling. "You're going to be okay. No big deal. No big deal."

His face is white, so white it looks like chalk, and I think I'm going to pass out.

"The police are coming, and I bet they're bringing an ambulance. They are, I'm sure."

The cops should be here by now. They should be here.

I cry out with relief when he puts a freezing cold hand over mine. "I'm okay, Gracie. Stings like hell, but it just nicked me."

He sits up, eyes cutting toward the foyer, reminding me that Jake's getting away. Jake will find a way to spin this entire situation, and we are the one's trespassing. In South Carolina, that gives him every right to shoot him full of holes.

He'll say that Beau beat up Amelia, and I helped, and that he came home to find her bleeding and miscarrying and did everything he could to save her. I glance back toward my cousin, needing her help, her reassurance, her advice, and find her missing from the doorway. From the kitchen.

Another gunshot—deafening, heartbreaking—rings out from the front of the house. My mouth falls open but no sound comes out, and the noise pries Beau's pained eyes wide open. I look down at my hand, helping staunch the sticky flow from the mayor's arm, then back at the spot where Amelia should be, stuck in place with no way to win. I'm torn in two, needing to know if Millie needs help but not wanting to leave Beau, when she appears in the doorway. Her face is a nightmare, but under the blood and the bruises, she's vacant.

The pistol, the same one that shot Beau, hangs from two fingers.

"Millie. Millie, what happened? Where's Jake?"

She lists from side to side, then falls to her knees, staring at the silver weapon as though it holds the secrets to the universe. Tears fall from her eyes, but mine are glued to her thighs, bare under her sundress.

Spotted with blood.

Then her eyes are closed, and no matter how loud I scream, she doesn't respond. Her chest rises and falls, Beau shivers, and I can't move. There aren't any other sounds, and whether Jake is dead, injured, or gone I have no idea, but he's the least of my problems at the moment.

The wail of sirens slump me forward, relief mingling with my wild panic over these two people who mean so much to me. I press my forehead to Beau's. "The police are here. I hear the sirens, just hold on."

"Police! Open up!"

Beau's hand finds strength, presses against his own arm. "Go let them in, Gracie."

I hear the heavy door burst open before I take two steps and a handful of cops, EMTs, and even a couple of firemen pour into the kitchen; it's the sweetest thing I've ever seen. The flurry of activity blurs before my eyes, and their questions jumble in my ears. A policeman settles me in a chair at the kitchen table.

"He's been shot. You have to help . . . help him. And she's bleeding. She's pregnant. My cousin." I hope the string of words makes more sense to them than it does to me.

The EMTs work on Beau, but he's sitting up, calmly answering questions. Even the fact that the EMTs cut his shirt off to display a tanned, muscled chest, can't make me feel okay.

Knowing Beau's going to be fine does nothing but double my concern for Millie. One of the EMTs gets on the radio and asks for a second ambulance, asks them to hurry.

The request echoes in my brain, bounces off the walls of my skull and amplifies again and again. Hurry. Hurry. *Hurry.*

"Ma'am?"

I look up into the kindly eyes of an older, graying officer with a belly that says he's spent more time eating donuts than catching criminals.

The rest of the day's events swoop in, clutching me in eagle talons of panic. "Did you catch Jake? Jake Middleton, he's the one who did this."

"He the dead guy in the foyer?"

"He's dead?" I'd be relieved if my boyfriend and my cousin weren't bleeding. "What happened?"

"I'm rather hoping you'll be able to tell me."

"I . . . he . . . we didn't mean . . . she never . . ." I can't get anything out. The fact that Jake's dead won't make sense.

The EMTs help Beau into the chair beside mine, and his ice-cold hand covers mine.

"Plenty of time for that," the cop says, ever gentle. "I'll get you a glass of water and send you along to the hospital in one of the ambulances. You're not looking too good."

I don't tell him the injuries aren't from today, because I don't want them to make me stay here and answer questions instead of going with Millie. There are more people in the kitchen, more shouting as they load her up on a stretcher and roll her away.

ଊ

This hospital is different, but it looks the same. Smells the same. They have tried to cover up the drab starkness with stupid paintings that are abstract smears of pastels, but it's all hopeless, inside and out. I'm waiting for the doctors to tell me if Amelia's going to be okay, and Beau's still squirreled away somewhere getting checked out. He's been gone too long, and the worry that it isn't just a scratch bunches my muscles into leaden balls.

I hate the sense of déjà vu, mostly because it's not a figment of my imagination. In a similar room, in a similar place, Mel waited for good news about Will that hadn't come.

I've been worrying about him, too.

A doctor walks in and over to me. I clutch the wall, desperate for good news but knowing better than to expect it. "Can I see Beau now?"

"Your cousin, Amelia Middleton?" I nod, my heart in my throat. "She's going to be fine, though we are going to bring in a plastic surgeon to consult on her facial trauma."

"And the baby?" I cringe away from him, as though space will make the news easier.

"He seems to be handling the stress, at least for now. We had to perform some emergency procedures to stop the bleeding, and she'll need to stay on bed rest for some time. There may be permanent damage."

He's alive. I cling to that, instead of the pebbly drywall. "Can I see her?"

"Of course. Follow me."

Amelia's alive, breathing, and even awake, though she looks even more hideous now than she did earlier. I sit on the side of her bed and grab her hand, tears gathering in my eyes at her weak smile.

"You look like shit, Millie."

"I'm afraid to look in a mirror. On the plus side, I never liked my nose, anyway." Her voice is nasally, all wrong.

"Amelia, the police want to talk to me. What happened?"

"I tried to stop Jake from leaving. He came after me again and then I had the gun. I . . . I killed him." Her eyes meet mine, incredulous but not sad. "I killed him."

"What are we going to tell the cops?"

"The truth. I'm not living the rest of my life looking over my shoulder." Her hands flutter over her stomach. "I'll be like Anne Bonny, pleading my belly to the court."

"Don't talk like that. Beau and I will back you up."

"Of course you will. We stick together."

"To the end."

"To the end."

We fall silent, listening to the beeping of machines. A nurse hustles in later, waking Millie when she's just nodded off, and we both straighten our backs.

"One of you asked to be updated on Beauregard Drayton's condition?"

"Me," I squeak, fighting the urge to cringe again.

"He's going to be fine. The bullet went straight through, but tore up some muscle. He's asleep, but I can take you to him if you want."

"Go, Gracie," Millie urges when I glance at her for approval.

I pull the second half of the diary from my purse and leave it on her bedside table. "Read it. You'll understand why I had to come."

"I'm glad you did."

Epilogue

It's a couple of days before Beau's released from the hospital, because he picks up an infection, and another three weeks before Will will complete enough physical therapy that they let him go, too. He's alive, though, so there isn't much more we could ask for.

Amelia has moved in with me, and she's confined to her bed for at least another week. The doctor says he might be able to remove the stitches in her cervix by then, because the baby seems to have stabilized after the trauma of his mother's near-death experience. Jake is buried, and no charges are filed. Beau and I backed up Amelia's claim of self-defense, and the state of her face and the kitchen left little room for argument.

Anne's gone, which kind of surprises me since Mrs. LaBadie hasn't resurfaced. Millie and I don't know what we think as far as the curse is concerned, but until the little peanut she's cooking turns thirteen, we'll both be hypervigilant about his safety. I guess Anne thinks it's enough that we know to look out for him, and doesn't feel the need to stick around to supervise.

It's hard to blame her. Two hundred years is a long ass time to hang around people who mostly stare right through you.

I lock the front door of my grandparents' old house, which Amelia has convinced her parents to let us occupy for the time being. As though there was any doubt, once his daughter asked him for something, that Uncle Wally would deny her.

I'm happy to have a home. To have Amelia. Still, this whole thing left me feeling unmoored. Different. I'm not sure who I'm going to be now, or how it might affect me in the future, but there's nothing wrong with waiting and seeing. In theory.

Will's scheduled to leave the hospital in less than an hour, and Mel's invited a few people and ordered a cake to celebrate. I'm approaching the coffee shop, where Beau promised to meet me, when the sound of Leo's guitar catches my ear. I stop and toss him a dollar, give him a smile.

The song ends and he puts down the guitar. "Hey, Gracie. Marcella wants to know when you're coming back to the library."

"I don't know. Mr. Freedman keeps asking. Soon, I think." It's weird to think about going back after what happened with Mrs. LaBadie, but I need a job, and there isn't anywhere else in town that would give me any semblance of satisfaction.

Unless I want to hang out my shingle as Gracie harper, ghost whisperer.

Definitely not.

As much as I admit to—on the rare occasion—missing Anne, not having to deal with her insistent presence is a relief. It had been a lot of pressure, not letting her down.

"Where are you headed?"

"I'm meeting Beau, then we're popping over to the hospital to celebrate Will's release."

"Oh." His eyes narrow and he sucks in a breath, as though there's something he wants to say. In the end, the air blows out with no words.

My head tells me to ignore it, but letting go has never been my specialty. "I know you don't like Mayor Drayton, Leo, because of what happened with your sister."

He rubs his hand through his long hair, and does the inhale, exhale again without talking. Then his eyes meet mine, hesitant but also determined. "There's more than just that, you know, that makes me wish you'd stay away from him."

"Hey, Gracie!" Beau strides up behind Leo, his eyes glued to the back of my old nemesis's head. He kisses me on the cheek and nods to Leo, then asks if I'm ready to go.

"Yeah." I smile up at him, glimpsing nothing hidden in his expression, nothing unsure about his interest in me. Because of his injuries, mine, and the fact that a ton of my time has been spent taking care of Amelia, the two of us haven't had much time to explore what's happening between us.

But we will. And, I'm consistently surprised to find out, I *want* to.

The bad blood between him and Leo has nothing to do with me and there's no reason to ignore my instincts, which promise he's a good man. He's not Jake, he's not David. I don't know if he's as good as Gramps, or even Will, but I'm willing to find out. If he has secrets, they're his to tell, when and if he's ready to trust me with them.

No matter how truly I believe that, I can't help but glance over my shoulder as we bid Leo farewell and head toward the hospital. He watches us, fists clenched, but gives me a small smile when he catches my look.

"Good day?" Beau asks.

"Good day. Amelia might be able to get out of bed next week, the baby is doing great. Will's going home. What more can a girl ask for?"

"I can think of a few things," he murmurs my direction, sending all kinds of tingles down my spine.

"I'm sure you can. And I'm dying to hear about them tomorrow night when you take me to dinner."

He squeezes me tight with one arm as we stride into the hospital, then take the elevator to Will's room. Grant runs up to give me a sweet little hug before announcing—loudly—that his daddy gets to go home. My eyes meet Mel's and we share a moment of happiness between two women who have loved the same man and who, in the end, love each other at least as much. The room grows chaotic as more people show up. Mel cuts the cake, handing over the first piece to Grant, which he promptly drops on the floor, icing first.

"I'll go grab some towels," I tell Mel, urging her to stay in the room. "I could use a minute of quiet, anyway."

Beau doesn't notice me slip into the hallway, and as much as I love my friends and makeshift family, after weeks of near solitude that room is a lot to handle. I wander down the hall to the nurses' station and ask where I can find the janitor, then walk a few more doors to his storage closet.

Inside, there's a yellow mop bucket holding a gray-tinged mop, shelves of cleaners, and stacks of towels. I grab a couple towels, snag a spray bottle of floor cleaner, then turn to go, and drop all of the gathered supplies onto the floor. They clatter and roll, but the noise hardly registers.

There's a figure between the exit and me. He's wearing a man's clothing, some kind of period dress, though the fact that he's mostly see-through makes the era hard to pin down. His face is drawn, angry, and when he sees that I've noticed him, he extends one long finger straight toward my chest.

Oh. Hell. No.

THANK YOU

For reading *Not Quite Dead*, and for buying books and supporting authors in general! If you enjoyed this book, I would appreciate a review on the site where you purchased it – they're so helpful in assisting other readers in finding books that might appeal to them.

Also, if you enjoyed *Not Quite Dead*, you might enjoy my other books, so please check them out if you're so inclined:

Broken at Love

By Referral Only

Be My Downfall

Staying On Top

ACKNOWLEDGEMENTS

Novels may be written by a single person, but everything else—from the idea, to the cover, to the finishing touches—can't be done alone. This particular book was written years ago, during a National Novel Writing Month, so my first thanks go to that program, which inspired me to get the first draft out of my head and onto a computer. Past that, my critique partner Denise Grover Swank read the (seriously lacking) old draft and encouraged me to revise, somehow seeing the potential for something greater inside the mess of early writing mistakes. She's not just my critique partner but one of my closet friends, my confidante, a pioneer, the person who tugs me back from the brink of madness, an inspiration, and a woman who always, always has a bottle of pink champagne in her cabinets. May we all strive to be more like her.

I'd be remiss without thanking the other early readers of this book—Cait Greer, Leigh Ann Kopans (another person without whom I might not be sane), and Diana Paz. They all have amazingly brilliant books for sale that I recommend without hesitation, so please look them up.

My agent, Kathleen Rushall, is such a support and source of motivation, even for the books she's less involved in—knowing she's on my side gives me mountains of confidence. My editor, Lauren Hougen, my proofreader Cynthia Moyer, my cover designer Eisley Jacobs, the wonderful photographer who staged the cover image, Iona Nicole, and my formatter, Lucinda Campbell—this book would be nothing, really, without the combination of your immense talents, creative and otherwise.

My family, who has put up with me for years—including my own beloved grandfather, who inspired much of the character of Gramps in this novel. It seems like he's been gone forever, but everything he was and all of the moments we shared, the knowledge passed on, is never far from my heart. To my boyfriend, Paul, for putting up with my deadlines, the not-too-often showers, and the nights he falls asleep to the sound of the clicking keyboard—I appreciate the way you make it okay to be myself and to still be with you, too.

To Anne Bonny, a woman who knew her mind, thank you. I'm not saying that murdering and stealing is the way to go, but you're a lady who showed the rest of us that it's okay to be who you are, no matter what the world is going to think.

Rock on, ladies.

ABOUT THE AUTHOR

Lyla Payne has been publishing New Adult romance novels for a little over a year, starting with Broken at Love and continuing with the rest of the Whitman University series. She loves telling stories, discovering the little reasons people fall in love, and uncovering hidden truths in the world around us – past and present. In her spare time she cuddles her two dogs, pretends to enjoy exercising so that she can eat as much Chipotle as she wants, and harbors a deep and abiding hope that Zac Efron likes older women. She loves reading, of course, along with movies, traveling, and Irish whiskey. Lyla's hard at work, ALWAYS, and hopes to bring you more Whitman University antics and at least one more Lowcountry ghost tale before the end of the year.

If you want to know more, please visit her at http://lylapayne.com

If you're a fan of Young Adult fiction—science fiction or otherwise—please check out her work that's published under the name Trisha Leigh. http://trishaleigh.com

Made in the USA
San Bernardino, CA
01 April 2014